WILDCAT

Adam Paulhus

WILDCAT

Histria SciFi & Fantasy

Las Vegas ◊ Chicago ◊ Palm Beach

Published in the United States of America by
Histria Books
7181 N. Hualapai Way, Ste. 130-86
Las Vegas, NV 89166 USA
HistriaBooks.com

Histria SciFi & Fantasy is an imprint of Histria Books encompassing outstanding, innovative works in the genres of science fiction and fantasy. Titles published under the imprints of Histria Books are distributed worldwide.

Library of Congress Control Number: 2024944044

ISBN 978-1-59211-502-0 (softbound)
ISBN 978-1-59211-518-1 (eBook)

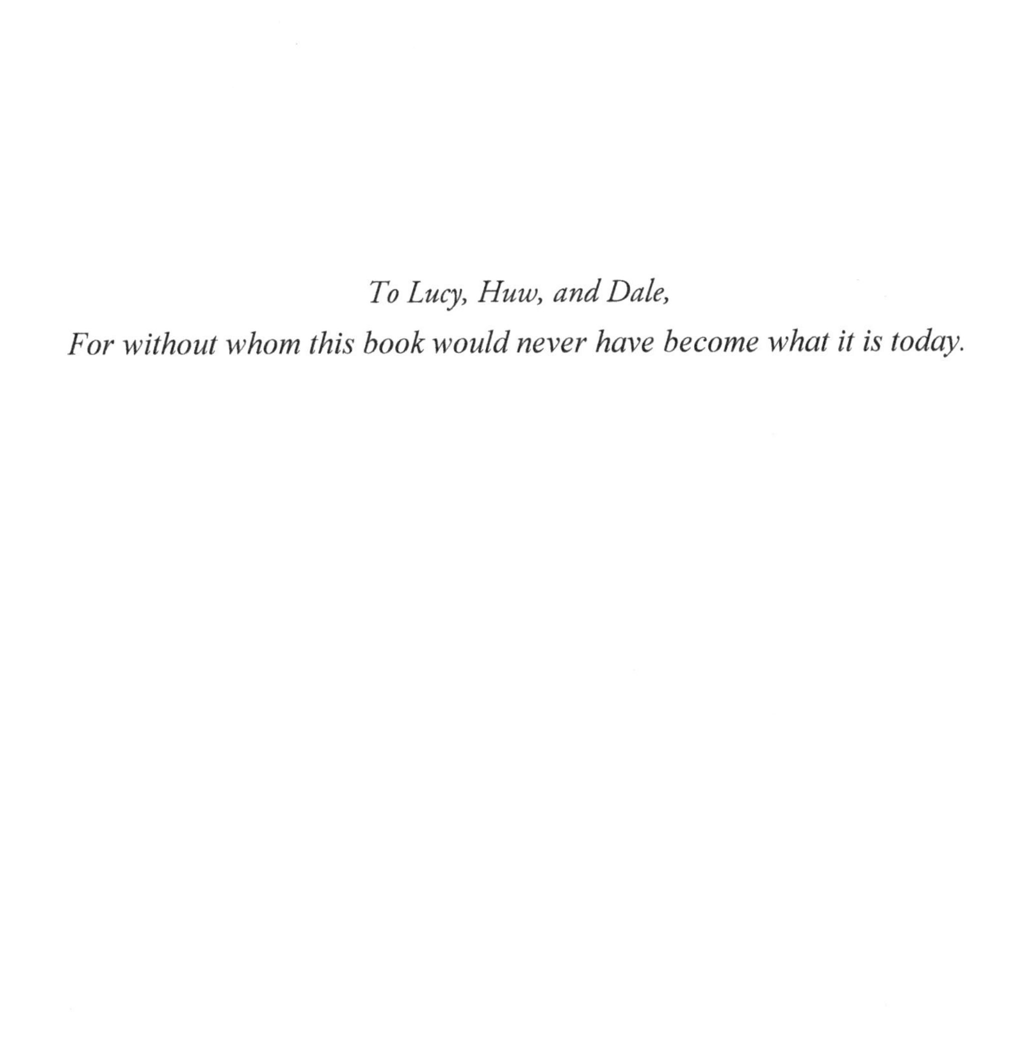

To Lucy, Huw, and Dale,

For without whom this book would never have become what it is today.

PROLOGUE

Corsatari Ignasius "Skyline" Oran absently watched his Low-Range Detector. Ahead of his Shrike fighter was a blue blip on the orange sphere indicating the position of his escort target, the Altherian business liner *Future's Dream*. To Ignasius's right was a green blip, another Shrike—his wingman, Litscari Nyra "Stalker" Yprall—gliding into position. On cue, Ignasius heard the radio in his helmet come to life.

"Skyline, Stalker," Nyra said. "In position."

"Skyline copies." He looked to his right to verify her position. Some two hundred meters from him, he could make out the triangular shape of the Shrike, as well as its high tail, adorned with an orange hawk, the symbol of their squadron. "Maintain speed at three klicks per second and hold position. Halfway inside the gray zone we turn back."

"Stalker copies."

Ignasius relaxed in his seat. With his rookie partner in position, there was nothing more for him to do except watch his L-RaD. *Not that anything will show up*, he thought. *The Altherians know the drill the same as us. Halfway, no farther.* When *Future's Dream* came back in a few cycles, they'd be back in the gray zone to pick up the ship and escort it to the colony. *Such is the way of peacetime.*

"What are you going to do with your time off?" Ignasius asked his wingman.

"Probably go visit my brother on Ashimara," Nyra replied. "I haven't seen him since he left home."

"Ashimara is supposed to be exceptionally beautiful this time of year. It's right in the middle of their growing season." Ignasius could almost picture the fields of green and gold stretching for endless kilometers across low hills and level ground. He imagined standing in a room with his wife at the highest floor of the tallest hotel in one of the cities, looking out over the seemingly infinite fields, which fed so much of the New Federation.

"What about you, sir?" Nyra's voice yanked Ignasius back to the present. "What will you do with your time off?"

"I have to finish moving to Surillin with my family," he explained. "Once that's done, I'll probably just try to spend as much time as I can with my daughter."

"Surillin? Why move to one of the colonies?"

"The governor was so gracious of our friend's help in building the colony that he gifted him a house in case he ever decided to move to the New Federation permanently. He said he would never, so he gave me the house as thanks for escorting him all these years." Ignasius laughed.

"I would have never thought an Altherian could be so generous," Nyra said, laughing.

"They aren't all bad," Ignasius responded. "Mika is a prime example of that."

"How old is your daughter?" Nyra asked after a brief silence.

"Ten," Ignasius said. "She turned ten just a couple of cycles ago. I wish I could be home more often for her."

"You aren't thinking about retiring, are you, sir?"

Ignasius laughed hard. "No. Not yet at least. I think I've got a few more years left in me, but I want to be home when she starts high school."

As the conversation between the two pilots died down, silence again enveloped Ignasius's cockpit. He glanced down at his L-RaD. It was still just the three of them, and they were almost at the halfway point in gray space. Another few minutes, and they would be on their way back home. Ignasius watched his L-RaD and occasionally looked out of his canopy at the non-existent view. Ahead of him was just the long, sleek, white business liner, its black windows lining the midsection of its sides. Beyond *Future's Dream* and Nyra's Shrike, all that Ignasius could see were distant stars. The closest, still more than a system away, shone brightest in a blueish hue.

"Skyline, Stalker, this is Roost, do you copy?" Ignasius jumped to attention at the sound of wing command.

"Skyline."

"Stalker." The pair checked in in turn.

"Mission update, prepare to copy." There was a brief pause in the radio transmission. "Fighters Skyline and Stalker are to destroy hostile ship *Future's Dream.*

I say again, fighters Skyline and Stalker are to *destroy* hostile ship *Future's Dream.* Updating data." At once, the blue blip on the L-RaD turned red.

"Roost, Skyline." Ignasius keyed his radio immediately. "That can't be right. *Future's Dream* is a friendly and civilian vessel."

"Skyline, that is your mission." The voice on the other end of the radio was firm. "Engage and destroy the hostile ship. Transmit confirmation of mission."

"Roost, I will not until you tell me why we are destroying a civilian vessel." Ignasius was almost yelling at his superior. *This doesn't make sense,* he thought. *Mika is a good man. He is on our side.*

"We don't have time for this. It must be done before the halfway mark. Stalker, Roost. Confirm mission."

"Roost, Stalker confirms," Nyra said flatly. "Stalker will destroy hostile ship *Future's Dream.*"

"Stalker, what are you doing!?" Ignasius called to her as though his voice would carry across the vacuum of space and into her cockpit. Instead, it simply went through their radio.

"I'm carrying out the mission," Nyra responded. "There must be a good reason for why we are doing this."

Ignasius watched as Nyra deployed the hardpoints of her Shrike. Two missiles, one on each side, lowered from their storage within the fuselage.

"Stalker, wait." Ignasius breathed out heavily before he spoke again. "I'll do it. You don't want this kind of blood on your hands. Besides, Mika was always my friend." Hitting a switch on his flightstick, he deployed his own hardpoints.

"Stalker copies," Nyra said. "Retracting hardpoints."

Ignasius stared at his L-RaD. He stared at the small red square that marked his friend's ship. He knew that the moment he turned his safety off, his Shrike would begin locking on to that ship. Immediately, his friend would know he had betrayed him, and he could never tell him why.

"Skyline, get on with it." The voice of wing command came through his helmet.

"Skyline copies." Ignasius took another breath and held it. He flicked off the safety on his flightstick. At once, he heard the beeping of the targeting system. It didn't matter how long he waited; there was no way that *Future's Dream* could outmaneuver a fighter craft. But he didn't want to wait. He didn't want to leave his friend wondering why any longer than he had to. The instant the beeps of the targeting system became a solid tone, Ignasius depressed the trigger twice, sending two missiles streaking toward the business liner.

CHAPTER 1

With only a gentle hum, the four metal lifts began to lower the coffin into the ground in perfect unison. A dozen people watched, headed by a man wearing a black robe with light green lines from his shoulders to his waist. He was on his knees with his eyes closed, his voice droning on toward the conclusion of his speech.

"Each one of the Gods placed their hands at the back of the Omasye and guided him through the Great Rebellion so that he in turn could guide each one of us," he said in a quiet voice filled with conviction. "Just like the Gods, the Omasye continues to watch over each and every one of us, guiding us toward our future. The Omasye certainly kept his watchful eye on you, Mika, until the very end. However, we, just like the Omasye, must trust that the Gods know best, and when it is time for one of his precious Altherians to join the Gods, the Omasye cannot stop them. The Gods must certainly need Mika's light elsewhere. Though his body rests here, his soul will continue to serve to guide the Altherian Empire toward its glorious future."

Natalie Annikki, with her head low, couldn't stop more tears from falling. She knew the preacher was wrong: there was no body. They hadn't recovered one. They were burying an empty wooden box that merely represented her father. Natalie wished she had known that when her father said goodbye to her four cycles ago it would be for the last time. She would never get to tell him about her high school graduation, or what her and her friends did for her seventeenth birthday. Now, flanked by her aunts and uncles, she realized that she was alone and had been alone since her father left on his last trip. In total silence, the tears fell even faster now, only to be blown off course by the cold wind of northern Jontunia.

Natalie remembered the men who came to her door just a few days ago. She thought that her father had come home early, and she had run down the stairs from her bedroom to greet him. Instead, she opened her door and saw two men climbing from an unfamiliar car.

"We're sorry... your father... flying home from the New Federation..." Everything they said to her was so blurred together and flimsily strung in her mind that it was more like recalling a nightmare than a real event.

She looked up at where the coffin had been laid. The machine had been taken out, and the hole was being filled with dirt. This was the proof: the empty coffin, the aunts and uncles that Natalie hadn't seen in years, all of it was proof that it hadn't been a nightmare. Her father was really gone, and she was alone. The family that she had left would be on flights back to their homes soon and would probably never come to Rikata again. Even now, as the last of the dirt began to cover the wooden symbol of a man, his brothers and sisters turned to leave.

Some left without a word. Occasionally, Natalie heard whispering between them as they left. One or two placed their hand on Natalie's shoulder, pausing before they left. And then they were gone. The only family members she had left, heading back to the airstrip at the edge of town to leave forever. When she looked up, however, she was not alone. Standing at the edge of the freshly buried grave was a woman in a black dress. She wore a black coat as well to shield herself from the still cold summertime winds. When she saw Natalie looking at her, she turned to face her.

"I'm sorry," the woman said. "You were his daughter, right?"

Natalie nodded.

"Mika was a colleague of mine." She looked over her shoulder at the grave. "He was a good man. I'm sure he was a good father for you as well."

Natalie felt the tears pooling in her eyes again. She didn't want to cry in front of a stranger. She was sure that the woman could already see the redness of her eyes and the flush of her skin trying to keep herself together. "He was," she said, though the words came out much quieter and hoarser than she wanted. "He was gone a lot, but when he was home, he was always teaching me new things."

"Did they tell you much about his death?" the woman asked.

Natalie looked past her at the grave. "I didn't ask them for details," she said. "They just told me that he had finished his work on one of the Halerian colonies, and while crossing the border back into the Altherian Empire his ship was attacked and destroyed."

"They didn't tell you who destroyed his ship?"

Natalie shook her head. "They said it was unknown, but that it was probably an identification error from either a Halerian or Altherian patrol."

The woman was silent for a couple of moments. "They told us the same thing," she said. "They came to the firm's headquarters on Sintunisia the same day that he was supposed to be arriving."

"They came to tell me three days ago now."

The woman looked at Natalie. "What will you do now?"

Natalie shrugged. "I'm not sure," she said. "I've finished school, so I'm just waiting on some applications to pan out. I probably won't be staying here, though."

"If that's the case, perhaps you will consider continuing your father's legacy in the future." The woman produced a plastic card from her jacket. "Your father did great things. If you're ever interested, we would be more than happy to pay for your education and give you a position within our firm." She handed the card to Natalie.

Natalie took the card in her hands and looked at it for a few moments. In fine blue writing, it said: *Rebirth Colonial Development*, and in much smaller letters: *Giving planets a new life as a home for all of us.* Below that was one phone number, labelled "applications."

"Whenever you make your decision on what you want to do," the woman told her, "just call that number and tell them your name. Everyone would love to help continue the Annikki legacy."

Natalie looked up at the woman. "Thank you," she said. The tears were coming back in earnest. "This means a lot to me. I'm glad my father meant this much to your company."

"He was one of the best," the woman said. "He will be missed on Sintunisia, but I know he will be missed even more here. Take as much time as you need, and if this is your calling, then reach out to us when you're ready." She turned to leave. "Take care, Ms. Annikki."

The moment the woman turned her back on Natalie, the tears came streaming down, following paths that many had followed before. Natalie clutched the plastic card with both hands as she watched the woman leave the cemetery. Her vision was blurring, and she could do nothing but turn away, back to face the grave of her father, where she stayed for another hour.

***

The walk back across town to Natalie's home was nearly silent. There was little activity in the small town, and in the fading light of the sun going below the distant mountains, most were at home relaxing or preparing dinner. As fast as the shadows were growing over the town, the temperature was dropping faster, heading toward the night temperatures of just above freezing.

The house sat atop one of the larger hills in the town, overlooking much of the east side of town below. While the hill cast its shadow on the rest of town, Natalie's home was awash in the fading orange glow of the day's remaining light. From here, the distant cemetery was just visible, followed by the town's airstrip and the flat ground of the forest and lake beyond. Natalie hardly took a glance back at the town before she climbed the three steps to her door and went inside.

There was much to do. In the days since learning about her father's death, Natalie had found herself unable and unwilling to carry out many, if any, of her daily chores and activities. Now dishes were piling up in the kitchen, and dirty clothes threatened to overrun the confines of their hamper. Though she had work to do, along with preparing her own dinner, Natalie moved sluggishly through her home. Once a place of comfort, it suddenly felt empty, as though it had been long abandoned. It shouldn't have felt any different, Natalie knew. Her father wasn't supposed to be home from work yet. It should be normal to be alone in the house. After all, for the past eleven years, she had seen her father only four times per year, each for about one cycle. For eleven years, she saw him twenty-eight days at a time. Yet now everything about her house felt different, empty, and wrong.

Natalie stopped just after the front door, peering down the halls and up the stairs to the bedrooms. Even though Natalie's father had only lived in the house some four cycles a year, his absence now made Natalie feel more alone than she had ever felt before. For the first time in her life since her father had gone back to work following her mother's departure, she was bothered by the fact that she was alone. As she put her dinner in the oven, she could feel the tears rushing back to her as her mind waded through sudden loneliness.

She sat down on the floor, leaning against the counter wall, her legs tucked close to her chest. She glanced up at the digital display hidden in the wall before her; the sixth cycle of 2592, and the second day. The first tears escaped her and slid down her cheeks, and she rested her face against her knees. *Why?* her mind asked. *Why him? Of the millions who cross the border everyday, of the billions of Altherians, why him?* She knew that she would never have that answer. After all, her father's death was a fluke; a mistake, a one in a billion chance that *someone*, on either side of the border, misidentified his ship. It didn't matter who did it; the result was the same. Knowing who made the mistake would do nothing to bring her father back. And it certainly wouldn't make Natalie's pain or loneliness go away.

After a few minutes, Natalie lifted her head up. She took the end of her emerald-green hair, which lay across her right shoulder in a ponytail, and held it across her mouth. She closed her eyes, and after a minute, her mind slowed. She felt her tears stop, the old ones already beginning to dry on her skin. *I have to keep going*, she thought. She pushed herself up from the floor and glanced at the oven timer. She still had over half an hour before her dinner would be ready. *Enough time to get some stuff done at least.*

Natalie first made her way to the laundry room. Looking at the mountain of dirty clothes waiting by the washing machine, Natalie sighed. She regretted not doing a load of laundry just a day sooner, at least a day before the men had come to her home and shattered her life. Now there was more than just one load of laundry to do, and the second would have to wait until after dinner. Once she finished starting the first load of clothes, Natalie returned to the kitchen and began filling the sink with hot water. The countertop next to the sink was stacked with dishes, pots and pans, and a large bowl of cutlery. Her dinner, which lay in the oven, was out of necessity. She had used up everything to cook with on the stove. As the sink slowly began filling, Natalie grabbed a cloth, dampened it, and then set about wiping down various surfaces around the house.

Though Natalie was happy that she was at last occupied, she found unwanted memories creeping in with each room. She remembered holidays, birthdays, and watching movies with her father in the living room as she wiped down the coffee table. In the study, each book brought back memories. The seemingly endless books on history and politics, the one shelf of only mystery novels that her father enjoyed so much. Another shelf contained only books on historical colonization, from the first planet, Suntara, which took a millennium to fully develop, to the modern era of rapid terraforming. Everything brought back memories of her father, and Natalie felt her eyes well up with tears again and again.

When she returned to the kitchen, she stared at the sink. The water steamed around soapy bubbles. *What's the point?* she thought. *If everything is going to make me cry, I should do nothing instead.* She frowned and shook her head. *I can't. That won't get me anywhere.* A lone tear broke free, and Natalie shook her head again. She began placing dishes into the sink. Even as another tear slid down her left cheek, she kept working, scrubbing at each dish and placing them neatly in the rack for drying.

***

Sleep didn't come as quickly for Natalie as she had hoped. Every minute of peace was interrupted by memories of her father, life without him, and her own future. No matter how much she turned in her bed, repositioning herself and adjusting the warm blanket around her, she could never find sleep. When her body, rather than her mind, gave in, sleep was more like an extended blink, a dozen seconds when Natalie closed her eyes and opened them to face the morning light.

Beams of light came through the thin curtains and fell on the far side of the room, lighting up her desk and dresser. The bed, nestled against the wall under the window, remained in the fleeting shadow. Rolling in her sheets, Natalie turned away from the light filling her room and faced the still-dark wall. About five minutes later, she rolled onto her back and stared up at the ceiling. Sighing, Natalie threw the sheets off her and sat up. The light from the window hit her face, and she squinted, looking out the window in disgust before turning to face the other side of the room. Stretching, Natalie shook out the remnants of her bad sleep. She stood up, and without taking anymore pause than to glance at her bed, left the room and headed for the kitchen.

Breakfast didn't take long to make; a simple meal of eggs and toast with a cup of coffee was all Natalie cared to make. As she ate, she looked up at the digital display in the kitchen, and then outside. It looked like a beautifully clear and warm day. *That's the end of the cold then, I guess,* Natalie thought. *It'll be properly summer in no time, just sweat and bugs.* She shook her head just before taking a big bite out of her toast. *It's probably already baking down south.* She looked back outside. *At least it doesn't last long here.* Natalie returned to her food, finishing the last few bites quickly.

After a quick washing of the morning's dishes, Natalie went back to her room. Opening each of the drawers of her dresser in turn, Natalie took out each article of clothing she would need for the day, tossing each one onto the chair at her desk. When she had finished, she found that she had taken everything out in the wrong order, sighing as she lifted everything else just to reach her socks. Quickly, Natalie changed from the dark green tank top and black shorts she wore to bed and into a simple white T-shirt and dark blue jeans. Next, she grabbed her backpack, which was sitting against the end of her bed, and put it on her desk. Opening the pouch, Natalie picked up two books from her desk and slid them gently into the bag. The first was *Jontunia's Hidden Wonders*, a thin book with an image of a forested river valley on it. The second was *The Altherian-Halerian Interstellar War*, a much thicker hardcover book with the flags of both the New Federation and the Altherian Empire on its cover. Closing the bag, Natalie put it on and left the room, grabbing her house keys off the wall before heading outside.

Going from her house to the town's airfield never took long, as Natalie walked along the road and down the hill she lived on. A short walk to the east end of town and then a little way north brought her to the edge of town and placed the airfield control tower and its four small hangars well within sight. Natalie continued walking until she got just past the airfield's center. Stepping off the road and onto a lightly trodden dirt path, Natalie walked through a grassy field for a couple of minutes before the path began climbing a hill close to the fence on the edge of the runway. At the top of the hill, Natalie had a near perfect view of the airfield. She could see the entirety of the runway, as well as any activity in front of the first two hangars.

Plopping her bag down on the cool green grass, Natalie sat down next to it, facing the airfield. Natalie frowned slightly as she peered into the airfield. There was little activity from what she could see. Rikata's only plane of any notable size was sitting quietly outside the first and largest hangar, its twin jet engines rotated forty-five degrees upwards to aid it in taking off from the small runway. But the plane was not getting ready for take-off, and instead a pair of technicians in orange jumpsuits walked around the plane, stopping every now and then to touch, check, or adjust something on the plane. Accepting that there might not be anything to watch for awhile, Natalie turned to her bag, from which she drew the first book, the thinner of the two, and opened it to a bookmark near the end.

Natalie was well into the second, much thicker book, when she heard steps climbing the hill. Looking up from her book, she smiled at the woman climbing the hill. She was older, somewhere in her early forties, and was wearing a faded green technician's jumpsuit, and her hair was pulled back into a hasty ponytail.

"Good morning, Natalie," the woman said. "What'cha readin' today?"

"Good morning, Elle." Holding her page with her thumb, Natalie flipped the cover of the book forward to show her. "It's about the first interstellar war, when the Halerians invaded us. I'm re-reading some of it."

Elle took a careful seat on the grass next to Natalie. "My father told me tons of stories about that war when I was growing up. Next year will be what, fifty years since the start of the war?"

"Yeah, the capital has already started preparations for the anniversary. They're expecting people from across the empire to come to Jontunia to pay thanks to the 3rd Mobile's defense of Altheria." Natalie looked out at the horizon. "I'd love to see it. My dad promised to take me, but…" Her voice trailed off, and she looked down at the grass.

"Sorry to hear about your father," Elle spoke quietly, placing a hand on Natalie's shoulder. "I wanted to be at the funeral, but the boss gave me a private contract that he said I couldn't refuse."

"It's okay, thanks." Natalie looked up at the airfield. "A private contract, huh?"

Elle shook her head and looked out at the airfield as well. "Technically speaking, I can't talk about any of its details. In fact, according to our logs, it didn't even happen."

Natalie looked at Elle. "What?"

"Moving some people from the capital to here and back. I flew out before dawn yesterday to pick them up in Garun and get them here by sunrise. And then they told me I had to wait in the plane until they came back, which was only by the evening." Elle shook her head again. "Just a weird one, y'know. I got back here late last night, and now my plane has got a knock in the left engine. Probably from too much flyin'. She's gettin' too old for this kind of stuff."

"I'm sorry to hear that," Natalie said. "It definitely sounds like a weird job."

"Yeah, at the end of the day, it pays well though." Elle paused. "It's a shame though, I wanted to take you up today too."

Natalie smiled. "There's always another day."

"How's your application coming along?" Elle asked, changing the subject.

"Oh, uh, I don't really know," Natalie stammered. "I guess I'm just kind of waiting to hear back from the OSC at this point."

Elle sighed. "I'm sure they'll take you. The OSC is desperate for pilots. But they do take their time, don't they? That was one thing I never missed about it. It was like every question went all the way to the Omasye himself."

Natalie laughed. "As long as I get to fly, I think I can deal with that."

"I'm happy to hear that," Elle said, smiling. "I was worried that with everything that happened you wouldn't want to leave Rikata. I was afraid that you'd give up on flying."

Natalie shook her head. "No, I know that this is still what I want to do. I'll admit that things have been... harder since..." As her voice trailed off, Natalie felt a hand on her shoulder. She turned to see Elle's reassuring smile.

"I understand," Elle said. "I suppose, for me, my parents lived long lives and so I was well into my own life when they died, but it was still the hardest times in my life. Grieving is all part of the process, especially when it is so fresh, but you will keep moving forward. If Jontunia stopped spinning every time someone lost their parent, we would never see another day. Your world may have stopped spinning right now, but you'll get back up and going soon. I'm sure that your application will be accepted soon, and then you'll get to fly."

"Yeah... got it." Natalie sniffled a little, but no tears had escaped this time. "I think I'd rather it gets accepted sooner than later. Having something to do would help me a lot right now." She looked down at the open book on her lap.

"So, what parts of the war are your favorite to read about?" Elle asked, looking at the book and then at Natalie.

Natalie smiled when she heard the subject change. "Well, I think it's pretty well mandatory for every Jontunian to say, 'the 3rd Mobile's defense of the homeworld.' At least, that's what it seemed like in school." Natalie paused in thought before continuing. "But for all its remarkable moments, I've always found the *Ardonis Moon* and its little fleet's defense of Suntara to be more inspiring. For less than eight hundred ships to win against over four *thousand*, it's incredible."

Elle looked up at the sky. "It really is," she said. "All of those people whose names are known across the empire now—"

"All it would have taken was for one of them to not be there," Natalie interrupted. "They made decisions that no one else could, risking everything to protect their home."

Elle smiled. "Most of them died doing it, y'know."

"But they pulled off the impossible; that's what's so amazing about their stories."

Elle sighed, still smiling. "I suppose so," she said before standing up. "Well, I should probably get back to work. I'm sure the techs could use the help." The pair gave their goodbyes, and Elle departed down the hill. Natalie returned to her book, opening it back up to where her thumb had held the page. She read for awhile longer before her stomach told her it was time to eat. Carefully putting the book back into her bag, Natalie left the hill overlooking the airfield.

After getting lunch from a quiet shop near the center of town, Natalie walked back toward the east side of town. This time, however, she stopped short of the airfield, instead arriving at the gate of the town's cemetery. Quietly, she walked along the rows of tombstones until she reached a now all-too-familiar row. Not far along was a patch of misshapen grass and dirt clumps, and a simple tombstone with her father's name etched on its face. Natalie stopped at the foot of her father's grave and stood in silence for a few minutes.

I don't get it, she thought. *How could anyone make this kind of mistake? Who would have? The Halerians? Altherians?* She shook her head. She would never know. Chances were, nobody really knew except for the people who did it. Natalie knew that space was too vast, and the gray space between the New Federation and Altherian Empire too sparsely monitored, to ever find the truth. *It could have easily just been some pirates. That would explain why they couldn't recover a body.* Her mind began to flash images of the pirates she had heard of in stories, and the things they did to those they captured—dead or alive.

Natalie closed her eyes and looked up at the sky. When she opened them, she was staring up at the dark blue of the distant atmosphere above the clouds and closer to the edges of space. She could just make out the green tint, which faded in the atmosphere. It was the green coloration of the Salerum Cloud, the nebula that shrouded Jontunia and her moon from the outside.

I could be up there soon, she thought. *Me, a pilot in the OSC. I could fly the same space that my father did. And that he died in.* The second thought interjected itself before Natalie could shut it out. She looked back down at the grave in front of her. *Should I really be doing this? What would I be protecting? I have no more family. I should just be happy with what I have here.* She looked back at the town, at the hill in the distance where her house sat. *What do I have here anymore?*

It was nearly an hour before she returned to her home. On the short path to the front door of the house was a small metal mailbox, which Natalie flipped open as she walked by, expecting it to be empty. She had to stop and step back after the white of an envelope flashed past her vision. She took the envelope inside with her. It was addressed to her, and the front of it had OSC on it in large, bold letters, with Omasye Space Council, Jontunia underneath in much smaller letters.

Natalie hardly had her bag off before she tore the envelope open in the kitchen. Inside the envelope was one sheet of neatly folded paper with Natalie's name and address at the top. Natalie unfolded the letter and began reading. Quickly, it was apparent that it was an offer to join the OSC as a pilot like she had applied for. The letter briefly mentioned that the training base was in Sardubra, and that the course was eight cycles long. Finally, it stated that if Natalie wanted to accept the offer, she needed to be in Narhava by the nineth. Natalie spun around to double-check the wall display: it was the third.

Then the doubts from the cemetery came rushing back. *Do I even go?* she thought. *Is it right to leave? To leave everything behind? My home, my things, my father's things? Leave it all behind? I want to leave. I have to leave. But what would become of everything here?* She paced from room to room in the house, as though the thoughts were a ghost and she simply needed to find the room it didn't have the key to. But there was none. Even when she made dinner, she thought about leaving or staying. And when she went to bed, she had to fight off the same thoughts to sleep.

***

"I could take care of it," Elle said as she sorted through an unorganized toolbox. "You've no family left here, right?" Finding the tool she was looking for, Elle shoved the drawer closed with her elbow.

"Yeah, I'm the only one now," Natalie said quietly, shifting on her feet. "Are you sure though? I don't know if I'll ever be back."

Elle smiled as she climbed the stepladder under her plane's left engine. "You think I *don't* know that?" She laughed. "Which one of us has done this before again?"

Natalie couldn't help but smile. "Alright, that's fair, but only if you're certain you want to do it. I don't want to impose."

"It's not an imposition, dear, and whenever you retire, you'll want a home to come back to. Trust me." Elle reached deep into the underside of the engine and began turning something with the tool. "Grab that plastic bin."

Natalie did as she was told, holding the plastic bin under the spot where Elle was working. "Alright, then it's settled. I'll come drop off the spare key tomorrow," Natalie said, watching as a metal bolt dropped from inside the engine and into the bin with a thunk. "And I'll put my key in the mailbox when I leave."

"Four days, right?" Elle asked.

"Yeah," Natalie paused. "Four days."

Dinner sizzled pleasantly on the stove as Natalie cleaned the counters on the other side of the kitchen. *I'm not abandoning anything anymore,* she thought, smiling. *Thanks to Elle, I won't have any regrets. Everything will be here whenever I come back.* She repeated the last sentence again, gazing across the room.

"Whenever that is," she said. She knew deployments in the OSC were often for years at a time, with only short periods spent back at a fleet's home planet for resupply. Her smile had vanished. *Will I ever see this place again before I retire? When will* that *be?*

***

Natalie stared at the wall display while stirring her cereal in its bowl. *Three days.* She looked outside. It was cloudy, the dark sort of clouds that meant rain would start to fall any minute now. She wouldn't be going to the airfield today, not in this weather. Chances were, Elle wasn't going to be working either. Next to her bowl on the table was the acceptance letter from the OSC. It faced her, the top third folded up and in perfect view, its words immediately readable each time Natalie looked down at her food. Natalie flipped the paper over. *Am I just running away?* She stared at the book she had been reading, which was sitting on her bag in the chair next to her. *I want to fly though.* What better way to spend one's life flying, Natalie had thought when she applied, than by doing it in the defense of her home and her people? What if she could be like the heroes of the last war?

It had started to rain about halfway to the cemetery. By the time Natalie got to her father's grave, the grass was a shining wet, and the still-visible dirt had become saturated and had begun to turn to mud. Water beaded and rolled off Natalie's olive-green jacket, dripping onto the grass as Natalie stood silently over the grave.

"I'm not wrong for wanting to leave, am I?" Natalie asked the stone. "Is it wrong to leave all of this behind?"

Natalie shuffled her feet and looked down at the ground as if she were expecting to hear a response. The only sound that came was the quiet ruffle of leaves as a weak breeze swept through the cemetery.

"I love this town." Natalie looked back out the entranceway to the cemetery and at the rest of the small town. "But there's nothing left for me here. There's no future." Tears, the first of the day, began to fall onto the grass, blending and disappearing with the rain. "I don't want to leave you, or home, or this town, but I have to. Is that okay?"

Again, the stone didn't respond. It never would. After a handful of minutes, Natalie turned away from her father's grave. She sniffled back the last of the tears.

"I need a career. I want to fly. The only pilots here are retirees." She turned back to the stone. "Maybe I'll come back and be just like them. To do that, though, I need to go. Goodbye, Dad."

As though the stone would see and judge her, Natalie turned her back on the grave and left the cemetery in a hurry before the tears could come rushing back to her, stronger than ever before.

She spent the better part of the afternoon cleaning up the house to make things easier for Elle. Natalie washed all the dishes, bagged all the trash, and set about cleaning the floors, tables, counters, and walls of the entire house. Taking only a brief break to cook herself dinner, it was night before Natalie realized. Walking through each of the rooms in the house, she found that each one was well cleaned and prepped for what might be years of disuse. Satisfied with her work, Natalie went to bed. When she would wake up, it would be her last full day in Rikata.

It was still raining when Natalie woke up, the sounds of thousands of water droplets pattering the window of her bedroom. Natalie spent much of the day slowly packing the things she would take with her. Suspecting that she wouldn't be able to come back home after training, she made sure to pack some of her personal belongings that she would want with her in her "new" life. One was a small stuffed animal, which had been sitting on the corner of the nightstand. It was a cat, a gift her father had given her after one of his trips to Altheria. Natalie picked it up and sat on the bed holding it. She knew that of everything she owned, she couldn't leave this behind. A single tear formed from her left eye before falling across her cheek. Natalie brushed it away, returning herself to the task at hand. She took the stuffed animal and put it in the bag with everything else. Soon, she had everything she felt that she needed neatly packed away into one duffel bag. She brought the bag downstairs, leaving it by the door before going into the kitchen.

The only other thing to take with her would be the acceptance letter from the OSC. Placing the letter inside a fresh envelope, Natalie took it to where her jacket was hanging and placed it in the inside pocket. *Everything's set now*, she thought, looking around at her bag and the clean kitchen. It was already late afternoon, with the sun beginning to shine through the kitchen windows in an orange hue. Natalie decided to take the rest of the evening to relax and catch an early night.

The next morning, Natalie didn't waste time getting out of bed. She quickly got dressed, pulling on some warm pants over her legs, and a light T-shirt and sweater over her slim upper body. After a quick meal, followed by cleaning the used dishes, Natalie threw on her jacket and grabbed her bag. The sun was up, and the clouds of the previous days were clearing. Natalie put her key in the mailbox as she left. She hoped that Elle would be at the airfield to get the other key.

The walk to the airfield felt slightly longer with the big duffel bag on her back, but Natalie didn't mind. The air was still cool, so she didn't get uncomfortably sweaty. When she arrived, the small plane she would be taking was already sitting outside its hangar, facing the runway. Natalie paid for her ticket and walked out onto the tarmac. Elle was working on her plane like usual.

"Hey, Elle," Natalie said as she got close. "I have that key for you." She fished it out of her pocket.

Elle smiled, taking the key. "For a bit there I thought you'd changed your mind," she said. "I'm glad to see you're still going."

"Me too. The house is all cleaned up for you, so you can do what you want with it while I'm gone."

Elle gave Natalie a hug. "I'll take good care of it for you." She looked at the other plane, its passenger door open and its pilot waiting outside. "Looks like you'd best be going now. I'll see you soon."

The plane Natalie boarded was small, with only a dozen or so seats, and not even half were filled. She took a seat alone and waited. She hoped that eventually she would return, but she knew it would be many years from now. Natalie hoped that by then the fighting between the Altherian Empire and the New Federation would have ended, and she would be satisfied having contributed to that. The plane taxied to the end of the runway, and as it took to the sky, Natalie watched the small town she had known for the past seventeen years become smaller and smaller, eventually vanishing on the horizon.

CHAPTER 2

Natalie landed in the city of Narhava just before midday. The sight of hundreds, maybe thousands of towering skyscrapers and what seemed like an endless flow of people was overwhelming for Natalie coming from a small town like Rikata. The city seemed to go on forever, and no matter how far she traveled along the city's metro train system, the city never seemed to slow down. Mass transit was the only land-traveling system offered, and on her flight in, Natalie saw thousands of buses and metro-trains running through Narhava, like blood in the veins of a body.

With her directions to the OSC center, Natalie arrived by late afternoon that day to finish the next step of her application. The result was hours of filling out the necessary paperwork and getting her medical tests completed. While waiting for confirmation, she stayed in a nearby hotel, using what money she had to pay for bed and board. Two days later, she was given instructions for transportation to the Omasye Space Council's main training facility on Jontunia. It was the same training base mentioned in the acceptance letter, a facility in Sardubra, the southernmost continent of the planet. The base was in a remote region, deep inside the mountains and rivers of the continent, where the OSC trained citizens of Jontunia how to fight the enemies of the Omasye. The training grounds were divided into multiple bases, each one specializing in an element of the military.

The first thing Natalie noticed when she got to the base was the heat. Despite being in the southern hemisphere, where it was currently winter instead of summer like in Rikata, the temperature was much higher. Compounding this was the fact that it was just as humid as it was in the north, and Natalie could feel the sweat forming on her skin from the moment she arrived.

A large bus took her and other recruits to the pilot training base, one of the sub-bases of the massive training facility. Once they got off the bus, the recruits were quickly organized into a classroom for a short briefing, mostly on dress and deportment. They were then taken outside where they were given a quick lesson on basic military drill.

After a few hours, the recruits were taken to the barracks to be issued their uniforms, and then to their quarters. Natalie was given a small room in the barracks, along with a stack of paper containing information on her training, rules of the base, eating times, and more, even drier material. Every recruit was expected to know all the information in the papers by the next day. It took her the rest of the day to read it all. She had just enough time to get some rest, knowing that training would begin in earnest tomorrow.

The sounds of alarm bells and shouting woke Natalie. She jumped out of bed, throwing on her uniform as quickly as she could. *What? What's going on?* Her still half-asleep brain moved her body through motions as it tried to process what was happening. She turned first to make her bed, and then to the mirror at the end of the room. Satisfied with the way her clothes looked, she rushed out into the hall while putting her hair in her usual ponytail. She stood in her doorway, looking up and down the hall.

Training staff in uniform were moving through, shouting into the recruit's bedrooms. Farther up the hall, she saw other recruits standing at attention in front of their doors. Natalie followed suit, standing at attention until the staff came by. One of them looked at her top to bottom, only stopping for a moment. Apparently not finding anything wrong, they moved on without word. *Is this what it will be like every morning for the next eight cycles?* Natalie thought.

Glancing down the hall, she saw one of the soldiers berating another recruit, a young man unshaven and half-dressed, who had obviously only made it out of his room just in time. Some other recruits laughed when they saw the man, but they in turn received only hard stares from the soldiers, which put them silent in a hurry. Once the men had reached the end of the hall and had finished checking each recruit, they dismissed the recruits for breakfast.

The mess hall was an unadorned, wide space full of tables and chairs, and the far wall was replaced by a long metal counter, where the base's cooks served the meals. Some of the recruits had already grabbed their meal trays and were standing in line waiting to be served when Natalie arrived. She followed, grabbing a tray from the beginning of the counter and eventually received a simple breakfast. She sat at an empty table away from the main group of recruits. She was only a few minutes into eating when she sensed someone approach her table.

"What are you doing," the voice of a man said, "sitting here all by yourself?"

Natalie glanced across the table, watching a tray be set down across from her, followed by a young man taking a seat himself. Natalie recognized him as the man who had been berated in the hall earlier for not being dressed. He was dressed now, but still unshaven. He was a handsome man, with short, thick brown hair, and he looked strong and tall. He was smiling when he sat down and looked up at Natalie.

He introduced himself, outstretching his right hand toward her. "Name's Darren Verra."

Natalie shook his hand, replying. "My name is Natalie Annikki." She looked back down at her food right away, continuing her meal.

"Well, it's a pleasure to meet you, Natalie Annikki." Darren Verra paused, subtly looking over Natalie's figure. "You're pretty small for someone who wants to be in the military; you sure you're in the right place?" He finished speaking, putting a large mouthful of food in his mouth.

His comment irked Natalie, who was silent for a few seconds. "That's some awfully big talk for someone who couldn't even get dressed this morning," she replied. "Are you sure that *you're* in the right place?" She continued to eat as Darren chuckled, still trying to finish his mouthful.

"Well, I guess you've got me there." He swallowed the last of his food. "But, hey, discipline has never been my strong suit. Not something I've ever much cared about. I just wanna fly, make a name for myself. I couldn't care less if my clothes are perfectly ironed," he lifted his hands in air quotations, "or if I meet the "model soldier" requirements. I know what I'm here for, and I know I'm gonna be damn good at it. All this discipline bull, just not something I feel the need to care about."

"It'll be pretty hard to be good at this without proper discipline." Natalie was becoming more annoyed. He already thought he was going to be top stuff. This man was so confident in his abilities, but couldn't even exhibit the most basic requirements? "If you think you're going to be a good pilot, you'll have to fix that."

Darren took a drink before speaking. "Maybe," he scratched the short hair on his chin and jaw, "but when I do, I'll be the best pilot here. You, on the other hand, you might wanna bulk up. It looks like you might not even be able to pull back on the stick without breaking your arms." He laughed and then shoveled more food in his mouth.

Natalie stood up, having finished her food. She looked him in the eye before walking past him. "I'll think about it," she muttered. As she walked off, "idiot" slipped out under her breath.

Immediately after breakfast, the recruits began their first class. The classroom was plain and uninteresting, and large enough to contain the hundred-odd recruits comfortably. Natalie found a spot to sit, specifically away from Verra, who was already sitting down in the midsection of the room. All the seats filled up quickly, and the class soon began.

One of the instructors stood at the front of the class, and a projector lit up an image of the OSC symbol on the wall.

"Welcome to your first proper lesson," the instructor said. "I'm certain that you are all familiar with the basics of each of the Omasye's Commands that govern each of the core functions of our great empire. Today, however, you will become intimately familiar with the inner workings of the Omasye's Space Command, from the very top in HQ on Altheria, down to the lowest spec of dirt within the organization, otherwise known as recruits."

A couple of the recruits laughed at her joke, but most silently stared on as the projector switched to a slide of the OSC's structure.

"From HQ, the OSC is divided into two distinct groups: the Mobile fleets, and the Defensive fleets." The instructor now had a laser pointer, which she used liberally. "The seven Mobile fleets are the tip of the spear in our fight against our enemies, and..."

Natalie could already feel herself losing interest. She wanted to slump onto her right arm and shut her eyes, or at least stare at the wall. She knew she couldn't, as a second instructor was watching the class like a hawk, making sure no one was falling asleep or not paying attention. *I know all of this,* she thought. *Can't they just give me a test and let me get on with the stuff I don't know?*

After an hour of lecturing things that Natalie already knew, the subject changed to the training schedule for the recruits.

"Every morning before breakfast, except for on weekends, you will all be formed up at the training yard no later than 0500," the instructor explained. "After some good PT, you will be dismissed for breakfast at 0555. Lecture class will begin at 0700, and will begin by covering the basics of flight, but will get more complicated over the coming weeks. Lunch is from 1200 to 1250, and then you will all be formed up in the training yard to learn military code, drill, and rifle training. For those of you who make it to the second cycle, the afternoon classes will be replaced by simulation training. In either case, these training periods will last until dinner, from 1700-1830. After which will be your main physical training class, which will run until we decide it does. Sometimes this may be replaced by military training such as tactics or pilot survival training. You get an hour of free time before lights out, one hour before moonhigh. Any questions?"

When nobody answered, the instructor nodded and changed the projector to another presentation, this one about military conduct. Natalie yawned, and she was relieved an hour later when lunch came around and they were dismissed from class. Lunch, just like the classes, was boring. Natalie found a spot by herself in the mess hall, and Verra nor anyone else bothered her.

After lunch, the recruits formed up together the main training building. The instructors from the morning had been exchanged for two new instructors.

"Now I know you were told that each day your afternoon classes would be on basic military skills," the lead instructor of the pair explained. "Today, however, things will be slightly different."

At once, the other instructor began calling some basic drill commands to get the body of recruits marching toward the largest of the various sets of hangars on the base. It wasn't a far distance, but it took the recruits around some smaller buildings until they came out between two hangars. When the recruits got to the front of the hangars, four different military craft were waiting. They were split in pairs by size, and each pair sat in front of one of the hangars.

"Today, we decided that we would introduce you to the four options you have as pilots in the OSC," the instructor said.

The instructors took the recruits to the two larger craft first, specifically the largest ship there. It was much larger than the other planes, and Natalie had quickly deduced it was a transport. It was bigger than the passenger craft, which came to the airstrip in Natalie's hometown. It had a very wide wingspan, stretching to what Natalie guessed was around a hundred meters. Forward propulsion came from two massive dual-function ion-jet engines, which were located in the corners where the wing met the fuselage. The fuselage itself appeared very rounded, especially near the front where it sloped downward over a large glass canopy covering the cockpit.

"This here is the Phantom-class Heavy Transport, the main heavy lifter of the OSC." The instructor walked under its nose and toward its forward landing gear, of which the tires were almost his height. "These titans are referred to as planet builders, because if a fleet can deploy enough of them, they can build a base the size of this whole training facility in a week. Or, if you fly the Phantom-Heavy, you'll hear the nickname planet razer. The heavy is a strategic bomber, replacing all of the cargo capacity for large conventional ordnance, enough for one plane to level a small town."

The instructor carried on, going over its transport capabilities and matching them with the capabilities of the bomber counterpart. The Phantom seemed to interest a few of the recruits, but Natalie remained thoroughly uninterested. In its transport variant, it would never see a frontline fight, and its bomber variant excelled at staying away from enemy guns, high in the atmosphere and out of sight from enemy fighters.

They moved on to the next ship, which also appeared to be a transport, albeit much smaller than the Phantom. This one was a craft that Natalie had seen before. It had been in books that her father had bought for her, and she examined it with a keen interest. It was a Dolphin-Class Light Transport, the main transport in the Omasye Space Council. It was light, just under thirty meters in length, and was amazingly fast. Its powerful twin engines pushed thrust out exhaust ports on either side of the fuselage, just above the rear ramp. Four large exhaust ports on the fuselage rotated to bring even more thrust to propel the craft forward or divert all thrust to slow it down to land vertically. It had a large wingspan, but still much shorter than the Phantom. The Dolphin was similarly unarmed. *This is more like it,* Natalie thought. This was the frontline transport of the OSC, and its variants typically took on the most dangerous roles, like the Thunder Dolphin, which was the main anti-ground and fire support craft, armed to the teeth with cannons and missiles. With speed and maneuverability, Natalie wondered what the Dolphin was truly capable of at its limit.

Natalie did not get to ponder the thought for long, as the instructors moved the recruits to the third craft.

"This is the Hunter-class bomber," the instructor said. "In atmosphere, they operate light duties bombing targets with precision ordnance. In space, however, they are some of the deadliest craft in the battle. They can utilize armor-penetrating torpedoes to break the hulls of capital ships, causing significant damage. A few well-placed torpedoes from a Hunter can cripple a ship the size of a cruiser."

As the instructor continued, Natalie looked over the features of the bomber, supplementing it with the information from the instructor. It was about the same length as the Dolphin, with a wider fuselage, but still narrower after the wingspan was considered. The wide cockpit accommodated a crew of two; a pilot and a weapons master, the latter in charge of aiming and dropping the payload. The ship was slow and had little defensive ability, relying on protection from the ship next to it, a sleek, small craft sitting on its rear landing gear as if it were a moment from leaping skyward.

Natalie studied every curve and line of this smaller plane in detail. Near the front were two cannons, and on its wings it had three machine guns protruding from each. It had long curved wings that elegantly tapered rearward. In the rear, tall twin vertical stabilizers swept back in an elegant curve, and six smaller stabilizers swept in much the same fashion. These six made up the horizontal stabilizer, and two stabilizers rotated forty-five degrees away, up and down on each side of the craft's tail. As Natalie stared at the craft, itemizing each of its deadly features, she heard one of the instructors introduce it as a Spectre-Class fighter. She turned her attention to the instructor and then looked back toward the fighter, still listening intently.

"This is the primary strike craft in the OSC," the instructor explained. "Six .50 caliber machine guns and a pair of 30mm cannons make it the deadliest fighter in the skies, not to mention its capacity for six missiles, either air-to-air or air-to-ground. Its primary role is to engage and defeat enemy fighters, and in doing so it can also be assigned to provide escort to transports and bombers. In the sector, it is regarded as both the most heavily armed and the most maneuverable fighter."

Natalie stared on at the plane. Her eyes passed over every detail three or four times. Natalie was captivated by this formidable craft, and by the end of the tour she wanted to do nothing other than learn to fly a Spectre.

The next stop on the recruits' orientation to pilot training was a massive warehouse-looking building. Inside was a single large room, filled with closed metal machines. They looked strange, big gray boxes on what looked like hydraulic mounts. Not all the machines were the same either. Some were small, and others were quite large, with visible doors and ladders on them. Some had steep slopes to some of their "walls," and others were much shallower, but longer.

As Natalie stared, one of the instructors began speaking. "These are the base's simulators," he said, motioning his hand toward the gray machines. "You will all learn how to fly every one of the four craft within the simulators, and about a cycle from now, you will come here to take your first tests at flying each machine. Do well with that machine's craft, and chances are a couple of cycles from now you'll be flying the real thing. The classroom is your home for the first cycle, but these machines are your home for the cycle that follows." Natalie looked on eagerly. She now saw the path to what she wanted. *Come simulation day, I'll be the best Spectre pilot in the class,* she thought as the instructors led them through the building.

The day's orientation ended when they reached the mess hall once again. The recruits were dismissed for dinner, and many sat down together, discussing in high spirits which strike craft they'd like to fly. Natalie took her meal tray and sat as far away from her classmates as possible. She didn't join to make friends. She joined to protect the Altherian people, and to fly.

She had just started eating when she heard a familiar voice. "Still not joining them? In fact, I think you moved even farther away; wow." Natalie didn't have time to respond before Darren sat down across from her. He quickly pushed a spoonful of mashed potatoes into his mouth, chewing through halfway before speaking. "So, it seems that everyone else knows what they want to fly." He was difficult to understand, his mouth still full of food. He paused for long enough to swallow before continuing. "How about you? Know what you want to fly?"

Why does this man keep coming around? Natalie thought to herself. *He must really be an idiot if he hasn't realized I don't want him here.* "The Spectre," she answered curtly. "The Dolphin if I had to." She took a drink.

Darren paused for a moment before speaking again. For the first time, Natalie noted that he had stopped eating. "The Spectre, really?" His surprise carried into his voice, making it even more obvious, although it was already written all over his face. "Or the Dolphin? Not at all what I'd expect from someone like you."

Natalie felt as though he were going to annoy her again, but she decided to ask anyways. "Someone like me?" Sarcasm slipped into her voice, but Darren seemed to ignore it, if he had even noticed.

"Like I said this morning," he replied quickly, "you don't exactly have the physique expected for a Spectre; I had you down for the Phantom. Y'know, slow, steady, the computers take care of a lot of it for you. But a Spectre or a Dolphin? It's all pilot and muscle. No computers for you there."

Just as I thought: idiot. "You really think that you know it all?" she started, her tone harsh. "By the way you're talking, I bet you want to be a Spectre pilot then, right?" Darren nodded, his usual smile evaporating for a moment. "And you think you're already qualified to tell me if I can or can't do the same? What makes you so sure that you've got what it takes?"

He paused in silence for a few seconds, a little taken aback by Natalie's sudden flash of anger. "I guess we'll see." Darren stood up with his tray. "Training will tell, and that starts with PT tonight."

Natalie met up with the other recruits in the training yard, where all the physical training would take place. The training yard was located a little way outside of the general base structures and consisted of various wooden obstacles as well as a dirt path, which led deep into the forest. Natalie had arrived with only a few minutes to spare, and at the top of the hour, the instructors began the exercise.

"Welcome to PT session number one," an instructor, a man built like an ox with thick arms and a powerful chest, grunted at the recruits. "Your first night with us will determine who is cut out to become a pilot in the OSC, and who is just pretending."

The exercise went on for two gruelling hours, putting the recruits through many intense physical activities. Natalie was certain that she had never run more in her whole life combined. Many recruits did not last through the first hour. A quarter of the remaining recruits did not last the final hour. The instructors, all while yelling at the recruits, sent them over every obstacle in the yard at least two dozen times, and the number of individual exercises that they did was beyond count.

Natalie's arms and legs felt limp. They felt as though they would become putty, that the bones within them had dissolved and she would collapse into a boneless mass of skin and guts with a head. But she refused to quit. Even when they were forced to run through the forest and through a cold river, she didn't give up. Every step of the way, each time she felt as though she was ready to give in, she reminded herself why she was there, and why she would not quit.

If this is the price, then it is worth it, she told herself.

By the end of the training, she stood with the rest of the recruits that had passed the test. Many did not meet the high standards of the OSC, but Natalie could count herself as one of them. She was proud of herself. She felt even more proud when she saw Darren looking on as they were dismissed for the night. He too had passed, but he could no longer hold his fitness over her.

***

The days quickly fell into a routine for Natalie. The classroom lectures continued to cover the basics of flight as well as teaching the recruits proper military conduct and basic skills. Occasionally, these morning classes were used for teaching a deeper understanding of each craft the recruits would fly. Instructors each led small groups of recruits around one of the ships, talking in depth about something about the ship. They were shown and taught about the general characteristics at first, but soon they moved into more detailed lectures including flight controls and how to fly each craft. The days when Natalie was chosen for a tour around the Phantom or the Hunter, she was mostly bored but still paid attention. *Part of being a good pilot is knowing the aircraft that fly around you just as much as your own craft.* She would remind herself of that each time she was learning about something other than the Spectre or Dolphin. On those days when she learned more about those two crafts, she soaked in all the information she could, making sure she knew the ships inside and out. Darren Verra no longer bothered her during mealtime, instead socializing with the rest of the recruits, which Natalie was perfectly happily with.

As the days turned to weeks, the instructors began recommending that the prospective pilots decide what craft they would like to fly, as well as to begin taking time outside of training to learn more about the craft. At the beginning of the second cycle, the recruits would start running simulations on all the craft. Tests would be run at the end of the second cycle to determine if the recruit were qualified to fly their selected craft. During this time, Natalie visited the base's library and picked up several textbooks. All of them covered information about the Dolphin and Spectre, from technical data to flying techniques and historical articles of past combat experiences. She spent the weeks of preparation reading on the Spectre whenever she was out of classes, spending her evening free time outside, on a small hill near the barracks on the west side of the base. Natalie enjoyed the peace and quiet outside, the only infrequent sounds coming from the transports that landed at the airfield. Occasionally, she saw Darren nearby, but he kept to himself, instead seemingly wandering the area with no real goal in mind. Natalie wondered what he was doing, but more often than not simply ignored him to focus on her reading.

This hill was also the best area to view the base as a whole. She had spent her time at the airfield in Rikata on a similar hill, where she could watch all the comings and goings of aircraft, as well as the service vehicles that often ran about the base. The military training base here was far larger than the simple airfield in Natalie's hometown, however. The base had four runways, the larger two crossing each other on the far side of the base from where Natalie's hill was. The smaller two ran parallel to each other, situated to the south, one running east to west and the other running west to east. Each had its own set of hangars, control tower, and service building. Each runway with its set of dedicated structures was the size of the airfield in Rikata. On the northwest side of the base were all the barracks, training, and administrative buildings. There were at least two dozen buildings, ranging from small one-story storage buildings to the massive five-story barrack buildings, which housed not only the recruits but the military staff that lived here. Near the far edge of the buildings, closest to all four runways, was one massive tower, twice as tall than any building. At the top, the tower was completely glass, the final four floors having a 360-degree view of the entire base and its surroundings. This was the central control tower for the entire base, which ran not only air traffic but also base security.

Natalie's hill reached the height of the barracks, but the tower made it look puny by comparison. Natalie wished she could go to the top of the tower and take in the sights of the surrounding landscape.

For now, she accepted, she would enjoy the sights from her hill. Often, as the evening light grew weaker and Natalie finished her reading for the day, she would set her books aside and take in the landscape. Other times, as the moon and stars started to get brighter, she would lay on her back, staring up at them. She wondered how many of the stars in the sky she would visit, traveling to many different worlds, just like her father did. *There's so much to see,* he would say to her when she was a child, *why would anyone want to stay on the ground forever?*

CHAPTER 3

The end of the first cycle of training couldn't end any faster for Darren Verra. Day in and day out of sitting still in classes, taking notes, and being tested on things he found tedious and unimportant was beginning to drain him. He was here to fly, dammit, not be lectured to on how or why the traditions of the OSC exist. For all he cared, they didn't need to exist in the first place. Luckily for Darren, the final week of these basic military classes came and went relatively quickly.

With the start of the second cycle, the daily schedule changed. The basic military classes in the afternoon were replaced by simulator training. Right away, the aspiring pilots would be exposed to their trade on the ground by being put inside virtual substitutes of the real thing. This, to Darren, was real progress, even if he hadn't left the ground yet. And swapping half a day of lectures for a chance to feel the controls of *any* craft was better than nothing. The recruits were taken to the simulation building, where their afternoon was broken up to give them the same amount of practice time with each craft. For the first two days, however, things were slightly different. To get the recruits warmed up to each craft, they would take extended flights, doing two of the craft each day. This initial "test run" allowed each of them to get a feel for the requirements of each individual craft as well as giving both the instructors and the class a benchmark for where everyone sat. Darren anxiously awaited his turn to prove that he was a natural, and all he needed was the controls of the Spectre in his hands to do it.

After the two days, the recruits would carry on with regular practice with each of the four planes. They were handed the cycle's schedule that told them which simulators they were at and at what time. At the end of the cycle, they would take their flight tests. These final tests would determine which of the four craft they had the option of continuing their qualification on when real-world flying began.

As Natalie was handed her schedule, she saw that her simulation testing began with the Hunter-class bomber. She was brought to a wide machine with three small metal steps leading to a hatch-like door. Natalie grabbed the handle on the door, which was located at the door's base. She pulled the door outward and then pushed up; the door opened upward like a wing of a bird. She climbed through and into the cockpit space, which was low but spacious. Even Natalie, who was by no means tall, had to duck as she moved to the flight seat.

As she sat down in the pilot's seat, one of the instructors, who would be serving as the weapons master, climbed in after her. He took his seat to Natalie's left, a seat surrounded by switches and two small joysticks used for guiding missiles and bombs. He also had a screen in front of him that could switch between two cameras on the Hunter itself, or small cameras equipped to some of the large weapons the bomber carried. When both were settled, he gave Natalie the go-ahead to begin, and Natalie strapped herself in and began going through the startup procedures. The cycle of classes and teachings inside the Hunter had taught Natalie all she needed about the controls inside the cockpit, and she had a reasonable expectation for how the craft flew. When she pushed up on the final switch, the machine came to life, and the simulation displays lit up, displaying an environment based on the area around the training facility. The Hunter-class bomber sat on the concrete a few hundred metres from the hangars. As the heads-up display lit up with orange numbers and text, Natalie prepared for takeoff.

The Hunter could not take off vertically with a full payload, but its powerful engines could accelerate it to takeoff speeds in a short distance. Natalie made certain the engines were in this mode before she gradually applied throttle, turning the craft away from the hangar and toward the base's runway. As she lined up with the runway, she pushed the throttle forward, and the Hunter began to accelerate, pushing both Natalie and the instructor back in their seats. She pushed the throttle farther, until it reached its limit. She kept one hand on the flight stick, watching the velocity on the HUD climb to takeoff velocity.

As the craft reached its necessary speed, Natalie pulled back on the stick, and the Hunter climbed skyward. It may have only been a simulator and a craft that Natalie took no interest in, but Natalie felt a rush of adrenaline as the Hunter climbed through the air. The machine they were in accurately simulated how flying a real aircraft felt, the machine bouncing and swaying with the movement of the bomber. It was the closest one could get to flying without being in the real thing. *One step closer; soon I'll be flying for real,* she thought as she banked the bomber to turn toward their destination over the hills.

Almost three hours after climbing inside the gray machine, Natalie took the three metal steps to reach the concrete floor outside. Her flight had gone flawlessly, but Natalie left the machine even less interested in the craft. The first simulation run was just a simple exercise of flying the craft around the base area, followed by a landing, verbally guided by the instructor. The Hunter was not hard to fly. It flew mostly in straight lines, as any attempts at a tight maneuver sacrificed too much speed to be effective. If there was anything to be said for the Hunter, it was fast while flying in those straight lines. The craft was capable of supersonic speeds, a worthy asset to bomb targets and escape quickly. Although the instructor seemed pleased with Natalie's performance, she wasn't looking forward to flying the craft for the rest of the cycle.

As the recruits moved to the day's second scheduled simulation test, Natalie saw that Darren Verra was heading to fly the Spectre. *I wonder if it will go as well as he believes,* she thought. But a moment later, she came back to her senses. *Why am I even thinking about it? Why would I even care?* After all, he was just a cocky guy who thought he could rule the stars. *Maybe struggling will give him a reality check.* Still, she couldn't bring herself to hope that he would fail. No, she found herself hoping he would do well.

An instructor called her name, waiting on her to move to her second flight, this time aboard a Dolphin. As she followed the instructor, she felt some excitement building inside her. It wasn't the Spectre, not yet, but at least it was something she wanted to do. The Dolphin had interested her greatly, and she had spent a good portion of her preparation week reading about the limits of the light transport. Now she had the opportunity to try it out herself.

The simulation machine for the Dolphin was quite different than the Hunter's. It was taller, enough for Natalie to easily stand inside, and was also narrower, with just enough width to fit the two seats and the instruments around them. Natalie strapped herself into her seat while the instructor did the same next to her. On the signal, Natalie started the machine up. The displays depicted a familiar scene, much like the one she saw earlier: the same hangar, the same weather conditions, exactly as it was with the Hunter's flight.

Natalie began the startup procedures, firing them and bringing the engines up to temperature. The Dolphin was designed to take off vertically or in a short distance even fully laden with soldiers and all their gear. Natalie positioned the jump jets on a steep angle and quickly pushed the throttle forward. The Dolphin leapt into the air as if it were weightless, and Natalie quickly maneuvered the engines to a forward position, causing the transport to accelerate rapidly. The machine pushed Natalie farther and farther into her seat as the plane gained speed. She pulled back on the throttle as the craft reached an ideal speed and began her standard flight, a quick trip through the area just like before.

The Dolphin was nimble, even more than she had expected. Despite being called a "light" transport, the craft still weighed over thirty tons. Yet it flew with the agility of a heavy fighter; it was astounding to Natalie. She loved the feel of the craft, one that seemed capable of anything despite its apparent size. At the end of the flight, Natalie approached the base's runway, dropping the landing gear to come in for a conventional landing. As Natalie gently touched down, her instructor promised that vertical landings and high-speed landings would come soon. The Dolphin was incredibly fun to fly, and the promise of more intense flights left Natalie smiling as she climbed from the simulator.

With the last flight finished, the recruits were dismissed for food and some free time before the daily exercise regime. Natalie sat in her usual seat, away from the rest of the recruits. When she glanced up from her food, she saw Darren Verra standing across from her. After a quick glance at him, she turned her attention back to her food, but he set his tray down and sat in the seat across from her.

"Long time no see!" he exclaimed. "Or at least, no talk." He laughed to himself before beginning to eat his meal, taking large spoonfuls of food. Natalie continued to eat, not responding. It took less than a minute for Darren to speak again. "So, how's your flying going?" he started, pausing to finish the food in his mouth. "What ones have you done so far? I did the Dolphin and the Spectre; by the way, the Spectre went *excellently*. Guarantee you that's what I'll be trained for. Probably going to be top of the class for the test too."

Natalie continued eating for a bit longer before feeling obligated to answer his questions. "It's all going well, thank you," she began, looking up from her food at him. He was smiling as usual but had still obviously not developed much discipline, as his hair was still unkempt, and his face was scruffy from days between shaves. "I've tested the Hunter and the Dolphin." She returned to her meal immediately after finishing.

"Yeah, and how did they go?" Darren asked, still trying to make conversation. The air about him seemed different today, Natalie noted; he seemed genuinely interested in how things were going and wasn't there just to flaunt his own success. She decided that she could be friendly with him, so long as he stayed this way.

"The Hunter went fine, although I would be glad if I never flew the simulator for it ever again," she said, and Darren stopped eating, paying attention to every word. "The Dolphin was fun. I played it safe for the first flight, but I can't wait to get back in the sim and push it to its real limit. I think there's potential for it to be faster and more maneuverable than the instructors recommend."

Darren was surprised, pausing for a moment before speaking. "I didn't get that same feeling." He was speaking low, in a more serious tone than normal. For the first time, Natalie felt like he wanted to have a real discussion. "When I flew it, it felt too clunky. Like turning was a huge ask."

"That's closer to how the Hunter handles, but not the Dolphin." Natalie lifted her hands and mimed as she continued. "The Dolphin has four vector-thrust engines, and you control their throttle and position in pairs, left side and right side. However, each one can be controlled separately by its own throttle and positioning stick when unlocked. So, if you are quick enough with your hands, you can rotate each one individually and change their thrusts to make the craft turn in a very specific way, very quickly too, on account of the massive thrust those engines give. The way it sounds, you never really played with their vectoring except to take off. But that's where the Dolphin's maneuverability comes from, its ability to vector thrust in any direction at any time." As she finished speaking, she reached for her cup and took a lengthy drink. Darren sat still, processing everything she had just said in silence. As Natalie put down her drink, she looked at his expressionless face. She decided to give him some time and continued eating her meal.

In time, he began speaking again. He sat back up straight and seemingly found his focus again, looking at Natalie. "I may have been wrong about you, y'know," he said. "You might just get that Dolphin."

"Unless I'm near the top of the class for the Spectre," Natalie responded. "Then they'd have to give me my choice of where I end up." She finished her meal as Darren nodded in agreement. *Maybe I was wrong about him too. If he can talk like this, maybe he isn't so bad.*

Darren departed ahead of Natalie, with three of the other recruits. They laughed and joked about things as they walked to their usual hangout spot. The group had met early in the training and typically spent almost all their recreational time outside the simulation building, where they were now.

As the group began chatting about the day's events and other topics, Darren's mind wandered. It drifted back to his earlier conversation with Natalie Annikki. *I've completely misjudged her,* Darren thought, feigning interest in the actual conversation going on around him. *She's got spirit, that's for sure, and it may be that she has the ability as well.* Darren thought about the pleasantness of their conversation, and how genuine Natalie had been when advising him on the Dolphin. *Maybe she's not as cold as I originally thought; there might be a real nice girl under that shell.* Darren smirked slightly as he thought this, without intention. However, the most vocal of their group, a recruit named Rygil Pryst, noticed.

"What'cha thinking about, Verra?" he said in his usual loud voice. "Must be something good to be smilin' like that."

Darren Verra's smirk instantly vanished, and he turned his head to meet Pryst's stare. Rygil Pryst was not an attractive man, at least not by the standards of any woman Darren had known back home. Pryst was short, around five and a half feet, like Natalie. His face was plump and round, and his nose was too big. His brown eyes, however, were seemingly always leveling a challenging stare at anyone who made eye contact. His cropped blond hair was his only redeeming physical quality, appearing quite soft. He was a talkative man and usually made for entertaining conversation, one of two reasons Darren befriended him. The other was that he was also convinced he was going to be the best Spectre pilot in the class.

Darren shook his head. "Nothing, just going over maneuvers in my head."

Pryst was laughing, and soon the other two joined in. "Come on, buddy," Pryst began, tapping Darren on the shoulder. "Don't lie to me. You were thinkin' about that green-haired girl you were having dinner with, weren't you!" Darren's silence quickly doomed him. "Ha! I knew it!" Pryst lifted his arms high in the air as he confirmed the truth, like a sports player who had just scored. "So, Verra buddy, you making your move on her soon? Is that what you were thinking about?" He stepped close to Darren, who bumped into the wall of the building behind him.

"It's nothing like that," Darren said, his voice serious. "I simply find her interesting to talk to. She wants to be a Spectre pilot, just like us. And I think she's actually got the talent to do it." Darren wasn't sure if he fully believed anything he was saying, but if it made Pryst back off, he was okay with it. "I have no interest in her beyond some friendly conversation. And if she proves to be as good as she intends on being, I'm sure we'll be flying with her in the future." Pryst seemed satisfied with the response, backing off while letting out a puff of air.

"Well, no matter how good you think she is," Pryst began, crossing his arms, "there's no way I'll believe she's a challenger to our position. The top two are ours." Pryst held his pose for a few seconds, arms crossed, his head pointed skyward. Then he dropped his arms and let out a long laugh. The others joined in, and Darren, relieved that he was not on the firing line anymore, did as well.

The next day, the recruits gathered again in the simulation building and soon began the second half of their initial testing. Natalie had spent the previous night preparing herself for today. Today, she would fly the Spectre in the simulator for the first time. First, however, she had to fly the Phantom. Of all the flights she had to do she was looking forward to this one the least. Spending the previous evening reading about it on her usual hill had prepared her but had also dulled any excitement she had about it.

Nothing about it appealed to her: well over a hundred tons, engines that seemed to succeed at only barely getting it off the ground. The job was routine as well, waiting for cargo to be loaded, which made the craft even heavier, then take off, slowly, fly to the destination, usually far away, slowly, and then land, gently and slowly. It was all boring, made worse by the fact that the computer systems inside the Phantom took care of almost everything. The pilot was seemingly there only to watch.

As she climbed into the massive simulator that was the Phantom cockpit, she cursed every second of it to herself. She sat in the seat, strapping herself in, and waited for the all-clear to begin. *It's just a few hours. Get it over with and move on to the Spectre.* And she did. It was the same usual flight as the other two, but at a much slower, wider pace, as the Phantom had to take long wide sweeping lines to make full turns. She landed it as gracefully as a massive plane could, coming to a slow stop on the end of the runway. When Natalie left the massive gray machine, she wished to never see the cockpit of a Phantom ever again.

Natalie spent the few minutes between exercises excited. She knew that there was only one flight remaining, the one that she had been looking forward to all this time. She was finally going to get her chance in the Spectre, the craft that she had dedicated most of her time to learning.

When Natalie reached the gray machine that was the Spectre simulator, she was fully prepared. The machine was the smallest in the building, a narrow machine, but still as long as the Dolphin's. This was to accommodate the second seat, the instructor's seat, behind the pilot. Natalie climbed into her seat and pulled on the harness. It was a five-point harness, unlike the harness used in the other craft. Natalie strapped herself in and waited on the instructor. With the all-clear, she began to run through the startup procedure she had memorized. She flipped the switches in order, as if it were something she had done every day all her life. She flipped the last switch, and the simulator hummed to life. The displays lit up, and Natalie found herself looking around in a virtual cockpit, so close to reality Natalie could almost forget she was only in a gray box.

Takeoff went well as the Spectre accelerated and leapt skyward, but when she banked for her first turn, the light but sensitive stick was almost fighting against her every movement. As she tried to force it to her will, it snapped out of her hand, and Natalie quickly reacted to gather up the plane and regain control before she crashed. The Spectre was incredibly sensitive to inputs, and nothing like Natalie had expected. Most turns ended in her either losing control of the flightstick or the plane jumping on her slightest movements, overzealously rolling or turning the plane.

Twice, Natalie failed to land, her approach either too fast or thrown off by the Spectre's unwieldiness. The third approach, Natalie took good measure to come in slow and straight, landing in much the same fashion as the Dolphin had. When she landed, her instructor patted her on the shoulder before climbing out of the gray box. *What happened?* This was the only thought Natalie could manage as she pulled her green ponytail in front of her face again, pressing it to her nose and mouth. She remained this way, silently, for another minute, calming herself before she felt she was okay to get out of the cockpit.

CHAPTER 4

Even before the metal tray clanged against the table, Natalie knew what conversation was coming, one she had been dreading ever since she stepped out of the final simulator.

"So, how'd it go?" Darren Verra asked in his usual cheery voice. Natalie didn't look away from her food. "The Spectre specifically, of course," Darren clarified when there was a moment of silence. "I'm sure neither of us care about the Phantom." He began to chuckle but stopped when he noticed Natalie's silence. "Hey, are you okay?" His voice had lost its cheeriness.

"I couldn't get it," Natalie began, her voice quiet, and she still did not look at Darren, her eyes still fixed on the mashed potatoes. "The Spectre, I just couldn't get a hold of it. It was too wild, and it fell out of my control too many times." Finished speaking, she reached for her ponytail, holding it with one hand against her chin.

Darren took a few moments, but soon he said, "The plane is the hardest thing to fly in the Space Council. Hell, it might be the hardest to fly in the whole galaxy. It can't be for everyone."

"I guess that makes you right then." Natalie poked at the potatoes with her fork as she spoke. Darren seemed surprised by the remark as Natalie continued. "A cycle ago, when you told me I wouldn't be good enough for the Spectre. You should be happy you were right."

Darren shook his head. "Whether I am right or not, I didn't want you to fail." Natalie looked up, despite herself. His voice was soft, almost comforting. "I think I wanted to see you beat my expectations and be able to fly the Spectre." He paused for a moment, thinking before continuing. "Look, this first run may not have gone the way you were hoping, but we have a whole cycle before the final tests. Maybe you'll be able to get the hang of it before the end of the cycle."

Natalie wasn't sure what to do with this unexpected kindness. She was sure that he would have laughed and said he told her so, but here he was trying to comfort her and encourage her. She found that she kind of liked having someone she could talk to about her flying. It wasn't that she disliked talking to people; she had always felt more comfortable alone in her own thoughts, unconcerned about what others thought or did. *What changed?* she thought. *How have I been tricked into talking to him so much?*

The next day, regular simulation training began. Each day, a recruit had an hour or two with each craft, switching through according to their schedules. They were given an extra hour for the craft their instructor felt they were most suited for, which for Natalie was the Dolphin, and Darren, the Spectre. During Natalie's simulation time with the Hunter and Phantom, she would fly regularly, instead thinking most on how to improve her Spectre skills. When she flew the Dolphin, however, she quickly began trying more complex maneuvers, the plane's movements and capabilities coming to her naturally. Flying the Dolphin quickly became the most fun part of Natalie's day.

Flying the Spectre, on the other hand, was certainly the most frustrating. Her second flight went the same as her first, and when she climbed out at the end of the session, she felt like the endeavor was pointless. *I'll never figure this out,* she thought as she walked back to the mess hall. *Maybe I should just stick to flying Dolphins.* Her thoughts continued to swirl as she arrived at the mess hall. *No, I can't give up, not after only two tries. I'll keep going until the end of the cycle; I'll find something to help me.* Having reassured herself, she picked up her dinner and sat down at her usual table. Soon after, Darren joined her. Their conversation was quiet. As Natalie explained her continued difficulties with the Spectre, Darren interjected with his own suggestion.

"You know," he began, and Natalie stopped speaking. "I feel pretty comfortable with the Spectre. What if I tried to help you out during our recreational time? Yeah, I'm sure I could teach you how—"

"No," Natalie interrupted, her voice firm and serious. She had been holding her ponytail to her mouth, but it fell to her shoulder now. "I can learn it on my own. I don't need help from you or anyone else." Natalie quickly stood up and departed, leaving Darren behind.

After the day's physical training, Natalie spent her recreation time visiting the base's library. She found more books on the Spectre, including some detailed accounts of its flying characteristics from other pilots. After finding five more books to go with the pilot accounts, she checked them all out and brought them back to her room. Two stacks of books sat on her desk, one containing books on the Dolphin transport, while the other stack—now twice as tall as the first—contained only books on the Spectre. Natalie had been using her recreational time every day to read as much as she could and had finished most of the Dolphin books. *Now I only need to focus on the Spectre.* She picked up one of the books, titled *Spectres in Flight: A History of Spectre Flights and Trials in Atmosphere.* Satisfied with her selection, she took the book and exited the room.

In Sardubra, the days were long, and the nights were short. Even though it was only two hours before midnight, the sun had not set completely yet. The air was cool, but still comfortable, the day's heat fading over the horizon with the setting sun. Natalie climbed her usual hill on the edge of the base, sitting down on the soft grass, under the single small tree, its leaves a beautiful display of greens. This was possibly the only place that Natalie felt at peace, disconnected from the life inside the base. Natalie sat down at the top of the hill and began reading. No one ever bothered her there; she hardly ever saw anyone while she was there. The only person was Darren, who would occasionally wander the area but never onto the hill.

Natalie remained atop the hill until just before lights out. When she got back to her room and laid her book down, she already felt like she had learned something and would soon start improving. As she went to bed though, she reminded herself that it would take time. *One night of reading is not going to magically make me capable,* she reminded herself as she changed into black, thigh-length shorts and a dark olive tank top and climbed into bed. *Ability will be a combination of reading and simulation time.*

***

The virtual Spectre touched down hard onto the runway, the right wheel hitting before any other and bouncing up, sending the left wheel and front wheel harder into the pavement. As the Spectre slowed to a crawl near the edge of the runway,

Natalie cursed. She was dripping with sweat inside the simulator, her hands aching under their intense grasp of the flightstick.

It had been six days since the start of simulation training, and as Natalie climbed out of the Spectre's simulator, she had not made any noticeable improvement. She only had two weeks before final testing began, and her goals seemed to be slipping away. She remained frustrated throughout dinner, which she ate alone. *There has to be some sort of solution*, she thought as the recruits began their daily physical training. *There must be something more I can do to get better with the Spectre.* Being that the physical training didn't require speaking to anyone, Natalie had plenty of time to think about the problem; by the end of the session, she had an answer. She quickly showered and got dressed to maximize her recreational time and begin executing her new idea.

Darren Verra wandered around the edge of the base alone, looking out at the trees that surrounded the area. He enjoyed the outdoors, especially in Sardubra. The continent was full of beautiful river valleys and thick forests of green. This base was in a dense forest just outside a mountain chain, similar to his hometown located only a day's drive away. He had grown up in a mining family, like most living near the mountains of Jontunia. He had watched his father, older brothers, and uncles work underground, coming home dirty and sore, and more often than his mother would have liked, injured.

Darren was also expected to become a miner, but he had other ideas. He had spent many an evening just as he was now, wandering in or near the forests that surrounded his town. He had concluded that he would never become anything in this town, only a miner. He knew that the only thing he wanted in life was to do something that he felt mattered, and in doing so try to give himself, and even his future children, a better life.

He had no idea why he decided on flying, or the military at all for that matter. More than likely, he found that it was a lack of options. He believed that someone from a mining town couldn't be qualified for any business jobs. But the military seemed so much more achievable, and it was always hungry for manpower. If he was skilled enough to do something more than grunt work, then it would be worth trying. That's why, when he turned eighteen, he became a pilot in the Omasye Space Council, rather than starting at the mine. His family was shocked, confused, some even angry. To them, he was throwing them all aside to die amongst the stars, alone and in the cold void, but to him, he was going to do something with the Verra name. His children wouldn't be miners; no matter what, he would succeed in his career and give them the best life he could.

Darren's wandering thoughts were cut short when he realized he was nearing the northwestern edge of the base, where the hill Natalie always read on was. He never looked to the hill directly, for fear that she may notice him watching and would leave. Darren could never make sense of Natalie, no matter how hard he had tried. A girl that never wanted to talk to anyone and spent all her free time reading, who seemed to have hated him when they met, but prior to her Spectre test had been incredibly friendly. And yet with their last conversation, she had reverted to her original self. *Why did she get so upset?* After all, he was only trying to help. He shook his head; he would never fully understand her, he accepted. The only thing he had realized was that the two shared the same determination. No challenge was too great; they would try until they hit an absolute answer, yes or no. He saw that now, as Natalie seemed determined to succeed with the Spectre. He took a side glance at the top of the hill, to see if he could tell what she was reading, but instead he ended up stopping and turning his head. Natalie was not on the hill; she was nowhere to be found.

Darren Verra had searched everywhere he thought Natalie would be. She was nowhere outside, nor was she in the mess hall or her room. It was getting close to lights out, and at this point, he was genuinely worried. *Has she given up?* The thought briefly passed through his mind as he walked across the base to the simulation building. He pushed open the metal side door and was above the simulation machines, on a black steel catwalk. From there he would be able to quickly find her if she happened to be in the building. He scanned up and down, looking at each machine. Every single one he looked at was silent, and Natalie was nowhere to be seen. Just as he was about to give up, he saw the metal door of one of the Spectre machines swing open. A woman stepped out, climbing back to the floor, her green ponytail still draped over her shoulder. Darren breathed a heavy sigh of relief before quietly stepping out of the building. He knew he couldn't let her find out he knew what she was doing. *She's trying to learn, but without anyone else,* Darren thought as he stood outside. *But why? Why can't she just accept other people's help?*

His thoughts were abruptly cut short when he heard another door, one around the corner but at the same cat-walk level, open and close with quiet deliberateness.

Natalie is down below, he thought. *She will go back through the basement hall to the main entrance. Was someone else watching?* He couldn't help himself. With hurried, but quiet footsteps, he reached the corner of the building. Carefully, he peered around the corner until he saw the figure of Natalie's other spectator.

By her uniform, Darren knew instantly that she was an instructor. Her black hair, usually made up in a tight bun, was in a long ponytail that ran down the length of her back. Since she was facing away from him, Darren had no way of identifying her. She was standing still, looking at her phone, which Darren could gather because of the light emanating from her front.

Must be checking in on how her students are fairing, he thought, backing away from the corner. It was nearly lights out. If he were caught here instead of at the barracks, he knew he would be in a world of trouble.

***

Natalie walked across the simulation building; her pace quickened by the frustration of another two hours wasted trying to bring the Spectre under control. Every flight was the same as the others: take off, fly carefully with only minor maneuvers, and then attempt some more proper maneuvers. This usually led to a furious fight with the craft, as it jerked out of control and began its rapid descent toward the ground. As the simulation reset, the process repeated itself: Takeoff, attempted maneuver, crash.

How does anyone fly that thing? Natalie thought as she climbed into the Dolphin simulator. *Darren said just to be smoother with the inputs; what the hell does that even mean? I've tried everything, the balance of that piece of shit is off.* She placed a pair of technical manuals on the co-pilot's seat as she shut the door behind her.

Plopping herself into the pilot's seat of the Dolphin, Natalie ran through the startup procedure with one hand while doing up her straps with the other. As she clipped in the last of the four straps, the twin engines sprung to life. *At least I'll have this to fall back on.* With her right hand gripping the flightstick tightly, Natalie placed her left on the vector thrust controls, disconnecting their synchronous movement. She preferred the feeling of the individual control of each of the four thruster pods. Individually, she had access to near omni-directional movement at a moment's notice.

Engaging only the front two pods, Natalie pitched the Dolphin up as the craft's nose rapidly lifted off the ground. With a swift movement from the left hand, Natalie disengaged the front pods and sent all power to the rear exhaust, shooting the craft upward at a steep angle, the simulator's forces pushing Natalie back in her seat. Instantly, Natalie was smiling, the rush of adrenaline wiping her mind of the Spectre's challenges.

Bringing the Dolphin level high over the base, Natalie rotated the left pods to face downward and the right pods to face upward. Reengaging all four pods, the craft was sent into a high-speed roll. Natalie's quick fingers rotated the pods in sync with her hand on the flightstick, turning the roll into a swooping dive to the right. She then cut hard to the left, and the Dolphin's wings briefly stood vertical with all four pods facing the underbelly of the craft. In mid-air, the Dolphin quickly skidded to almost a complete stop before Natalie returned full power to the main exhaust, accelerating away.

Natalie leveled out, pulling back on the throttle and bringing the Dolphin into cruising speed above the base. She smiled, relaxing in her seat. "Why can't the Spectre fly like this?" she thought out loud. "It would be so much easier with pods like these." Suddenly, an idea, a new one, burst into Natalie's thoughts, and her smile vanished. Leaving the Dolphin cruising level, she reached over to the co-pilot's seat and grabbed one of the technical manuals.

The manual in her hands was for the current generation of Spectre fighters, and her fingers raced through the pages to find its technical features. Natalie stopped on a page detailing part of the systems the Spectre used to aid the pilot in maneuvering in space. A diagram on the top of the page indicated several small rotating nozzles along the underside-flanks of the fuselage, as well as four smaller nozzles on the topside of the aircraft, behind the cockpit. These nozzles could be used by rerouting power from the Spectre's engines and would be used to make minor corrections, such as when entering a hangar space or navigating a narrow area.

This was nothing new to Natalie, as all craft in space had these kinds of nozzles for low-speed maneuvering. What interested her more, however, was the fact that while most craft used pressurized air for these tiny thrusters, the Spectre used power directly from its engine, like the Dolphin did with its vector-pods.

"It'll probably be limited in power though," Natalie mumbled as she continued to read the page. Scanning the rest of the information, she found the specifications of the power rerouting system. "Unregulated?" she said as she read it over again, and then a third time. "Can I run max power through this? I need to see the controls." Quickly, she flipped to another page of the manual, this time the control surfaces inside the cockpit. After a minute of searching, she found a button that released the control module for all the Spectre's maneuvering thrusters. When not in use, the control module folded underneath the throttle controls on the left side of the cockpit, but when in use, it folded out beside the controls. Next to the button's description on the page was a reference to another page, which detailed the control module.

Natalie opened the new page and found a diagram of the control module and details on each component. From the diagram, Natalie could tell that it was similar to the one on the Dolphin but simplified into a fly-by-wire type system. With its own throttle and two joysticks, the system would automatically route power to the correct nozzles based on the pilot's inputs. Natalie imagined that this was similar to the controls for any craft's maneuvering thrusters, but the Spectre's unregulated rerouting system made her curious. Shutting down the simulator mid-flight, Natalie quickly unbuckled and grabbed her other manual before climbing out of the Dolphin, a plan in mind.

***

Natalie stood inside the simulation building with the rest of the recruits. The cycle had at last come to an end, and the recruits were about to begin their final tests, tests to determine what they would fly for the rest of their careers. Each of the next four days would be spent running a test mission on one of the crafts. The tests were scheduled in the same order as each recruit's simulation schedule; Natalie was beginning with the Hunter-class bomber. *One last time,* Natalie thought as she climbed into the gray metal box. *One more flight, then I never have to see it again.*

The flight started as any other, on the ground at the base, but today, she was flying a long combat run to bomb enemy ground forces. For Natalie, it was another boring flight, and she couldn't wait to be done with it. She was glad, however, that the Hunter had such great straight-line speed. It could fly at supersonic speeds, drop its payload, and accelerate out before anyone even had a moment to react to it. The downside was the speed loss the Hunter had to undergo to drop its payload on target. As well, this deceleration process had to begin well in advance of the target's location. This left it very vulnerable, and with only basic countermeasures in the form of flares, Natalie felt uncomfortable with ever flying into real combat. Any enemy fighter in the area could, in theory, get behind a Hunter while it was flying at supersonic speeds and simply wait for it to decelerate for its attack run. She was thankful that she was simply doing a simulator run and not making a career out of flying a defenseless plane with no maneuverability.

By the end of the test, Natalie was ready to leap from the machine and never even look at it again. Four hours of flying one of the least exciting planes in the Omasye Space Council had drained her. Natalie's night went by quickly, mostly spent reading on the Dolphin, the plane she would fly tomorrow. She was confident, as she had spent the cycle perfecting her abilities with the plane. She had practiced basic roles as well as high speed and often dangerous maneuvers to maximize the maneuverability of the Dolphin. Natalie went to sleep that night more excited than she had ever been before.

The Dolphin test was set up the same way as the Hunter test. She was given a mission to fly from her base to the objective, complete it, and return to base. When the simulation started, her view was the same clear skies as before, only this time she heard approaching footsteps outside her craft. The screens in front and to the side of her tracked her head movement, rotating the camera as she looked around. Looking over her left shoulder, Natalie saw a small squad of virtual soldiers approaching the Dolphin. She quickly reached for the ramp release, a small yellow handle near the center of the cockpit. The hydraulics in the rear of the craft quickly lowered the ramp, and Natalie heard the low thump of the ramp hitting the tarmac. Since the simulator only encompassed the cockpit of the craft, Natalie waited for the simulation's panel to tell her that all soldiers were strapped in. She raised the ramp and began to throttle up the Dolphin. She had to drop the squad off quickly near hostile forces, so she flew in low, just above the trees, hugging the curve of the hills.

As she approached the landing site, she remembered that the goal was to pass, not to try any tricks. As much as she wanted to see just how quickly she could get the Dolphin on the ground, she had to pass a test. Natalie began rolling back the throttle and rotated the engines to bring the transport to a semi-quick halt above the site. She dropped the altitude as early as she was clear of the trees and dropped into the clearing with speed, efficiency, and a surprising level of grace. The soft tires of the landing gear thumped on the ground, jolting Natalie in her seat as the transport came to a stop. She pulled the yellow handle to lower the ramp and waited for the all-clear from the simulation's side display. During these moments, Natalie took deep breaths; flying the Dolphin was still the most exciting thing she had ever done, even if it were only a simulation. Though the instructors weren't allowed to speak during the tests, Natalie saw her evaluating co-pilot smile as he made some notes on his clipboard. Clearly, Natalie thought, she had impressed him already.

The next day's test was even more boring than the Hunter test, further cementing that Natalie would never again fly a Phantom, in simulation or real life. She took off from the familiar runway, flying for nearly two hours to another airport. Nothing eventful happened on the flight there, and most of the time Natalie felt as though she could climb out of the simulator, get a drink, and return before anything happened that required her attention. She landed at the other airport, which was the first time since takeoff where she actually controlled the craft. She parked near a building for five minutes, and the simulator did a slight time skip while the craft was loaded with cargo. Now loaded with cargo, Natalie's Phantom was even heavier and slower as it pulled onto the runway, and Natalie pushed its throttle up, taking off to return to the base she began at. Again, not a single time did the craft require Natalie's assistance until it was time to land.

Natalie went to bed that night restless. Her next flight would be inside the Spectre. *I just need to pass,* she thought. *Then I might have a shot at flying it for real.* Eventually, Natalie was able to fall asleep, but it felt like no time before she was back inside the simulation building.

Natalie climbed into the Spectre's cockpit and strapped into the seat. *I can do this,* she told herself as the instructor climbed into the seat behind her. *I practiced too hard to fail now. I will succeed.* The machine turned on, and Natalie began running through the startup procedure. As the engine hummed to life, Natalie began to release the brakes. As she did so, she released the maneuvering thruster controls, which came up next to the main throttle. Natalie rolled out to the runway while the instructor explained the mission. She was to fly to an area with known enemy air presence and take down any hostiles. As she took off, one hand on the flightstick and the other on the secondary control surface, the plane felt natural for the first time. She had by no means passed yet, but in this moment, it was close enough, and Natalie loved every second of it.

She flew at high speed to the area where enemy craft were to be waiting, and soon after arrival, picked up her first target. She had used her travel time to gain altitude and arrived well above the enemy. As she pinpointed the target's position both on display and visually, she rolled the Spectre to the right, aided by the re-routing system and the secondary controls, and dove like a hawk upon a field mouse. The target never even had time to react before Natalie streaked by in a hail of cannon fire, which ripped the enemy fighter to shreds. Natalie pulled back hard on the stick, leveling out. Through every maneuver, Natalie used the maneuvering thrusters to correct any discomfort she felt in the stability of her Spectre. With the unregulated rerouting system, Natalie could even use the vectoring thrust to help her maneuver faster and sharper. She now banked hard to engage another enemy close by that was now turning in her direction. The Spectre, having the better maneuverability, came out of the turn first, and Natalie fired a missile off before the enemy could come around completely. The missile impacted in a brilliant fire-ball, and Natalie had recorded her second kill. As she moved across the sky, ma-neuvering to advantageous positions over her targets, she was thrilled. It all felt natural now, with the aid of the vectoring thrust she had mastered on the Dolphin. It was tough, yes, as the Spectre was the most demanding craft in the OSC. She had to put every ounce of strength into her turns to get the best turn rate; the machine was tough, as it bounced and moved around with her movements, and it would only be tougher in a real Spectre. But she loved it; it felt right, like it was where she belonged. It felt like home to Natalie, and she knew that she would never give it up.

***

"So, how did your final test go?" Darren Verra asked between mouthfuls of food. It was dinner time, and the mess hall was a talkative room, with recruits sharing everything about their final tests and predictions on what they would be selected to fly. Natalie Annikki had sat quietly in her usual spot, but inevitably, Darren had come to join her, curious about her Spectre test. Despite the cold ending of their last conversation, Natalie didn't refuse his company.

"It went very well," Natalie started, smiling toward him for the first time. "I felt perfectly at home in it, and I can't wait to fly the real thing."

Darren smiled back. "Wow, is this the first time I've seen you smile?" Natalie laughed as he continued. "Remember though, if your results are as high on the Dolphin as I think they are, they'll stick you on that if your Spectre results aren't high enough."

Natalie hadn't thought much of it since the day of the Dolphin test. "I'm not worried. I'm sure my results on the Spectre will be high enough that I will get to choose."

"I guess we'll see," Darren said before taking a drink. "They put up the test rankings tomorrow afternoon, during our free time. We should go look at it together." He smiled as he finished his sentence but did not continue eating as usual, instead waiting on her response.

Natalie paused. "Sure, of course," she answered, a tad surprised. "Why with me though? Why not with your usual friends?"

"Are you not one of my usual friends?" Darren asked. "Besides, I need to see how you did. Top of the class in a Dolphin is one thing, but if you score high on the Spectre too, that'll be somethin' to see."

Natalie laughed. "Just don't make it some sort of spectacle, okay?"

Darren returned the laughter, but then cut it short. "Can I ask you something?" Natalie nodded. "Why did you turn down my help before?"

It took some time before Natalie responded. "It's just a personal philosophy I've had for a long time, so to speak." Her voice was quiet. "If I can't to do something on my own, it's hard to ask other people for help. It's like, if I can't do it on my own, why should I even bother with it? I didn't mean to be so harsh; it's just how it is."

"You never considered that sometimes you might *need* help?"

"I grew up having to learn things on my own." Though she didn't really mean to, Natalie's voice came across with an air of pride in it. "I haven't had someone help me do anything I couldn't do since I was eight. If I couldn't do it, I didn't do it, or I learned on my own."

"What about teamwork?" Darren asked. "Is there any room for that?"

"Not really. If someone needs help, I'll gladly help them. If I'm flying and in trouble and someone comes and saves me, then I'll be thankful. The only thing that is different is that I won't ask for that help."

Darren nodded but was silent for some time. Natalie finished her meal and looked up. He seemed lost in thought and was slowly eating. "Well, I'll see you at PT then," Natalie said, picking up her tray and standing up.

"Yeah." Darren seemed startled out of his thoughts. "See you then." He watched Natalie walk away.

The next day's morning classes were spent mostly in discussions between the instructors and the class, discussing how people felt toward each craft they flew during the test. The air was light-hearted, and everyone seemed excited to see their results later that day, even the ones that were on the edge of passing any of the tests. Throughout the discussion, Natalie remained quiet, listening, while Darren was very vocal during anything regarding the Spectre. He still seemed adamant that he would be top of the class, and at this point, no one challenged him on that belief. Others, whom Natalie recognized as Darren's friends, supported him, but also advocated that they would be right behind him on the scores. Natalie ignored them as best as she could. She did not care about scores, so long as she got to fly Spectres.

Later that day, when the recruits were finishing their lunchtime meals and preparing for their free time, many began gathering in groups to check their simulator scores. Natalie watched from her peripheral vision far from the others in the room. Multiple times, people asked Darren if he was going to tag along, and each time she saw him gesture a polite refusal. As she watched, she tried to figure out why he would abandon his friends; why was she more important than them? Natalie certainly wasn't one of Darren's friends, or at least she didn't see it that way. And yet he was turning them all down to spend time with her. *Maybe I'm reading into this too much. Like he said, he's probably interested in his competition.* That's all they were: rivals. But then why did she hope that he'd do well? Natalie couldn't come to a proper conclusion, and her thoughts were cut off as she saw Darren begin walking toward her table. Quickly, she finished the last of her drink and stood up as he reached her.

"Ready to go?" he asked. He was smiling as usual, and his voice was friendly and soft. "I don't want to rush you, so take your time."

"No, no," Natalie helplessly stammered. "I'm fine. Let's go." She picked up her tray and dropped it off as the pair exited the mess hall.

The rankings were located on a wall near the classrooms on a large information screen, and when Natalie and Darren arrived, there was a large gathering of recruits. Not many were looking at the rankings anymore, instead discussing among themselves. As Natalie and Darren approached the group, many of them stopped talking and turned their attention to the pair. Natalie began to feel uncomfortable. Darren slowed his pace with Natalie.

"What's going on?" he quickly whispered to Natalie, but she simply shrugged, having no idea herself. The two kept going, and as they approached the wall, the nearby recruits moved out of their way. As nonchalantly as he could, Darren spoke to Natalie as they looked at the long lists on the screen.

"So, let's start with the Dolphin, eh?" he said, looking at the screen. Names were scrolling across the screen in four columns, and at the top of each a static title carried the name of each craft for its corresponding column. Darren soon pointed to a list titled "Dolphin Light Transport." Natalie's eyes moved from the title and to the list. It was scrolling from the bottom of the rankings to the top, and as Natalie scanned the list, she did not see her name. She was confident her name would be in the top half, so she continued to watch the names tick by at the top of the screen.

Many names, probably well over half of the class of over a hundred, scrolled by; Natalie didn't know most of them. She saw Darren's name, about a quarter way from the top. She continued scanning the names as they went by, and as the list neared the top, she realized she hadn't seen her name yet. She became excited and nervous, the possibility of her placing in the top five growing increasingly high. The names kept going by, none being hers. Third from the top, not her; second, still not her. Then finally, the list reached the top; she had placed top of the class for the Dolphin transport. Excitement overwhelmed her, and she turned to Darren to share her surprise and happiness, but he seemed to be in another world. He was staring at another section of the board, his mouth partially open, and himself unmoving. Natalie followed his gaze to the section of the board titled "Spectre Fighter." Her eyes fell onto the top of the list, as it slowly scrolled downward, and the shock overtook her as well. Darren Verra's name was listed in second place, but above, at the very top, was Natalie's own. *Both? Top in both the Spectre and the Dolphin? How?*

Quickly, Natalie tapped on her name, opening a more detailed panel. She had flown the Spectre well, but she never thought she flew it better than anyone else in the class, surely. The panel, now just showing Natalie's grading with the Spectre, broke down her score into a few categories. Most of the scores were only just above average. Even her raw flying skill only placed her just outside the top five. But there was a final score, this one based on improvement. This score was almost at the maximum the instructors could give. Natalie stared at the total, eyes wide, even after the screen timed out and returned to the class ranking.

As the shock began to dissipate, the realization of Natalie's position began to set in. She was top of the class in two strike craft; she would have her choice, and she knew she would take the Spectre. Then she could get on with her career, a career on the frontlines defending her fellow Altherians. She would become the people she read about in her history books.

Natalie realized that everyone was still staring at her and Darren. She grew uncomfortable, and she turned to Darren, who was still staring at the board. "Come on, let's go," she said as she tugged on his arm. But he didn't move. He kept staring at the rankings, even as they scrolled through a second time. She sighed loud enough for him to hear, turned, and quickly walked away from Darren and the crowd of staring eyes.

CHAPTER 5

"Real world training begins in two days," the head instructor said to Natalie. "You can choose either the Spectre or the Dolphin, but not both."

Natalie was standing in a room with a dozen instructors, including the head instructor for the entire base. The others were a mix of the higher positioned instructors for both the Dolphin and Spectre. For them, it was a big event. It was almost unheard of for someone to qualify at the top of two different craft, and each one of them wanted their say in getting a possibly future great pilot.

"Spectre pilots are hard to come by," one of them opened her side of the debate. "Increased conflicts with the pirates are reducing our numbers almost faster than we can replace them. Last I checked, the Dolphins had no business in the pirate skirmishes."

"There are enough undeveloped worlds that require our pilots," a Dolphin instructor responded. "The 3rd Mobile spreads its Dolphin fleet across its entire area of responsibility. Pirates, as well as Dominionists, have been known to build small outposts on worlds within our territory. It is the Dolphin pilots, in conjunction with the OGC, who handle those cases. Our pilots are being burnt out."

"Let's hear what the young recruit has to say before you two jump at each other's throats," the head instructor intervened. "Ms. Annikki, where do you want to go?"

Natalie didn't hesitate in her response. "Spectres, sir. I love flying the Dolphin, but the Spectre is what I truly want to fly."

"Now hold on a minute," the same Dolphin instructor as before spoke up. "Your skills with the Dolphin, at least in the simulator, are very promising. You could easily be flying special forces, or missions that few other pilots could dare to take on. You would be invaluable to the Dolphin ranks. If you go Spectres, you will just be another nameless fighter pilot among thousands of others. Not to mention the danger of—"

"Let her go where she wants," another Dolphin instructor interrupted. Natalie immediately locked eyes with her, but the instructor turned away. Her black hair, and something about her face, reminded Natalie of someone, but she didn't know who. *My mother? Do I even remember what my mother looks like? So familiar...* The woman carried on speaking. "If she wants to fly Spectres, then we have no right to try and convince her otherwise. If she proves to be as capable as she seems, she can always be picked up for a second certification later in her career. Who knows, maybe in a few years she will *want* to fly Dolphins. We need to let her make that decision herself."

The other instructor grunted. "Fine. Mark my words, though. We are risking losing potentially a great Dolphin pilot to a pointless death as a fighter pilot."

The head instructor turned from the others to Natalie. "So, Ms. Annikki, the Spectre program is your final decision, yes?"

"Yes, sir." Natalie smiled.

When real world training began two days later, the class of recruits was split up by their selected craft. They only ever saw their now former classmates during meals and free time. The class of Spectre pilots was down to thirty members. They spent their classroom days being taught the intricacies of their fighter, soon delving into the flying characteristics and recommended combat procedures. The recruits had much to learn if they were to fly the plane for real. The simulators had tested only some of the skill and ability a Spectre pilot had to possess. Flying for real would quickly reveal the other physical and mental demands. Outside of the classroom, a great deal of time was spent inside the simulators. Throughout this, Darren never spoke to Natalie. Natalie spent more time wondering why than she felt she should have, but in the end assumed he was simply jealous.

About half a cycle after Spectre training started, the recruits were taken out to the hangars once again. As they approached the area, Natalie could see the outline of a Spectre-class fighter, but next to it was another plane, one that Natalie knew was not Altherian. Its design gave it away, as all Altherian strike craft had large, swooping wings and smooth shapes to their fuselages. This craft was sharp and angular with an aggressive stance. As the group came nearer, the instructor began introducing the craft.

"Everyone, this here is possibly the most important lesson of your careers," she said, coming to a stop near the two crafts. "This is your primary adversary, your biggest threat, and your main prey. This, for us, is the biggest threat in the sky, and the main enemy of the Spectre: the Shrike Fighter and the fastest strike craft in the known galaxy. It is Halerian by design, operated by the New Federation Space Fleet in the same capacity that the Spectre is operated by the OSC. This one here was given to the air base by a New Federation defect many years ago. In the coming cycles, it will be your job to know how to face one and win. If you don't, you will die."

The two crafts sat opposite one another on the tarmac just in front of the hangars. The two fighters were a great deal different from each other as Natalie learned, both from observing and from listening to the instructor's lecture. The Shrike was much smaller than the Spectre. The Spectre had a narrow fuselage and a very wide wingspan, which gave it its impressive turn rate, but the Shrike had no wings, save for its rear stabilizers. It carried only one vertical stabilizer, shaped like a shark's fin, and four angled horizontal stabilizers, like that of the Spectre.

The Shrike was shaped like an arrowhead, and at its rear was more than twice as wide as the Spectre's fuselage. Its nose came to a sharp point, and the cockpit sat roughly equidistant from the nose as the Spectre's cockpit. The Shrike had a smaller gun armament, carrying only four 12.7mm machine guns to the Spectre's six 12.7mm guns and twin 20mm cannons. The two craft shared the same missile payload, six, either anti-air or anti-ground. However, while the Spectre carried two on each wing and two in its fuselage, the Shrike carried all six inside its wide fuselage. The Shrike remained in a stance directly opposed to the Spectre. While the Spectre sat on its haunches, ready to leap into the sky, the Halerian fighter's nose lay lower to the ground than its rear, as though it were bowing to the gathered crowd, or as if it were a trained animal, waiting for its rider to mount.

The instructor went over the advantages and disadvantages of the two fighters when they engaged each other, which proved to be nothing that Natalie hadn't already guessed. The Spectre had a vast advantage in its turn rate, but only in flat turns. The Shrike could roll and perform corkscrew maneuvers on par with the Spectre due to its small size. The Shrike was also faster, in both acceleration and atmospheric top speed. A good Shrike pilot could use the craft's speed to perform hit and run attacks, coming from blind spots faster than the Spectre pilot could react. This was accompanied by the Shrike's tight maneuverability, allowing the craft to slip out of sight from any Spectre that attempted to follow them through a corkscrew. A Spectre pilot had to out-think their opponent and not follow the

Shrike into tight maneuvers. Instead, they had to predict where the Shrike would finish its maneuver and use the Spectre's superior turn rate to align itself from a distance. The Spectre's heavy armament meant it would take only one burst to hit the Shrike to destroy it. Getting that first burst was the primary goal for any Spectre pilot.

"Take this lesson to heart," the instructor said, turning from the planes to the class. "It is invaluable for your entire flying career, and that starts tomorrow." The instructor paused just long enough to take in the looks of the students and the whispering of recruits to one another. "Starting tomorrow, you will learn to fly the Spectre for real, and in a few weeks, you will all begin combat training."

Natalie smiled. *Finally, the real thing,* she thought.

Natalie managed to sleep after lying in bed for hours, her mind racing at the thought of flying. She read the notes she had made from the simulators three times over and barely got enough sleep to be rested and ready for flying. The recruits were taken back to the hangars, where five Spectres waited. However, these Spectres were training models, designed to carry a recruit and an instructor who could override their controls if something went wrong. There were only five modified Spectres available, so many of the recruits, including Natalie, had to wait their turn.

Natalie watched her classmates fly all day, some of them a little rough or shaky; some of them, notably Darren, flew like an experienced pilot. Finally, it was her turn. As the canopy closed around her, Natalie felt the tingling in her fingers and feet. She itched to prove that she was just as good as the best in the class on day one. She began her startup sequence, running through it with ease, having done the same thing many times over in the simulator. As she pressed the final button, she felt the engine behind the cockpit spur to life in a low rumble, which sent vibrations throughout the craft. The sensation Natalie felt was unlike anything before it. *This is finally it,* she thought, checking her controls. *I'm finally going to get to do it.*

Carefully, she taxied the Spectre to the end of the runway until it was lined up to the strip of tarmac, a pathway to everything Natalie had dreamed about. She pushed the throttle forward and was immediately thrust back into her seat as the Spectre accelerated hard down the runway. Then, once the plane had reached the right speed, Natalie gently pulled back on the flightstick, and the wheels lifted off the ground; Natalie was flying. The ground and the nearby mountains seemed to fall away, and Natalie was hit with such a rush of adrenaline and emotion that she thought she might pass out all on her own. She pulled back on the stick farther, and the Spectre leaped skyward, rapidly gaining altitude until she leveled out high above the air base.

Natalie couldn't help but laugh. This feeling, a feeling she knew she wanted since she was a kid, was real. She never needed any confirmation of what she wanted to do with her life, but here it was anyway, all around her and throughout her body. All her senses confirmed for her that she was born to fly. Flying level, Natalie let go of the flightstick and twisted in her seat, looking around at the sky and the world now below her.

The view was more stunning than she could have ever imagined. The air base was set near the mountains, and Natalie could see everything from her cockpit. She could see into the forest and river that ran south and west away from the base, as well as the high mountains and deep valleys, which flanked the north and east areas of the base. The mountains, primarily gray, gave way to white near their peaks and a lush dark green near their base. Multiple lakes dotted the area, sparkling in the distance from the bright sunlight. The view was far better than anything Natalie could have gotten at the base; even the high primary control tower couldn't compare.

Most of all, however, she was surprised by how natural the Spectre felt in her hands; she felt as though she could already do anything she wanted. Her inputs were perfectly smooth, and her control was flawless. Even as the instructor asked her to do some more complex maneuvers and turns, she handled them with ease. When she finally landed some three hours later, she had never felt better nor more confident in her skills.

***

The weeks went by in a flash. By the end of the cycle, the instructors let them loose, giving them the single seater Spectres to fly, to learn and become more accustomed to the craft by themselves. Natalie toyed around with some increasingly more complex maneuvers that she read about in one of the flight tactics books she had, but much of her time was spent secluded, flying around in the mountains, diving deep into the valleys and enjoying the beauty of it all.

One day, while flying in the mountainous area northwest of the base, Natalie found a beautiful valley between two tall gray mountain chains. As the mountains swept downward, the gray gave way to the forests below until it became a wide blanket over the rocks of the valley. The two sides finally met in a wide sparkling blue river, which came down into a freshwater lake, which was calm and undisturbed. Only the tiny ripples from the wind made the lake shimmer and sparkle. The area was so astonishing to Natalie that she decided that this would be the area she would stay each day. Occasionally, she noticed another fighter come into her area, sometimes coming to pass in a mock-combat run, which Natalie avoided with ease. She did not care much for these games, but she was not going to be made a fool of either. She wished she knew who it was, so at the very least she could ask them to cut it out, but their Spectre, like hers and all the other training models, was unmarked, a flat gray with a white T on the tail to mark it as a trainer. For all Natalie knew, it wasn't even the same Spectre every time.

During their meals, Natalie began to hear some talk from the other recruits seated away from her. They were talking about someone who was continually attempting to jump everyone else during their flight practice. *Must be the same person who keeps finding me,* she thought. *At least we know it's one person then.* She scanned the room of Spectre recruits, but no one revealed themselves. Everyone either continued eating their meals or joined the conversation to share their encounter with the rogue pilot. The class was small though, with only thirty pilots. Natalie figured it wouldn't take long for them to be exposed.

Throughout the cycle, class time was spent teaching the pilots basic combat manoeuvres, becoming more advanced as time went on. They taught them primarily about flying in an atmosphere, with space flight coming later in the training. After only a cycle of solo flying, the instructors believed the recruits were ready to begin combat in the real world. The recruits were to begin their first combat training classes slow, but more complex maneuvers would soon follow. Natalie was excited, as she was at last getting to learn the maneuvers needed for her to defend herself and anyone from any threat.

First tests involved the recruits making passes at slow-moving instructors in other Spectres. The instructors would fly straight, and each test involved the recruit attacking from a new angle. These tests were designed so that the recruits could get a feel for aiming as well as closing speeds but were no different than what Darren had already been doing all cycle against the other recruits, Natalie believed. Soon, the instructors began maneuvering away from the recruits as they made their passes. It was now the recruit's job to predict the defense from the instructor and make a clean attack. Many recruits struggled to get good passes or line up good shots on the instructors in these more complex tests, but a handful of pilots, Natalie included, aced the tests after the first few attempts.

A week into the real-life combat training, the instructors began showing the recruits proper defensive maneuvers against their primary foe, the New Federation's Shrike fighter. The instructors took on the role of the attacker for these tests, and it was the recruit's task to pick the appropriate defensive maneuver depending on various factors, such as the Shrike's angle of attack and closing speed. Many of the recruits struggled with this, even for longer than the attack drills. Natalie and a select few others, Darren included, soon adapted to the idea of defensive flying, using the classes' maneuvers as guidelines and improvising changes as they saw fit. It was this ability to adapt that quickly showed who the most capable pilots in the class were. By the end of the third week of combat practice, however, the entire class could attack and defend to the satisfaction of the instructors.

Darren stood off to the side of Pryst's Spectre. The latter was walking toward it, ready for his next flight. The class was near the end of their most recent training class. This time, the recruits were to fly up in pairs and practice attacking and defending at the same time, switching after either the attacker had a clear victory, or the defender had turned the tables on them.

"Good luck out there," Darren said.

Pryst took a half-glance back at his friend. "*Pfft*. I don't need luck against *her*." He pulled on his helmet and reached for the ladder release on the Spectre.

Darren fought off the urge to shake his head. He looked to his left, down the row of Spectres on the tarmac, to where Natalie was climbing into her own plane. He wasn't lucky enough to get a match against her, and now that today was the last day of this training activity, he was sure he wouldn't get the chance, at least not yet. But he had watched her fly against many others in the class. Even if Pryst was the third-best pilot in the class, he had been unable to beat Darren, who was the only other undefeated pilot next to Natalie. Darren was already sure of the outcome as he walked away from Pryst's Spectre and stood off by the hangars with the rest of the class.

The outcome of both rounds was not a one-sided route like Darren had predicted. Pryst held his own while playing the role of the attacker, and even managed to create distance between himself and Natalie at the start of his defending round. Though Pryst had been able to show his skill as a pilot in the opening movements, both rounds ended the way Darren expected. While Pryst was the attacker, Natalie had been able to shake him, flying low over the trees surrounding the base and down into the nearby valley. When the pair re-emerged, Natalie was behind him and giving chase. In the second round, Pryst didn't last even half as long. His defense was easily broken by Natalie, who had predicted the next maneuver long before Pryst started it, allowing her to cut the distance in a sharp maneuver high above the base.

When they landed, Pryst walked directly to where Darren had been watching from. Natalie had stopped close by, and when she climbed down the ladder of her Spectre and turned around, her and Darren made eye contact for the briefest of moments before Pryst arrived by his side. As the pair walked away, Natalie couldn't help but continue watching. Though Darren turned his head to his friend every now and then to add a word to their conversation or to simply show that he was listening to Pryst's frustrations, he never once glanced back at where Natalie was still standing next to her plane.

Natalie had only just started eating when another tray rattled onto the table. Hopeful that it may be Darren finally coming to speak with her again, Natalie looked up. Her hope quickly turned into disappointment as she met Pryst's eyes staring from his plump face.

"Mind if I join you?" Pryst said, seating himself before Natalie could respond. "Just wanted to go over a few things if y'don't mind." Natalie was surprised and said nothing to Pryst at first. "See," Pryst continued, taking Natalie's silence as an acceptance, "you shocked us when you placed first in the simulations. You shocked our buddy Verra most, but I said we should wait to see you fly for real. Now I just want to know how you beat me."

Natalie took a moment to think everything over. She had never thought much of this man, beyond her initial impressions. He was unattractive with an equally unattractive attitude. Every time she overheard him speaking to the other recruits, he was boasting about how great he was, flying or otherwise. However, she was forced to recognize that he was a decent pilot. He had given her the greatest challenge by far, and Natalie now understood why he placed third on the simulation tests. But here he was, seemingly searching for answers as to why he wasn't the best.

"You weren't bad," Natalie began in her usual calm, soft voice. "To be honest, you were the best challenge out of everyone I faced." Pryst seemed to be following, but his face was still desperately searching for answers. "As to how I beat you, I can't really say. The only thing I noticed was that you were very predictable." Pryst's expression shifted to that of shock. "Seconds before you made most of your moves, I knew what you would try. In fact—"

"Wait, wait, back up," Pryst cut Natalie off, raising a hand. "Seconds before? How is that possible? I wouldn't have even began making my move by then." His voice was increasing in volume, and his face betrayed his bewilderment.

Natalie sighed. "It isn't about seeing you begin your maneuvers and reacting." Natalie's voice remained low, but she knew that her tone was shifting into that of a teacher talking to a student. "It's about predicting what you're going to do next. And you don't do anything unpredictable. The only times you almost got the better of me were due to me making slight errors in my counters, errors I'm certain I won't make again."

Pryst took a few moments before speaking, allowing Natalie to eat some of her dinner. When he began, his tone sounded more agitated than anything else. "You're telling me that I'm too predictable? That's not the way the opponents that I beat described me."

"And what did Darren have to say about your performance?" Natalie retorted, quickly becoming fed up with Pryst's tone. She was trying to help him the best way she could, but she didn't have all the answers for him.

"He's a better pilot than I am, simple as that." Pryst's was clearly becoming angry with Natalie, and it showed in both his voice and on his face.

"And I'm not?" Natalie asked, looking to end the conversation. Natalie stood up, picking up her empty tray. "I'm trying to tell you why you lost, that's all." She walked away from Pryst as his face contorted in rage.

The next day concluded the practice sessions for the recruits. Natalie again was paired with a lower skilled pilot and bested her handily. Through the usual routine, Natalie was again eating in the mess hall when Pryst again sat down at her table.

"Can I help you?" Natalie asked as she glanced up from her food. Pryst seemed to be back in a calm mood and showed no anger over yesterday's discussion.

"You can, but I want to start by apologizing for losing my cool yesterday," Pryst began, his apology shocking Natalie, although she didn't show it. "See, I gave it some thought, and I want you to try to better explain how I am 'predictable.'"

His use of air quotes over that word irked Natalie since he seemed to be refusing the truth. Still, if he was willing to apologize and try again, Natalie saw no reason to turn him down. "I don't know how else to explain it," she began, realizing the issue. She couldn't tell him why he was predictable; he just was. Whether that was Natalie's skill or Pryst's lack thereof, she could not say. "It's like I said yesterday, I can tell what you're going to do a couple of seconds before you do it. I don't know if you are following the book too much or if it's something else. I just don't know."

Pryst put his elbows on the table, putting his hands together and leaning his head into them. "This is the best you can do?" he said, staring down at the table from his pose. "The best you can do is tell me that the answer is either I am not a good pilot or that you are so much more skilled than I am that I haven't a chance at beating you?"

Natalie didn't enjoy that description of the situation, but he wasn't wrong. "If I had any other reason, I would tell you." Her voice was about as soft as it could be, trying carefully not to provoke Pryst into anger like yesterday. "As I said, it may be possible that you are following the book too much. Try taking the maneuvers the instructors taught us and come up with variations of them. There are always more maneuvers than they can teach us; it comes down to the situation."

"Bullshit," Pryst said, lifting his head. Pryst's face looked too similar to yesterday's now, Natalie saw. As much as she tried to help him, it seemed he just couldn't deal with what he was being told. "So, you're just some gifted pilot that knows everything?" His voice was harsh, anger fighting disappointment. "You know what, Annikki? You might be just that good with the stick. But a proper good pilot would tell me exactly what I'm doing wrong."

Natalie sighed, for her attempts to help him had collapsed. "I told you," she started, trying to remain calm in the face of what she perceived as unending stupidity and arrogance. "Pryst, I've told you too many times now that you do the expected maneuver every time. Once in awhile go left instead of right, okay? That's all I've got, and whether you accept it or not is none of my business." Again, Natalie picked up her empty tray and left Pryst to deal with his own emotions. However, as Natalie placed the empty, dirty tray with the others, she realized she couldn't continue to deal with people like this.

He'll be back tomorrow asking the same thing. And if he doesn't, someone else will. Natalie had noticed the other recruits talking about her, overhearing them ask questions like that of Pryst's. It would only be a matter of time before they too came to her directly. It was in that moment that Natalie made the choice that she would no longer eat in the mess hall. She would pick up her food and take it to her hilltop, where she normally read her books. After all, Natalie preferred being outdoors, and if it meant she didn't have any more uncomfortable discussions, it was a total victory in her eyes.

CHAPTER 6

As the fifth cycle of flight school began, the instructors gave the pilots special equipment on their Spectres; one was the target locking computers for their missile systems, and the other was a special computer that predicted and simulated the trajectory of cannon and machine gun rounds to determine whether a hit would be achieved. The equipment would then log each of these events. The recruits were moved into the first specifically competitive portion of their training, where each day the instructors would take the pilot's equipment and update a scoreboard, keeping track of each recruits' kills, as well as how many times they were killed in return. To achieve a kill, the rookie pilot had to either achieve a solid missile lock on another pilot's aircraft or hold them within their gun sights for three seconds.

Most of the recruits understood that this was their best opportunity to show just how good they really were. By now, the recruits had learned that the fighter squadrons of the Altherian Empire's 3rd Mobile fleet, Jontunia's home fleet, were monitoring the new recruits. With limited recruits across the planet and many seats to fill, the squadrons did a draft picking, with the best squadrons in the fleet having first pick. Essentially, the best rookies joined the best squadrons, so placing well in the first truly competitive part of the training was paramount to each and every one of them.

During the first day of "the deathmatch," as it quickly became known among the recruits, the pilots had to adjust and get used to the new targeting equipment as well as attempting to keep an enemy within their sights for three seconds. As always, some recruits adapted and learned quicker than others. Both Natalie and Darren adapted the quickest, each scoring a large multitude of kills before the end of the first day's session. As the days continued, however, Natalie pulled a lead over Darren, and by the end of the week, Natalie had established a wide gap over any of the other recruits. But while Darren had lost one fight already, no one had been able to beat her, an achievement that had gotten her referred often as "unkillable."

Natalie decided that with her large lead, she could return to her river valley and enjoy the peace of flying in the beautiful Jontunian mountains. At the end of each day, she checked the scoreboard to see if Darren was closing on her too much. If he was, Natalie would spend her next session building the lead again. Doing this, she found that she could return to her valley every second or third day.

One day, around three weeks into the deathmatch, Natalie was checking the scoreboard at the end of another session. Nearby, a pair of recruits were in discussion, just loud enough for her to listen in.

"I don't know what's happened to him," the first recruit, a man, said. "He scored so high on the sim test, and yet now…" His voice trailed off, but the woman he was talking to quickly finished his sentence.

"Now he's total garbage. He'll be last place soon if he doesn't figure it out." Conversations like this, either about the impressive skills of a pilot or the contrary were often being talked about around the scoreboard. Most of the time, the recruits were merely guessing who it was they had seen flying, telling stories of their different encounters in the sky. Rarely, but like right now, the pilots knew who they were talking about.

"Maybe he's just lost his edge," the man replied. "I'm sure he'll figure it out soon."

"It's like he's forgotten how to fight," the woman said. "But I don't know how. He won't tell me anything."

The man grunted in agreement before changing the subject. "I fought both of them again today."

"And how'd that go?" the woman asked.

"Like always," the man said, disappointed. "One is too fast. You don't even have time to react, and they've already got you. The other one is impossible to keep up with. I don't even understand their maneuvers half the time."

"I tried to fight the second one yesterday," the woman started. "I jumped them right after they made a kill. But as soon as I got on their tail, they put themselves right down on the deck and used the trees to shake me. Before I knew it, they were behind me, and I couldn't get away from them."

"Maybe I'll try to find that one tomorrow," the man said. "But sometimes they're impossible to find."

"Yeah, I've noticed that they disappear every couple of days. Some of the others are saying they go off into the mountains somewhere."

Natalie wasn't surprised to learn that at least one of the two pilots was her. Clearly, the other pilots had noticed her repeated absence, or at least, the absence of one plane. If they didn't know it was her, Natalie thought, that would be for the better. She didn't need any more Rygil Prysts happening.

***

Natalie Annikki sat comfortably in her flight seat, traveling at a moderate speed high above the glistening freshwater lake at the base of the valley. She had spent most of her flying session practicing some more complex maneuvers, mostly in massive speed reduction to lose someone that was behind her. Feeling that she had practiced enough, she decided to fly around the valley, taking in the picturesque sights. Of course, she had seen them many times before, but Natalie never got tired of it. She felt a great sense of calm and wellness here, elevated by flying over the land. Here made her feel certain that flying was the best experience in the world more than anywhere else.

It was this calm serenity that almost let another Spectre get the better of her. If she hadn't just happened to glance to her right as she rounded one of the mountain peaks, she would have lost her "unkillable" title. Instead, she caught the silhouette of a Spectre coming fast through the opposite side of the valley looking to make a surprise missile lock. As soon as Natalie identified the threat, she plowed the stick down and hard to the left, turning back into the mountains she had just been exiting. Her hope was that she could lose her opponent in the dark shade of the white capped mountains, but this was not the case. As she leveled out between two low peaks, she heard the first warning tone. Natalie snapped the stick right, bringing her fighter into a wide turn against her opponent, who was coming in behind her. The warning tone had meant that the other Spectre's missile system had begun establishing a lock on her plane. Natalie was certain she would not allow them to come so close again.

As Natalie completed her wide turn, the two Spectres crossed paths for the first time. Natalie kept her Spectre in its turn, knowing that her opponent would have to maneuver around the mountains to turn into her. With one move, she had gained the advantage, and to Natalie, that was all she needed to win. As she came back through the mountains, she caught the other Spectre in the valley below, having dove after crossing the mountains. Natalie dove down toward her target, who was hugging the valley floor. She gained considerable speed, enough to close quickly on her target, which she would use to either establish a missile lock or put them well within her gunsights. As she leveled out with the treetops, she could see the other Spectre just ahead. Her missile's targeting computer quickly began establishing a lock, the first beep going off in her helmet.

Due to the complexities of establishing a missile lock and path for the complex, hypersonic missiles employed by the Altherian Empire, it took six seconds, marked by three equally spaced tones, for the computer to have a solid lock, signaled by a solid tone. In combat, a missile could be fired after the second tone, but this would not guarantee a hit; the final tone signaled that the computer had created a path for the missile around any obstacles between it and its target.

As Natalie continued to cut the gap on her opponent, the second tone sounded. In combat, since they were both traveling in open air with minimal terrain changes inside the valley, Natalie could fire a missile with a high probability of success. But for the training, a solid lock had to be achieved. Just before the final tone, however, the lead Spectre suddenly pulled up, shedding a massive amount of speed as well as gaining altitude. Natalie was caught off guard, and due to her massive speed advantage, could not follow in such a tight maneuver.

She flew past, pulling the stick hard toward her, the Spectre climbing in a vertical loop to round back to her enemy. *They did exactly what I was practicing earlier.* Natalie suddenly realized as her plane climbed from the valley floor. *Had they been watching me practice? How else could they have so perfectly recreated the move?* But if they had been watching Natalie practice the move, then they knew the final step to make it a guaranteed success. As the slower plane climbed and fell behind the faster, it would level out, traveling in the same previous direction, thus arriving behind their opponent. The only way for the faster plane to recover would be to complete a vertical loop, using their speed to get above the slower plane, and then loop down on top of them. But at such a low altitude, completing a vertical loop was risky at best, a death sentence at worst.

As Natalie came to the top of the loop, upside down, she saw her opponent completing her maneuver. They had most certainly been watching her, but who could have been so skilled as to match her on their first attempt? Natalie remembered the conversation she heard yesterday. *It's the other one,* Natalie realized. *Finally here to challenge me?* There was no way she could lose to them. Natalie rolled the plane into the descent, determined to complete the loop. Natalie gripped the stick and pulled back as hard as she could, but her Spectre was losing too much altitude, too fast. "Come on!" Natalie shouted, putting all her strength into her arms. Her opponent had obviously spotted Natalie at this point as they banked away from their position, turning to where she would come out of her loop, if she did at all.

The maneuver that Natalie had perfected, and had now just been copied, was working better than Natalie ever thought possible. Even with the faster plane looping to meet the slower at the point of the maneuver's origin, if the slower plane's pilot saw the opponent quick enough, they too could turn back to meet them, easily taking them as they came out of their dive. It was surely a small window, as the slower plane would have to build some speed to make the hundred-eighty degree turn back to their opponent. But a skilled pilot, such as Natalie clearly faced here, could make it work, as they were doing now.

Natalie Annikki's Spectre was barreling straight down now, toward the forest below. She still had some time, and it was now that she felt the plane begin to come out of the loop. But she would continue to shed altitude until she had completely leveled out. She continued to pull on the stick, so hard she was sure it would snap off in her hands. The rerouting system was working as hard as it could under Natalie's hand to help, but even so, it was getting close. The green valley floor was growing ever closer, but more and more, her Spectre began to pull out of its dive. Just as it reached treetop height, the forest gave way to the glistening lake at the base of the valley. Natalie was fortunate, as her Spectre only leveled out a few meters off the water, below the trees. As she climbed to a safe altitude, she looked around frantically. The other Spectre was nowhere to be seen. They should have been behind her at this point, catching Natalie at the exit of her dive. But instead, they had seemingly exited the valley. Natalie's shipboard Low-Range Detector picked up no contacts, but in the mountains, the L-RaD was unreliable.

She continued to gain altitude until she came out high over the mountains. It was then that she picked up her opponent's signature on her spherical display, already several kilometers from the mountains, heading toward the air base. *Did they give up? Why didn't they continue their pursuit? They had me; why didn't they commit to it?* No answers came to Natalie's questions. The only person who held the answers would be the pilot themselves, whoever they were.

***

Darren met Rygil Pryst as Rygil was climbing out of his Spectre at the end of the day's session. This was the routine for Darren, meeting Rygil at the end of the session, then going to get dinner from the mess hall together while discussing the day's events. As of late, however, the discussion was always the same. Rygil was angry and frustrated, always shouting about how nothing he was trying was working, and how he couldn't explain where he'd gone wrong. Darren had noticed the way Rygil's flying had changed ever since the start of the deathmatch. Rygil had always been calm and collected in the flight seat, but rarely attempted any abnormal maneuvers. To Darren, this made Rygil a good and consistent pilot, but not a great one. But since the start of the deathmatch, Rygil's by-the-book style of flying disappeared; instead, he executed seemingly random maneuvers. He was unpredictable yes, but his maneuvers were easy to counter since they were often done at the wrong time. Because of this, Rygil had only managed to score a handful of kills, the lowest in the class, and his overall ranking plummeted. Darren had even flown with Rygil to try to get him back on track. He had tried to teach Rygil how to counter his own maneuvers, but instead ended up giving up, handing Rygil a thinly veiled free kill. He had hoped it would bring back some of Rygil's confidence, but instead, Darren now had one death to his name, and Rygil still sat at the bottom of the board.

One thing Darren had noted was that any time Rygil asked for advice and Darren told him to go back to the book, Rygil flat out refused. He had completely cast aside all the teaching the instructors had given over the past five cycles, and somehow couldn't see that he had cast aside his flying ability at the same time. After the first week of the same conversation, Darren resigned himself to just being an earpiece, only listening instead of answering questions Rygil may pose during his ranting.

Instead, Darren thought of his own flying and often of Natalie and her flying. It had been two days since Darren had challenged her in her river valley, and still her flying behavior astounded him. She had an aggressive and wild flying style, and even in the setting of the deathmatch, a simulated fight, she had put it all on the line to try to beat him. *She's trying too hard,* Darren thought as he ate dinner and Rygil ranted on in the background. *Maybe this is just her style. Wild and aggressive, all out, all the time.* Darren conceded to himself that had he not seen Natalie practicing her maneuver prior to their engagement, he would have lost to her easily. *I guess it's settled then,* Darren thought, momentarily refraining from eating. *She really is the best pilot here.* Satisfied, Darren continued eating, all the while listening to Rygil attempt to reason out his own problems.

CHAPTER 7

The sixth cycle of schooling was the final cycle of the deathmatch, so every recruit was concentrating more and more on honing their skills and climbing the leaderboard. A higher finishing position would surely mean a great deal in the eyes of the prospective 3rd Mobile squadrons. However, Natalie was in no rush. She had a tremendous lead in the deathmatch, so she would continue to practice in her valley while keeping an ear out for how the other recruits fared against each other.

Today was no different than any other as Natalie enjoyed the peace of the river valley. She was flying her Spectre at a cruising speed, tucked close to the mountain, just above the line of trees. It had been almost twenty minutes since she had finished her usual practice. Now she flew along, enjoying her private area of peace, when she happened to glance at her L-RaD, noticing a new contact. She hastily put her pen back inside her notebook and tucked it away before sitting up straight and preparing herself for a fight. *I wonder who it'll be this time,* she thought as she guided her Spectre to face her opponent.

Taking a quick look at the L-RaD told Natalie that her opponent was coming in high and fast, faster than any other Spectre she'd seen. Remaining level, Natalie pushed the throttle to the max and flew in the direction of her enemy. She would make them dive on her earlier than they anticipated, and then dodge at the last moment. Natalie would know when to dodge based on the L-RaD's altitude display, which used thin lines either above or below the detected craft that would indicate if they were below or above Natalie's Spectre.

As Natalie closed in on her opponent, she saw the line between her and them on the L-RaD shortening; they had started their dive. Natalie waited until the indicating line was about to vanish, then snapped the stick forward and to the right, her left hand bringing extra directional power from the rerouting system. Her own dive should have been in the opposite angle of her opponent's, and she was already starting a corkscrew, which would bring her behind them, as their speed would have caused them to pass her.

Suddenly, Natalie heard a warning tone, which sent fear and shock through her. Two seconds later, she heard the second tone. She yanked the stick back into her, trying to pull out of the dive. *How are they behind me?* Even as her Spectre began to climb and she felt the g-forces push down on her, she knew it was already over. She heard the third warning tone and accepted her fate, leveling out over the valley. But there was no final warning tone, not even the subtle ticking notification of someone targeting her Spectre. On her L-RaD, the other craft was close behind her but began closing before moving to Natalie's right. Natalie turned her body as much as she could to look out the right side of her canopy.

There she saw her opponent drawing itself up alongside. But this was no Spectre; it was a Shrike. Natalie recognized the markings on its tail, indicating that it was the one from the base. It pulled up so its nose was even with her right wing before suddenly pulling up and accelerating away. As it left the valley, Natalie still wasn't sure what happened. All she knew was that even if the leaderboard didn't show a defeat next to her name, she knew that she had lost this fight, and so easily too.

The class of aspiring Spectre pilots stood together on the tarmac, ahead of one of the hangars that housed their planes. Three of the instructors were standing in front of them, two with their arms crossed, and one pacing the length of the body of recruits. The entire group had been silent since they got there some ten minutes ago.

Natalie looked up at the clear blue sky with its slight green tint. Beads of sweat had already formed on her forehead. The sun was beating down on them, making the summer heat all that much worse.

"Are we not teaching you well enough?" The voice of the pacing instructor brought Natalie's attention back to the ground. Though his question seemed directed at no one, when none of the recruits answered, he stopped pacing. "Are we not doing our jobs right? Someone answer me!" he faced the recruits and shouted at them. Then, taking deliberately heavy steps forward, he came within a foot of one of the other recruits. "Tell me what we're doing wrong, now!"

The recruit almost fell backward into his fellow recruits. "You aren't doing anything wrong, sir!" His answer came out loud and at a rate of speed that was almost impressive.

The instructor stepped back, seemingly satisfied that the recruit had played into his hand. "So, if it isn't our teaching, then is it safe to say that all of you are dog shit pilots?" He asked the whole contingent this time. "Because I cannot wrap my head around the fact that not even one of you can put up even a half decent fight against the enemy. Didn't we tell you that the Spectre is better than the Shrike? Each and every one of you has lost against the Shrike, and not a single one of you even looked like you were trying. We have the best plane in the sector and you *useless* wannabes are making it look like it was designed by my kid!"

One of the other instructors stepped forward. "Where's our leading pilot?" he asked. "Annikki, where are you at?"

Crap. Natalie raised her hand from the middle of the group. "Here, sir."

"You're supposed to be the best one here," the instructor said calmly. "At least that's what the stats say. So, tell me, which is better for a tight, high-speed maneuver? Say, for example, a corkscrew-style maneuver."

Natalie felt the weight of her defeat three days ago suddenly drop on her shoulders. Despite all the cursing internally, she knew she had to respond to his question. "The Shrike is better, sir," she said reluctantly.

"Correct." The instructor smiled. "Now tell me why you thought it would be a good idea to use a corkscrew maneuver against me the other day."

The rest of the class was suddenly staring at her. A few tried to chuckle quietly. "I thought you were a Spectre, sir."

"A Spectre, really?" His voice was climbing. "Does the enemy fly Spectres, Annikki? Are we in the New Federation right now? Am I a Halerian? Do *you*, Annikki, want to see Altheria burn, is that it?"

"No, sir!" Natalie responded swiftly.

"Then you'd better start paying attention, all of you." The instructor's voice fell back to a low but firm tone. "The enemy flies a truly capable aircraft. The Spectre may be better, but it is not invincible, and the enemy won't hesitate to exploit any sign of weakness. The deathmatch that you have all been participating in is *not* for your gain. It is not for you to prove that you are better than everyone else. It is for you to learn the weaknesses of your own craft. It is so you can learn to never expose any of those weaknesses against the enemy. Start paying attention in class and start reading on your own. If you can't beat us in a Shrike when we were trained on Spectres, how are you supposed to beat those who have dedicated their entire careers to flying Shrikes?"

Natalie walked along the row of administrative buildings with a pair of new books in her hand. She knew she had to start dividing her reading time between the Dolphin and Spectre, and more importantly now the Shrike as well. She knew that she would re-challenge the Shrike if she could, and there was no way she was going to suffer the same embarrassment as before. The Shrike was a formidable opponent, but so was the Spectre. Natalie continuously worked out where her Spectre could beat the Shrike, and where the Shrike could beat her. The Shrike was faster, but the Spectre could turn sharper. The Spectre had more weapons, but the Shrike was smaller and harder to hit. Natalie quickly found that the only way to beat the Shrike was to put it in its weakest traits. Force it to try to turn, never follow it in a corkscrew, and definitely don't try to run away from it in a straight line.

She knew it would only be a matter of time before the Shrike found her again, or she found it, but she was confident that when it did, she would be ready. She would know everything about both the Spectre and Shrike, and while she wasn't sure if she could best the experience of the instructor flying the Shrike, Natalie knew that she could put up a good fight, enough to garner the attention of the top squadrons.

As Natalie neared the base post office, she turned left to go inside. She had received notice earlier in the day that she had mail waiting for her, and now that the day was done, it would be the best time to pick it up.

In line ahead of her was one other woman. When Natalie stepped in line behind her, the woman turned around. Immediately, Natalie recognized her as the Dolphin instructor who had argued in favor of Natalie flying Spectres.

The woman smiled. "Oh, a different recruit!" she said cheerfully. "Sorry, it's not often I see non-Dolphin recruits around."

Natalie's eyes shifted from the woman to the counter behind her. "Hello, ma'am," was all she could think of to say.

"Here to pick up some mail from home?"

"I'm not sure, to be honest," Natalie responded. "The only person who would send me anything is an old pilot I knew back in my hometown. Maybe she just wants to see how I'm doing."

"That's so sweet of her," the woman said, taking her package from the counter. "It's good to have someone keeping an eye out for you. Well, have a good evening!"

"Thank you, ma'am," Natalie said.

When her mail was handed to her, she found that it was just a single white envelope, addressed to her. However, there was no return address. She tucked it between her two books and headed for her dorm.

Setting the books on top of the others, Natalie sat down at her desk and delicately opened the envelope. At first, she stared at it, confused. She hadn't felt any paper within the envelope as she was opening it, and now that she was looking at the opening, she confirmed that there was no letter inside.

Is this a joke? she thought, dropping the envelope onto the desk.

Just as it impacted, a small white square was propelled out of the envelope and onto the desk. Turning it over, Natalie revealed a letter E on the square. She picked up the envelope and flipped it upside down, causing a few more squares to tumble out. Pinching the sides, she opened the envelope wider and scraped out the last of the white squares. Then, she turned all of them over until all the letters were facing right side up.

There were five *E*'s, two *D*'s, two *I*'s, and one of each: *A*, *B*, *C*, *G*, *N*, *O*, *R*, *U*, *V*, and *Y* for nineteen letters in all. Natalie stared at them, spread across her desk.

This has to be a joke, she thought again. *There's no way anyone could unscramble this. You could make anything you wanted out of these letters.*

For a few minutes, possibly to simply humor whoever was playing this trick on her, she attempted to unscramble the letters. She started with making simple words, such as *no* or *you,* before experimenting with larger words like *endeavor*. When she made these words, they were loosely assembled, crooked, and spaced apart by some millimeters.

If they were all together at one point though, she began thinking, *they should have all fit on one line.* Carefully, she began putting letters close together to make their edges flush. When she did this, she found that a word like *endeavor* was crooked in places. By lining up each letter with another, she could examine them for how well they fit together. This, coupled with some logic and spelling, helped speed things along.

Still, it took Natalie nearly half an hour longer to create her sentence. When she had it, she sat back and stared at it.

There's no way this is the message, she thought. She examined each letter, its position on her desk relative to the other letters. She examined each line, every angle, to make sure that each letter was perfectly in line with the next. Despite her desire to be wrong, all the letters appeared to be exactly where they were meant to. With the realization that the words on her desk were the intended message, Natalie could do nothing but stare at them.

YOU ARE BEING DECEIVED.

The message seemed to stare back at Natalie. She knew what each of the words meant by themselves, but together, the message was almost meaningless.

Deceived? About what? Or into *what? And by who? How?* Every possible question formed in Natalie's mind in a flurry, each one existing just long enough to be recognized and then dismissed. After all, she didn't *feel* like she was being deceived by anyone. *Or is that the point?* Even if she were being deceived without knowing, she had no idea who would be deceiving her or over what.

There was also nobody to ask. The letter had no return address, and nothing inside the envelope indicated any sort of origin. The message could have come from anyone.

It's probably some stupid prank, Natalie thought. *Someone just trying to make me paranoid.* She thought about sweeping all the letters into the garbage, ignoring the whole incident, and moving on. She didn't have time for somebody's pointless game. Still, it would be worth keeping track of in case she needed to bring it up to her superiors. Taking a small notebook from the edge of her desk, Natalie quickly scribbled down the message onto a blank page with the date next to it. Then she swept the individual letters back into their envelope and wrote the date down on the envelope as well.

Hopefully this is the only thing I'll hear of it, she thought as she tucked the envelope into her drawer and set her notebook on the corner of her desk. *But if not, at least I'll have proof.*

***

Darren had been on his way to the outer perimeter of the base, where he usually spent his recreational time walking and enjoying the evening air, when he was stopped by three other recruits. Darren recognized them immediately as three of Rygil Pryst's friends, and though he had only limited interactions with them, Darren knew their names. As they led Darren to a more secluded area to talk, he suspected that this was about Rygil's flying, considering it had been getting worse since the beginning of the deathmatch. The group of four made their way toward the eastern edge of the base, far from the buildings and any other people. When they stopped, Darren's suspicions were immediately proven correct.

"Do you have any idea what has happened to Pryst?" the first asked, a young woman with short jet-black hair, who Darren knew as Ismarie Yisha. "He's become the worst pilot in the whole class."

"I haven't got a clue," Darren said, already not enjoying this conversation. "As far as I can tell, he's trying to completely rebuild his flying style. Or he's just gone mad." Darren's sarcasm was reactive; he had nothing to give them, and he was sure they had nothing to give him.

"This isn't the time for jokes," one of the other recruits snapped. This one was tall, black hair shaved down to its roots, named Ayair Sayol. "Something, or rather *someone,* has caused Pryst to change. We need to know what he was told so we can help him." The two other recruits nodded in agreement.

Darren let out an exasperated sigh. "Sorry, Sayol, but I've got nothing. He won't tell me anything. He just rants about how shit he's become at flying." Sayol was immediately in Darren's face.

"Calm down, Sayol," the third and final recruit said softly. She was short, shorter than Natalie to Darren's eyes, her bright blonde hair done up in a tight bun. Darren recalled her name being Jenevieve Fritallia. She seemed to be the calmest and most reasonable of the group. Sayol backed down, taking a few steps away from Darren, but not once breaking eye contact. Darren couldn't care less, instead focusing his attention on Fritallia as she continued. "We know you have spoken to Natalie Annikki on multiple occasions, Verra." Fritallia paused for a moment.

What does she have to do with this? Darren wondered, becoming uneasy. "You stopped speaking to her after sim testing though, so you probably aren't aware. Pryst went to her for advice on flying just before the deathmatch began." Darren couldn't hide his shock. Pryst never spoke well of Natalie, so why would he go to her for advice? He recalled that Pryst had also sought him out for advice on combat, but Darren had been unable to provide it.

"Do you really believe that she is responsible for ruining Pryst's ability?" Darren asked the three of them. "She has no reason to try to bring down any of us—she's already the best in the class by far."

"Tch, maybe you just don't know her," Yisha said bitterly. *Why am I defending Natalie?* The thought flashed through Darren's mind alongside a rush of heated anger. "The two of them got into a heated argument the first time they spoke. Rygil went to her a second time just a few days before the deathmatch started. And that's when his flying went downhill."

"Whatever she told Pryst," Fritallia concluded, "has caused him to become a failure as a pilot."

"*If* Natalie is even responsible," Darren began his own conclusion to the discussion. "She had no intention for this outcome. She is kind and will help anyone who asks her. I have no doubt that she gave him her honest advice. Perhaps he has simply misinterpreted it." As Darren finished, he turned and walked away, headed for the opposite side of the airbase.

He found himself too irritated to relax during his walk, his mind unable to focus on anything other than the accusations. *There's no way she'd do something like that.* Natalie had always come across as kind if a little cold. When he had struggled with the Dolphin simulator, Natalie offered her methods to help him fly it better, even without him asking. There was no possible way she would act so maliciously. *Maybe I should talk to her about it.* Then Darren recalled the last time they had spoken. It was when the sim test scores had been ranked, and Natalie had beaten him in the Spectre. He couldn't explain why he never spoke to her again, just that for some reason he couldn't. He didn't want to believe that simple jealousy had ruined their relationship. He decided speaking to her now on such a subject may not be the best choice. *Then I will have to talk to Rygil.* Satisfied with his conclusion, but with his thoughts still whirling, Darren returned to his dorm early.

***

Natalie brought her Spectre level just above the trees at the base of the river valley. Mentally, she logged where she had done well and where she had improved on her latest maneuver. As she ran through the maneuver in her mind, she began flying back toward the mountain she had started at. Throttling up, she glanced down momentarily at her L-RaD, only to see an orange marker bearing down on her. Again, it seemed that Natalie had been caught unawares by her opponent. This one was already almost on top of her, coming from her right, and fast. She banked and arched over the mountains on her immediate left, taking the Spectre down the steep slope. Halfway down the slope, she pulled back hard on the flightstick, toward herself and to the right, taking the craft out of its dive and leveling out just over the trees at high speed, still hugging the mountain. The opposing pilot kept themselves hidden until the last possible second, and the speed… This was no recruit; this was an experienced pilot. She looked around for the enemy, spotting it a way down the slope, just coming out of its turn. It was a sleek, triangular craft: a Shrike. Finally, after two weeks, it had returned.

So far, Natalie had not heard of any recruit beating the Shrike in combat. She had even overheard Darren discussing how the Shrike had gotten the better of him. She knew the scores were based on how close you could get to beating the Shrike, not by actually beating it. However, Natalie would still give it her all in this fight, as in her mind it was no different than any other.

If you want to come challenge me, I will fight. But I won't lose this time. With her height advantage, there was no way the Shrike would win an acceleration fight, as it had to climb the mountain. Natalie rolled left, banking hard down the mountain toward her opponent. The Shrike's pilot did not try to turn and climb, instead turning away from Natalie's Spectre, accelerating farther down the mountain, before pulling out high above the valley. Natalie followed, losing some ground. *I'm not close enough for the lock, but I am far back enough that I'll be able to predict any movement he makes.* Natalie was able to keep this distance despite the Shrike's faster speed because she could see his maneuvers. Every time the Shrike turned or attempted a maneuver to shake Natalie, she followed him through, often cutting the distance in the corner due to the Spectre's superior turn rate. For several minutes, the two fighters danced through the valley, between the peaks of the mountains, back down to the freshwater lake, their exhaust kicking up the water below. Then they went back up through the valley and did it all again. Neither party could get the upper hand. Every time Natalie closed to gun range on the Shrike, the pilot would use his speed advantage to run away, but every time he tried to turn to shake Natalie, she cut his turn, closing the range. And so, the dance continued for many minutes, a test of skill and endurance. But Natalie was determined not to give up the fight.

As the pair flew high over the valley, the Shrike rolled over and dove, trying to loop back on Natalie. He would pull up hard, climbing back to Natalie's altitude, trying to attack her from below. If she followed, she would lose even more ground, and he would be able to climb and dive on top of her, taking her out. *He won't get to my position fast enough.* Natalie pushed the Spectre's throttle, pulling away from the Shrike's maneuver exit, and turned hard to the right, as hard as Natalie could pull back on the stick. The Spectre came out of its hundred-eighty degree turn just before the Shrike came up from its dive to Natalie's altitude. It was committed, didn't have the speed to turn away, and could not loop back fast enough to enter a new dive. Natalie was quickly upon him, making her gun kill as she swept by. The Shrike turned away, briefly staying in the area before flying back to the forests closer to the base.

Natalie was relieved and brimming with confidence as she flew through the shadows of the valley in the setting sun. She had beaten the Shrike, piloted by an instructor with years of experience on her. She was the first, and so far, only, rookie pilot to accomplish this task. *All my hard work is paying off,* Natalie thought, smiling inside her flight helmet. *This will practically guarantee me a place in the top squadron.* That top squadron was known as the White Tails, one of the oldest squadrons in the 3rd Mobile. The White Tails consisted of only Spectre pilots, all of whom were double or triple aces. Even outside the 3rd Mobile, in the inter-fleet competitions, the White Tails were one of the best, having won the yearly competition several times. To be a White Tail was to be one of the best pilots in the Omasye Space Council. Today, more than any other day, Natalie felt as though she could join that elite squadron.

***

Darren Verra walked along the outskirts of the air base under the slowly setting sun, hanging just above the forest surrounding the base. Today, however, Darren was not alone. Beside and just behind him walked Rygil Pryst, quietly keeping pace. Darren had asked Rygil to walk with him just after dinner, but since they had begun walking nearly ten minutes ago, not a word had been spoken. As they reached the southeastern corner of the base, Darren decided to break the silence.

"So, I heard you've been talking with Natalie," he began in his usual nonchalant tone. "Mind telling me what that's been about? I could have sworn you thought she was too uptight for you." Pryst's pace noticeably slowed at the mention of Natalie, and Darren slowed to match.

"It was only twice," Pryst responded quickly, his voice defensive. "And it was pointless. I asked her for advice, and all she did was bash my flying."

Natalie wouldn't do that, Darren thought. *She was probably giving her honest take of how she beat him.* But for the sake of getting answers, Darren decided to go along with it. "Alright, and what did she say about your flying?" Darren probed, hoping not to set Pryst off.

"She said I was predictable." To Darren's amazement, Pryst started to explain everything. "She said I stuck to the book too much, with no difference from what I had been taught by the instructors. She could see the next move I'd make before I'd even begun to make it because I always went with what we had been taught."

"So, your answer was to cast it away completely?"

Pryst's voice dropped low. "She said I should be more unpredictable. So that's what I did. But I don't understand why it works for you and her but not me."

"'Cause we didn't throw the book away," Darren responded quickly. "We reference the book when needed, but not every situation is a perfect book-cut situation. We can change what we do. I think you've misinterpreted her advice." Everything began to click for Darren now. Natalie hadn't intentionally sabotaged Pryst's flying ability; he had merely taken what she had told him to the extreme, probably out of spite to her comments.

"Maybe I did, but I doubt it," Pryst said after a few moments of silence. "There's somethin' about her, somethin' that makes me think she never wanted to help me in the first place." His tone had shifted to something almost sinister, a tone that worried Darren Verra. Pryst thought far too highly of himself to believe he could have made a mistake like Darren was accusing him of.

"I'm pretty sure you've got it wrong." Darren tried to salvage the situation, while also ending the discussion. All he wanted to know was what had actually happened, and now that he knew, he had other things he would prefer to be doing. "I'm fairly sure she tried to actually help. She's not the kind of person you think she is. But I can't talk you out of making your own interpretation. Just don't do something stupid with it." With that, Darren said his farewell and turned back toward the base.

As he did, he saw the flash of a shadow dart behind a nearby building. Hastening his pace, Darren came to the building. Turning the corner, his eyes locked with those of a short, young woman as she was undoing the tight bun of her hair. Long blonde locks fell over her shoulders as his eyes registered who it was in the shadow of the building. Her eyes were full of what Darren could only perceive as hate, a sinister look scrawled across her face. Fritallia didn't say a word. She walked past Darren, toward the recruits' barracks. Darren stood still for minutes, staring at nothing in silence. He knew that the only people he didn't want to know anymore than they did would now hear everything. Darren knew Natalie was innocent, but he also knew that Fritallia and the others would see this as proof that she was responsible. Darren's heart and mind were quickly flooded by guilt, guilt that he had been the one to coerce the evidence from Pryst's mouth.

Natalie Annikki sat on the grassy hill at the northwestern edge of the base. As always, she had come to it after dinner. It was so quiet, completely undisturbed by the usual activity inside the base. It was here that Natalie would read, in the quiet serenity of the evening light. She held her current book against her lower thighs, with her legs bent to form a comfortable incline.

Natalie usually read one of the textbooks from the base's library, but today, with Natalie feeling at her peak confidence level in her flying, she had decided to take a break from studying military craft. Instead, she read a book about the many species of cat that populated Altheria. Natalie was still determined to own a cat on Jontunia after she retired from the military. They had been one of the last things her father had shown her of the world outside Jontunia before he died. She had been able to do a small amount of reading on them just prior to her father's death, but now was the first time she could sit down and read a great deal about them. She had read that cats had been mankind's companion for thousands of years and had even been reserved for kings and queens. Even after humans had begun conquering the stars, they couldn't help but bring their loyal animals with them, and now, in relatively small numbers, cats inhabited the sector, just like humans. The more she read about their history on Altheria and their place in a human's life, the more she was eager to own one.

But it was more than that. Her father had shown her what a cat was. If she were to get a cat, it would be her father's final gift to her, as she would never have known them without him. Natalie pulled a small picture of her father out of the breast pocket of her olive-green jacket. The picture was one of the few she had been able to take with her when she left home. It was from the second time he had visited Altheria, years ago. In the picture, her father was holding a cat from a pet store, which he had told her had at least a dozen of these animals that were so rare on Jontunia. The cat had long brown hair with black spots and lay happily on its back in his arms. Natalie held the picture with the book, smiling to herself, and losing herself in memories. He would have brought back one just like the one he held, just for his daughter.

"What'cha reading, Annikki?" a female voice from her right said suddenly. Natalie was seemingly ripped from her thoughts. Natalie looked up from her book and was looking at a young man standing on the hill, low enough that their eyes were level. He was familiar, but Natalie didn't know him. He simply stared at her, unmoving. Knowing this was not the voice that had spoken, she then glanced to her right. There she saw two women about her age, both walking slowly up the hill. One was smiling, but the other wore a frown, her eyes piercing Natalie's. The smile suddenly felt fake, and Natalie felt a sense of unease quickly rising in her stomach.

"H… Hello. Can I help you?" Natalie tripped over her words. She recognized the three as fellow Spectre trainees but had never spoken to them before.

One of the women, wearing a tight black tank top and military fatigue pants, with short, jet-black hair shook her head before speaking. "No, I don't really think you can help us anymore. See, you've already done quite enough. We're just here to make up for what you've done. *Sayol.*" The woman nodded toward Natalie while speaking what sounded like a name.

That's when two arms came around Natalie from behind, grabbing her own arms and pulling them behind her. Natalie let out a small yelp of surprise and spilled her book and photo on the grass. She was pulled toward her assailant just enough to cause her legs to give way, falling flat on the side of the hill. Natalie realized that the man in front of her was gone. He must have circled in behind while she had been focused on the two women to her right. She felt herself begin to panic, but she knew she had to remain calm and tried to bring her mind back in order.

The other woman, a short blonde in a black flying jacket and training shorts came up the hill, stopping in front of Natalie. "You look pitiful," she said, smirking, staring down at Natalie in her restrained position. "I expected the top of the class to put up a fight instead of submitting so easily. Maybe that's all you are, just some weak little girl, trying to look like the big tough hotshot pilot. That's it; the hotshot pilot who thinks no one else deserves her time or knowledge, so she just feeds them bullshit to get them away from her."

"I don't know what you're talking about," Natalie retorted, wincing as Sayol tightened his grip on her arms. "I've done nothing of the sort!" Quickly, her mind began unraveling the cause of the situation she was in. *Rygil,* she realized.

"Tch, listen to her try to hide what she did to Pryst," the woman spat. "You listen here, you bitch." She crouched down immediately next to Natalie, speaking into her right ear. "We know exactly what you've done. Your buddy Verra got Pryst to spill everything. You deliberately gave Pryst bad advice, knowing he was desperate enough to go through with it. You ruined his flying career." She pushed on Natalie's side, causing her to wince at the pain caused by the pull in her restrained arms. *Darren is in on this?* Pain struck something in her chest. *No, there's no way that's true.* She shook her head as the blonde woman spotted something on the ground.

"Hmm, what's this here?" The blonde reached down, forcing Natalie's left leg aside. She then stood up, holding Natalie's book in her left hand and the picture of Natalie's father in her right. *No, leave that alone,* Natalie pleaded, but the words wouldn't come out. "Lovely picture you've got here, Annikki." She quickly glanced at the cover of the book then back to the picture and back to Natalie. "Heh, your old man must have good money to get animals from Altheria. Maybe you're just some rich girl who thinks she owns the world." Natalie shook her head, staring down at her legs.

"Please, you've got it all wrong. I swear I haven't done anything wrong," she pleaded, just wanting to end this nightmare. "Please just let me go."

"Sounds an awful lot like begging," the blonde responded, laughter in her voice. "I'll cut you a deal then, okay? You never come near any of us again, got it? Oh, and I don't mean just us three and Pryst either; I mean the entire class. I don't want any chance of you trying to sabotage some other poor recruit. If I see you say one word to another recruit, the next time we do flying practice, there's going to be an accident." Natalie nodded her submission, and the girl threw the book at Natalie, hitting her square in the chest. She then crumpled the photo in her hand and threw it into the trees close by. She signaled the others to leave, and Sayol threw Natalie down to the ground. A few moments later, when Natalie was sure they would be out of earshot, she began to cry.

CHAPTER 8

Darren Verra stood on the tarmac of the airfield, next to the hangars with the rest of the Spectre recruits. It was the day after the deathmatch had concluded, and the instructors had gathered the recruits prior to daily flight practice to instruct them on the next portion of their training. Occasionally during the instruction, one of the massive Phantom heavy transports would spur up and take off down the large runway on the other side of the base, drowning out the words of the instructors. Each craft's class was getting close to the end of their eight-cycle training, today being the beginning of the seventh cycle. The eighth cycle was reserved for pure practice, as well as the final exam in front of the squadrons.

The routine for the next cycle would be formation flying. This was nothing new to any of them, as proper flying procedure in a wing or squadron was taught to the recruits from day one. To Darren, it felt as though they spent more time making sure their flying looked prim and proper than making sure they could actually win a fight. Darren knew which he cared about more as he yawned. Deciding it couldn't be helped, however, Darren went along with it. There was an aspect of teamwork to fighter combat of course. He also figured that proper tandem flying would be of some benefit to learning how to utilize one's wingman to win the fight.

The recruits were soon instructed to pair up and get ready to begin practice. Darren decided to wait while some of the class formed their pairs. As he expected, Yisha and Sayol paired up, as did Pryst and Fritallia. As the recruits paired off and began to move toward their Spectres, Darren noticed that one recruit wasn't moving, instead glancing down at her flight boots and subtly around her immediate vicinity. She was holding her deep green ponytail to her lips and appeared to be muttering something to herself. He thought about walking over to her. The two still hadn't talked since the sim tests. He began to step in her direction. Two steps in, however, Natalie abruptly turned away and set off toward the hangar where her Spectre was located. Darren stopped instinctively and glanced around. None of the other recruits were still around, having all paired up. Darren quickly decided that he would wait until after practice and try to speak with Natalie.

Darren was quietly standing near the door to the mess hall, fixing his short brown hair when he saw Natalie coming down the hall. Darren called out to her. She glanced up from the floor. As she met Darren's eyes, her own lit up briefly. Darren admired the vivid hazel coloring, which gave her eyes the appearance of two small stars. "Hey, I was wondering if you'd like to be my flying partner for the rest of the cycle," Darren asked in the sincerest tone he could. Something in him really did want to fly with her, and he was sure she hadn't made any other friends to fly with. "If you've got someone else already, that's fine, I don't mind," Darren added, smiling toward Natalie. As he did though, Natalie's eyes faded, and she looked away from him. She shook her head and continued walking into the mess hall, never saying a word, leaving Darren dumbfounded in the hallway.

Darren took his tray and looked around the mess hall. Clusters of recruits chatted away over their meals, and, as per usual, Natalie was taking her meal out the door with her. Darren looked away from her after a moment and headed toward a table. Whatever her issues, he was certain that right now she just wanted to be left alone. So instead, Darren put his tray down at the end of a table and sat down alone with his dinner.

Not long after he sat down, he heard some others setting down their trays a few seats down from him. Glancing to his right, he saw Pryst, Sayol, Fritallia, and Yisha together. None of them seemed to notice him as they sat down. Darren soon returned to his meal but found himself drawn to the conversation just within earshot.

"She's history now," he heard Fritallia's voice. "She'll be bottom of the barrel, if she even passes now."

Darren could see Pryst speaking out of the corner of his eye but couldn't understand the words. Thankfully, Yisha responded at a higher volume. "Oh, we gave her a good scare for sure," she said with a smile on her face. "And you'll never believe it; she's just a rich stuck-up bitch, living on Daddy's money!"

"Yeah, her dad's some bigshot businessman," Fritallia added. "She had this picture of him holding some animal on Altheria. I bet she's got one at home too."

"Did you see the look on her face when you threw it in the woods?" Sayol asked excitedly. "That shit was priceless!" He laughed.

Darren looked down at his half-eaten meal. He didn't feel like eating anymore, and he certainly didn't feel like listening to the others. No, there were better things to do now.

***

Darren walked around the perimeter of the base after dinner as per his usual routine. However, today, his thoughts were focused solely on Natalie Annikki. Almost every day he had seen her, she had carried herself with confidence, always looking ahead. But today it was as though the Natalie Darren knew wasn't inside her, leaving just a shell of her to walk the base. He was glad he had overheard the others' conversation at dinner. At least now he knew what had happened, or at least some of it.

Before Darren had even reached the foot of the hill, he could see that Natalie wasn't there. *I'm sure it happened here,* Darren thought as he climbed the grassy hill. Reaching the top of the small hill, Darren looked around him. He could immediately understand why Natalie liked the hill. Despite not being remarkably high, Darren had a vantage point above the nearby administrative buildings, the closest structures to the hill. He could even see most of the runway used by the Dolphin transports. He couldn't quite see the opposite side of the base, the Phantom's area, as it was blocked by the central base buildings.

Behind the hill was the edge of the forest, a section of which Darren had not explored out of fear of disturbing Natalie's reading. However, if they had ambushed Natalie here, then her father's picture was probably somewhere nearby. He entered the woods on a narrow path. The forest was consistent around the whole of the base, a mix of pine evergreens and larger trees with brilliant green and red leaves. The ground was tumultuous with roots and leaves making journeys off the paths harder to navigate, as the leaves often hid roots poking above the dirt. Figuring the picture was near the immediate edge of the forest by Natalie's hill, Darren began walking through the woods.

As Darren wandered around the trees, he scanned the ground around him for any oddity. Eventually, he saw something white near the base of a nearby tree. He began making his way around the other trees to investigate. It was the photo, crumpled up into a ball, resting at the base of a tree. Darren picked it up and began unfolding the crumpled paper. Unfolded, the photo revealed a man in a dress shirt with graying black hair holding a furry animal the likes of which Darren had never seen before. *I guess this is it then,* Darren thought as he carefully placed the photo in the breast pocket of his shirt.

***

The fifth day of formation flying had gone by, and as Darren put his flight helmet down on the small desk in his dorm, he considered his options. Natalie had continued to set off to her own plane without speaking to anyone, and still Darren had found himself without a partner. *If neither of us get partners, there's no way we'll graduate, at least not in the highest squadrons,* Darren thought as he changed from his flight suit to his standard fatigues. From the moment he had learned of the draft system, he had aimed for the best squadron, the White Tails. He had his suspicions that Natalie was aiming for the same, and he found it unacceptable that he would allow both of them to miss out on the opportunity, at least not before finding out what had happened. If the worst scenario came to pass, where Natalie had pretty well quit flying Spectres, Darren would borrow some other recruit to practice. Darren was about to leave his room but turned back to grab the picture of Natalie's father from his desk, placing it in his shirt pocket.

Natalie paced around the doorway to the cafeteria for a few minutes. Other recruits, some from her class and others from the Dolphin, Phantom, and Hunter classes, walked by and into the building for dinner. Only after these minutes of pacing did she stop, face the doorway, and go inside. Even if she didn't want to, Natalie's eyes scanned the room for Pryst and the others. She found them within moments, sitting together at a table near the center of the room. She shook her head and turned her attention to the meal line.

She waited in line, watching the kitchen staff walk in and out of the kitchen itself and into the serving area, bringing up more food or taking the place of one of the servers who was going on break. Most wore some combination of white cooking clothes, but some wore the flat, olive-colored military fatigues. All of them wore either a black or white round hat, tall but not top heavy. One gave her some dry-looking pasta, even with the sauce, and another gave her some steamed carrots to go with it and handed her the tray.

At first, Natalie turned to head back toward the doorway. On any other day, she would have gone back to the hill where she read, and she would have eaten there. Even now, with a plan in mind, she had to fight her instincts that told her to go through that door. She slowed to a stop near the front of the cafeteria, half-turned toward the tables and half toward the door. Her head drooped, but suddenly shot up. Natalie fixed her eyes on an empty table and started walking.

"You've got to be kidding," someone said from some table nearby as she walked around an occupied table to her own.

"You think you can just come back in here after avoiding us for so long?" another voice asked, which Natalie didn't respond to.

Unfortunately, someone else did. "Yeah, instead of avoiding helping us, she's just going to ignore us completely."

"You think you're just so good that you don't need to bother wasting your time with anyone else." This voice was familiar, and as Natalie subtly glanced around, she saw that it was the black-haired girl from before. Contempt filled her eyes as she continued. "You're despicable, and you'll have no friends in the future. You're going to die alone, with no one helping you when you need it. Just like you deserve."

Natalie wanted to leave. She already hated her decision, and she looked down at her food, trying to find the composure to start eating, to ignore the others and eat like they didn't exist.

"Any pilot can tell that you aren't a team player," one recruit said as they walked by. "You're just a loner, in it for yourself."

"The instructors sure like her," another recruit, walking with the first, pointed out.

"I bet they do," the first responded. They spoke loudly and more in the direction of Natalie than to their friend. "I wonder when the last time was that she slept in her own bed." He laughed. Others joined in, and soon recruits that passed Natalie's table dropped off words like "slut" and "whore" as they went by.

Natalie was moments from grabbing her tray and leaving when the room suddenly fell deathly silent. The silence was abruptly broken by the sound of a metal tray clattering against Natalie's table.

"What are you doing?!" Rygil's voice was clearly heard from a way away, obviously yelling at whomever had placed their tray on Natalie's table.

"Piss off, you bloody idiot. You're stupid in thinking that this girl was actually trying to sabotage you. If you think that she had to worry about you threatening her position on the boards, you really are living in some fantasy world. Might as well go join the peace-terrorist Dominion in theirs." With that, Darren sat down at the table. Natalie looked up, a single tear beginning to slide down her cheek. All Darren did was smile at her.

"I thought you were with them," Natalie began, her voice weak. "They made it sound like you had gotten Rygil to explain what I had spoken to him about, and that you all had taken it the same way."

Darren shook his head. "I had Rygil explain everything to me so I could figure out why the others were suspicious of you, but they listened in without my knowledge and twisted it all. I know you just wanted to help him." Darren appeared so comforting, immediately erasing the cycles of the pair not speaking. Natalie too began to smile, now that she had confirmed that her only friend hadn't abandoned her. "Hey, you know what, let's eat somewhere else," Darren offered, hoping to get Natalie away from the people still glaring at her. Natalie nodded, and the two quickly stood up, taking their trays with them out of the mess hall.

The pair stopped at the top of Natalie's hill and took a seat along its slope, looking over the base. Natalie began eating, and Darren let her be for a few moments, watching. She didn't seem to notice at all. Occasionally, she would look out at the base, but Darren only saw relief in her eyes. He didn't quite know what it was about her, but he was starting to understand why he felt the way he did. After watching for a few moments longer, Darren decided to break the silence. "If you don't mind me asking, what did they do to you?"

Natalie slowly stopped eating and took a drink before responding. She had regained her composure by now, as far as Darren could tell. "They held me here, yelling at me and pushing me, before threatening that if I talk to anyone in the class ever again, they'd stage an accident against me."

Darren could already feel his temper rising. "I'll make sure that doesn't happen."

Natalie stifled a laugh. "How could you possibly do that?"

"I don't know, but I'll find a way. I'd fly into them if I had to," Darren reassured her.

Natalie was silent, but Darren saw a hint of a smile at the edge of her lips.

Suddenly remembering what was in his pocket, he changed the subject. "Oh, I found this." Natalie looked over at him as he drew her father's photograph from his pocket. "I'm pretty sure this belongs to you. It's a little damaged since it was crumpled up and in the dirt, but it's still in decent shape." He handed it to Natalie, who was completely stunned at seeing the photo again.

"I thought this was gone forever. They stole it from me. How did you find it?" Her eyes were alight, and her voice rose in a way that caused Darren to smile.

"I overheard them bragging about throwing it into the woods," Darren said. "I figured you'd want it back, so the other day I went looking for it. I saw that photo crumpled at the base of a tree just over there." Darren pointed into the woods near the hill.

"Well, thank you," Natalie began, her voice falling soft. "This picture means a lot to me; it's the only one of my father I could take with me."

"Maybe you can ask him for a new one when you graduate. A new picture for a new chapter." Natalie's eyes dropped to the grass. "Did I say something wrong?" Darren asked, concerned.

"My father," Natalie started and stopped, the words sticking in her mouth. "My father was killed just before I came here." Darren placed a hand on her shoulder, which she found rather comforting.

"I'm so sorry." Darren was silent for a moment, looking as though he was trying to think of something to say. "Dammit, I'm an idiot."

Natalie let out a short laugh, choking back the tears that nearly formed from the memory of her father. "You are, but not because of this," she started, looking back up to him. "You had no way of knowing. But you're an idiot for betraying all your friends just for me."

Darren shook his head. "Never. They're all jealous, vengeful people, and you're the sincerest person I've met here. You're honest, and you don't bear any ill will just because someone critiques you." Darren paused for a few moments, letting his words sink in. "I also want to know what that thing your dad is holding is."

Darren laughed, and Natalie laughed too, taking the picture back out of her pocket. "It's called a cat," she said, handing him the picture. "Boring name, I know, but they seem really cool. On Altheria, they're everywhere, and people keep them for pets. You can import them here, too, but they're really expensive. My dad showed me one after a business trip to Altheria, and since then I've wanted to get one. He said he'd get one for me when I started my career. I think I want one now more than anything."

"Do they all look like that one?"

Natalie shook her head. "There's so many different breeds it's hard to keep track of them. And the pattern of their fur can vary so much. Some even look like their wild relatives."

"Wild?" Darren asked.

"On Altheria, there were big wildcats that were apex predators long ago. Nowadays, though, there are so few left that they are kept in strict conservation areas. But for a long time, they were the deadliest animals in the wild."

"And these 'pets' are descendants from those wildcats?"

"More or less." Natalie laughed.

"Well, this one looks very soft," Darren said, handing the picture back to Natalie. "One of those things my family would never be exposed to. Born on the wrong planet, in the wrong town." Natalie looked at him quizzically, prompting him to continue. "I grew up in a mining town. My brothers, my father, my grandfathers, and so on have all worked in the mines that supply the production of ships and weapons for the OSC. Bad work, worse pay, and we were all destined to do it the moment we were born."

"Except you," Natalie interjected. She leaned a little closer to Darren.

"Except me," Darren agreed, nodding. "I decided that there was more to life than mining, getting injured, and being poor. I decided that the Verra name had the ability to become a great name, if only we could leave that town. So, I decided to be the first to leave. My family has practically disowned me, but you know what, I was alright with that. I don't want my kids to be miners. I don't want my sons to come back from work every day sore and bruised, or worse. And I don't want my daughters to be worried that their husbands or sons might not return from work. The military wasn't the ideal solution, but it was all I could do." Darren's voice trailed off, his eyes full of sorrow.

"You miss them, don't you?" Natalie asked quietly. Darren nodded. "Do you regret joining the OSC then?"

Darren shook his head. "No, at the end of the day, I can't regret anything. I've always put the past behind me. And besides, I'm doing what I set out to do, make something of my name for my future children. And I've met someone like you, and I could never regret that." The two locked eyes for a few moments, trying to read each other's feelings. Natalie was the first to pull away, returning to her original sitting position.

"I never thought you would have come from a background like that," she began, looking out across the base. "I don't really know what I thought though."

"What about you?" Darren asked inquisitively. "Where did you come from, why are you here?"

Natalie sighed and smiled before beginning. "I came from a small town in Accullad, far from any notable city. My father was a businessman who went on trips across the Altherian Empire and New Federation, but my mother left us when I was little. She decided that the New Federation was a better life for her, but not for us, I suppose. I wanted to fly, more than anything." Natalie paused before continuing. "And I wanted to save people. I applied to the OSC, and then my father died just before I got accepted. He was killed crossing the border after a business trip. He ended up being one of the innocent people I wish I could protect." Natalie took a breath, looking away from Darren. This was the first time she had said everything aloud, and she instantly wondered why. *Because it's him,* she realized, looking back at Darren.

"What about your mother?" he asked. "Is she still alive?"

"I don't know." Natalie shook her head. "She never tried to contact me after she left. I don't even know where in the New Federation she is, or if she is still alive."

"Would you want to find her?"

"Maybe, but there are tens of billions of Halerians. It would be beyond impossible. Maybe someday I can get a hold of the immigration records and find her. Even then she probably changed her name and left behind everything that I knew about her. Finding her would be years away. Honestly, by the time I found her, she might be dead anyways." Natalie stared off into the distance at nothing in particular.

Darren nodded, taking a moment to absorb what he had been told. "I guess we're both pretty similar, at least in determination. I won't give up until I've secured a future for my family, and you are determined to protect and save as many people as possible. Our goals are different, but I know that neither of us would quit until they are realized."

"Maybe we're more alike than either of us realize," Natalie responded, smiling. "What a strange thought that would be, seeing as outwardly we're total opposites." The pair laughed and continued talking throughout the evening, discussing their families, their interests, desires, and anything they could think of. By the end of the day, the two had agreed to become flying partners for the remainder of their training. Starting the next day, Darren and Natalie paired up for practice. In the evenings, they continued to talk with one another. Natalie had never been happier.

Then another letter came. It was almost the end of the cycle, and the last of the true training was beginning to wrap up. When Natalie picked up the letter and saw that there was again no return address, she returned immediately to her room and spilt the envelope's contents onto her desk. Again, small individual letters scattered about the wooden desk. This time, however, there were far fewer letters.

With much better efficiency, Natalie began lining up letters to test their original order. After only a few minutes, she had the message.

THEY LIED.

Natalie shook her head. She wanted to yell at the paper letters on her desk. She wanted to demand they tell her who sent them to her. She wanted to force them to explain their real meaning. She knew that such things were never possible.

Do I just wait? She thought. *Wait until whoever is sending me this tells me more or reveals themselves? I wouldn't even know where to begin looking for answers. This could be about anything.*

Placing her notebook flat on her desk, Natalie began the same ritual as before. She dated everything and wrote the message underneath the first one.

Maybe one day whoever this is will actually tell me something, she thought after she had put everything away. *Maybe they can at least point me in a direction.*

CHAPTER 9

The sun was beginning its descent toward the mountains, but it still shone bright over the base, which was busy with dozens of aircraft making their final landings of the day, to be put away until the next morning when they'd again leap to the sky. On the smallest of the many tarmac strips lining the base, the Spectres fell in line one after another, each making a swift and quiet landing before taxiing into their designated hangars. For the recruits flying these planes, it was routine, practiced over many cycles of training. It was the final cycle for the recruits to hone their skills before the final examination and draft.

For Natalie Annikki, her whole day was now a routine, and it was beginning to become stale. There was little else to master when it came to flying Spectres, and this began to bore her. Until she reached outer space, where the maneuvers were tighter, quicker, and more complex, she had little to practice.

Natalie landed her craft and was climbing out when she heard a voice behind her. "Looks like you've done your training already," a gruff, male voice said. Natalie climbed off the Spectre's ladder and turned around. She immediately recognized the man as one of the Dolphin instructors present when she had made her decision to fly Spectres. He was older, the hair on his head almost completely silver. His short, thick beard still showed some black in it, but most of it was a silvery gray. He was tall, and Natalie stood with the top of her head just reaching his shoulders.

"Well, sir, to be honest, I believe I've mastered everything for the Spectre," Natalie replied as she adjusted her olive-green flight suit. "Until I get into space, that is."

"Well, after pulling your file and watching you fly for a few days, I agree completely." The man scratched his thick graying beard. He took a step closer before continuing. "You and your classmates are already going to be certified Spectre pilots. All you're doing now is honing your skills and making sure you look pretty when the top squadrons come visit. As long as you pass the final flight test, you're in."

Natalie hadn't thought of this, but now it made sense. After countless combat drills, formation flights, and maneuver exercises, there was nothing left for the instructors to test them on. All that remained was their final demonstration before graduation.

"I should introduce myself." The man cleared his throat before continuing. "Light Commander Aidle Gyr, one of the lead instructors for the Dolphin training program at this base." He spoke with confidence and continued after a pause, letting Natalie think on his position. "You have basically a spare cycle before the final few weeks, when those top squadrons will be scouting out here. This is the proposition I am giving you: You expressed interest in the Dolphin light transport, and you scored at the top of your class during simulation tests. Your file says that you are a very quick learner, so I think you could get a double certification, for both the Spectre and the Dolphin. Of course, as you chose to fly Spectres first, you will not be picked up by a Dolphin squadron. You will be an especially useful resource, however, able to take on that role in a pinch."

Natalie took a moment to think. The Dolphin had been very intriguing to Natalie and flying it in the simulators had only increased that. She felt as though there was much more potential to the craft than what she had ever been told in class. Coupled with the versatility of the craft, its platform covering four separate roles including special forces and high-speed ground attack, Natalie could not deny that she was very interested in flying one for real. Getting out of the stale routine was also a bonus.

"If you say I can get it done in a cycle, so I don't compromise my position with the draft, then I'll take you up on that offer." Natalie smiled, outstretching her right hand to make the deal with the instructor.

Gyr nodded and smiled, shaking her hand. "You need your sim certification for the Dolphin first. Get that done, and then we can start the actual training." With that, he stepped back from Natalie, turned, and departed the hangar, going back toward the area of the base where the Dolphins trained.

It took only a few days for Natalie to qualify for real Dolphin flying. Having flown the Dolphin in the simulator cycles before and a few times during her spare time since, it still felt familiar to her. It took her almost no time to get into rhythm with the ship. With her certification in hand, she went to see Light Commander

Gyr to get training underway. Immediately after showing him her certification, he led Natalie to the section of the base Natalie had not been before. It was not the Dolphin training yard, which was in full use by the Dolphin class, yet it had its own set of hangars and a small runway, which was about the same length as that of the Spectre's training yard.

"You may not be aware," Gyr said as they walked through the area. "But this base was originally constructed to test new Dolphin variants, as well as updates to existing models. It is occasionally still used for that purpose, but much of that role has moved to another base on the planet, one dedicated entirely to that role. As such, this area is not considered nearly as important as say, your Spectre training yard, and therefore doesn't warrant the high-class hangars and prep decks you have. But you can see that the Dolphin requires about the same operating space as the Spectre. As I'm sure you've guessed, that's because the plane uses its vectoring thrust system to aid it in acceleration and deceleration, therefore reducing the needed runway length."

Natalie looked around the space once more. It was distant from the rest of the base, farther into the trees than any of the other areas. The entire space was surrounded by green grass, and trees lined the area not far away. From here, the base was oddly quiet. The great Phantoms taking off could hardly be heard, and the grumbling of the Spectres could not be heard at all. The area seemed so peaceful, almost disconnected. The only link to the main base was the narrow road, which Natalie and her instructor had taken to arrive.

Soon, the pair had arrived at the two main hangars of this "mini-air base," and it was here that Natalie saw four Dolphins sitting together in a tight semi-circle. Each one seemed slightly different from the next. The first had the same appearance as the Dolphin the entire class of recruits had been shown early on in their training. The rest appeared to be variations on the standard Dolphin. The Dolphin was long, over five meters longer than the Spectre and was at least twice its width in fuselage. Both shared characteristically broad, sweeping wings, although the Dolphin's were proportionally larger. The Dolphin had one central, tall vertical stabilizer against the Spectre's two, and it had standard horizontal stabilizers rather than the Spectre's six angled stabilizers swept similarly to the main wing. The four vector thrust pods were easily visible on the Dolphin split evenly on both sides, with two just behind the cockpit and two just under the twin-engine's exhaust ahead of the rear ramp.

"Before you start flying, I'm going to give you a crash course through the four variants of the Dolphin." Light Commander Gyr turned to face Natalie. He scratched his graying beard, pausing in thought before he began. "So, you've spent a fair bit of time being told about the ins and outs of the base model, the Dolphin Light Transport. This is the one that you will spend most of your time flying if you stay in a Spectre squadron. Flying from ship to port or planetside, you and your squadronmates will fly one of these. You already know what it does, excelling at bringing and extracting small groups of soldiers from hot zones very quickly. I'm sure you've already gathered from your sim time that it has exceptionally high maneuverability despite its weight and size. You won't be able to take on Shrikes directly, but you can make it tough for them, and hopefully someone in a Spectre will come save your ass. So, let's skip over the base model and into the other three you see here. We'll start with this big girl."

Gyr stepped toward the next model of the Dolphin, resting his hand on its nose. This one appeared to be heavily armed, as it had many pylons along its broad wings, and gun ports that appeared to be remarkably similar to that of the Spectre's.

"This here is the Thunder Dolphin," Gyr said, running his hand from the nose of the craft along the left side of the cockpit. "This is the most devastating ground attack plane in the galaxy. Six fifty cals, four twenty mill cannons, and an impressive payload capacity for high explosive rockets and anti-tank missiles. The fuselage here," his hand ran along the main fuselage, "this is, to be blunt, a bomb. Every ounce of fuel, and the entirety of your cannon and MG rounds are stored in the fuselage. This whole section is armored though, and unless a Shrike has a direct line on you, most likely his MGs will bounce off. And small arms stand no chance. However, you're heavy and barely fast enough to match the Dolphin LT. So don't expect as good of maneuverability, but you'll still have plenty for attack runs at low altitude."

Gyr stepped away from the Thunder Dolphin, turning toward the next Dolphin in the semi-circle. This one was all black, with no visible weapons. As Natalie inspected it closer, it appeared that the thrust pods were slimmer and shaped in a very sleek manner.

"This black beauty is the Dolphin-SF, or Special Forces." Gyr walked the length of it as Natalie watched. "It has no external armament, as it is built entirely for stealth purposes. It carries specially modified engines, which emit a very low heat signature but are also higher power than the base Dolphin. What this makes is a very fast, and very hard to detect transport. It operates solely at night, flying operatives in and getting them out before the enemy knows what's up. It is made as light as possible but coated in a special material that makes it harder to detect. It is a fragile but fast and stealthy craft."

The final Dolphin was gray, and had no windows save for the glass canopy of the cockpit. It appeared totally sealed, its small, unmanned turret protruding from the forward section of the fuselage.

"This is the Dolphin M," Gyr said, and Natalie noticed his voice changed slightly, as if he were speaking to an old friend. "The *M* in this case is for marine. The Dolphin M is the only craft used for boarding operations in space. These craft carry the marines that go inside enemy vessels and attempt to capture them, or, in the case of their use in the Omasye Security Council, eliminating terrorists or pirates that have taken over civilian vessels. She's like the Dolphin LT, but she's got extra armor to go into the toughest spots in the fight." He stopped, staring at the cockpit of the craft.

"You flew a Dolphin M before becoming an instructor?" Natalie guessed.

"That's right." His eyes were filled with the memories of the past, his voice carrying the sound of the nostalgia of flying. "I flew for the OSC on active duty for many years, including in the war against the Insubel Dominion, over twenty years ago. When the Dominionists took the challenge to us, I volunteered to transfer to the 5th Mobile, the frontline fleet for the war. One of these old girls got me through some tough missions over the course of that year," Gyr continued, resting a hand on the nose of the ship. "In and out of enemy cruisers, carriers, and once even a heavy battleship; I would never fly anything other than one of these."

The connection between a pilot and their craft, Natalie thought. *Will I have that same connection in twenty years?*

***

The next day, Natalie Annikki began flying the Dolphin for real. Light Commander Gyr took her to the base model Dolphin she had seen yesterday, in the same secluded section of the base. Natalie climbed inside the left side of the cockpit, a tight, two-seat cabin at the front of the craft. Gyr climbed in on the other side.

"Alright, you've flown the Spectre, so I shouldn't have to worry about your basic flying practice," the instructor said as Natalie went through the startup procedure. "Just take a bit of time to get used to the feel of a heavier craft, and then do what you do. I'll pipe up if something is wrong."

Natalie flipped the switch for the starter, and the ship's twin engines rumbled to life. A smile broke across Natalie's face as she basked in the sound of the powerful engines. She moved her left hand to the throttle, flipped a small switch underneath that read "VTOL," and began slowly moving the throttle forward. Outside the craft, the four exhaust ports on the fuselage of the craft rotated ninety degrees until they stood vertical, pushing the Dolphin into the air. Natalie held the stick stable, and the craft hovered a few meters above the ground. It felt almost surreal to her, to have such a large, heavy craft balanced in the air so perfectly. Of course, she had done it in the simulator plenty of times, but the real thing felt incredible.

She clicked the switch from VTOL, and at the same time she pushed the throttle forward. The Dolphin swiftly accelerated forward, and Natalie pulled back on the stick to make it climb skyward. She flew about the area around the base, the feeling of the Dolphin coming naturally to her hands. About an hour into her flight, the instructor asked her to make a touch and go at the short strip where they had taken off. Her first time, she went slowly and gently, as though she were returning to the base in clear skies. The second time he asked her to perform the same maneuver, Natalie decided to do a combat landing. Coming over the strip at high speed, Natalie used the thrust vectoring control to rotate the exhaust ports 180 degrees, opposite of her direction of travel. Then she pushed the thrust to maximum, bringing the craft to a very swift halt. As it began to fall from the sky, she once again switched it into VTOL mode, using the thrust of the exhaust to slow the Dolphin to a hover near the ground. She then slowly let off the throttle, letting it drop onto the dirt. She waited three seconds and then pushed the throttle to maximum. In one swift motion, the Dolphin lifted off the ground just as Natalie returned the exhaust to its normal flight mode, launching the Dolphin into the sky.

Natalie performed these touch and goes a handful of times over the next three hours of flying. By the end of the day, she felt great confidence in her abilities with the Dolphin.

The older instructor seemed to agree, smiling at her when they had climbed out of the cockpit. "That's quite some skill you've got there," he said as he shook her hand. "Not sure I've ever seen anyone who could pick up a new ship quite so fast. You'll definitely get this done before the cycle is up."

"Getting some side lessons in?" A female voice came from the hangar behind the pair and the Dolphin.

Natalie turned to see a Dolphin instructor, the one she remembered from the post office, and more importantly, the one that had spoken up in support of her choosing the Spectre all those cycles ago. As she approached, Natalie couldn't stop herself from tracing all her facial features with her eyes.

What is it about her? she wondered. *Why does she seem so familiar? It must have been a coincidence. Now the feeling is just because I've seen her here before.*

"Sir, are you still trying to change this young pilot's mind?" the woman asked. This time, Natalie could read the nametag on the woman's flight suit: Damos.

"Not at all, Captain," Gyr scoffed. "I got approval to fast track her capabilities, since she is clearly so talented. I'll have her certified on the Dolphin just in time for her final exam on the Spectre."

Captain Damos smiled. "That's incredible! I can't remember the last time any recruit showed this much ability. And to think that there were some who thought that we were debating over an unknown quantity back then..." For a moment, she looked to the sky, as if lost in thought, then suddenly back down at Natalie. "You must be excited too, getting both the Spectre and Dolphin."

"Yes, ma'am," Natalie said somewhat sheepishly. "I never expected it, at least not while I was still training. It's almost a dream come true."

"It's a dream for the OSC as well, having someone as talented as you." Damos leaned forward to bring her eyes level with Natalie's. "Pilots like you are virtually non-existent, you know. Tell me, where are you from?"

"Uh, you probably won't know it," Natalie said, injecting a slight laugh into her words. "It's a tiny town called Rikata." When Damos stared dumbly at her, she continued. "It's, uh, way up north. In Accullad, in the mountains on the northern part of the continent. Nobody knows where it is unless they've been there."

Damos stood straight and placed her hands on her hips. "Well clearly we should be recruiting from there more often!" She smiled. "Why'd you join? Were your parents OSC?"

Natalie shook her head. Her training told her to maintain eye contact with her superior officer, but the subject forced her to look away multiple times. "No. My mother left when I was little, and my father was a colonial engineer. He died just before I got accepted into the OSC."

Light Commander Gyr looked down at the runway pavement and scratched the back of his head. Damos frowned. "I'm sorry, that's really unfortunate," she said. "I'm sure they're proud to see you becoming such a promising young pilot."

"Thanks, ma'am." Natalie too looked at the ground.

"Well, I should be going now," she said. "It is getting late, and dinner is waiting at home. Good luck with your flight exams!" She waved back at Natalie as she walked back toward the hangar.

"I keep running into her," Natalie thought out loud, watching Damos turn the corner of the hangar. "But she seems like a kind instructor."

Only when she was long out of sight did Gyr speak, letting out a long sigh as he led into what he had to say. "I shouldn't say anything, but you aren't part of the Dolphin class anyway." He spoke with a sudden quietness that put Natalie on alert, though, his rough gravelly voice still came through. "There's something off about her. She only showed up at the base about a cycle after all you recruits got here, after we already had all the Dolphin instructors we needed. She's always just "around," but never actually doing any teaching, and that just rubs me the wrong way." He turned away from the hangar and looked beyond the runway, out toward the distant snow-capped mountains. "It just doesn't feel right, her being here."

There was a long silence between them. Gyr continued to stare at the mountains, and Natalie's vision shifted between him and the direction Damos had gone. *A supervisor? Watching the course to evaluate its effectiveness?* Natalie tried to process different scenarios. *All the Spectre instructors teach and fly and always interact. Maybe the Dolphin program has had some problems lately…* It was the only conclusion that made sense. An officer placed among the instructors to secretly evaluate the standards of the course. That's why she would be so hands off, just observing, not interfering…

"Try to pretend I didn't say anything," Gyr suddenly said, snapping Natalie's attention away from the captain. "If there's a problem, it's us instructors who have to face it, not you. Especially when you aren't even in the Dolphin program." He gave a gentle smile, and Natalie nodded.

"Thank you for the lesson today, sir," Natalie said, coming to attention and saluting.

Gyr returned the salute. "Same time tomorrow, we'll get on with the next phase."

***

Natalie carried her tray across the mess hall, filled with her dinnertime meal. She walked toward her usual table but had to walk past the main group of Spectre pilots on the way. Many glanced in her direction, distrust and enmity in their eyes. As the distance grew between her and the group, she heard some of them whispering.

"Have you noticed she doesn't even show up to fly anymore?" one asked in a low but rushed tone.

Another snorted in disgust. "She probably thinks she's so good she doesn't need to fly anymore. Look at her, walking around like she owns the damn place. I bet she thinks she's going to be a White Tail."

Another man laughed at that remark. "With her attitude? No way, not a stuck-up pilot like her."

Natalie soon moved out of earshot, sitting down at her table in silence. *Same things as before,* Natalie thought as she began eating. *Whatever, I don't need to worry about what they think.* She remained in thought for a little while. Suddenly, the metallic sound of a tray hitting the table brought her back to reality. She looked up from her food, catching Darren Verra's eye. He smiled warmly as he sat down across from her.

"Lot of talk about you nowadays," Darren began as he started eating. "I mean, there was a lot of talk about you before, but now that you've stopped flying Spectres? Oh boy, I swear all I hear is them talking about you. Not too kindly either. Imagine if they knew what you were really up to!"

"Well, they'll have to get over it," she replied. "I'm not going to give up a double cert for their sake."

Darren paused, his spoonful of food hovering just before his mouth. "If you did, you know, it might help make you seem more human and less… advanced AI," he said.

Natalie couldn't help but laugh with Darren. "You've figured me out!" she exclaimed, playing into it. "I'm an advanced AI, developed in secret against the Oranis Convention. Please keep my identity a secret, or they'll melt me down and turn me into a fridge." She placed a finger over her mouth and laughed. "I'm only getting to do it 'cause one of the older Dolphin instructors was kind enough to give me the training."

As their laughter dwindled, Darren kept speaking. "Well, I guess you will be getting everything you wanted," he teased Natalie, twirling his fork in front of her. "You get your pretty fighter, and your, ah, flying boat." He laughed again.

"It's a lot more maneuverable than you think," Natalie retorted, still smiling. "One of these days I'll get you in one with me, and I'll show you just how maneuverable it is."

"Well try to leave it until after the graduation," Darren responded, his smile slowly fading. "You don't want to show off your Dolphin flying skills to the White Tails. Keep sharp with the Spectre, yeah?"

Natalie paused, glanced up at the ceiling in momentary thought, and then nodded. "You're right. But I'll be done with the Dolphin soon enough, and I'm sure I'll put on a good show for the White Tails when they get here."

In the silence that followed, Natalie slowly ate away at her food. *A White Tail, the best of the best,* she thought. *Of course that's what I want. My goal, my dream. What better way to protect people than by being with the very best? And if Darren is there too… I hope he is. I have to be a White Tail if he is too.*

***

Natalie signed her name at the bottom of the certification on Light Commander Gyr's desk.

"Congratulations, Annikki," he said. "You are the fastest trained Dolphin pilot I've ever seen. Even in wartime it takes longer than two weeks of real flying."

"Thank you, sir," Natalie said proudly.

"Of course, you did cut out the tests on stealth flying, boarding parties, and ground attack, so you'll only be qualified to fly the base model until you do those courses." Gyr rested against the edge of his wooden office desk. "But as a Spectre pilot, you won't need any of that."

"Maybe one day I'll learn them anyway. They could come in handy down the road."

Gyr smiled. "You never know where the Omasye will need your skills. And with your talent, I'm sure that learning the other variants will be a simple task. I still can't believe that someone can learn maneuvers that quickly. It's uncanny. Two attempts, and then you're doing it almost as well as I am."

"It's just so comfortable for me," Natalie said, crossing her arms over her flight suit. "Way more comfortable than the Spectre. Everything I do in the Dolphin just feels so natural."

"And yet you chose to fly the Spectre." Gyr laughed.

"The Spectre takes me to where I can make the biggest difference. That's where I want to be."

Gyr looked down at the floor for a moment but didn't say anything. Then he cocked his head up, looked at Natalie, and smiled. "If you're half as good with the Spectre as you are the Dolphin, you'll do great things."

"Thank you, sir." Natalie could hardly contain her happiness and pride. She felt like she had grown two inches taller just from being in this room.

"Now you'll receive your proper cert, the verified copy of this one here, after your graduation." Gyr stood up and grabbed the paper from the desk. He held it with both hands, studying all its details. "Just come to where the Dolphin graduation is, and I'll be there to give it to you."

Natalie nodded her understanding and was then dismissed. Even an hour after being dismissed, as she sat on her usual hilltop, her excitement continued to course through her.

One down, she thought, looking out at the base. *One more to go. Then I'm a true pilot in the OSC. I'll be off Jontunia, flying to defend all Altherians. I'll fly to defend Rikata and to make my father proud.*

CHAPTER 10

Natalie Annikki pulled on her olive drab, one-piece flight suit before repositioning her dark green ponytail to sit on her left shoulder. Zipping up the flight suit, Natalie turned to look at herself in the mirror and took a deep breath.

Today was finally it. After so many cycles of training, the day for the final examination had come. Tomorrow, Natalie knew that she would be a pilot in the OSC. The only thing that was left to be determined was whether she and Darren Verra would make the White Tails. Natalie took another deep breath. It was time for the recruits to assemble outside, and she could already hear the bustle of the other recruits leaving their dorms and heading downstairs. Natalie turned away from the mirror, stepped out of her dorm, and joined the rest of her class on their way outside.

Darren had never been the nervous type, but today he was battling with himself. This was the opportunity he had been waiting for, the opportunity to prove that he was one of the best. He couldn't screw this up, not after all the doubt and anger from his family. Darren was one of the first people outside, even after meticulously dressing and grooming himself to look presentable. Now he stood alone in his thoughts for what seemed like an eternity, until he caught the familiar figure of Natalie stop next to him.

"Are you ready for this?" Natalie asked.

"I think so," Darren started, still staring forward. He knew his voice gave away just how nervous he was. "Just a lot of pressure, having to prove myself right here and now."

Natalie laughed but looked serious. "Weren't you so sure of yourself when we first started?" She reached up, patting him on the back. "You're going to do fine. Just do your best, and I'm sure you'll come away with everything you wanted."

Darren turned his head to look at his friend. Her hazel eyes sparkled in the morning sunlight, and the slight smile on her face told him that she believed every word she said. "You're right," he told her. "The two of us are going to be White Tails at the end of the day."

Shortly after all the soon-to-be graduates had assembled themselves outside their building, the instructors walked them to the Spectre hangars. Natalie could see a nearby group of men and women in uniform watching the young pilots. Natalie had never seen them before and assumed them to be the squadrons of the 3rd Mobile. Natalie knew that one of them was from the White Tails and would decide her and Darren's fates. She forced herself to refocus on the test they were about to undergo.

The recruits were quickly briefed on the first stage of the exam. They would begin with a combat scramble-style takeoff, with all the recruits quickly boarding their craft and taking to the skies, cleanly and without delay. Once all the recruits were flying, they would assemble into a full squadron formation, doing two passes over the base. As the instructors finished the briefing, one stepped forward and shouted to the assembled recruits, "Scramble, scramble, scramble!"

All at once, the recruits were running to their own planes. Natalie's plane was stored three hangars down the line, but she arrived at it quickly, nonetheless. She immediately grabbed and twisted the handle, which dropped the small cockpit ladder and opened the cockpit, sliding the canopy along the height of the fuselage. As Natalie climbed up the ladder, she heard other Spectres starting up.

The first Spectres in line. Natalie dropped into the cockpit, hitting a switch inside. As the canopy closed and the ladder retracted, Natalie strapped on the five-point harness and ran through the startup switches. Her plane grumbled to life before settling in a low idle. Looking forward, Natalie spotted the first of the Spectres take off. She was not worried for time, knowing that the Spectres in the hangar before hers hadn't taken off yet.

Once the engine of her plane warmed up to operating temperature, Natalie released the brakes, allowing the plane to begin slowly rolling out of the hangar. She went through her control checklist, watching behind her to check her ailerons and rudders while wiggling the flight stick. With everything in order, she began to raise the throttle, coming out of the hangar a little quicker now. If the hangar prior to hers was on time, they would be turning onto the runway and pushing to full throttle just as she came out of her hangar. Natalie breathed in deeply and out through her mouth, preparing herself for flight.

As Natalie's plane cleared the entrance of her hangar, she looked to her left for the other Spectres that should have been ahead of her. However, she saw only one, just turning onto the runway. It was on time, but the other one was missing. Just as the first came flush with the runway and began accelerating, Natalie spotted the second coming out of the hangar late and in a hurry to make up time. Natalie saw that it was coming out too quickly, on a collision course with the Spectre already on the runway. The pilot of the second Spectre must have realized this too; the plane jerked away from the runway, but into her path.

Her breath caught as she made sense of the situation. She couldn't accelerate forward to avoid him, as she would collide with the first Spectre, but if she remained how she was now, she would be run into. Making a snap decision, Natalie engaged the Spectre's rerouting system. Small thrust vents opened along the rounded bottom of the fuselage of Natalie's Spectre, diverting most of the engine power from the rear exhaust to the bottom of the plane. Only a second after engaging this mode, Natalie pushed the throttle to maximum. The light Spectre quickly leapt into the air, barely clearing the incoming plane. Already airborne, Natalie switched off the system, allowing her Spectre to quickly accelerate forward and away from the base. Natalie breathed another sigh of relief before banking her Spectre toward the area where the class would form up.

The last of the recruits caught up to those already airborne and assumed their position within the formation. At the beginning of the training, the positions had been randomly assigned, and the recruits had learned to memorize the formation. This was the easiest part for Natalie. All she had to do was keep her position, watch the spacing, and follow the next plane in the formation. They flew at a slow cruising speed, both to allow the others to catch up and to allow the evaluators below to study them closely.

Even as the formation turned back toward the base, not one of the Spectres fell out of line. The first pass over the base was from the south. As the class reached the north marker, they turned in formation and came back across the base. This time, however, as they came across, the formation split into three parts. One carried on southward, one turned east, and the other went west. Natalie was part of the group turning west, which at a farther marker turned back east at the lowest altitude of the three groups. On the final pass, Natalie's group flew under the other two, with all three intersecting over the base at the same time. It was like how Natalie imagined air shows in the southern cities must be like, but much slower.

Her formation, now heading north, was in the middle, and the group now heading west was at the highest altitude. As the three groups flew past, they concluded the formation flying part of the exam. *Looks like it went well,* Natalie thought. *It is the easiest part, but if anyone screwed up, the ones on the ground would have seen it.*

The second phase of the exam was solo flight procedure, particularly with landings. The pilots were instructed to fly in one after another at a predetermined spacing and make a series of touch-and-goes on the runway. With each pass, they were given different objectives: The first pass was a normal approach; the second was a combat landing, meaning harder, faster, and shorter. The final was an emergency landing, with no engines. Natalie was almost bored throughout this, having to wait for her turn each time. It was almost easier than formation flying, as the procedure for landing in different conditions had been drilled into the young pilots from day one. As the touch-and-go testing ended, every pilot landed and taxied back to their hangar for the next test.

The final portion of the examination was much more exciting for Natalie. The recruits were to engage in a round-robin style tournament. The order of the tournament was made by the instructors prior to today, allowing each pilot the same amount of rest between each sortie. Natalie found that she was rather entertained watching her classmates duel each other, analyzing each of their patterns and flying habits. She also found it interesting to see the difference in skill level between the classmates. It was clear when one was superior to the other, often ending the duel in under three minutes. Sometimes, however, two closely matched pilots faced each other, and these were the most intriguing duels. Natalie would watch intently, trying to predict the outcome as best she could.

Natalie's own duels went much quicker than most. There were only a handful of pilots that could challenge her for longer than a handful of minutes. Most made predictable moves or committed some sort of error in judgement that allowed Natalie to get an easy line on them. Many of them were still competent pilots, Natalie observed, and those that were of an average skill looked to be decent enough to hold their own in combat. Natalie could only hope that they never faced any highly skilled enemy, at least not alone.

Over the course of the combat portion of the exam, Natalie faced only two real challenges during the duels. The first employed trickery, often faking a maneuver before snapping into a completely different one. As with any other opponent, Natalie hadn't found a problem getting behind them, but no matter how hard she tried, she couldn't get a solid bead on them. High above the base, her opponent had free reign to do any maneuver no matter the cost of altitude, and without fear of landmass or structures blocking them.

Natalie arched her Spectre to come level once again over the base. It had been nearly ten minutes. Ahead of her, her opponent banked left and turned to remain just beyond Natalie's gun sights. The missile seeking indicator beeped twice before going silent as the leading Spectre left the view of the chasing's missile.

As the lead plane began to level out, Natalie watched for the slightest twitch. Her missile tone began to beep again, but she knew that her opponent would break off before the lock was established. Time seemed to slow in that instant as Natalie waited for her opponent, her enemy in this moment, to make a move. As the lead Spectre began to twitch right, its rudder slowly shifting to increase the yaw, Natalie ignored it, believing it to be another feint. She instead focused on what she believed the real maneuver would be: a hard diving left. She began to twitch her plane to the left pre-emptively, expecting her opponent to turn.

The moment that Natalie committed to her turn, the fake maneuver became real, and suddenly the lead Spectre rolled hard right, turning opposite to Natalie. She was caught off guard and quickly had to turn back to the right, rather than a left as she had anticipated. This cost her a lot of ground, and as they completed the maneuver, Natalie found that she was well on the back foot with her opponent coming around above her and slowing to get behind.

With no other option apparent, Natalie slammed her stick forward, sending her Spectre into a steep dive. Her opponent followed, and the two Spectres began to level out low over the base. Reacting only on instinct, Natalie realized that she now had her opponent where she wanted them, in a low altitude environment where they couldn't fake maneuvers. All she had to do now was get behind them.

Natalie pushed her Spectre to full throttle and began weaving through the hills outside the base, then into the base and around the taller buildings.

After only a few turns, the chasing Spectre fell away. When Natalie came around one of the massive Phantom hangars, she saw the other Spectre flying slowly, still at low altitude. She closed the gap in an instant. Noticing Natalie coming, they tried one final feint. They began to turn left, but Natalie simply smirked inside her helmet and guided her plane to the right. Seeing Natalie turn opposite to them, they again tried to turn the fake into a real maneuver, but upon turning left found the high hangars of the Phantoms in their path. They jerked out of the maneuver, straight into the Natalie's clutches, who made her final pass.

Natalie was the first back to the hangars, parking and shutting down her plane. The other landed a few moments later. Natalie quickly dismounted and jogged to their hangar, curious about her opponent's identity. As she rounded the corner of the hangar, she saw the pilot take off their helmet, allowing their golden blonde hair to tumble out. Fritallia promptly cast her helmet into the cockpit in frustration and then climbed out of her Spectre.

For an instant, Natalie's stomach turned, and she frowned. *Of everyone, why her?* Then her thoughts turned, and she looked up from the concrete floor. *No. It doesn't matter what happened before, I have to do this.* Natalie walked toward Fritallia, and as she neared, Fritallia looked at her, making eye contact. A scowl came to her face, growing as Natalie got close enough to shake her hand.

"You almost had me there. That was a good fight," Natalie said, stretching out her right hand. "You've been the toughest today by far. I think that's something to be proud of."

Fritallia glanced at Natalie's outstretched arm but did not shake her hand. She instead looked back up at Natalie, her scowl still present. She scoffed before sidestepping around Natalie and walking out of the hangar. Natalie watched her leave in silence before walking out on her own to rejoin her class.

***

Natalie flew around the outskirts of the base, waiting for the radio call telling her to begin the duel. It was the final duel of the exam, and Natalie knew exactly who she would be flying against. The instructors had saved the most anticipated duel for last, the duel between the two best pilots in the class: Natalie Annikki and Darren Verra.

The radio crackled to life, and Natalie heard the voice of one of her instructors. "Best of luck to you both; you are clear to start the duel." The radio then clicked off, and Natalie pushed her throttle to full, turning toward the base.

This is it, Natalie thought. *I can't leave any doubt behind from this fight.*

The duel was by far the most physically demanding fight Natalie had gone through. Shortly after the two made contact, they began to push each other to the limit. Each attempted to get the better of the other, but each time the other had the perfect counter-maneuver. Neither had been able to get behind the other for longer than a second as the two spiraled, rolled, and flipped through the skies above the base. For those watching on the ground, it was like watching two dancers, perfectly in step with one another across the blue sky. Ten minutes passed, with neither gaining any sort of advantage. Natalie managed to bring the fight to ground level, but unlike her duel with Fritallia, Darren could match her in this tricky environment. And so, the duel continued, the pair going from tree-top to high in the sky, and back down again. Throughout the duel, the pair tried to find a maneuver to get the better of the other, and the role of hunter and hunted changed frequently.

Almost twenty minutes into the duel, Natalie had brought the fight back to low level. The two planes weaved across the wilderness outside the base, hugging the hills, diving down in and out of the nearby rivers, racing across the trees back to the base, all while turning and weaving to counter the other's attempts to get behind them.

Once they got back into the base, however, Natalie hatched a plan. She allowed Darren to fall in behind her whilst using the buildings to stop him from getting a missile lock. She led him around and between the hangars as well as the tall barracks and administration buildings. Carefully, but at high speed, Natalie led Darren to exactly where she wanted. The pair rounded one of the buildings, coming face to face with the main control tower, the tallest building on the base. Seeing the tower, Darren quickly broke off, pulling up and to the right, coming over the lower hangar near the tower.

Natalie, however, at the same time, carried on forward. At the last opportunity, she rolled the plane over to the right and used the full power of the rerouting system. Thrust was diverted from the rear of her plane to its belly, which was now facing left. Natalie's Spectre launched to the right, and Natalie switched off the rerouting system, completing a roll and passing safely by the tower. In under a second, Natalie had seemingly jumped around the tower and had cut just enough speed to fall behind Darren, who was now above the buildings, in the open. Clearly unsure of where Natalie had come out, he was an easy kill. As Natalie flew away, slowing her plane down, she breathed a sigh of relief. Sweat was slipping from her forehead and down the sides of her face. She could feel the dampness inside her gloves, and her breathing was sharp. Her heart rate would not even think to slow down until she landed.

Natalie landed her Spectre just behind Darren. As she took off her flight helmet, she heard a familiar voice coming closer.

"You're absolutely insane, you know?" As expected, it was Darren, calling to her from halfway across the hangar. He was walking toward her with a brisk pace but smiling. Natalie placed her helmet in her seat and adjusted her ponytail to rest on her left shoulder. She then descended the ladder to meet Darren, who had arrived at its base. "How do you even get that kind of thought in your head?" Darren asked, laughing and poking her arm. "I'm pretty sure you've left the instructors speechless with that one, not to mention the scouts from the other squadrons. You're bloody crazy."

Natalie smiled, swatting away his poking finger. "Sometimes you have to be a little crazy to win. We are too evenly matched for either of us to win conventionally."

"I guess that's why you're the better pilot then," Darren started, his tone shifting to a more serious one. "You don't have doubt or fear and focus on what you need to do to win. I saw that tower, and my mind froze up. The only thing I could do was find an escape route, no matter the cost."

"I'm not sure if that really makes her all that much better," an approaching instructor said firmly. Natalie shifted in her boots at the man's intimidating tone. Instinctively, her vision fell to the floor. "While it was a good move and won the fight, it was reckless, a move that put your own life needlessly in harm's way. There are other ways to best your opponent than games of chicken. And if this is how you fly in a mock duel, how reckless would you be in a real battle?"

"I flew exactly as I would in a real fight, sir," Natalie responded, looking the instructor in the eye and trying to shake off the impact of the scolding. "If I am confident in my abilities, there is no reason, at least in my mind, that I shouldn't go the limit of my own ability. If that means I perform a maneuver that is too risky for some to follow through with, doesn't that give me the advantage?"

The instructor sighed. "I said before that it was a good move, a damn good one, beyond even my comfort level," he conceded. Natalie breathed a sigh of relief, believing he was finished. "But." Her ease vanished. "A reckless move like that can have implications beyond what you may be aware of. What if another plane that you didn't see flew by while you did something like that? If both of you are unsighted to each other, then it is a recipe for disaster. Further, what about your wingman? If you do something crazy around a large ship, you could find yourself far from your team, and a lone pilot is an easy kill in the real world. Out there?" The instructor pointed skyward. "There are no clean duels. There are only melees, where you live and die by the one watching your back."

Natalie was without an answer. In her mind, she had done nothing wrong. But this instructor was delivering a lesson with such seriousness that she couldn't dismiss it. There had to be some truth in it, she knew. *But if I fly like this, I can shake anyone on my back,* Natalie thought. *Then my wingman doesn't need to protect me.* Her thoughts, as well as the instructor's lesson, were interrupted by the rest of the recruits and training staff, even the scouts joining the trio in the hangar. Many of them were applauding, some of the instructors saying that it was the best duel they'd ever seen. Darren and Natalie stopped in front of the crowd, taking in the moment. They glanced at each other and smiled before offering their thanks to everyone present. The first instructor shook his head, knowing that at that moment he was alone in his distaste for Natalie's reckless flying.

CHAPTER 11

Natalie and Darren walked through the mess hall, which was nearly empty, rather than the usual bustle of hungry recruits. As they approached the counter, one of the cooks handed them a bottle of champagne and a pair of glasses. The pair thanked him and then set off to Natalie's room. It was the day after the final examination, and in a few hours, all the recruits would be graduating and receiving their postings. Since the duel yesterday, the class was buzzing with rumors that Natalie and Darren were certain to be picked up by the White Tails. Whether they both ended up in the same squadron or not, they wanted to celebrate together.

Natalie led the way into her room, shutting the door behind Darren. "You can just sit on the bed," Natalie said, gesturing toward the neatly made bed. However, as she approached her desk to grab the chair, she suddenly froze. In the center of the desk was her notebook, and next to it were the envelopes containing the cryptic messages she had received. Almost leaping across the room, she began checking the notebook and envelopes for any tampering.

"What's wrong?" Darren asked, watching from the bed.

Natalie didn't turn to face him, her eyes glued to her things, her hands frantically opening envelopes. "It's, uh, it's… What the hell!?"

Darren jumped to his feet. "What is it, Natalie? Is it something I can help with?"

"No, no, it's just…" her voice trailed off. "Someone was in my room. These things weren't out when I left. Someone came looking for this and…" Natalie opened her notebook to the page where she had written the messages. Except that the page was no longer there. She stared at the rough tear-line inside the notebook. She stood there frozen for a few more moments until Darren spoke again.

"If someone's been in your room, we should get the instructors," he said, already moving toward the door. "They'll call the military police."

"No!" Natalie exclaimed, causing him to stop. "Don't. We don't know who might be involved in this."

"What are you talking about?" Darren asked. "Natalie, what's going on?"

Natalie sighed then stepped back and seemingly fell onto the side of the bed. Darren came and sat down next to her. "Something really weird has been going on, but I don't know what it's about," Natalie said quietly, staring down at her hands in her lap. "A while ago I received the first of two letters. No return address, and inside the envelope was just a bunch of cut-out letters. Both of them were like that. When I deciphered what they said, the messages were: "You are being deceived," and "they lied." I wrote both messages in the notebook and hid the envelopes in my desk. But someone found them." She turned to face Darren. "Someone broke into my room to find these messages, and they took the deciphered copies I made. Darren, I think someone is spying on me, but I don't know why. I don't even know what these messages are about."

"Has anything suspicious, other than the letters, been going on that you've noticed?" Darren asked.

Natalie shook her head. "Not that I've seen at least, but who knows. If someone is breaking into my room to get at this stuff, though…"

"But you haven't seen anyone?"

She shook her head again.

Darren smiled. "Well in that case, just keep an eye out and try not to worry too much. And don't tell anyone. You don't need more que—" Suddenly Darren's eyes were looking beyond Natalie, and the words he had tried to stay were stuck within his open mouth. Then, as quietly as he could, he rose from the bed and approached the door. Natalie simply stared on in confusion. She wanted to ask him what he was doing but decided to wait for it to play out.

Darren pressed his ear to the door, then in one swift movement grabbed the door handle and swung it open, himself halfway jumping into the hall. Natalie watched him stand there, his head taking glances up and down the hallway. After a few seconds, he carefully stepped back into the room and shut the door. He then took great care to continue staring at the lower edge of the door as he returned to the edge of the bed.

"What was that about?" Natalie asked.

Darren was still staring at the door. "There was a shadow at the base of the door. When I was talking, it moved." He was practically whispering.

Natalie looked at the bottom of the door. Along the edge, the gap between the door and the floor simply carried a glow to it from the light coming in through the hallway windows. "Are you saying someone was listening?"

Darren nodded. "I'm certain that someone was there, and they went to leave when they had heard enough."

"I'm kind of scared now," Natalie said, looking back to her friend. "If they heard everything…"

"All they've heard is you say that you are more clueless than they are," Darren said, his smile beginning to return. "They can't exactly do anything with you if you don't know anything about the people they are really looking for." He pointed to the envelopes on the desk. "Just be careful. Chances are whoever is trying to rope you into their conspiracy hasn't given up yet. Maybe if they send you something else take it to the MPs. Or leave a message for whoever it is that's watching you. Tell them that you are on their side."

"I just want to know what this is about," Natalie said with a sigh. "It's like I'm in the middle of an elaborate scheme and I've been given the role of the ignorant bait."

"I'm sure you'll know in time." Darren picked up the bottle of champagne from the floor. "Just be safe. For now, though, we have something to celebrate."

At once, Natalie's smile came back. She nodded and leaped up to get the glasses from the desk. Darren opened the bottle, and she held out both glasses for him to fill. After filling them, Darren moved the bottle close to the desk and then took one of the glasses.

"Well, here we are," he said, holding the glass up to Natalie. "In a few hours we'll be graduated, and then we'll be getting ready to leave."

"Hopefully we'll still be together when that happens." Natalie lifted her glass in return. "To our graduation, and to the hopes that we are both White Tails." The two clinked their glasses and took a sip.

Darren placed his glass on the edge of Natalie's dresser and then turned to face her. "I'm really glad we were able to become friends," he started, smiling at her. "To be honest, after the initial scores had been posted and you were placed above me, I had a tough time with it. I don't even know why, even now. I'm sorry that

I stopped talking to you for so long because of that." His smile had faded, and he looked down at his hands.

"When you stopped talking to me, I really couldn't stop thinking about it," Natalie said, her voice becoming quiet. "I didn't have any other friends here, and then when the others started coming after me, I really did feel lost."

"I'm sorry," Darren said before Natalie could continue.

Natalie smiled. "It's okay. When I needed you most, you were there. You pulled me back from becoming totally lost." She placed her hand on his leg. His eyes shifted to her hand, then back to her face. "You don't know how happy I was when you started talking to me again. And now we're going to be White Tails together, and I feel like I'm going there with someone I can really trust."

Her own words made her nervous, and reactively she pulled the end of her ponytail to her lips. It was only a couple of seconds, but it felt to her like hours, reliving every decision she had made up to this point. Darren was simply staring back into her eyes, smiling, but no doubt going through the very same thoughts. Natalie felt her body leaning toward him and let herself relax. She simply let go of her hair, letting it fall from her mouth, and closed her eyes.

Natalie first felt Darren's hands on her waist, followed by his soft lips against her own. The flood of sensation and emotion threatened to overwhelm Natalie, and her eyes began to well up with tears. Her hands seemed to move on their own, climbing up Darren's back to his shoulders. Natalie felt that she could stay in this moment forever, the moment that she knew deep down she wanted since they had become friends during sim testing. The moment she had been longing for after Darren had stopped talking to her, the moment that she had wanted after he came to her rescue and gave her back her father's photograph. This moment, which felt like ages, only lasted a handful of seconds, but Natalie knew she didn't want to let go. As Darren pulled back, his lips releasing hers, her hands moved to the back of his neck and head, her fingers burying themselves in his thick brown hair, and she tried to pull him back to her.

No. The strange sound had slipped from Darren's lips, in a low, soft voice. Natalie opened her eyes to look at him, and his eyes no longer betrayed the same feelings. Now they revealed something she could only describe as fear.

"We can't," he started, his voice hoarse. "Not if we are flying together. We can't be together... like this. Not in the same squadron." He let go of Natalie's waist, and he pulled back completely, forcing Natalie to let go of him. "I'm sorry, I want this as much as you do, but you know that this kind of relationship is impossible, and against military conduct." He shook his head, as if he were trying to convince himself too.

"I… I understand," Natalie said, the words sticking in her mouth. "You're right, as usual." She forced a smile, but the tears forming in her eyes betrayed her feelings. "Who would have guessed you of all people would be teaching me about military conduct?" Her laugh was choked by her emotions, but she saw Darren smile. He reached around her and pulled her toward him, pressing her head against his chest.

"I guess we've both come a long way from when we started training." He laughed, but Natalie could tell he was still hiding his feelings, albeit better than she was. "It's not like we're going to have to be strangers. We'll always be together to have each other's backs, no matter where our job takes us." His left hand was holding her snug against him, and his right had begun stroking her soft green hair. "And if you ever need me, to listen to your struggles or to save you, I'll be there."

Natalie again felt the moment that she never wanted to leave, but she knew she had to, or at least take on a different meaning. "I'd like you to continue being my best friend," she said, feeling safe and secure once more. "And if you ever need me, you know I'll be by your side in a heartbeat."

"I'd like that," was all Darren said, and he held her a little tighter. The pair remained this way for a few minutes, both not wanting to see the end of their truest moment with one another. Eventually, however, they had to separate. The graduation ceremony was soon to be upon them, and it would not wait, not even for the best pilots in the class.

***

The class of graduating Spectre pilots was gathered in one of the hangars. It had been cleared out save for a single Spectre and a podium on a small dais. Their class was not massive, with only two dozen new pilots standing together in their dress uniforms. They all faced the podium, which was lined on either side by instructors and representatives from the recruiting squadrons. A few minutes after the soon-to-be graduates had been assembled, the lead instructor stepped up to the podium. His stiff, booming voice echoed around the hangar, surely allowing even a passerby outside the hangar to clearly hear. He began with the usual pleasantries and congratulatory praise to the recruits, but soon carried into the main body of his speech, his final message to the new pilots.

"To most people, today is just the 10th day of the 14th cycle. The year is winding down, and in a cycle and a half's time we will be getting ready to celebrate the new year. But for all of you here, today is different. Today marks the end of your training to become pilots for the greatest organization anyone could fly for. When you receive your proper uniforms tonight, from those squadrons that have chosen you, know that you are making a commitment to uphold the honor of the OSC." He tapped the badge on the right side of his chest, a bright green, reversed *S* with a white *O* in the upper cavity and a white *C* in the lower, all on a black oval. "This is the symbol of the protectors of the Altherian Empire, the first line of defense against those who wish to do harm to the Omasye's people. By putting on your uniform, you are saying you are willing to do anything the Omasye may ask of you, including die to protect his people. When you put on your flight suit and fly against your enemy, know that you are doing it to protect your family, your hometown, your planet, your leader, and your beliefs." The recruits were captivated by the speech and listened closely to his every word as he continued. "Take all of this to heart and use it to fuel your courage to face your enemy and use it as a reminder that you must win to continue protecting that which you hold dear. I cannot tell you exactly what challenges you will face. The Altherian Empire has enemies across many of its borders, and the vast expanse of the unknown on its opposite borders. Some of you may have successful careers fighting against pirate incursions. Some of you may face our greatest enemy, the New Federation, the greatest threat to our ways. Some of you may even venture into the unknown, for the first time since our ancestors ventured away from the safety of Altheria. I cannot say what fate will befall each of you, as only the Omasye knows the plan of the Altherian Empire." His volume increased as he reached the climax of his speech. "All I can say is that no matter the challenge, no matter the odds, no matter the fight, you must fight to the last breath, together, unified against the enemies of our great Empire. I can only wish that many of you will live to settle down peacefully, safe, knowing that the generation of pilots behind you will continue to defend the unity of the Altherian Empire in your stead, as you are in ours. Remember, only in unity can the light of Altheria continue to shine." With that, the head instructor bowed to the recruits and stepped away from the podium to the growing applause from both the recruits and the other attending personnel.

Another one of the instructors stepped up to the podium to explain the next phase of graduation. "Each of the squadron representatives will step forward and call the recruits chosen to join their ranks," she explained, in a well-practiced set of instructions. "If you are called, come forward and receive your new flight suit and helmet. There will be two for each squadron, and you and your new squadronmate will each choose the callsign for the other on the spot, to carry with them for their entire career."

As soon as she stepped back from the podium, the first squadron began calling out their chosen pilots. It wasn't said, but it was clear to the recruits that the squadrons were moving from the least prestigious squadrons to the elite. Regardless, each recruit seemed overjoyed when being given their personal flight suit and helmet and took pleasure in naming their new squadronmate's callsign.

Natalie watched on with intrigue, nervously waiting for her or Darren's names to be called. As she watched, she took note of where Rygil and his friends ended up. Rygil seemed to have bounced back somewhat from his earlier issues, but still found himself in a lower prestige squadron. His new squadronmate gave him the nickname "Boomerang." Yisha and Sayol made it into the same squadron, a decently respected squadron called the Twilight Talons. Yisha gave Sayol the name "Torchlight," and Sayol gave Yisha "Killswitch" in return. Fritallia ended up in an equal squadron, the Depth Takers, and was given the callsign of "Sunfire" by her new squadronmate.

Finally, after what felt like a year of waiting, the representative for the most prestigious squadron in the 3rd Mobile, the White Tails, stepped forward. There were only two recruits left waiting, and he walked up to the both of them, a flight suit and helmet in each hand. On the breast pocket of each of the flight suits, which was folded so the pocket was visible, was a single white feather. It was the same patch as on the man who gave them their new uniforms.

"Natalie Annikki," he said, holding out the flight suit and helmet with her name on it. "Darren Verra, welcome to the White Tails, both of you. You are some of the best pilots I've ever seen go through this program. Congratulations." Natalie took the flight suit and helmet and turned to face her best friend. Both were smiling as Darren received his flight suit. "So, what are you going to give her as a callsign?" the White Tail asked Darren, nudging his arm with his elbow.

"Wildcat," Darren said without hesitation. "Wildcat because you are the craziest and most lethal pilot I think I'll ever see. Both in our final duel and the day you almost crashed just to beat me." Natalie laughed, blushing somewhat but still smiling. Suddenly she stopped, realizing what he had just admitted.

"Wait, you're saying you were the one back then? You beat me—why didn't you finish the job?"

Darren shrugged. "I don't know. You almost died just to win a training match. I knew that if our roles had been reversed, I would never have even tried that. I don't have the guts to do it. Because of that, it didn't feel right to make the kill official."

There was a lasting silence between them before the White Tail turned toward Natalie and nodded his head. Natalie thought for a second before answering. "Phoenix," she said with certainty. "Phoenixes are reborn, and you were reborn from the arrogant, cocky kid I met you as on day one to my best friend today, and I could never have been happier about it."

Darren blushed slightly this time, laughing. However, he was stopped short by the same female instructor giving them their next order. She explained to the new pilots that they were to pack their belongings tonight, as they would be getting on a Phantom first to an orbital station high above Jontunia. Afterward, they would board a shuttle craft to Jontunia's moon, Tralis, the main staging hub for the 3rd Mobile the next morning. From there, they would travel to the carriers they would call home for most likely the rest of their careers.

With this news, the graduation came to an end, and the fresh pilots returned to their rooms to pack and rest before their long voyage. Before Natalie returned to her room, however, she had to find someone and thank them once more.

Natalie knew that the Dolphin class was having their graduation at the same time, and, more than likely, most of the instructors would still be there to celebrate with the graduates.

When she arrived, she smiled to see the crowd inside the hangar. Almost no one had left yet. From just outside the hangar, she began scanning the moving, chatting, laughing heads for Light Commander Gyr. After a minute or two, she began making her way into the hangar. *Maybe he's just near the back,* she thought.

Natalie passed clusters of people, instructors, and freshly graduated pilots. She scanned the faces of each group but didn't see Gyr anywhere. At last, she reached the back of the hangar, but even in the final group, Gyr was nowhere to be found.

With no other option, Natalie approached one of the instructors. "Excuse me, ma'am?" The woman, a full Commander, turned around. "I'm looking for Light Commander Gyr, do you know where he is?"

The woman scanned Natalie top to bottom. "What's a Spectre pilot doing here?"

Natalie shifted in her boots. "Light Commander Gyr helped me get my certification on the Dolphin before the final exam. He told me to come here to get my official certification."

The woman looked briefly surprised. "Well, first of all, congratulations on a double cert," she said. "However, I'm afraid that Gyr was transferred suddenly to another base. He left late last night."

"Oh," Natalie blurted out. "That's really too bad. I wanted to thank him for everything…" Then Natalie remembered the other reason for coming to the hangar. "What about my certification? It must be here, right?"

The woman glanced around. "I don't believe that it's here, unfortunately. It was probably sent to the mailroom with any other outgoing mail. If you don't pick it up before you leave, it will catch up with you on whatever ship you are stationed on."

"I'll check there right away then," Natalie said, turning to leave. "Thank you, ma'am."

The post office was just a few minutes from closing when Natalie arrived. She asked the clerk at the desk if anything had been dropped off for her and then waited while the clerk went into the backroom.

When they returned, they were carrying one item. It was a large, beige envelope.

"This was dropped off by one of the officers here," the clerk said. "We were gonna hold it to send to you after you shipped out, so good thing you showed up. Anything else that shows up with your name on it will be chasing you to your next posting."

Natalie took the envelope. "Thank you," she said and left.

Natalie returned to her room and opened the envelope. From within, she slid out her certification for the Dolphin, the same paper that she had signed in Gyr's office. Except now it was official, a proper, verified document that proved that she could fly the Dolphin just the same as she could fly the Spectre.

I'm sure that both side by side on my wall will look pretty good. A smile grew across her face before she carefully set the paper down.

Then she began packing what few belongings she had. Most were textbooks, followed by some clothes, and the few personal effects she had, such as the stuffed cat her father had given her. Everything she owned, including her military uniforms, fit in two large bags and a backpack, and Natalie was finished before it had even gotten dark. Looking around the room to make sure she left nothing behind, she decided to go for a walk before the sun set.

Natalie had almost completed a lap of the base when she came up to her hill. As she reached the top, she stopped and looked around the outskirts of the base. The sun was just beginning to dip below the mountains. Rays of light shone over their crests, lighting the treetops near the base. This would be the last time in a long time that she would see the sun set on Jontunia. Tomorrow morning, she would fly away from the only world she knew and enter what was, for her at least, the unknown. She knew that for many years she would see the world from what was essentially a metal box floating through the depths of space. Surely, she would see the surface of other planets, but they would never be her permanent residence. No, that would belong to a room in a ship with a population about half that of her hometown, but with none of the beauty that came from the snow that blanketed the place where she grew up, or the thick forests and clear rivers that surrounded it.

I wonder when I'll ever get to see this again, she thought. Or when I'll get to see home again. Suddenly, Natalie felt very homesick. She wished that before she left, just one more time, she could go home. *I can't. I have to leave.* This may only be the first step, but Natalie knew that it may be the most critical. She couldn't forget why she joined in the first place. *The defense of the innocent against any threat,* she thought. Natalie took one last look at the snow-capped mountains and green forests surrounding the base before leaving her hill for the last time.

Prior to returning to her room, Natalie stopped by the base's general store and picked up some paint and a brush. Returning to her dorm with the items, she placed them on the now clean desk and then retrieved her new flight helmet from the end of her bed. The helmet was black, and in small white letters at the bottom, on either side of the large, clear face shield, was written "Lt. Natalie Annikki." This was her helmet, a helmet that no other pilot had ever worn or would ever wear. Smiling, she set the helmet down on the desk and opened the paints she had bought.

The first was a crimson red. She dipped the brush into it and then carefully pressed the brush against the side of her helmet. She made three stripes on either side, coming from the top of the back, down toward the bottom of the front, stopping just short of her name. After doing this on both sides, Natalie carefully cleaned off the brush and dipped it into the second paint, a frosty white. Carefully, as neatly as she could, she wrote the word "Wildcat" on both sides of the helmet, overlapping the stripes. Satisfied, she cleaned off the brush and set it over the edge of the desk to dry. She closed the paints up and placed them in one of her bags with care. After all, Natalie thought, she may need to re-apply the paint in the future. By now, the sun had set, and Natalie decided to get some rest. She let her helmet sit on the desk to dry and draped her new flight suit on her desk chair—the flight suit of a White Tail. Changing into her olive-green tank top and short black shorts, she climbed into her bed one final time, smiling at her new helmet before shutting her hazel eyes.

CHAPTER 12

The shuttle lifted from its launch pad, located on the outskirts of the city, and soon accelerated to the great speed it needed to break Jontunia's grasp on it. It ascended rapidly toward the clouds above, through them, and into the soft blue sky of the lower atmosphere where the clouds below stretched endlessly in all directions. When the shuttle climbed higher, the sky became a darker blue, then a blue green color as the Salerum Cloud's haze mixed in. By the time the shuttle reached orbit, the haze had fallen to the background, the Cloud visible in the black expanse when focused on.

Natalie sat quietly in her seat, a soft blue chair, identical to those around her currently occupied by the other graduated pilots from her class. The windows of the shuttle had been closed during the ascent, but now that they had reached orbit and the vacuum of space, the long, tall windows of the shuttle peeled back their protective layer and allowed Natalie to see the cosmos for the first time in her life. Distant stars peered through the Cloud and into the bubble Jontunia occupied. The planet's moon, Tralis, was in the distance. Lights from a surface covered in buildings, docks, and shipyards gave the rock a sparkle and shine to it. When the shuttle turned toward the moon, Natalie's view of Tralis was replaced by the Cloud and Jontunia, which now appeared both to her left and below her. She could see the swirling of clouds below her, carried by air currents over the continents, familiar to her but never visited except for two: where she had trained to become a pilot, and where she had grown up. The latter was just visible, high in the north and covered by snow. It had already been nine cycles since she had seen it.

Thoughts of home suddenly brought in other thoughts. Natalie was aboard a small shuttle ship, a rather pleasant-looking rounded commercial liner, just less than twice the size of a Phantom. Natalie supposed that this ship was more than likely similar to the same ones her father would have flown in on his trips, the same as when he died. All at once, the excitement Natalie had originally felt since she had boarded the shuttle disappeared, and only the image of her father remained. Was it right to feel excited about her new career when her father's death had happened not long ago? It had been nine cycles now. Was that long enough?

Was she allowed to move on and focus on the career ahead of her? Was she going to forget about her father? No, she responded to her questions; she would never forget about her father. Did that mean that she couldn't enjoy her career?

Natalie pushed out these depressing thoughts, returning her focus to what was outside. She focused on the dark distance first, the bluish-green haze of the Salerum Cloud. The nebula, which wrapped itself around Jontunia, painted the distant expanse a dreamy color. Natalie thought how once, on Altheria, the first people in space must have thought they were so high. At first, she had felt the same way. Now, however, she saw that up here in the vacuum of space there was no "high." One simply existed in an ocean with no depth, no limit, no direction, and no gravity. One could be anywhere relative to anyone else, and the planets and stars alike were only grounded by their relative perspectives to one another.

Occasionally, another ship flew by Natalie's window, traveling through the system. Each one was different, and they became more frequent as the shuttle neared Tralis. Soon, the space outside her window was bustling with ships of all sizes moving around each other, flying to and from the moon. Some of the ships were small like the shuttle she was on, and others were much, much larger. In quick succession, Natalie's perception of how large a ship could be was replaced by a new larger, more complicated vessel, only to be replaced by yet another.

Many of the commercial ships Natalie saw were not any bigger than the shuttle, except for the freighters, which were many times larger. However, even these behemoths were dwarfed by many of the military vessels, their cannons protruding from them menacingly. Almost all of them were moving away from the moon, rather than toward it. Most of these ships were at least a kilometer in length, by her best estimates, but they too were dwarfed by a single ship that passed by the shuttle at a distance. Even from over a kilometer away, the ship spanned Natalie's entire window. She stared at it in amazement as it glided through the void. The ship was brick-like, with sharp angles and multiple box-shaped structures. Many large cannons were easily visible, the majority of which pointed straight forward in an intimidating display of military power.

"I see the ol' girl has caught your eye. That's a Devastator-class leviathan." Turning to see who had said that, Natalie saw the White Tail from her graduation standing next to her. He smiled and continued. "They're some of the most powerful ships ever built. Twelve kilometers of enough guns and planes to take on a small fleet on their own." Natalie turned back to look at the ship, which was now turning away from them and toward where the other OSC ships were headed. "That one is the OSC *Trinity*, one of three leviathans in the 3rd Mobile. She's one of the oldest ships in the whole OSC, along with her sister ship, *The Heart of Jontunia*, the fleet's flagship."

"Where are all of the ships going?" Natalie asked, watching more OSC ships follow behind *Trinity*.

"The 3rd Mobile doesn't stay in the Cloud for long," the White Tail replied, sitting next to Natalie. "Jontunia has the 3rd Defensive fleet to protect it, so we don't need to stick around. We're here for our supply pickup, which happens about once every five cycles. That includes of course picking up any new blood that have joined the ranks. I'm sure when we board the carrier we'll hear where we'll be going exactly." Suddenly, the lights in the cabin changed from their standard white glow to a soft orange, signaling that the ship was about to dock and for all passengers to remain seated.

The shuttle slowed; after a few minutes, a metallic *clunk* echoed through the ship as it shuddered and docked with the terminal on Tralis. The lights in the cabin switched back to normal, and the passengers began rising from their seats. Natalie found Darren near the exit door, retrieved their bags, and then they followed the White Tail out of the shuttle.

The three headed down the busy corridors of the moon's port, passing many workers, businesspeople, and ship crews. The hallways were well lit, and their gray corridors were strewn with metal crates and parts. As they turned down different hallways, Natalie glanced out their large windows. Ships were coming in and out of the docks, and often there were small one- or two-man pods moving about doing work on many of the ships.

The trio walked past where a freighter had docked, still floating above the port, held in place by large magnetic arms. Numerous cranes moved along the length of the ship, dropping their arms into its massive hold, plucking large containers out of the freighter. The containers were then carried to another area of the dock, where the small pod-ships were opening the containers and retrieving their contents. This freighter was clearly here to resupply the moon with parts for the ships that sought repairs or retrofitting, or with goods for the people on Tralis.

The White Tail led Natalie and Darren through a set of doors in a section of the port, and suddenly the atmosphere changed completely. Here, the hallways were full of uniformed personnel, all carrying the distinctive OSC badge.

"This is one of the military wings," the White Tail said, not looking back at the pair following. "There are five military wings in this complex. Four of them allow the servicing of our ships, as well as facilitating the shuttling of military personnel from the complex to orbiting ships. The fifth is the maglev that has a direct route to the main military complex on Tralis. That's where all the ground forces of the Omasye Ground Council are stationed when not in our fleet. It's also the main hub for OSC ships to dock and resupply."

"So why are we here instead of at the military base?" Darren asked as they walked past some uniformed men lifting metal crates onto a trolley.

"Because our captain, Commodore Vystra, likes to do things differently." The White Tail laughed before continuing. "He doesn't like docking the carrier. Says he shouldn't have to rely on ground crews to resupply his ship. So instead, we sit in orbit around Tralis, and he makes the Dolphin crews go down to this wing en mass to pick everything up and bring it aboard, where the crew then unpackages and resupplies everything themselves."

The White Tail led them to a two-piece white door, but before he touched the control panel, the door opened with a sudden hiss. A tall woman in a flight suit and carrying a helmet stepped through. "Hey, tuna fish, you're late," the woman said, playfully punching his arm. "Did you get some good pickings down there? I hope the ones they told us about were worth it." It was only then that she noticed Natalie and Darren, who were standing awkwardly nearby. "Ah, you two must be the ones then. Name's Captain Trisha Valentine, otherwise known as Valkyrie. I'm the second in command of the White Tails."

Darren spoke before Natalie, reaching out to shake Trisha's hand. "Name's Darren Verra." He spoke confidently, but Trisha was still looking at him expectantly. "Oh yeah, uh, Phoenix." Natalie couldn't help but smirk seeing Darren so suddenly disarmed.

"So, the bird, right?" Darren nodded, causing Trisha to smile. "Pigeon." Natalie snickered but quickly fell silent when Trisha turned to face her.

“I’m uh, Natalie, er, Wildcat, Annikki,” Natalie stumbled through her introduction. “It’s a pleasure to meet you, ma’am.” Natalie shook Trisha’s hand, who was smirking widely at her.

“Likewise, Kitten,” Trisha said, laughing. “The instructors from your base talked a big game about you both. It’s rare that they get anyone skilled enough to call Jinsu planetside to do any scouting. I hope you live up to the hype.”

Both Darren and Natalie looked at Trisha quizzically before the silence was broken by the other White Tail, who had been standing silently nearby. “I guess I’ll introduce myself now then.” The man pushed off the wall he had been leaning on. “I was trying to keep the mystery up until we were home, so I could introduce myself with everyone else, but now that Valentine here has ruined the party, I guess now will do. I’m Lieutenant Jinsu “Swordfish” Hyltide, the scouter for the White Tails, as you both know. It’s good to formally meet you.”

Jinsu shook hands with both Darren and Natalie, smiling. For the first time since he had first spoken to them, Natalie had a chance to study him. He was about average height for a man, close to Darren’s height, and had short black hair. He was skinny, far less athletic looking than Darren, but was dressed primly and properly with not a thread out of place, unlike Darren. Both Jinsu and Trisha looked young, but still older than either Natalie or Darren, perhaps somewhere around thirty.

“So, does Captain Valentine do this with everyone?” Darren asked, glancing at Trisha, who had stepped back and was checking some notes. “With the nicknames I mean.”

“More or less,” Jinsu replied before turning back to the door. “You’ll see when we are aboard *Endurance*.”

Jinsu put on his helmet and stepped through the door, signaling the others to follow. Darren and Natalie followed behind him together, putting on their own helmets, with Trisha Valentine bringing up the rear. The group went down a dimly lit, short hallway with the door closing behind them. Natalie fidgeted with her helmet, making sure everything was secured to her suit, before pulling the switch to make the inside of her suit airtight. The flight suit with the helmet on held enough oxygen for a pilot to go from the air-filled section of a ship or base through the airlock and to their plane inside the hangar.

As they reached the end of the hallway, Jinsu pressed a button on the door. Two green lights lit up on either side of the door, and after a pause, the door slid open. Jinsu then led the others through, revealing a small hangar. The hangar was lit by many bright lights lining the ceiling corners, shining down onto the pristine Dolphin that was resting on the gray metal floor. The Dolphin was gray, with a single green line running down the side of the fuselage, before angling up with the rear ramp, coming all the way to the tip of the singular, tall tail.

Natalie and Darren entered the Dolphin through the rear ramp, sitting near the front of the cargo space. Natalie attached her suit to the corresponding mount behind her, which funneled air in and out of her suit. Jinsu and Trisha climbed into the cockpit through the front doors and buckled into the pilot and copilot's seats. Looking through the open door between the cargo hold and the cockpit, Natalie watched the pair quickly run through the startup sequence. The Dolphin rumbled to life, its powerful engines pushing heat through the four vectoring pods on the exterior of the Dolphin.

With the engine started, Jinsu, from the copilot's seat, hit a switch, and a bright green light in the hangar turned on. Immediately, the hangar's turntable floor rotated the Dolphin one hundred-eighty degrees. Large metal doors, marked by yellow warning patterns, began separating, revealing the busy moondock outside. Even in the quieter military wing, ships were still continuously flying in and out. Natalie sat back in her seat, deciding to let her mind rest for the trip to her new home, *Endurance.*

***

The intercom crackled to life with the sound of Jinsu's voice. "We're coming up on her now. You can look through the front canopy if you'd like to see the box that is your new home."

Natalie loosened her seatbelt and leaned forward, turning to look through the cockpit. Just as Jinsu said, Natalie could see the OSC *Endurance,* floating quietly against the green-blue backdrop of the Salerum Cloud. Natalie noticed Darren doing the same as her.

"She's a Tempest-class carrier, the main class of carrier in the Omasye Space Council," Jinsu explained. "Thirteen hundred meters long, 3,800 crew members, plus an additional 1,200 pilots. Comes standard with four hundred Spectres, along with about two hundred strike craft of a mix of bombers and transports. Some change these numbers, but not *Endurance*. She's an old girl, one of the first Tempests ever built, but she's reliable, and tough. And now she's your new home."

Endurance certainly had the appearance of a carrier: long and flat, with its main bridge the tallest point on the ship offset from the rest of the hull on the left side. Height-wise, the ship was short, adding to the look of its length, and it was sleek, coming to a fine point at its bow. From some angles, it carried the appearance of a short sword, piercing through the haze of the Salerum Cloud. *Endurance's* only engine, a rather large engine, sat atop the hull on the left side of the ship and extended well beyond the stern of the main hull. It was on this structure that the bridge connected with the rest of the ship.

From the pilot's seat, Trisha expertly brought the Dolphin to the hangar opening along the left side of *Endurance's* hull. Natalie counted five hangar decks stacked one atop the other from this opening. Each one was busy prepping other planes or guiding returning planes into the hangar. The technicians dedicated to each of the aircraft aboard *Endurance* moved about with purpose inside the airless hangar, protected by their work suits and helmets. The Dolphin gently touched down, its wheels absorbing the light impact with ease before the engines began to shut down in a low hum. Once the engines were silent, the four occupants began to climb out into the green walled hangar space.

The hangar was large, covered in planes, engineers, and pilots busily going about their tasks. Natalie and Darren climbed out the back ramp and regrouped with Jinsu and Trisha, who were standing near the front of their Dolphin. Jinsu was looking back for them expectantly, and when they neared, he signaled them to follow as he and Trisha led the way to the exit of the hangar. As they exited the airlock into the rest of the ship, the four took off their flight helmets. The two senior White Tails led the way through a series of off-white corridors before coming to a stop ahead of a simple salmon-colored door.

"This is the locker room of the White Tails," Jinsu said, turning to the new recruits. "Soon you'll get your own lockers and will be able to store your flight suits here whenever you aren't flying. For now, however, we'll just be meeting your new squadron mates." Jinsu pushed the door open and stepped inside, and the others followed.

The locker room was separated in two sections, dividing the women and men of the White Tails. Each section had ten lockers, five on each side of the section opposite the other five. A thin V-shaped panel blocked the view into the sections from the immediate entrance. Jinsu Hyltide led the way to the men's side, where three pilots were waiting. The first pilot Natalie saw was a tall man standing at the front of the section. Natalie guessed he was in his mid-thirties, and he had short dirty blonde hair and confident brown eyes. Everything about him seemed to emanate self-assurance, and he stood with a commanding presence.

"Let's get all the introductions underway then, shall we?" Trisha Valentine said, stepping into the space between the two groups. "These two are our newest additions, a kitten and a pigeon." Trisha smirked, motioning to Natalie and Darren in turn. "Lieutenant Natalie Annikki and Lieutenant Darren Verra, or Wildcat and Phoenix." Natalie lifted her right hand in a small nervous wave before Trisha continued. "This man here is our squadron leader, Captain Tanner "Archon" Kislo, or "peasant" for short."

Tanner Kislo laughed as he stepped forward. "Kislo works just fine for everyone except Captain Valentine," he said as he shook Natalie and Darren's hands. "Welcome aboard *Endurance*, and welcome to the White Tails. I'm sure Hyltide picked some good ones."

"Yes, that remains to be seen," Trisha said, stepping past Kislo to the next person, a woman about the same height as Jinsu, who lifted herself from the bench she had been sitting on. "This lovely lady who is full of emotion right here," Trisha grabbed the woman's shoulders and held her out front, causing the woman to frown, "is Lieutenant Varya "Wyvern" Kishpin. Or, as I like to call her because it pisses her off oh so much, my little lizard."

Varya's brunette hair was drawn into a short ponytail, and her expression gave away no emotion. She was in her full flight suit and holding her helmet, in contrast to Kislo, who was dressed in standard fatigues. *Coming in from a flight or going on one soon,* Natalie thought.

"Call me Wyvern." Varya stepped forward, her voice calm but serious. "It's a pleasure to meet you." She shook Natalie's hand before stepping back in line.

"Finally, we have the squadron's sweetheart." Trisha stepped behind a short girl with deep red hair, lightly pushing her forward. "Lieutenant Claire "RedSky" Riftfell, the nicest girl you'll ever meet. Unless you're the enemy, that is."

Claire was slightly shorter than Natalie herself. Her hair was blood red and reached just below her ears. She had clearly just come back from a flight, as her flight suit was halfway undone and wrapped around her waist, revealing a white, sweat-soaked tank top underneath.

She stepped forward, smiling and giving off a well-composed attitude. "You can call me whatever you want." She placed her helmet on one of the benches and shook Natalie's hand, then Darren's. "I'm sure you'll both feel right at home here soon." Claire then stepped back toward Trisha. Both Claire and Varya were younger than the rest, around their mid-twenties.

"Wait, she doesn't get a nickname from you?" Darren asked, looking at Trisha expectantly.

"Nope, and she won't get one from you either," Trisha answered immediately. "So don't even think about it."

Kislo spoke up, stepping into the center of the group again. "Alright, now that we've all met each other, let's get our two newbies to their rooms. Hyltide, take Verra to his room, and Riftfell, take Annikki to hers. Then you both can go rest; you deserve it after your flights. Valentine, you're with me, and Kishpin, you've got a flight to do yourself. We can regroup in the mess at 1800 Ship Time for dinner and drinks and get to know our new friends." With that, the White Tails broke up, each heading out to their own destination.

Natalie followed Claire through a series of hallways, all busy with the sounds of machines and personnel moving up and down the ship.

"This is the engineering section of the ship, the closest section to the hangars," Claire said as they walked the gray halls. "This is where they conduct repairs on all the planes in *Endurance,* as well as the carrier itself. They can even manufacture new parts, and in the extreme circumstances where it's necessary, they can manufacture an entirely new plane." The pair passed some wide, tall open spaces with large yellow machines and a slew of metal parts and boxes. "We live above all of this, at the top of the main hull. We also have a viewing area into the top hangar bays, where our Spectres are, as well as a few direct staircases to every hangar entrance. Other than the engineers, who live between us and this section, we are the closest to the hangars. I just wanted to take you through this section so you could see more of the ship." Claire smiled at Natalie, who smiled back. The pair then turned through an automatic door and up a staircase.

They climbed many flights of stairs and passed doorways reading "engineering" and "residence," both preceded by a wrench symbol. They eventually passed a sign that had a knife and fork symbol and the word "messdeck" on it, and the next floor up had a generic plane symbol and the word "residence" again.

"This floor and the two above are where all of *Endurance's* pilots live. All of us White Tails live on this floor, though." Claire led Natalie through these doors and down the hallway, with walls a clean white-like color that was soft on the eyes. After a brief walk down the hall past a few rooms, a right turn down a second hall, and past a few more rooms, the pair reached a door with a nameplate reading "Lt. N. Annikki."

"Here you are, room 23." Claire fished through the pockets of her half-drawn flight suit and produced a keycard, which she then swiped lengthwise on the nameplate. A small green light on the end of the plate lit up, and the door unlocked.

As Claire tucked the keycard back into her pockets, she caught Natalie glancing in her direction curiously. "Master key," Claire responded, smiling. "Both Captain Kislo and Trisha have one. This one is Trisha's. You'll have your own key waiting for you on the desk inside."

"So where does everyone else live?" Natalie asked, looking up and down the hall.

Claire stepped past Natalie, motioning to Natalie's left. "The first two rooms in the hall are Kislo's and Valentine's. Across the hall from you is Jinsu Hyltide, but don't expect to see him coming in and out of that room much." Claire let out a short laugh before proceeding. "The next two rooms are mine and Varya's, and then finally Darren Verra for all of the White Tails. Other squadrons occupy the rest of the rooms on this floor and the other floors."

"So, this room…" Natalie paused, looking over to Claire. "Was it someone else's in the White Tails, before I showed up?"

Claire's smile vanished. "Let's not talk about that quite yet." After a pause, her smile returned. "Come, let's see your room!"

Claire motioned toward the door and waited for Natalie to enter. Natalie pushed the door open and stepped inside, Claire following behind. She found the light panel on the wall to her right and lightly tapped the bottom selection of the touch screen, the button to turn on all main lighting. The space lit up in a soft white light, revealing Natalie's new residence.

Walking from the small entrance hall, Natalie stepped into the main living space. The place was clean, with an open space containing a couch, a small but comfortable looking chair, and a display installed inside the wall. Behind the couch was a small desk with a built-in computer and a leather chair. Moving along the wall beyond the living space, Natalie reached the door to the bedroom, a simple square room containing a bed, a nightstand, and a dresser. From the bedroom, there was a small door. It led to the bathroom, which also had a shower, and was accessible from the living room as well. She set her bag down on the end of what was now her bed and turned back to Claire, who was waiting by the door.

"It's nice here," Natalie said, smiling while taking in the room once more. "It's a lot nicer than I expected, honestly."

Claire Riftfell smiled, shifting her leaning position on the door frame. "It's nice, but to be honest, it's nothing special. It's the standard naval officer room, the same rooms you'll find on any other ship in the OSC. I don't mean to offend or anything, I just—"

"I'm not offended, don't worry," Natalie interrupted, raising a hand to silence Claire whilst stepping across the room toward the door. "I knew that all the officer's quarters were the same. It doesn't change the fact that I like this place." She smiled at the red-haired woman, who smiled in relief back at her. "So, Darren has a place just like this, huh? He'll be the most excited of all, if not completely bewildered." Claire was looking at Natalie with a quizzical look. Natalie shook her head before responding. "Don't worry about it."

Soon after, Claire headed back to her own quarters. Natalie unpacked her things, slowly making her quarters her own. Occasionally, she considered the fact that someone else once lived here, and she questioned what could have happened to them. Remembering Claire's reaction, Natalie suddenly felt nervous. She pushed the question from her thoughts. It wouldn't help her to think so much about it, and the place was hers now anyway. She finished unpacking the last of her things before finally placing her helmet on top of her dresser, next to the neatly folded flight suit, which a small stuffed cat sat atop. Natalie sat down at the end of her bed. This small, apartment-like place was her new home, *Endurance,* her new town.

She was finally beyond the first step in her career and her lifelong goals. From now on, she would fight to protect the innocent people of the Altherian Empire. If she could help it, no one would know the pain of losing a family member to senseless violence and hate. Natalie glanced over to the nightstand at the head of the bed, where she'd leaned the picture of her father against the lamp. Briefly, she thought of home. It had been over half a year now since she had left, and she wondered what had changed back in that small, snowy town. *Probably nothing. That old town never changes, at least not quickly.* Natalie smiled, stood up, brushed off her pant legs, and stepped out of the room, turning out the light.

CHAPTER 13

Every second light flicked from its light blue hue back to its normal yellow-white glow, signaling the successful completion of *Endurance's* mass-acceleration into near-faster than light speeds. The rest of the lights continued to glow the vibrant light blue, indicating that the carrier was maintaining its incredible speed. Natalie tapped her fingers against the pants of her light olive military fatigues and counted to ten before reaching for the safety harness. As she unclipped the belt on her lap, she felt a tap on her right shoulder. Looking over, she saw Claire, smiling and leaning toward her.

"Not so bad for a first jump, right?" Claire asked.

"No, it didn't feel like anything really," Natalie answered, rising from the fold-out jump seat mounted in the cafeteria wall. Around her, dozens of others aboard *Endurance* did the same. This was standard procedure for just about all of them, but for Natalie, this was completely new, being only her third day aboard *Endurance*. "I'm not really sure what I expected, but I didn't feel anything."

"Assuming everything works correctly, you won't feel a thing," Jinsu Hyltide said as he and Darren Verra approached. "If you do feel it, then something in the MAD Drive has gone wrong."

"MAD Drive?"

"Yeah, every capital ship in the sector uses a MAD Drive." The group of White Tails began walking out of the cafeteria, into the crowd of the rest of the crew. "The Mass-Acceleration Device, or MAD Drive. A highly unstable device capable of launching a ship into near-faster than light speeds in a matter of seconds. How it all works in depth is beyond me, but all I know is that those things are finicky tech and will sooner vaporize the ship and everything within a two-klick radius than go outside of the bounds set by its design."

Escaping the crowd, the four White Tails started down one of the many long corridors of the Tempest-class carrier. "What are these 'bounds'?" Darren asked.

"Well for starters, there's a minimum time and therefore distance that you have to jump," Jinsu continued. "If you were to jump any less than the minimum time, a so-called micro-jump, the MAD Drive would become critically unstable, and the ship would be doomed. Maybe not vaporized, but definitely not in good shape. The second bound is a maximum jump time of six hours. After that, the device needs to cool down, settle or recharge or something; again, that's beyond me. But every six hours of jump time means we have six hours of downtime while the MAD Drive figures itself out."

"Is there no way to jump any longer than six hours?" Natalie asked. "What if you only decelerated a small amount, relying on the MAD Drive less?"

"Even if you could do that, Omasye Space Council law dictates that every six hours all NFTL transit must cease, so the ship can get a new bearing and then it can launch again when its MAD Drive is ready to go. This stops anything cataclysmic from happening, like a fifteen-kilometer-long leviathan from traveling at NFTL speeds straight into a planet."

"Sorry to interrupt the Q and A session here," Claire said before any other questions could be raised. "But Jinsu, where are we going?"

"I'm taking the new cubs around the ship," Jinsu responded, half laughing. "They should probably get to know their way around here."

The four pilots continued down the long corridors of *Endurance* until they reached a set of stairs near the rear of the ship. They climbed up several floors to an open but busy deck. Natalie saw displays and workstations all around, stretching far into the room. Personnel in dark gray and green OSC ship uniforms were moving about, and there was the sound of many conversations happening at once. There were stairwells inside leading up to the next deck, with signs reading "engineering" and "command." As Natalie looked around, Jinsu began explaining. "This is the wing command deck. Every one of the fifty squadrons has a wing coordinator that operates at one of these consoles and acts as the liaison between the head of the entire wing and the pilots."

Natalie looked deeper into the room. "So, if there are fifty coordinators, how do they communicate with the wing?"

Jinsu pointed into the center of the room, where an elevated platform stood above the other displays. This platform was encircled by displays save for the steps up to the circular space. "That is the wing command console. There are some ten or so officers that watch everything happening in the vicinity of *Endurance.* They can see each squadron and assign them new objectives, which will pop up on the squadron coordinator's display."

As Natalie and Darren took in the room and the busy work of the ship's officers, another man approached them. "What's going on here, huh?" It was Kislo, coming from the right side of the room. "Hyltide, you showing the kids around? And I'm guessing Riftfell got roped into this too?"

Claire nodded.

Jinsu smiled at his superior. "I think it's important that they know how everything around here works, and how to get around."

"Always the teacher… Well, keep it up then." Kislo turned to leave.

"What are you doing here?" Claire asked Kislo. "You know we aren't flying for the next week, not until the transit is complete."

"I wanted to check our predicted waiting points on our trip to the pirate's border." Tanner Kislo smiled at his squadronmate. "Those six hours of downtime between jumps will be of good use to keep our edge. And we can get the new recruits up to speed on zero-g flying."

"I can take care of that for you," Jinsu answered. "I picked them, so I'll make sure they're as good as they looked on Jontunia."

"I figured you would." Kislo laughed as he turned to leave again. "I'm going to add training to your list of permanent jobs to go with recruiting."

Jinsu laughed as well. "I'm surprised you didn't years ago." Kislo gave a thumbs up as he walked away, and Jinsu turned back to the others. "Alright, any other questions before we leave?"

"What's on the decks above this one?" Natalie asked, pointing to the other stairwells.

"The deck immediately above is central command. On that deck, they can coordinate with the fleet, with every section of the ship, and command the steering of the ship. It's sandwiched between the engineers and the pilots so they can reach both decks quickly to pass new information."

"Do they really need the same amount of space as the wing does?" Darren asked.

"No, the command deck has considerably less floor space. The walls are much closer in, and between the interior and exterior walls, there are many layers of armor to protect command. It's the most heavily armored section of the ship. You'll notice on our way back down the branch section between the main hull and the bridge where we are now is very narrow. That's because the rest is armor to stop the bridge from being disconnected from the rest of the ship." Jinsu motioned toward the exit doors, and the rest of the group followed as he began walking out of the wing command deck.

"Next we'll show you the recreational facilities onboard," Jinsu told Natalie and Darren as they started back down the narrow stairs. "A ship this big has plenty of room for its crew to blow off steam."

"You'll like this part," Claire said to the two recruits. "The rec center has almost anything you can think of to keep you active."

Jinsu pressed a button on the wall, opening the white sliding doors with "recreation" on the sign above. "You know what?" Jinsu said, nudging Claire's shoulder. "If you're making me do the rest of the ship, how about you show them around the rec center?"

"Now why would you go and do tha—" Claire stopped when she saw Trisha on the other side of the door. She was carrying a gym bag over her shoulder and was wearing a dark T-shirt and some tight blue jogging pants. "Oh! Captain Valentine, good morning."

"Don't military me, sweetheart," Trisha said, smiling, and both women laughed. "What's going on here? You and the tuna fish taking the little ones around town?"

"Pretty much." Claire turned toward the two recruits. "Jinsu said they should know where everything is."

"Well, I hope they've been taking notes." Trisha locked eyes with each of the two in turn. "This place is like a 1300-meter-long apartment building that's also two hundred meters wide. It's like an entire town compressed and stacked on top of itself. You'll be getting lost for the first year you're here."

"Way to motivate the troops, Captain," Jinsu teased. "You'll scare them into only moving from their rooms to the cafeteria or the hangars."

"That's what you and Claire are here for isn't it?" Trisha shot back. "Well, just Claire now actually. I need to borrow you for a bit." Trisha moved past the group, grabbing the sleeve of Jinsu's uniform to pull him away.

"This wasn't even my plan though!" Claire shouted to Trisha as she jogged up the stairs. Jinsu turned and shrugged apologetically before he quickly ran up the stairs, trying to catch up to Trisha. "Damn her." Claire turned back to the recruits. "Sorry, her and Jinsu are pretty close friends, so this kind of thing happens a lot."

Claire led the pair into the recreational center, revealing a bright, well-lit place. To Natalie, it was as though they had just stepped off the ship and into a civilian gym. The immediate foyer had a central desk and labeled hallways toward both a women's and men's locker room and showers. Beyond the desk's sides were two more hallways, one marked with a dumbbell symbol and the other with a water symbol. Immediately behind the desk were two sets of stairs leading upward and downward. The area was less busy than the wing command deck, but still there were many people walking about, almost all in different styles of athletic clothing. Claire, Natalie, and Darren looked out of place in their light olive military fatigues.

"The rec center runs the width of *Endurance* and reaches to the central hangar bay along the length of the ship," Claire explained, naturally taking Jinsu's place as the tour guide. "On this floor there are two full-size swimming pools, as well as a large weight room; these are the two most often visited facilities. Down the stairs at the back is an obstacle course and a shooting range, mostly for any army personnel we have aboard the ship. Upstairs is a track and a soccer pitch for your running and competitive needs."

"I used to play soccer back home," Darren said, smiling. "How often does it get used? Are there teams within the wing?"

Claire smiled back to the young pilot. "We play squadron versus squadron. I'm the captain of our team since I'm the only one who really plays soccer in the White Tails."

"Well now you've got a second." Darren pointed to himself proudly with his thumb. "I can't wait to play!"

"Perhaps now we'll actually win more than a handful of games!" Claire laughed. "We aren't very good. The others try and aren't half bad, but the other squadrons, since they're bigger, often have better players than us."

As the two continued talking about soccer, Natalie listened but found the conversation hard to follow. After a few minutes, Darren and Claire were still talking and laughing but seemed to have moved from soccer to sports in general. *Seems they're both big sports players,* Natalie thought. She couldn't help but smile at the two getting along. *I think we'll fit in here just fine.*

"What about you Natalie?" Claire turned and asked suddenly. "Do you play any sports?"

Natalie half smiled. "No, sports have never been a big thing back home; the summer is too short."

"What about during the winter?" Claire asked curiously.

"Well, the town plays a lot of hockey, and there are a lot of skiing hills, but I don't really do any of that." Natalie smiled shyly at the questions. "I own a snowboard, but I don't do anything crazy with it. It's just for fun on the hills."

"Sounds like an unwritten book." Claire laughed and smiled mischievously. "I'm sure we can turn you into a soccer player in no time."

Natalie watched the engineers and pilots moving through the halls as she followed Claire. Navigating from one end of *Endurance* to the other seemed easy; there were main hallways near the flanks of the ship that led from one end of the ship to the other in an almost perfectly straight line. Since they had just been at the rear of the ship, where the recreational center and passage to the bridge were located, Natalie knew Claire was leading Darren and her toward the front of the ship, where the forward hangars were located.

On their way, the corridor shifted inward, and the right-side gray-metal wall was replaced by ceiling-high glass. On the other side of the glass were many Dolphin-M marine transports and Hunter-class bombers. Engineers went about their work on the planes without airtight suits, as the bay doors high above were sealed shut for the duration of the six-hour jump *Endurance* had just begun. Once the carrier slowed for its six-hour rest period, the hangar would be drained of air, and the large bay doors would open to allow planes to fly in and out. This hangar was a large rectangle nearly the width of the carrier and a quarter of its length, and it housed all the larger aircraft onboard. Just above the glass, Natalie could see the thick metal panels that would slide down and seal to the floor to cover the hallway during combat. These armored panels looked thick enough to block most strike craft rounds and some ordnance but were thinner than the regular hull armor.

Moving beyond the central hangar, the inside wall was now lined with doors and staircases at a steady interval. The trio were moving through the residences and engineering sections of the Tempest-class carrier. Here, nearly the entire crew of *Endurance* and its pilots ate, slept, and lived. The hallways were most busy here. Since the ship was traveling at near faster than light speeds, the pilots were off duty, and only the necessary maintenance was being conducted in the hangars. As such, most of the engineers and pilots were enjoying their free time and were socializing together in the residences. While the main corridor was intended to be always clear in case of emergency, many groups of crew members were moving up and down the halls, chatting and relaxing.

Claire, leading her two young pilots, weaved between slower groups as she made her way down the hall. As she neared her destination, she began explaining to the recruits. "When you two came in the other day, you flew into the side hangar entrance right?" Though rhetorical, Claire paused before continuing. "Well don't get used to that way of coming in. The only thing us White Tails have parked down there is the squadron's Dolphin."

"Wait, the White Tails have their own Dolphin?" Darren asked before Claire could continue.

Claire shrugged off the interruption with a smile. "Every fighter and bomber squadron has its own Dolphin, so the pilots can go moonside on their own time."

The trio came to a halt in front of a large gray door with yellow and black warning markers. Natalie recognized it as an airlock, similar to the one they used when they first boarded *Endurance.*

Claire turned from the airlock to her right, facing a short corridor and another door leading to some stairs. "You'll recall you came up those stairs when you first got here," she said before turning again to look back down the main hall. "The locker room we met in is just down there on the left."

The memory came to Natalie, and she nodded. "So why is the locker room up here then?" she asked. Claire simply smiled in return before pressing a blue button on the airlock.

Since the hangar on the other side was closed for transit, both ends of the airlock opened in unison, and the trio stepped through. Rows of Spectres filled the hangar, and engineers, as well as the occasional pilot, moved about the space. The hangar was long, as long as *Endurance* was wide. Every Spectre had its wings swept back, both to conserve space as well as for better performance in zero gravity. The trio had entered lengthwise inside the hangar and looking right across the short width of the hangar, Natalie could see the large airlock doors that stored the rest of *Endurance's* fighter complement. Letting Natalie and Darren take in the hangar, Claire slowly began walking to the next destination.

"This hangar," Claire started, ensuring the pair were following, "is where all seven White Tails' Spectres are stored. Unless we need major repairs, our planes are always ready on this hangar, so we can be one of the first into the fight." The trio were walking down a passage between two rows of Spectres facing each other. Many were being tended to by a single engineer conducting routine checks on his assigned fighter. Approximately halfway down the length of the hangar, Natalie saw the increasingly familiar white-colored twin tails of the elite fighter squadron. They were lined up with three on the left and the other four facing them on the right. Standing in front of one of the Spectres was an engineer having a discussion with a young woman in her flight suit. Her brunette hair was in a loose ponytail hanging over the collar of her clothes, shifting to the left or right with the vigorous movements of her hands.

"I just want a bit more in the vector jets," Varya said to her engineer, a man in an orange jumpsuit and similarly aged. "It doesn't flick quite as quickly as I think it could."

"Ma'am." The engineer had a defensive tone. "The strain you are asking from your plane is too much. This is the third time you've asked me to reduce the restrictor. If I go any farther, you risk overloading the pumps, tubes, even the airframe itself risks a fracture at those G's."

"But if you do this, I could finally match a Shrike in any maneuver."

"I'm sorry, Lieutenant, but the risk is far too great. I can't go through with this and risk you ending up just like..."

As his voice trailed off, Varya spoke. "I get it." She sounded disappointed but convinced. "You have my trust. If it's too risky, don't do it." The engineer nodded, waiting a moment before she waved her hand to dismiss him.

As the engineer walked back to the Spectres to continue his work, Claire stepped toward Varya. "How's our top pilot doing today?" Claire spoke in a cheery voice while smiling brightly.

By contrast, Varya sounded flat and emotionless. "I'm doing fine, thank you." She looked behind Claire, noticing the two new recruits standing politely together. "Taking them on the tour?"

"Yeah, Jinsu took off with Trisha and left me with them, but I don't mind."

Varya glanced away, sighing. Looking back to Claire, Varya put on a slight smile, though it looked a bit strained. "I guess it can't be helped." She then motioned the other two White Tails to come closer. "Neither of you have flown in space, right?"

"No, but Lieutenant Hyltide told us he would train us," Darren responded with excitement.

"That's good, you'll need as much training and experience as you can get before you get into combat." Varya's tone was cold and serious, her eyes moving between Natalie and Darren. "Flying in zero-g is the most taxing flying you'll ever do. The turns are a lot tighter, so the G's you'll pull are going to be a lot more than what you've trained with. You also need to understand that the combat is tight. This isn't like the old days on Altheria when jets engaged at 20 klicks, fired their missiles, and went home. The missiles don't work as well out here, so you have to rely on guns and close range to reduce the chance of a missile missing. If you can't master flying in space, you won't be on *Endurance* for long."

Natalie was taken aback by the lieutenant's speech. She had delivered what felt like a death sentence so matter-of-factly. "I think we'll do better than you expect," she responded, not afraid of challenging her superior's remarks. "I'm pretty sure we were selected for a reason, so we should have no trouble adapting to the new environment." There was silence as Natalie finished her rebuttal. Neither Darren nor Claire moved a muscle.

The first to move was Varya herself, stepping around Claire to get closer to the green-haired recruit. "Do you have any idea how many have come before you with that exact same thinking? How many of them never came back from their first fight? None of them ever listened to me when I gave them this speech. That kind of naive thinking is exactly what will get you killed," Varya said. She took several moments to look Natalie over. "I don't doubt that you're a skilled pilot, but understand that you must go into this with fresh eyes. Overconfidence will only put you at more risk." Varya, who was just a few inches taller than Natalie, was looking down on the inexperienced pilot as though she were a giant and Natalie a meager ant. Varya's golden eyes darted between Natalie's, burning with such intensity as though they would set Natalie ablaze.

Claire burst between the two, cutting the tension that threatened to swallow the entire hangar. "I think we ought to be heading out," she said in a nervous tone. "Wyvern, it's been a pleasure, and I'm sure these two know they can always come to you for sound advice, as our top pilot and proven veteran." Claire added the compliments hastily as she steered Natalie away and signaled Darren Verra to follow.

"What was that about?" Darren asked as they walked out of earshot of Varya. "She talks like we're already dead."

"I wouldn't worry about it too much," Claire responded, her voice finding composure. "If you want to understand her better, talk to Jinsu."

Claire led the two recruits out of the hangar and up the stairs to the residences. Stopping just a few floors shy of their quarters, Claire turned toward a set of rather nice double doors. "I have just one more place to show you two," she said with a smile, pushing through the doors.

Natalie and Darren stepped into a lively space full of tables and chairs, all made of fine wood. In the center of the room was a large display of all kinds of beverages, surrounded by a lavish rectangular bar, which had stools all around its perimeter. Many of the tables and chairs were occupied by men and women in the standard Omasye Space Council pilot fatigues, the same as the three White Tails that had just entered. Just as the white feather adorned the breast pocket of each of the three, other squadron emblems were carried by every pilot in the room.

Claire turned to the amazed recruits and smiled brightly. "Welcome to *Endurance's* pilots' mess hall!" she exclaimed, spinning back around and sauntering toward the bar. "All of the wing's pilots come here for drinks and relaxation." Claire stopped just before an empty corner of the central bar. "And this corner here is reserved just for the White Tails." At once, she plopped down on one of the stools, inviting the others to join her. Natalie sat down, but Darren held up his hand in polite refusal.

"It's too early for me," he said, beginning to turn away. "I'm going to go look for Lieutenant Hyltide."

"Good luck," Claire said teasingly before turning her attention to Natalie. "So, what do you think of *Endurance*?"

Natalie smiled. "It's becoming more and more like a new home."

"And the White Tails?"

"You're an interesting bunch for sure, but I like it." Natalie paused for a moment. "I'm not sure what to make of Lieutenant Kishpin though."

Claire tilted her head with a half-smile, her blue eyes dancing around, clearly putting her thoughts together. "Varya joined the White Tails only a year before I did. She has six years of experience, and in that time has become the best pilot we've ever had, even better than Kislo, who has six years over her." Claire paused, her face darkening. "She's been through a lot. We all share experiences, but she's somehow been closer to a lot of them. It's caused her to detach, in a way, from those she hardly knows. She won't let you in, won't be friendly with you, until you show her that you are good enough to stay for a long time. She's lost far too much to get attached to an unproven pilot."

Natalie sat in silence for a few moments. She felt as though she had opened a door better left closed. She couldn't imagine what Varya had been through. As a green pilot, Natalie had no clue what a pilot could see in combat to leave them as cold as she was. To be honest, she hadn't even considered those possibilities when she had signed up.

"What is she like?" Natalie decided to ask, moving from the dark path to hopefully a much lighter one. "Once she trusts you, that is."

Claire's smile returned. "She doesn't talk a whole lot, but she's actually really kind. She cares a lot about everyone in the White Tails. One day, I'm sure you'll even get to see her smile." Claire let out a giggle, causing Natalie to smile in return.

One day, she thought, *I hope we can all be friends and smile together. I think I've really found my new home here. I hope Dad is happy to see that I've found a place to call my own.*

CHAPTER 14

Natalie watched the engineers busily go about their work from the hangar's viewing platform just outside the pilot's quarters. Carts with racks of missiles, torpedoes, and ammunition belts moved this way and that between the planes, and when they reached their destination, the technicians would begin unloading the weapons, fixing them onto the craft that would carry them. When a Spectre or Hunter were loaded with weapons, they would be shuffled toward the hangar elevators at the sides and front of the hangar. From there they would be lowered into the storage decks, and another plane would take their place, ready to be loaded with weapons. By tomorrow, every strike craft in *Endurance's* inventory would be ready for battle, though that battle was still at least another day away.

The sound of boots on the metallic floor of the observation deck caused Natalie to turn around. She smiled when she saw Darren approaching her.

"Hey birthday girl, you gonna stand up here all night?" he teased, bringing his arm around the shorter Natalie to steer her toward the door. "Everyone's waiting for you in the mess hall, so come on. You only turn twenty-one once."

That's right, Natalie thought as the two started toward the door. It was her birthday. With the preparations for the incoming war, Natalie had lost track of the days. In her head, she laughed at herself. Even after three years of being aboard *Endurance,* she still found it easy to lose track of the days and weeks.

"It's too bad my birthday wasn't a week earlier," Natalie said. "Then you could have thrown this party on Jontunia."

Darren laughed. "Next time. I'm sure after the fleet rotates off the frontline the squadron will get another block of leave. Maybe then it will fall on your birthday."

Natalie sighed. "Maybe. One thing's for sure, though: next time, I'm going home for leave. Staying in a big city for three cycles was too much."

"I can't say I blame you," Darren said, chuckling as they climbed the stairs. "Who would've thought that Varya Kishpin was a big city girl? I thought for sure she came from some cold mountain just like you."

"Hey!" Natalie shouted teasingly. "Personality isn't defined by birthplace!"

Darren shook his head. "I swear, if the two of you had met during training, you would have been best friends... or mortal enemies. So cold..."

Natalie let out a disappointed *hmph*. "Yeah, well that isn't the case anymore. So, you can shut your mouth."

"Fine, fine," Darren relented. "But you know that if you want to go home for leave, you're taking Varya and I with you. It's not like I have anywhere to go, and Varya isn't spending her leave alone."

"You two are going to be so bored," Natalie said, unable to stifle her laughter.

The pair walked along the familiar halls and stairways until they reached the doors of the pilot's mess hall. Natalie drew her long, dark green ponytail to her mouth. "You've got nothing to be nervous about," Darren reassured her. "We're your friends."

"What if they've done some silly embarrassing thing for me this time?" Natalie asked, looking up at him.

"What would give you that indication?"

She let go of her ponytail. "Nothing, I guess. Claire promised that it wouldn't be any different from any other night."

"Then you've got nothin' to worry about," Darren responded, pressing the button to open the doors. "Claire doesn't lie."

The white sliding door to the mess deck parted revealing the pilot's mess hall. The other White Tails were in their usual place, at the corner of the finely crafted black stained wood bar in the middle of the room. Trisha was the first to spot Natalie and Darren's arrival, and Natalie saw her grab Jinsu's shoulder and get the others' attention. By the time she and Darren reached the others, they had all turned around.

Kislo raised his glass, soon followed by the rest of the group. "Happy birthday, Annikki," he said.

"Happy twenty-first, kitten!" Trisha shouted from her seat, followed by a chorus of "Happy birthday" and "Happy twenty-first" from the rest of their friends.

Natalie blushed. “Thanks everyone,” she said. She took a seat on an open barstool, and the bartender came by and gave her her usual drink.

“First one is on the house,” he said. “Happy birthday.”

“Thank you,” Natalie responded before taking a sip. She looked around. Nothing was out of the ordinary. Just like Claire had promised, things were just like any other night.

Soon enough, the group was chatting away, breaking into smaller groups. Glancing across the corner of the bar, Natalie saw Darren, Kislo, and Varya laughing together, and Jinsu and Trisha were having a quieter conversation next to them.

“One day they’re going to throw some big bash for your birthday, you know,” Claire said before taking a sip from her drink. “Probably after your fifth anniversary of being a White Tail.”

Natalie frowned, taking a sip from her own drink as well. “Talk them out of it.” She swirled the ice in her glass, watching it intently.

“Oh, come on, are you telling me you’ll never want a birthday party?”

Natalie turned on her stool to face Claire completely. “This is plenty.” She leaned on the bar, resting her left arm on the old wood. “I never had anything bigger than this back home. Usually, it was just me and my father, and when he was away on business, it was just me.”

“Then I think it’s time for that to change, or rather, in a couple years we’ll change that.” Claire playfully smirked, twisting on her stool.

“You’ve really got an evil side to you, don’t you?” Natalie teased, taking another sip of her drink. “You’re secretly more evil than Trisha, aren’t you?”

“It’s in the name.” Claire winked and laughed. “I wasn’t given RedSky for nothing.”

“Yes, I remember: ‘red sky at night, sailors’ delight. Red sky at morning, sailors take warning,’“ Natalie said, finishing her drink. “Trisha gave you it right?”

“Yes, she did,” Claire responded, beginning to blush. “It’s an old saying, pre-Federation. She said it was the perfect characterization of me in and out of the cockpit—or I guess the reverse—if you were to strictly follow the old saying.” She cocked her head to one side and winked, sticking her tongue out slightly.

"I can see why she named you that." Natalie giggled, causing Claire to blush even more. "I think it's pretty accurate. Delightful but deadly, if you will. So, if Trisha gave you RedSky, does that mean you gave her Valkyrie?"

From holding her glass, she pointed a finger out at Natalie before she finished her sip. "She's always there to protect me, from anyone or anything," Claire spoke quietly, her tone soft when speaking of her best friend. "I've made bad decisions before, upset people or let myself get hurt by others. But she always had my back. I'm sure you've seen it after all this time. I try to make up for it by protecting her in combat, not that she ever needs it."

"She'll never admit it, that's for sure." Natalie flagged down the bartender, who came over immediately with another drink. "But you've helped her out of some tight spots."

Claire laughed before responding. "We'll keep that between ourselves for now." She finished her own drink, signaling to the bartender for another. "So, what's the story behind Wildcat, eh?"

"Well, you know Darren gave it to me," Natalie said, glancing over at him, sitting with Jinsu, the two talking apart from the others. "He said it is representative of my 'aggressive and sometimes downright crazy' way of flying." Natalie rested her glass on the bar, instead reaching for her ponytail, which she twirled in her left hand.

"Sounds spot on if you ask me." Claire laughed. "I remember the first time I saw you fly in combat, way out in Sectra-86W, against that pirate cruiser that thought *Endurance* was an easy meal, away from its fleet. You had, what was it, two Sirens on you? And you traced the deck of *Endurance* at near max speed before diving through the narrow gap where the bridge meets the hull..."

"And both Sirens aborted, taking an earlier exit forward of the bridge," Varya's voice finished from behind them. "They had no idea that they had been baited into the turn, and you were already behind them... Sharing war stories now, are we?"

"It was Sectra-83W, but yes, sort of," Natalie responded, smiling at the new company. "We were discussing the origins of our callsigns."

"Which reminds me," Claire said, finishing a sip from her drink. "If Darren gave you yours, then you must have had a reason to give him Phoenix."

"That's right," Natalie replied, watching Varya pull another barstool over to the two of them and take a seat. "He was an ass when I met him." She shook her head. "So arrogant. But then, I don't know… he wasn't anymore. So, I gave him Phoenix, to symbolize his rebirth, so to speak."

"That's cute." Claire smirked teasingly, hiding behind her glass.

"Almost as cute as Valkyrie," Natalie jabbed back before turning to Varya. "So, Wyvern, you must also have a story behind your callsign, right?"

"My best friend, Myath, gave it to me," Varya responded in her usual unemotional tone. "Just like the both of you."

"So, what's the story behind it?" Natalie prodded before noticing Claire looking away from the pair and down at her glass sitting on the bar, which sat on the wood surrounded by a pool of its own condensation.

"The story is he's dead, and I'm still here," Varya said flatly, seemingly staring at nothing.

The conversation abruptly died, like a bird hitting a windowpane. Natalie couldn't wipe away the shock on her face. Claire was still looking away but had noticeably winced at Varya's response. Varya, however, was unchanging. She still stared forward, not giving away a single emotion.

The silence that passed was unbearable. "I'm so sorry," Natalie started, her mind desperately searching for the right words. "I had no idea, I shouldn't have asked, I'm so, so sorry."

Varya shook her head. "Don't worry about it," Her voice was still the exact same as before. "You couldn't have known. I just don't talk about it, that's all. It happens."

The bird had hit the ground. The three sat in silence for what felt like an eternity to Natalie. She couldn't find anything to say, but awkwardly smiled at Varya's forgiveness. Her mind ached, and she glanced repeatedly at Claire, hoping her friend would bail them all out of the awkwardness they had stumbled into. Claire, however, seemed to not even be part of the conversation, focusing more on her drink and the scenery of the mess deck than anything else.

In the end, Natalie's savior came in the form of a cake, carried by the bartender.

"Finally, it's here!" Kislo exclaimed as the bartender placed the cake in front of Natalie. Some of the others cheered. The cake was simple, a puffy rectangle with white frosting. On top were three lit candles. Two were together on the left, and the other was alone on the right. Cat ears had been drawn on the cake with chocolate syrup above the candles, and whiskers were drawn below.

Natalie smiled. She thanked her friends, and each smiled to her, taking a drink and shouting their well wishes. Natalie paused, staring down at the cake.

"Well, what are you waiting for? Blow out the candles!" The voice was Varya, standing just behind Natalie. Her voice held the cheeriest tone Natalie had ever heard from her.

Natalie looked back at her and smiled. Varya, smiling as well, nudged her toward the cake with a light touch of the hand on Natalie's back. Natalie nodded, bent to blow out the candles, and in a sweeping breath snuffed them all out, to the applause of the White Tails.

Kislo came to Natalie's side a moment later, holding a stack of plates and a knife. "Alright, everyone, come get your piece," he said, setting the plates down next to the cake. "Wildcat gets first pick though, being the birthday girl."

"Any piece is fine, thank you, sir," Natalie said somewhat shyly to her squadron leader.

"Hey, there won't be any of those formalities for the rest of the night!" he responded, handing her a hefty piece of cake. "Archon or Kislo, no Captain, no sir, nothing. I don't want to hear it, or else you owe me a drink." Natalie nodded, taking her cake to a seat at the bar. She decided to steal Kislo's seat, since he and a cake were currently occupying hers.

Behind her, Darren began outlining the slice of cake he wanted. "That's half the cake, you dumb pigeon!" Trisha Valentine scolded, lightly punching his side. Natalie laughed as she sat down, trying a bite of the cake. For something baked on a metal tube in space, it was surprisingly good, and she took another bite.

Soon after, a second plate was set down next to hers, followed by Jinsu Hyltide pulling up a chair. "How's the night going, Annikki?" He had yet to touch his cake, instead focusing on the young pilot.

"It's pretty good. Thanks for all this," Natalie said. She smiled at Jinsu, who was, as per usual for him, smiling in return. His familiar smile felt good. It felt like home.

Jinsu ran his left hand through his coarse black hair. "Well, you'll have many more years like this one. You know I tried to convince them to do this for you last year." He laughed, then glanced behind him. "But they told me you weren't ready yet."

"They were probably right, I don't think I would have been," Natalie said, laughing. "I wasn't sure if I was ready tonight until Darren forced me into the mess hall. Ah, your other half is coming. You might want to start running."

Jinsu laughed, faking fear in his tone. "If only I could actually outrun her."

Trisha stopped next to his seat, forcing him over until she could squeeze onto half of it herself. "What's going on here, hmm?" she asked, taking a drink from a tall glass.

"Just talking about how you could kick Jinsu's ass," Natalie responded, smiling.

"Oh, I do." Trisha replied quickly. "All the time. And not even just in the physical sense. I'm just better than him at everything." Jinsu let out a pained expression. "Oh, you know I'm only kidding." Trisha brushed her head against Jinsu's shoulder. "You at least stand a fighting chance at *some* things." Both Natalie and Trisha laughed at Jinsu's expense.

"This is starting to look like that stuff Kislo told you two to keep private," Claire spoke up, placing her hand on Trisha's shoulder. "Maybe you can save it for later." She winked at her best friend before reaching for her own chair to join the discussion properly.

Trisha scoffed at the remark, but still stopped. "Sometimes, sweetheart, you take the fun out of everything."

"Only for your own good," Claire said, tilting her glass toward Trisha. "Sometimes I provide the fun, like remember when I baited those two pirate fighters into that canyon intersection where you and Wyvern were waiting? Pretty sure you had lots of fun with them."

"Not as much fun as Wyvern," Trisha said, smirking. "That lizard plays with her food, forced him right into the canyon wall just because she could."

"Speak of the devil herself, here she is," Jinsu spoke up, laughing. "How's the night going, Wyvern?"

Varya was carrying two drinks between her right fingers, a plate with a slice of cake in her left hand. "I think it's going really well," she said, handing one of the drinks to Natalie, who took it with a confused expression and an awkwardly shaky hand. "Kislo and Verra are off talking about some nonsense back where they grew up on Jontunia. I hope Natalie is enjoying her first real birthday party with the Tails." Varya smiled, to the surprise of everyone.

"What's up with you, Wyvern?" Claire's voice was mixed with nervous laughter. "Are you okay?"

"I think I'm quite alright, Riftfell, thank you." Varya dragged a chair to the edge of the forming semi-circle around the bar. "I'm simply in a good mood. After all, it's our friend's birthday, and soon to be three years of being a White Tail. There's a lot to be in a good mood about. But enough about that, I thought I heard you sharing more war stories."

"We were just talking about how you like to play with your food," Trisha replied.

"It keeps things interesting." Varya tapped the side of her glass with her index finger while she spoke, droplets of condensation being flung off the side. "Why bother wasting precious ammunition on someone who will take themselves out of the fight?"

"That's awfully cruel, isn't it?" Claire asked.

"Funny for you to say that, Red Terror," Varya toyed. "I seem to recall an event where you led not one, but three enemy fighters into the side of their own cruiser on maneuver. You knew the cruiser was getting ready to accelerate to a new position and flew past his bow just before… The three behind you weren't so quick." Claire was silenced, leaning back in her chair.

"Hey, you lizard, don't be so mean to my sweetheart," Trisha spoke up, a playful anger in her tone. "She's saved your ass more times than you can count. Remember Jesnyr-098 last year? When you got caught by those two Sirens? They got your left wing, but then she showed up and got them both." It was Varya's turn to be silenced now.

Natalie spoke up this time. "Mistakes happen, but Wyvern is still the best pilot we've got."

Trisha snorted shortly. "You don't think you've usurped that title by now?" Claire and Jinsu nodded agreement from either side of Trisha.

"As much as I appreciate your praise, Annikki," Varya interjected, her voice having returned to its usual unemotional standard. "I have to agree with Valentine; You are certainly the best pilot we have." Natalie shook her head, forcing Varya to continue. "The only pilot who's never been hit, not by a single round, and yet you have just as many kills as Hyltide, a ten-year veteran."

Natalie was already twirling her ponytail and pressing it to her face when Trisha continued for Varya. "And your style! You make the Spectre do things I don't think even its designers knew it could do. You're undefeatable, kitten, and that's hard for me to say, because I'd beaten everyone in the squadron in a one-on-one before you showed up. And the lizard is the only person that's beaten me in return."

"You forgot that you beat her once, and the 'beaten in return' part was fifteen times," Claire added, causing everyone to laugh, except for Trisha. "But yes, Natalie, you're better than both our best pilots, and probably better than any White Tail before us, even before Kislo, and he's been here for fifteen years."

Natalie shook her head, her ponytail against her lips, her cheeks flushed red. "You all have been in way tougher fights than I have." She let her hair back to her shoulder. "Small flights of pirate fighters are nothing compared to the fights you have all fought. You've fought experienced pilots in equal planes, in much bigger fights. Save any praise for after the battle next weekdays."

Varya leaned over, softly pushing Natalie with her left arm. "Fine, but you watch; I bet you'll show us just how much better you really are."

"Until then, let's just enjoy the peace we still have." This was met with cheers and Jinsu calling for another round, causing more cheers.

***

As the night died down, the White Tails parted ways. After all, a great battle would start in a week, and it was vital that the time be spent preparing oneself for the unknown. Kislo took his leave far earlier than anyone else, needing to meet with the wing commander before he went to his quarters. Jinsu and Trisha were next to depart, Trisha wrapped around Jinsu's right arm as they walked out of the mess hall. The final four decided to leave together.

All seven pilots were well on their way to rest, save for two. Inside Darren's room, he poured two glasses of water. Carrying them from the tiny kitchen to the living space, he handed one to Natalie, who was relaxing on the couch. Darren placed his own on the glass table before sitting down on the couch next to his best friend.

"Hard to believe it's been nearly three years," he said quietly as he got comfortable. "Feels like it was just days ago that we were standing on Jontunia getting drafted to our squadrons."

Natalie smiled as she placed her glass on the table. "You're right. And yet it feels like we've known all of our friends for our entire lives." It was true; life aboard *Endurance* for the last three years, with its constant combat missions on the Altherian-pirate border, had brought the White Tails closer together than Natalie had ever imagined she would be with anyone. Each trusted the others with their lives completely.

"You know," Darren broke the silence without looking toward Natalie, "I haven't forgotten about us."

Natalie felt her heart stiffen. "What do you mean?" She was sure she already knew the answer, but she needed to hear Darren say it.

"That evening back on Jontunia, in your room." Finally, Darren looked to Natalie. His eyes were the same as they had been all those years ago. "I wonder sometimes, why we can't have that again?"

"Because things are different now. We're in the same squadron." Natalie didn't have to think long for the answer. It was like a pre-programmed response, as though she had expected this conversation.

"How is it any different? Being in the same squadron shouldn't change anything. Just look at Jinsu and Valentine. If they can have that, why can't we?"

"It's just..." Natalie realized she didn't have an answer. Darren was right; Jinsu and Trisha had a relationship that had begun long before either Natalie or Darren even joined the White Tails. Why would she try to resist? Did she not have feelings for Darren anymore? *No, that's not true,* something in Natalie answered her questions.

"It's just what?" Darren asked.

"I still feel that way." Natalie's mind was still battling her heart, though she didn't know why. "Something just doesn't feel right about it."

"Believe me, everything is fine." Darren moved closer to Natalie now.

"But what will Kislo say?" It was her mind's final defense against both Darren and Natalie's own desires. "He doesn't exactly approve of Jinsu and Trisha."

"He'll just have to accept it. We can keep it under wraps for as long as possible, and when he finds out, he'll have no choice."

Although something still felt wrong, Natalie's logical side had surrendered. As Natalie moved toward Darren, she knew it wasn't his debate that had won; no, it was part of Natalie herself that had overcome her mind. Desires buried for three years had silenced Natalie's logic.

As Natalie's right hand gripped Darren's shirt, pulling him toward her, she lifted her head toward his, closing her eyes. Darren didn't say anything; he knew that she had given in to her own desire. With his left hand, he softly cupped the back of Natalie's head, his fingers running through her soft green hair. When their lips met, they released three years of desire and inaction. Their minds went blank. There was only touch, smell, and taste now. Darren's right hand moved around Natalie's right leg from behind. He lifted and rolled her onto his lap. Natalie, now kissing Darren's neck, was silently willing.

Natalie pulled her head back and opened her eyes. As Darren opened his, in the endless seconds, the two searched for the three years they had lost. Darren pulled Natalie back toward him. His heart was beating so fast he felt as though it were going to leap from his chest. He felt every ounce of regret he had carried for three years suddenly lift from his shoulders. Now, as Darren felt Natalie's hands in his hair and on his back, he wished he had made a move sooner. But that didn't matter now. Darren had what he wanted. He knew now that Natalie, the woman that had captured his heart so completely, still loved him the same way she did three years prior.

Darren raked his left hand through Natalie's hair as he kissed her. His right hand slowly slid up from her thigh toward the small of her back. His fingers fluttered at her waist, pushing the bottom of her dark shirt aside, and his hand carried on.

The sudden rush of Darren's hand against her bare back reactivated Natalie's mind. At first, only the carnal sensations came through, but then more coherent thoughts. Was this really going to happen? Was this really what she wanted? What would this do to her relationship with the others? Would they accept another relationship like Jinsu and Trisha's? What if it didn't work out? How could they continue flying together if they hated each other? As Natalie felt Darren's fingers roll up over her ribs, the worst question of all came to mind: What if one of them died? At the same moment that Natalie's mind fell away in fear, she stopped kissing Darren back. In that instant, his hand had moved to cup Natalie's left breast.

As Darren's fingers pulled down on the cup of Natalie's bra, Natalie felt nothing. Her mind was busy entering a nuclear war with her heart at the center. Natalie's mind fired the first salvo: If Darren died, what would become of Natalie? If she accepted this relationship, accepted that she loved him, how could she continue in his absence? Would she even still be able to fly?

Natalie's heart returned fire. If she didn't accept it, she'd be useless, like a bird with clipped wings. In her heart, she had already accepted her feelings. Her hands were moving unconsciously, reinforcing her heart, though her mind took no note of it. As her mind readied its next round, Natalie's left hand was venturing to the crotch of Darren's pants, and her right was keeping a steady grip on his chest.

What if I died instead? Natalie's mind fired off a new round at her heart. *Would Darren be left broken like I would be?* It was enough to give her heart pause. If she died, and Darren were to end up in a broken state, that wouldn't be fair. She couldn't imagine causing the man she loved so much pain.

Maybe he'd move on, her heart responded, but it was on the back foot now. *If he were able to overcome the loss, that would be better than being broken.*

Though her heart was right, Natalie's mind knew it had won the war. *If Darren moves on, moves on, he'll find someone new. Eventually he'd forget about Natalie Annikki. It's better to end things now, when there will be less pain,* her mind concluded, and her heart went quiet.

Natalie opened her eyes, drawing back from Darren. Her brain became conscious of every feeling again. His firm chest in her right hand, the sensation she felt below her left. She felt his left hand on the back of her head, nestled in her hair, and she felt his right hand on her breast. His movements, like Natalie's, stopped the moment she pulled away. He opened his eyes, perplexed.

"We can't," was all she choked out, returning her hands to her sides.

"What? What do you mean?" Darren's mind raced in circles, his whole body aching in fear.

"It isn't a good idea." Natalie wanted to end things as painlessly as possible, though she knew it to be impossible. "We shouldn't be together like this."

"Why not?" Darren's eyes searched hers for answers but found none. "I don't understand, Nat."

His quiet, shaking voice threatened to undo the war her mind had just won. "It's too risky. If one of us dies—"

"That won't happen." Darren's determination was beginning to find its footing. "We promised to protect each other forever. We'll keep each other alive."

"I'm sorry." Natalie began to lift herself from Darren's lap. His hands, still in position, fell flat to his sides. "It's too much of a risk to place that much faith in a promise." Natalie made for the exit. She knew the longer she spent in the room the greater the chance that she would fall back in his arms.

Darren didn't move. His heart seemed to hardly beat at all. The door clicked closed on three years of wanting.

As Natalie stepped into the hall, she looked toward her room. It wasn't far, and the hall on that side was empty. *It's best no one knows what happened,* she thought, panning her head to her right. That hope, however, was crushed when she made eye contact with Varya Kishpin.

Having just returned from her usual walk to the hangar observation deck and back, Varya was caught off guard by the appearance of the young pilot emerging from Verra's room. It only took a few seconds to see Natalie's messy hair, and undone fly, not to mention the instantly scared and guilty look in her hazel eyes. Varya sighed, shaking her head. Without saying a word, she stepped into her own room.

Natalie was relieved she didn't have to talk to Varya, but she knew Varya knew. Hoping Varya would keep her mouth shut, Natalie ran to her door and silently flew inside before anyone else made an appearance.

Sleep was not easy for either Darren or Natalie. While Natalie continued to debate her decision, Darren was left wondering where he had gone wrong. Everything, everything, had gone right. Then Natalie changed. She was afraid. Too afraid. He knew he couldn't come close to understanding that kind of fear. But he could wait.

Once this war is over, Darren thought, *I'll make sure we make it out, Nat. You won't ever have to feel guilty over dying and leaving me behind.* They had promised each other, three years ago, to protect each other to the very end. That was a promise Darren knew he would never break.

CHAPTER 15

The seven White Tails arrived at the small conference room at nearly the same time. The room was one table surrounded by chairs facing a display that filled the far width-wise wall. Next to the display, and facing the central table, was a small podium. Dark, wooden shelves lined the long sides of the room, filled with framed photographs, trophies, and awards. Above the shelves were old and new flags representing the White Tails, and on the wall next to the door was a large, framed photograph of a long-ago group of pilots, the first to wear the white feather.

Both Jinsu and Trisha carried coffees with them, sitting down in silent submission to the after-effects of last night's party. Claire and Darren sat across from them, but likewise did not speak. Darren seemed to merely stare at the walls in absent thought, and Claire simply smirked at her two friends and their coffee. Kislo was standing at the front of the room next to the display with his own coffee in his hand. This left Varya and Natalie, who sat across from each other farthest from the display. As the last one settled into their chair, Kislo tapped a button on the podium, and the display turned on, lighting up the room even more and causing Jinsu and Trisha to wince.

"Alright, kiddos, the final battle plan has come down to the wing," Kislo said as the display brought up an image of many, many icons distributed across an astro-map. The three-dimensional map showed the formation of the 3rd Mobile Fleet on the left. On the right of the map was Dogor, the New Federation moon of the core world Gystamere. "Both the 1st and 2nd Mobiles are continuing forward toward their objectives at Lera and Crima, respectively. We are expected to begin our attack simultaneously with their efforts. Recent intelligence has shown that the Halerians are still unaware of our final objective, however, each day that the fleet gets closer to Gystamere, the fewer the options there are for us to be aiming for. Still, intel is confident that the New Federation will have little to no readied military presence around the planet or our beachhead objective, Dogor."

"What happens if an enemy fleet arrives before we do?" Claire asked, raising her hand.

"Depends on the size of the fleet," Kislo responded. "If it is clearly too large for us to take on, we may abort the attack. However, you have to keep in mind that our effort here is critical to the simultaneous efforts of the 1st and 2nd Mobiles farther along the border. If we abort, that frees up more ships to fight against our friends."

"Alright, so we're committed then," Trisha said, pulling her cup of coffee from her lips. "What's the plan then, Cap?"

Kislo flashed a thumbs-up before tapping the button to change the display to the next image. The display was now showing a detailed outline of the fleet's numerous fighter squadrons. "The battle begins in five days. Our initial approach on Dogor, under the current premise of extremely limited enemy presence, will be entirely by strike craft. The leading edge will be approximately half of the fleet's fighter squadrons, as each wing will need to retain some of their squadrons for the assault on Dogor itself. The White Tails will be taking the vanguard of this first attack. Behind us will be the bombers to mop up the capital ships before they can meet our fleet head on. Our job is purely to eliminate the enemy's fighter capacity and clear the way for the ordnance."

"What's the estimate of the enemy fighter strength?" Varya asked.

"Much lower than our own."

"So, there's no number?"

Kislo sighed, but still smiled. "No, there's no number. Expect no more than a couple hundred fighters. We'll be fielding ten times that at least, so don't worry."

Varya waved him off. "Not worried, just need a picture in my mind."

Kislo nodded. "We've been vanguard before for similar missions, so I am not worried about any of your capabilities in this battle. But we have to keep in mind that this is the first battle of a *war* against the New Federation. Everyone has to be on the ball every day from here on out. Keep your plane in order, keep yourself in order, and when we sortie, keep your wingman safe. We're a team, and we trust each other with our lives. Dogor is the first step; we don't know how long this campaign will be, or how many fights we'll have. So, let's make sure the White Tails stay in one piece. Any questions?"

Nobody moved. Kislo hit the button to turn off the display.

"I'll send out the formation for our squadron as soon as the wing finalizes the finer details of the plan," Kislo said, walking to the door. "Study it and make sure you know the squadrons that will be around us. Talk through maneuvers with your wingman, and let's make sure everyone in the fleet knows why we're the best there is." He held the door open.

One by one the other White Tails stood up and walked to the door. Each one nodded to their captain as they went by. Once they all left, he shut the door behind them but remained in the room. Kislo sipped his coffee as he stared at every award, every photograph, and everything else on the walls of the White Tails' conference room.

When was the last time the White Tails were in a real war? he wondered. Kislo looked at the images of the former squadron commanders. *Would any of them be able to do a better job? No. This is what I have prepared for my entire career. It doesn't matter what they would do instead. It only matters what I do.*

His eyes rested on one of the most recent framed images. The White Tails were all together, sitting in front of Kislo's Spectre. He held a trophy up. It was the trophy given to the best squadron in the OSC.

Was that already six years ago? he thought. *Myath, has it really been that long? Have you been gone for five years already?*

***

Natalie had been standing in line for almost an hour when she finally reached the front. Immediately upon reading her nametag, the clerk disappeared in search of Natalie's mail. With *Endurance* making port for the first time in ten cycles, there had been a lot of mail left on Tralis for the crew. Now it had finally been sorted, and the notifications had been sent to each recipient. This was routine. Even if it were routine, it meant for a busy day in the ship's mailroom, and a great amount of time spent by each crew member in line for mail from friends and family.

Natalie's mail came in a thick brown envelope, the standard indication that there was more than one letter delivered for her. Once she had it, she began the long trek back to the bow of the carrier where she lived.

The contents of the envelope were spilled onto the kitchen counter. There were three envelopes. The one at the top was from Elle, who still checked in at least once a year. Under her letter, however, were two unmarked envelopes addressed to Natalie. Her hands were almost shaking when she tore open the first one.

It's been years, she thought. *Why? Why now? What do you want from me?*

She spilled the contents onto the counter. Small packets tumbled out, which she picked up curiously. Opening them revealed the small, individual letters that Natalie had once been too familiar with.

She went back to her strategy from three years ago. She lined up each letter, testing each one with another until the words made sense. Then, she proceeded with the second envelope. Opening it revealed more small packets, and within those, more small letters. After nearly an hour, she had her two messages.

FATHER BETRAYED.

THE OMASYE KNOWS WHY.

Natalie turned away from the counter. She stared at her fridge, the sink next to it, and beyond, as though she was peering through the wall and into the hallway outside.

Betrayed? How? By whom? Why does the Omasye know? Did he order it? Was my dad killed by the government? What did he do? Why would they kill him? Why?

Her mind seemingly spiraled out of control. There wasn't a thought that could bring her back to reality.

What was my father involved in? Was he working for the NF?

The worst feeling was that she had no answers. And there was no one that could give them to her. Not if her father was working against the Altherian Empire.

Why keep me alive? Unless... Is it because I didn't know anything? If I asked about it, then they'd know... and then... Natalie shuddered. She had nowhere to turn, but her thoughts were trapped deep inside. What was she supposed to do?

***

Varya glanced up from her meal. Across from her, Claire and Kislo were in a lively conversation with Jinsu and Trisha, who were at Varya's right. On Kislo's left side, Darren was absently eating his steak, listening to the conversation but adding nothing. On Claire's right, Natalie pushed her potatoes through gravy and didn't say a word.

Varya thought back to what she had seen the night before. There was no mistaking why Natalie was coming out of Darren's room that late in the night. But if that had happened last night, then what was going on in front of her?

Did something happen? she wondered. *Could it end that fast? Or had it been going on for much longer? Did they have a fight then?*

When dinner ended, Darren was quick to grab Jinsu before Trisha could, and the pair left ahead of the others. Varya didn't need any more of an indication that something was up. When Natalie stood up to leave, she went with her.

The pair left the cafeteria together without saying a word. Varya checked behind her that the others were still seated. They made it as far as the first hallway out of the cafeteria before either spoke.

"You seem distracted," Varya said after checking behind her again. "Is something wrong?"

"It's nothing," Natalie said. Her voice was quiet, almost a mumble really.

"Is it about Darren?"

There was a long pause. "No."

Varya wanted to sigh but didn't. "Look, you can talk to me about it," she said with maybe more force than she intended. "Believe it or not, I was once—"

"It isn't about him," Natalie interrupted. "I'm serious, so please just drop it."

"Then what is it about?"

"I don't know if I can tell you." Natalie's eyes were cast onto the floor, and she seemed to only be following Varya's motions to navigate the halls.

Varya grabbed Natalie by the arm and pulled her off to the side of the hall. Now Natalie looked up at her. "You can tell me anything. What's going on?"

"It's better if you aren't part of it. It's best if I deal with it on my own."

Varya was about to raise her voice. She wanted to slap the sense back into her friend. But she didn't do either. "I'm not going to tell you what to do," her voice fell to a soft whisper. "But we're friends and teammates. You should be able to come to me with anything. So, until you get this figured out, I'll be here if you need me."

For the first time all evening, Natalie smiled. "Thank you," she said. Her smile, coupled with the way her hazel eyes seemed to shine at Varya, jump-started something Varya hadn't felt in a long time. She wasn't sure what it was, but it felt like a fond memory.

"I'll see you later, okay?" Varya said. "You know where to find me if you want to talk."

Natalie nodded and turned to leave. Varya watched her leave, but then looked down at the floor.

Is it really something other than Darren? Can it? She shook her head. *I have to know first.*

***

The next day, Varya watched both Natalie and Darren closely at every meal. Natalie still seemed to have her head in space, deep in thought about whatever it was that was troubling her. Darren, on the other hand, was entering conversations again, but still carried some hesitation. On more than one occasion, Varya caught him glancing at Natalie as she stared at her food and nothing more.

After each meal, including dinner, Varya walked with Natalie back to their quarters. The pair hardly talked any of the times. When they reached their quarters after dinner, Natalie thanked Varya again, but nothing more was said. Still, Varya felt something positive fill her chest. When evening proper came, she left her room in search of Darren.

He was at the bar with Jinsu when Varya found him. The two were sitting in a red leather booth with a low, round table in the center of the semi-circle booth. They each had a nearly full beer in their hands, and on the table were four empties for each of them. When Varya approached, the two looked up at her with surprise.

"Hey, Wyvern. What're you doin' here?" Jinsu said, his words lightly slipping into each other as he spoke.

"I came to talk to Verra actually," Varya said. "Mind if I borrow him for a second?"

"Why not? I don't own him."

Darren placed his beer on the table and stood up. "What's this about?" he asked. Unlike Jinsu, his words were still crystal clear.

"Just something I need clarification on," Varya said, trying to make a subtle smile.

The two walked away from Jinsu, nearly to the other side of the bar. When Varya stopped, Darren looked expectantly at her.

"I saw Annikki leaving your room the other night," Varya said. The pause she left between sentences was long enough for her to watch Darren's expression change at least three times. "You two haven't said a single word to each other since. What happened?"

Darren sighed. He ran his left hand through his hair and stared out at the rest of the bar. "We thought we were finally ready to get into a relationship." There was a long pause. "But it was pretty clear that she wasn't ready for it. She was scared that one of us would get killed in combat."

Varya felt her throat tighten. She took a couple of deep breaths and looked away from Darren for a moment. "That's a reasonable worry." She faced him again. "So then is that why you two haven't been yourselves?"

Darren let out a short, embarrassed laugh. "I suppose so, for me anyway. But I'm getting over it. Why? Has Natalie been acting strange?"

Varya glanced around them. "She hasn't been talking at all during meals. She just sits there, spaced out and hardly eating. When I asked if it was about you, she said it wasn't, but something is clearly bothering her."

"Any ideas?"

Varya shook her head. "I wanted to confirm if it was about you or not, even though she said it wasn't. If it isn't about you, I have no idea."

Darren turned to face his and Jinsu's booth. "I don't think she's too hung up on what happened, so it has to be something else," he said. "I think it's best if her and I keep our distance for a bit, though, so you might be on your own."

Varya nodded. She lightly tapped Darren's shoulder. "Got it. If you think of anything, let me know."

***

Today, Natalie walked a few paces ahead of Varya. They were on their way back from lunch. In the engineering wing between their quarters and the cafeteria, technicians and officers were clogging the halls. Some of them carried boxes, others pushed or pulled carts of heavy crates. They were all moving with different tasks but one singular purpose in mind: the final preparations for battle. In a little over two days, the entirety of *Endurance's* bombers, transports, and fighter craft would be called upon to take part in the opening moves of a new war. Today and tomorrow, the engineers were the frontline of a war not yet begun. After that, it would be the pilots and the Omasye Ground Council's soldiers that would take their place on a much more lethal frontline.

As Natalie weaved and bobbed her way through the river of people, Varya kept pace right behind her, close enough that she could have reached out to grab Natalie's hand to stop herself from getting lost—or rather, to stop herself from losing the one she was watching over.

A few minutes later, there was a right turn. It was merely another branch in the winding veins of the carrier, but here the crowds of engineers and busy technicians cleared. The pair had reached the pilots' quarters, a small sanctuary from the organized chaos behind them. Just then, as they finally broke free, Natalie stopped.

Varya, alone in her own thoughts, almost bumped into her from behind. When she looked up, she saw Natalie staring at another woman. She was a pilot, a captain, wearing the insignia of one of the Dolphin squadrons on board.

"Captain Damos?" Natalie called to the woman, who came to a stop just in front of her.

The woman shook off her mild surprise. "Yes?"

"Um, I'm not sure that you remember me," Natalie said, "but you were a Dolphin instructor when I went through flight school for the Spectre. I didn't know you were stationed on *Endurance.*"

Damos thought for a moment. "Sorry, we get a lot of candidates. I can't say I remember them all, especially if you were in a different program."

Natalie smiled sheepishly. "That's fine. How long have you been here?"

"I transferred from the school to *Endurance* just a couple of cycles ago when the ship came in for its resupply. It's been a long time since I've deployed."

"You picked a good time to do it, ma'am," Varya said. "It's going to be a long campaign, and who knows how we'll come out. We might need all the pilots we can get."

"Well, the Omasye says we'll be victorious, Lieutenant." Damos smiled. "If we trust in him, we will be successful for sure."

"I'm not worried about that, ma'am," Varya said, letting her tone shift slightly. "The big picture isn't my concern. My concern is what happens to my friends and me."

"I'm sure we'll be just fine," Natalie broke into the growing standoff. "We're the best squadron in the OSC, remember?"

Varya simply gave her a nod and a short, quiet *mm-hmm.*

"She's right," Damos said. "As the best squadron, you are all expected to play a big role in taking victory over the Halerians. As much as we may think of ourselves, we are all part of a larger whole."

Varya turned away. She decided that she would wait for Natalie a few meters down the hall.

Neither of the two women seemed to mind her stepping away. Varya leaned against the wall and watched them from out of earshot. Damos was a decent amount taller than Natalie, probably around six feet. She had to look down at Natalie, who was brightly expressing something. Varya liked the way that Natalie's whole face seemed to light up when she was excited about something. With the height difference between her and Damos, she was almost going up on her toes in excitement.

Probably telling her about the last few years, Varya thought. She wondered if Natalie mentioned her at all. *Why should I care?* She looked away, but not for long. Only a few seconds later, she looked back at Natalie, still alive in excitement, telling stories of their time fighting pirates on the other side of the empire. Varya smiled.

"Nothing on for the rest of the day, right?" Natalie asked when she reached her bedroom door.

Varya stopped at her own just down the hall. "No, we are on rest duty until the big day. I'll see you for dinner then."

She was just swiping her key card when she heard Natalie's voice. "Do you have a few minutes then?"

She knew she snapped her head around faster than she really should have. "Of course, what for?"

"I need to talk to you about something," Natalie said, pushing her door open.

Varya couldn't help but smile. "Oh, of course!" She bounded across the hall. Natalie followed her into the dorm.

Natalie flicked on the lights as the door shut behind them. "You can take your boots off," she said.

Once both had undone and taken off their black flight boots, they walked into the kitchenette next to the dorm's entranceway. Varya looked around the room. It was the first time she had ever seen Natalie's room—or at least since Natalie had lived in it. Around the kitchenette and in the living space were photos of snow-covered mountains. Against the back wall was a bookshelf almost filled to capacity. A quick glance revealed anything from history to geography texts and the occasional novel. The kitchenette itself was neatly organized, and the only thing on the counter was a black coffee maker sitting against the fridge at the edge of the counter. Varya slowly turned inside the room until she faced Natalie.

"What did you want to talk to me about?" Varya asked.

Natalie didn't respond immediately. She seemed to look around the room, searching for something, before she finally rested her eyes back on Varya. "Just wait right here." She took off to her bedroom.

When she came back, she carried some white envelopes and a small notebook. She placed them on the kitchen counter.

"These came in the mail the other day," she said. "One of them is from an old friend back home, but the other two had no return address." She picked up two of the envelopes.

"So, you have no idea where they came from?" Varya asked.

Natalie shook her head. She opened the first envelope and tipped it out onto the counter. A small flood of white squares tumbled out. On closer inspection, Varya saw that each one of them had a letter on it. About a foot from the pile formed by the first envelope, Natalie dumped the second envelope out, which created a similar pile of tiny letters.

"What is this?" Varya asked.

"Messages. The first ones I've received in three years. And most likely from the same source, too." Natalie began organizing the letters into words as Varya watched on.

"This was going on before?"

Natalie nodded. "Back in flight school. I never found out who was sending me these, and they never really made any sense to me. Once I got to *Endurance,* the messages stopped, so I just let it go. But then I got these."

Varya looked down at the messages. Haphazardly lined up on the counter, one above the other, the messages read:

FATHER BETRAYED.

THE OMASYE KNOWS WHY.

She shook her head. "I don't understand. What is this?"

"My father was killed coming back across the border just before I joined the OSC," Natalie explained. "I was always told that it was just some confusion in Gray Space, and nobody really knew who made the decision to destroy his ship. I was told it was an accident."

"What were the other messages? From before?" Varya took two steps closer to Natalie. They were only about a foot apart now.

Natalie turned away and grabbed the notebook from the counter. "One day during flight school, I came back to my room and found that someone had found the messages and had torn them out. But they left the envelopes behind, so I re-wrote the messages." She flipped through the notebook, pausing where a page had clearly been torn out. Then she flipped to the next page. "Here. The two messages were: you are being deceived, and they lied. Back then I had nothing to connect them to. But now… Varya, what should I do?"

Varya stood motionless for longer than she felt she should have. Natalie had never called her by first name before. "Let's take stock of what the four messages might indicate as they are now, all together," she said.

"Okay, well..." Natalie leaned over the messages on the counter. "If the first two messages are linked to the two new ones, then it means that what I was told about my father was a lie. And that he was... betrayed? Was he killed by our own people?"

"We have no way of knowing right now," Varya said. "Have you told anyone about this?"

Natalie shook her head. "No. That officer, though. Maybe I could tell her? She was a Dolphin instructor when I was in flight school. Maybe I could talk to her about it an—"

"No," Varya interrupted, her voice firm. She was staring at the words on the counter. "You shouldn't tell anyone about this."

"Why?" Natalie asked, taking a step back. "I need someone to help me with this. My father... I have to know what happened. I need to know what this all means."

"You are the only one who can know," Varya said, shaking her head. "You shouldn't have even shown me."

"You're my friend though," Natalie said. "I can trust you."

"Can you?" Varya snapped her head to face her. "You don't know who I am. You don't know who I know, who I might talk to. You don't know how loyal to the Omasye I am."

Natalie simply smiled. "If I thought you would report me, I wouldn't be telling you about this. I know I can trust you."

"You can trust me." Varya sighed. She placed one hand on the counter and leaned onto it. "But people could play the long game. I could have been one of those people. Believe me, if someone is really trying to catch you for anti-government thought, they'll present themselves just like me."

"But they have nothing to catch me for," Natalie said, her voice almost pleading. "I haven't done anything wrong. I didn't even know there was anything wrong until these letters started coming."

"That's exactly it," Varya said. "They could be using the letters to lure you into anti-government action, or they could see your possession of these letters as evidence of anti-government thought."

"What should I do then?"

Varya pushed off the counter, walked deeper into the kitchenette, then spun around lightly on her heels to face Natalie. "Don't take it anywhere, and don't tell anyone," she said. "Don't bring it to that officer, or Kislo, or anyone else. Does Verra know?"

There was silence for a moment. Natalie glanced down at her feet as though she were ashamed. "He knows about the first two messages." The words came out quiet. "Back in flight school, and not since. You're the only one that's seen the new messages."

"Let's keep it that way then," Varya said. "Don't tell him about the new messages, and don't bring it up anywhere else."

Natalie walked from the kitchen and into the living space. She let out a long sigh and seemed to study the floor before looking at Varya. "I need to know what's going on, but I can't talk to anybody. What am I supposed to do? Varya, my father was killed for a reason—one that's being kept from me. I have to know why."

She looked like she was going to cry. She moved in half turns, left, then right, as though her mind couldn't decide which way her legs should go. Her shoulders drooped, and her hazel eyes moved from the floor to Varya and back to the floor. Varya could hardly take it. In a few short bounds, she brought herself in front of Natalie and placed her hands on her shoulders.

"We'll find the answers for you," she said. "Both of us. We'll figure something out, and you'll get the answers you're looking for." She was barely a foot away from Natalie. The two stared at each other for a brief moment before Natalie smiled.

"Okay," she said, her voice like a whisper. "Thank you."

Varya let go of her and took a step back. "Now I don't know when we'll be able to really start," she said. "We have to get through the upcoming battle first, and then who knows how much downtime we'll really have. Is that okay?"

Natalie nodded.

"Good." Varya walked back to the messages on the counter. "It's best you hide or destroy these. Make sure nobody other than you and I know about them, got it?"

Natalie nodded again. Varya walked back up to her.

"All good?" she asked.

"Yeah," Natalie said. "I just never expected you to be so willing to help me."

Varya was silent. Her vision was cast to the floor. She stood there for a few seconds in front of Natalie, unable to say anything. Then, she spoke. "I… I want to help you," she said. "I don't know what you think of me, but for awhile I've wanted for us to get to know each other better, to depen—"

A knock at the door cut her off. Natalie scrambled away to shuffle the messages back into their envelopes. Another knock.

"Coming!" she called. Frantically, she took the envelopes and the notebook and tucked them behind her coffee maker. Then she jogged to the door and opened it.

"Hey, Nat!" It was Claire. "I was going to head on down the soccer pitch and see if I could get a game going. Wanna join me?"

Natalie glanced back behind her to where Varya was standing, but Varya hardly took note. She looked back to Claire and shook her head. "Sorry, Claire, but not today. I have some more things I want to go over before we fly out."

"Studious as ever," Claire said, laughing. "Alright, but don't burn yourself out. That brain of yours needs to be fresh for the fight. See you!"

"See you at dinner!" Natalie called after Claire before shutting the door. She turned back to face Varya. "Sorry, what were you saying before?"

Varya shook her head. "It doesn't matter." She walked back to the kitchen and pulled out the third envelope from the pile. She smiled at Natalie. "So, what did your friend send you?"

CHAPTER 16

Natalie "Wildcat" Annikki brought her Spectre into the White Tails formation, in tandem with Varya "Wyvern" Kishpin. They were the far right tandem, with Darren "Phoenix" Verra and Trisha "Valkyrie" Valentine on the far left. Tanner "Archon" Kislo led the center trio, with Claire "RedSky" Riftfell and Jinsu "Swordfish" Hyltide. They were traveling at space cruising speed, the wings of the Spectre folded back for better balance in zero-gravity combat. The White Tails led the way for *Endurance's* fighter wing, with the other squadrons taking up standard combat formations behind and to the left and right of the elite squadron.

Well behind the Spectres of *Endurance* were the Hunter-class bombers, still in orbit of the Tempest-class carrier and waiting for the word that the New Federation's own fighters had been removed from the battlefield. As the Spectres flew toward their target, the radios began to crackle to life with the voice of their squadron leader giving them the final brief.

Kislo's voice filled Natalie's helmet. "Alright, everyone, let's run through this one final time," he began. His introduction was the same for every mission. "We have about six minutes until contact with the New Federation Space Fleet ships above Dogor. Dogor is the first step in the 3rd Mobile's plan to take the planet Gystamere. This moon will be the beachhead, but first we need to clear the way for the boots. The word we've received from the recce's Space Detection Fields says that there's only forty-two hostile ships present, a mix of corvettes, cruisers, and frigates. There's two battleships and four carriers though, so expect enemy birds. Keep tabs on your L-RaDs; we don't know if they launched their birds before us or not. Should be a quick and easy fight. Intel suggests that their HMR Station isn't complete yet. The bombers will follow behind us, so let's give them a good show. The fleet wants to keep our big guns out of the fight today, keep them fresh for later. Birds only, but you've got a lot of friends. Fair hunting, loser buys the drinks tonight."

With that, the White Tails picked up their speed to combat interception levels. Soon, the details of the enemy ships could be made out. They were standing their ground in a tight formation above Dogor. As they grew closer still, Natalie could make out the tiny black shapes of the Halerian Shrike-class fighters, holding close to their ships. She knew it would be a dirty fight, as they always were when you brought the anti-strike craft turrets of the cruisers into the mix. But she also knew it would be a one-sided fight, unless the Halerians had some sort of trick up their sleeve.

Endurance alone could field four hundred fighters, and the 3rd Mobile contained four hundred Tempest-class carriers just like it, not including the larger heavy battleships and leviathans that could output over twice that number. The Halerians had only six ships that could field any fighters, and considering that they were at the dockyards, Natalie suspected they wouldn't be at full strength. As the Spectres pushed into the final committal to the fight, Natalie returned all of her focus to the task at hand.

The radio crackled with Jinsu Hyltide's voice. "There's a flight of ten Shrikes coming to us, right down. They're coming in fast!"

"Break formation and engage!" Kislo gave the command, splitting the three groups of White Tails. Natalie followed Varya as she dove right, spiraling to make it harder for the enemy to pick up an intercept point. Watching her L-RaD, she saw the rest of the White Tails moving in a similar manner but at different approach angles on the enemies. Just before the White Tails reached combat range, the Halerian ships broke up, and the dogfight began.

"I've got a good target lined up on our right, Wyvern." Natalie said, watching a Shrike peeling away from the pair.

"I'll follow you in then, switch!" Natalie reacted immediately to Varya's command, pushing the throttle forward and pulling the nose of her Spectre to the rear of the Shrike, which was trying to use its superior speed to pull away. But Natalie had enough momentum to carry herself into missile range, picking up a lock almost instantly. Quickly tapping the trigger, the missile was ejected out of the fuselage of the craft, and it fired off toward its target. Within seconds, it had found its prey. Natalie had no time to watch, however, as Varya had already picked up a new quarry. Now it was Natalie's turn to watch over Varya.

"Archon, one coming on your left, close!" The radio crackled with the chatter of the other White Tails.

"He's wounded; Phoenix, finish him off!" To Natalie, it was the soundtrack to the battle, as she maneuvered her own Spectre through the chaos, trying to find more prey.

"Wyvern, break off, I've got the lock!" Natalie watched her partner back off from the Shrike, followed swiftly by a missile from Claire's Spectre, somewhere above them.

"Good kill, RedSky, now move, you've got two coming on you!"

"I'm pulling up to engage them, Swordfish."

"Copy, Valkyrie, moving to assist." Above her and Varya, Trisha Valentine and Jinsu Hyltide began an engagement against the Shrikes that had been chasing Claire. Natalie could see it on her L-RaD display, watching the enemy targets dart away, attempting to escape the pair.

"Wildcat, on your right, one's trying to sneak up on you." Varya's voice brought Natalie back to focus.

"Got it, moving to evade." Natalie started her maneuver, banking the Spectre to the left and diving. "Follow me through, Wyvern."

"You know I will." Natalie smiled with Varya's assurance. Varya would loyally wait in ambush as the Shrike followed Natalie into her shallow dive. Coming from high above, Varya picked up a closing speed that the Shrike couldn't outrun, even if it saw her coming. Varya swept passed, a hail of 20mm cannon rounds exiting the fuselage guns and entering the rear quarter of the Shrike. Varya carried enough speed to then soar past Natalie before twisting her craft around and moving toward the rest of the White Tails.

"That was the last one," Kislo said over the radio. "Good kill, Wyvern. Everyone return to formation; I'm checking in with *Endurance* for further orders."

Natalie followed Varya up to the rest of the White Tails, and the group reformed, with Kislo leading them around to face the Halerian ships. As they did this, Natalie glanced at her low-range detection display, the bright blue spherical hologram spinning along with the angle of her craft as it turned to follow the others. Small green markers showed the locations of each of her teammates, with orange markers indicating other friendlies. Natalie was forced to do a double take, however, when she spotted one exceptionally large orange marker nearing the many red markers indicating the enemy capital ships.

"Archon, who's off our nose, heading 315?" she asked, keying her radio. "I thought we were keeping the caps at home."

Kislo responded a few moments later. "Looks like *Trinity* wanted some action. White Tails turn to heading 315 flat; we're moving to support the ol' girl." In formation, the flight rotated toward the Devastator-class warship and pushed their Spectres to intercept speed. They arrived quickly to find the leviathan facing off against all forty-two of the New Federation's ships. Around them, the fighter battle raged on, Spectres and Shrikes dueling in defense of their commanding ships. Though the Halerians were fighting hard, Natalie could see that not many of their fighters remained. While the White Tails dueled the vanguard of the enemy fighters, the rest of the 3rd Mobile's fighters had swept into the formations of the remaining Shrikes and had decimated their forces with sheer numbers. The White Tails weaved through more and more debris as they came closer to the battle, their hulls occasionally shuddering with the impact of smaller pieces of former fighters.

"Make a holding pattern out here, everyone. *Trinity's* got lots of support down there already, so we're gonna play the early defense on the rear. Move to intercept anything you see trying to sneak around her backside."

The White Tails spread out in pairs and then decreased their speed to a low idle. This speed felt like a crawl for the Spectre, but in reality, was still pushing two hundred kilometers per hour. Ahead of them, *Trinity* came into combat with the enemy capital ships. Her hull, twelve kilometers of high-strength composites, contained hundreds of guns, thousands of men, and all the supplies to maintain the floating city. This weapon of destruction now sped into the line of Halerian capital ships, her guns thundering away.

The first volley from *Trinity's* four main fifteen-meter-wide rail guns struck one of the battleships, felling it immediately. The ship, under a quarter of the Devastator-class leviathan's size, was struck in the bridge by one of the rounds and now drifted out of control, away from the battle.

Enemy cannons fired on the great ship, but its front was its most protected area. Rounds from the frigates and cruisers simply smashed themselves to dust on *Trinity's* thick hide or bounced off into the unknown void.

In response, *Trinity* let loose another devastating attack. The missile ports on the top hull of the ship opened, releasing a storm of fifty Alnair missiles. A single well-placed Alnair missile could destroy a frigate, and only a handful were needed to take a cruiser out of the fight. As the Alnairs rose from the ceiling of the leviathan, its flanks opened their own missile ports, releasing hundreds of Hushikis. The small, precise missiles sped off well ahead of the Alnairs, destined for whatever corvettes were on the enemy side. Anti-strike craft corvettes were the bane of the massive Alnairs, but a handful of ASC corvettes could not stop every Hushiki missile, and these missiles were coming to clear the way for the Alnairs.

Explosions lit up the battlefield as corvettes were struck down, followed within seconds by most of the frigates and cruisers in the Halerian contingent. The final battleship found itself with only a few cruisers, plus the four carriers hiding behind the combat ships.

Trinity powered onwards, even after the Halerian ships had escaped the angle of fire from her four main cannons. This was because the side hangar pods of the leviathan housed cannons that matched the battleship's own. As *Trinity* sailed past the remaining combat ships, she tore each and every one asunder with her side cannons. As the last cruiser drifted away, its hull fracturing under ammunition stores detonating, the Altherian fleet launched the last part of its plan of attack. The Hunter-class bombers, which had been waiting patiently behind the battleline, now rushed forward, ahead of *Trinity*, to the undefended carriers. The carriers were destroyed in minutes, the bombers launching their devastating torpedoes into the enemy hulls. Only *Trinity* and the hundreds of Altherian strike craft remained, amongst an expansive field of debris. The White Tails, still guarding *Trinity's* rear, had gone without prey since the first engagement.

"Alright, boys and girls, looks like we are returning home," Kislo said over the radio. "Rather, home is coming for us. The fleet's closing in to start the invasion pronto. We, however, have the night off. Relegated to sector patrols, so no moon hunts for us unfortunately. Also, Phoenix buys the first round tonight, since his kill was an already wounded bird." Darren Verra swore as the squadron turned toward *Endurance*, which was already close.

The rest of the fleet, the massive contingent of three thousand ships, was moving to encompass the moon in its entirety. As the White Tails flew toward home, Natalie Annikki knew that the invasion of Dogor had begun. The White Tails flew under and over the ships, and Natalie could see the Dolphin and Phantom transports, as well as their ground attack and bomber variants, streaming from the hangars. They were laden with troops, trucks, and tanks, ready to conduct ground warfare. Fresh Spectres were flying from the carriers to join up with them, ready to control the airspace above them. It would be many days before most of them would rejoin the fleet, instead being fielded from surface bases. Natalie smiled; the hangars of *Endurance* would be a lot less congested for a while.

***

Natalie lifted herself from her seat, and in an experienced fashion, swung herself onto the ladder and quickly down to the hangar floor. She twisted the ladder switch, causing the little ladder to retract into the fuselage. Turning about her, she saw the rest of the White Tails performing their final checkups and climbing out of their own craft. The hangar was already beginning to look sparse. At least a third of *Endurance's* fighters were heading to the surface, along with whatever Dolphin-class transports they had. Rather than the planes being lined wingtip to wingtip, there was now a comfortable gap between each one. Each one's pilot scurried about, checking for damage caused by enemy fire or debris. The engineers were moving through the deck as well, each plane's team getting to work. Natalie was so busy watching the other pilots that she didn't even hear Varya approach.

"Hey, Annikki," she said, startling Natalie slightly. Natalie turned toward her; she was still in her full flight suit with her helmet on, as there was no oxygen in the hangar. Natalie could see that she was smiling though, and Natalie smiled back. "Let's skip the start of the celebration tonight. I wanted to talk to you for a bit," Varya said, taking a few paces toward Natalie.

"Sure, of course," Natalie replied. "We'll go talk in my place." Varya nodded, and the two quickly set off for the hangar exit.

Natalie tossed her helmet onto the couch in her room and then took a seat after it. Varya followed, but carefully rested her helmet on the coffee table before sitting in the leather chair that matched the couch.

"Good work today," Varya started as soon as she was comfortable. "We don't usually pair up, but it's a lot of fun when we do. I know Riftfell is your usual partner, but I may have to ask Kislo to change that." She smiled mischievously, leaning back in the chair.

"Thanks, we make a pretty good team." Natalie smiled, flicking the end of her hair. "But that isn't what you wanted to talk to me about here, was it?"

Varya shook her head, her smile fading and her face darkening. "I wanted to talk to you about my first wingman, Myath. The one who gave me my callsign."

"Why?" Natalie asked. "I don't want you to open old wounds for nothing."

"It's fine." Her voice was stern. "I want to tell you about him, and it's a story I think you need to hear." Briefly, Natalie saw Varya's eyes light up before she started speaking. "He was amazing, both as a pilot and as a person. From the moment we met in pilot training, we were inseparable. We were top of our class and graduated hand in hand. We became White Tails nine years ago and fell in love at the same time." There was a long pause, and Varya stared at the floor in silence before continuing.

"No one else on any planet in the whole of the galaxy meant more to me than he did. And then one day, five years ago, we were on a mission. *Endurance* was tasked with a battlegroup to test the Dominionist border defenses. We were deep into their territory, thinking that they had no defenses. Turned out they were just leading us in to reduce the chance of escape. One day, we were flying a patrol, just the two of us, and we get jumped by five fighters. It was a long fight; it gets kind of hard to follow an enemy when his friend is up your ass, y'know? But we managed to kill them all. Both our planes were damaged, but his was worse. His engine was cutting out, and his oxygen tank had a leak. But we were going to make it back to *Endurance* and get the hell out of their territory." There was another long pause. Natalie could see the pain on Varya's face as she thought about what happened next.

"Life is cruel sometimes, y'know? You just scrape by, think that everything's going to be okay, and then life pulls the floor out from under you at the last possible second, just when you feel safe. We were making our approach to *Endurance*, which was on the move, getting ready to jump to Altherian space. So, we're approaching the side of the ship, making the adjustments we need to fly into the hangar. But then his engine gives up the ghost on him. And his oxygen supply is down to emergency levels and can't be sent to the maneuvering thrusters. So now he's got no control, and he's flying straight at the side of a wall." Natalie's heart sank; her entire body felt heavy listening to Varya's words. "We had just made it out of the toughest fight of our lives, and then I got to watch the man I loved fly into the side of our home, and I couldn't do anything about it."

Natalie had a hard time finding any words that would help. "I'm so sorry."

"I wanted you to know who I was, and how I became who I am now." Varya's voice was strangely soft. "And I wanted you to know him too. He was born on Jontunia, just like the rest of us. When I met him during training, he said he wanted to be a pilot just like his older brother and then become an even better one than he was."

"He must have accomplished that goal, being a White Tail, right?"

Varya laughed. "That's the thing; his brother was a White Tail as well. The both of them White Tails, the older one in line for a command position, the younger getting caught up in a romance with his squadronmate. They were as different as you could imagine, but they were equals in combat."

Natalie took some time to collect her thoughts before speaking. "His brother was a White Tail? Who was Myath?"

"Myath Kislo, Tanner's younger brother." Varya smiled. "They were total opposites. Tanner was, and still is, always by the book. But Myath wasn't. He flew like you do, wild and unpredictably, and out of the cockpit he was fun and always ready to talk."

Natalie couldn't hide her shock and couldn't find any words for a full minute before speaking. "Thank you for sharing, and I'm truly sorry for both you and Kislo."

"You should know that the relationship between Myath and me is the reason Tanner doesn't approve of in-squadron relationships. It's why he doesn't let Hyltide and Valentine express themselves openly." Varya paused, looking up at Natalie. "When I saw you come out of Verra's room the other night, I felt nostalgic for being your age and sneaking out of Myath's room at night. But then I also felt scared. I know you two called things off. He told me it was because you were worried about one of you dying. But you still love him, don't you?"

Natalie was silent for a few moments. "I'm not really sure." She still couldn't come to a concrete answer. "In a way I guess I do. But like Darren told you, I couldn't do it. I can't take that risk."

"But you said you do love him, one way or another." Natalie nodded. "When Myath died, I was broken. I couldn't function for a long time, long enough that if it weren't for Tanner being his brother, I would've been removed from the White Tails and quite possibly from the OSC entirely. You shouldn't fall in love with someone in this line of work. Don't take the risk of witnessing the death of the most important person to you. I took that risk, and I lost. Hyltide and Valentine are taking that risk every time they fly, and they shouldn't. I don't want to see you taking that risk either."

"I get what you're saying, but I'm just not sure I can do that. Sure, I told him I didn't want to be anything more than friends right now, but I still love him." Natalie paused. "And down the road I'll probably change my mind if he hasn't moved on from me. I can't just make these feelings disappear. This is the best it's going to get."

"I know, and I can't do anything to change your heart. Love is stubborn like that. But I can tell you that the risk is increasing exponentially right now. The New Federation isn't going to sit around doing nothing while we invade an entire planet. They're coming to protect it, and we'll be in a fight bigger than anything any of us have seen. I doubt that every White Tail is getting out of this alive. Love is hard, and stubborn at that, but you need to prepare yourself for the day when you lose the person you care for so much."

Varya's words stuck in Natalie's chest. She knew Varya was right. Gystamere was a core world for the New Federation, and the Halerians would not sit idly by while it was under siege. "Thank you, Varya." Natalie smiled at her friend. "I've experienced loss before, and while I don't think you can ever be fully prepared for it, I think I know how to deal with it better than most. I can't change my heart, so I have faith that Darren will pull through as well. In fact, I have faith that we will all pull through, because I care about everyone else in the squadron, especially you and Claire."

"Don't care for me, please," Varya responded, seemingly detached from her emotions. "I don't want anyone to miss me when I die." With that, she stood up, even as Natalie shook her head. She took her helmet and walked toward the door while speaking. "I don't want you to feel that sort of pain. I know that I don't want to feel it ever again, but more and more recently, I get worried that I'm in the same place I was five years ago." Then as she reached the door, she paused. "Don't die." With that, she stepped outside. Natalie thought she heard Varya whisper *please*, but it was too faint to be certain.

CHAPTER 17

Natalie set her tray atop the metal table next to her flight helmet before taking a seat. She glanced up at the ship clock: 0635, twenty-five minutes until she was due to be in the hangar for her shift on patrol. Plenty of time to enjoy her breakfast.

Endurance's general cafeteria always served good food, in Natalie's opinion. Today's breakfast was a pair of fluffy pancakes, some sausage, and well-seasoned potatoes. A mug of hot coffee steamed next to the plate. Just as Natalie began eating, a second tray noisily clattered onto the table, followed by the forceful placement of a blue flight helmet with white lettering reading "Swordfish" across the side. Looking up, Natalie smiled to Jinsu, who took his seat across from her. The two exchanged pleasantries and began their meal.

"So, Jinsu, what's the news today?" Natalie asked, pushing some potatoes around.

He laughed, trying to cover himself, rather ineffectively. "Why do you always assume I know everything that's going on?"

"Perhaps because you sleep next to the person who gets the news from the top," Natalie responded, pointing her fork at him. "So, let's hear it."

Jinsu sighed. "Well, if you insist." He took a sip of his coffee. "The 1st Mobile was reporting heavy losses and a stagnating frontline. They've requested for another fleet to be sent to relieve them, and soon."

"That's no good," Natalie said quietly. "The 2nd Mobile was already stopped just short of Lera." Jinsu nodded. "If the 1st is forced to turn back like the 2nd, then all eyes will be on us."

Jinsu pointed his fork between picking up his food. "That's not all. Word from Dogor is that the ground forces are facing much heavier and coordinated resistance than expected. The Halerian commander isn't fighting in the open, instead consolidating all of their forces in the bases and built-up areas of the moon. He's creating a war of close quarters, room-to-room fighting across the moon. Our tanks are useless, and our pilots are struggling to make precise air strikes on enemy targets. The fight has slowed to a crawl, and recent estimates say we will be stuck fighting on Dogor for at least a cycle."

"But by then the New Federation will surely be coming to provide aid," Natalie said grimly. "What are we supposed to do?"

"Trisha says the 3rd Mobile should start to back out," Jinsu said, looking down at his plate with disinterest. "If the 1st and 2nd have failed in their objectives, there's no logical reason for the 3rd Mobile to remain this deep in New Federation space. We're painting ourselves the biggest target imaginable right now. It's the 3rd of the 6th cycle now, and we were supposed to be done on the 25th of the 5th. We're six days past our stay. Every day we're here extra with no reinforcements increases the chance that the Halerians will come back to stop us."

"And why isn't the Omasye sending more fleets to reinforce us, or the others? Clearly three fleets are not enough to defeat the New Federation, even if they are the three strongest."

"Altheria reported a large spike in pirate activity on our border with Raider's Corridor, and so they've moved a number of fleets there, as well as the four fleets continually assigned to patrol our border with the Insubel Dominion. There may not be any reinforcements."

"Then we should probably just leave," Natalie said. Jinsu nodded his head in agreement. They sat in motionless silence for a minute before Natalie slowly began eating again. Quietly, as if she were attempting to eat without alerting anyone, she carefully pushed her fork into a soft cube of potato and slowly lifted it to her mouth. Suddenly, a loud alarm began blaring, and the lights switched to a red glow. She nearly jumped out of her seat, dropping her fork in the process. Natalie looked at Jinsu, eyes wide.

"What's going on?" she yelled. Even though she asked, she already knew the answer.

"I suspect the Halerians have returned," Jinsu replied, picking up his helmet and standing up. "We need to get to the hangar immediately." Natalie grabbed her own helmet and stood. The pair ran out of the mess, leaving their breakfast behind.

Jinsu and Natalie made it into the hangar together, forming up with the rest of the White Tails. Kislo was pacing in front of them but halted when the final two arrived.

"Alright, now that everyone's here, let's get this started," he began, his voice serious. "I will make this very, very brief. The New Federation has returned; there are no final reports but the recces, or the recces still alive rather, are reporting numbers and symbols indicating that both *Storm Bringer* and *Juggernaut* are here in full strength."

"What?" Darren exclaimed.

"Two fleets?" Claire looked from Kislo to Trisha. "There's no way…"

"I know this is a huge surprise. *Juggernaut* was tied up with the 1st Mobile until two days ago and arrived just behind *Storm Bringer*. An evacuation of Dogor has been called, but we need to get out there and hold off both fleets until we can get the troops back on board. We're moving out as a squadron, but don't expect to be able to stay together. Just try to maintain radio range and stick with your wingman if you can. Good luck, everyone. I expect to see each and every one of you back on board when the call comes out. Now go!"

In an instant, everyone was sprinting to their planes. Natalie reached hers. As fast as she could, she dropped the ladder, climbed up, threw the canopy back, and tossed herself into the seat. She made quick adjustments while the canopy closed and then began running through the startup sequence. The Spectre rumbled to life, and after checking that she had a clear exit, Natalie took off.

Outside *Endurance*, she was met with pure chaos. All around her, ships were burning, exploding, or breaking apart. Debris of all sizes covered the battlefield. Any standard battlelines had been given up—if they had even existed in the first place. Altherian and Halerian ships battled at point-blank range, and it was common to see ships crashing violently into each other. Strike craft were as common as debris, buzzing about the space, dancing and twisting, each trying to assert dominance over the other. Explosions, missiles, and cannon fire ruled the void.

It was hell incarnate, the messiest of battles, a fight between goliaths. Ten thousand ships and millions of people fought, burned, screamed, and died. And the moment they exited *Endurance*, the White Tails were in the thick of it. Natalie Annikki took a deep breath as the squadron formed up and moved to combat. Today would require all her focus if she was going to come out alive.

Their formation broke apart into their normal pairings, but as more Halerian and Altherian fighters joined the dogfight, even the normal duels were impossible to keep together. The battle was moving too fast, and within minutes, Natalie found herself unable to rejoin with Varya, and she could not stay in a location long enough for Varya to rejoin with her. The battle seemed to swirl around Natalie, who remained focused only on the target in front of her and any threats coming from behind.

Now and then she would see the flash of a white vertical stabilizer pass by, indicating one of her friends in the fight. Much of the time, however, it was simply nameless Spectres and Shrikes, chasing each other, each attempting to become the top bird of prey. Oftentimes, a target of opportunity would be present for only a second before being suddenly destroyed by another Spectre. Conversely, Natalie saw many a Spectre come out of a maneuver just to be viciously attacked by an unseen Shrike. If you were safe from the enemy behind you, there were many others at every angle waiting for the moment to strike.

Natalie keyed the radio, spotting her squadron commander in trouble. "Archon, stay on him, I'm coming in to get the one on your six."

"Roger that, Wildcat, just get on him fast." Kislo dove into a roll to follow the Shrike he was hunting. Natalie followed, positioning herself to dive on the second Shrike. During his roll, he was nearly stationary to Natalie, and a quick burst of her 12.5mm machine guns sent the Shrike spinning out of control before imploding in a small sphere of blue flame. As Natalie peeled away, a burst of machine gun fire came past her nose; a Shrike was moving onto her tail.

Natalie turned sharply to the right, pushing the throttle up. The Shrike would make a wider turn, buying her some time. Natalie moved toward a pair of cruisers who were busy fighting each other at a distance of only a hundred meters. Natalie swept between the Altherian Vanguard-class battlecruiser and the smaller Halerian Stingray-class cruiser, weaving through the narrow space.

Glancing at her L-RaD, she could see that the Shrike was still following. Natalie pulled up, curling over the top of the Vanguard before diving down in between the gaps in its hull. Still the Shrike followed, so Natalie turned back, tracing the left side of the battle cruiser, turning right again across the bow and under its massive cannons and then left, over the top of the Stingray. The Shrike was struggling to maintain its current range, and Natalie was evading any missile lock by putting the cruisers between herself and the Shrike at any opportunity. She knew she couldn't turn back on him. His speed was too great, and he would simply tear away from her before she could complete the turn, setting her back to square one.

Natalie knew she needed to find a friendly ASC corvette. The Hailstorm-class anti-strike craft corvette was fitted with two dozen radar-assisted flak turrets, lining all sides, top and bottom. It was the deadliest capital ship to pilots. As Natalie flew between structures on the Stingray, she scanned the battlefield for any of these corvettes. Every fleet fielded a fair number of them to cover the rest of the fleet, but now Natalie was struggling to find a single one in this chaos. The corvettes were small ships, and with three whole fleets at boarding range, it was easy for them to blend in against larger friendly ships. Looking in the distance was pointless, the ships blending into a canvas of gray and black, peppered in yellow and blue explosions.

A bright explosion brought Natalie's attention back to her immediate surroundings. The Stingray was losing the fight, and the Vanguard was backing away, signaling that the Stingray was soon to meet its end. Natalie quickly dove just moments before the cruiser erupted in several violent explosions. Glancing at the L-RaD, she saw that the Shrike behind her was not as fortunate, disappearing from the display.

Natalie circled back up to see how the Vanguard fared. The explosions had caught the bow of the ship, tearing it to pieces. Three quarters of the ship remained, and whilst still functional, the ship was severely crippled. Natalie suspected it would be forced to evacuate its crew before the compromised hull collapsed.

Natalie soon realized that she had separated herself from the rest of the White Tails. They were no longer displaying on her L-RaD, but she was still within radio range. She slowed to an idling speed, searching around her for any sign of her friends. As she searched, she noticed a dark shadow beginning to overwhelm her ship, blocking out the light of Gystamere's star. She glanced up, only to see the massive figure of one of a Devastator-class leviathan's fifteen-meter-wide cannons. Realizing she was inside what was essentially the maw of the ship, Natalie hit the throttle, pulling herself out to the side of the ship. Slowing, she saw the white letters of the ship's name pass by her, each letter larger than her Spectre. It was the OSC *Trinity*, accelerating slowly, as leviathans do, but carrying decent speed already. The twelve-kilometer-long ship showed signs of battle damage but appeared mostly operational. Deciding to support it in any way she could, Natalie turned to fly along with it. Already, there was a contingent of other Spectres, and they were flying about, fending off attacks from Halerian bombers and fighters. Natalie joined them, keeping tabs on *Trinity* whilst fighting enemy fighters and bombers.

Trinity was steaming toward a group of Halerian frigates, ships less than a tenth of its size. They were wolf-packing, hunting other frigates, as well as cruisers and the occasional lonely battleship. As Natalie flew with *Trinity*, downing several enemy planes, the frigates foolishly turned to make an attempt on the leviathan. *Trinity's* powerful main cannons could put shells through one end of the frigate and out the other, and usually a frigate did not survive more than two shells. The smaller cannons, still many times larger than anything on the frigates, would rip apart any that attempted to flank the leviathan. One frigate, which thought it was very clever for tucking in close to the bottom of the ship, was surprised by two turrets wielding cannons twice the size of its own. None of the frigates escaped, all being turned into lifeless hulks within minutes.

Natalie was in awe. She had never been this close to *Trinity* in action, and it was a seemingly unstoppable war machine. But even now, Natalie could see that the leviathan had sustained heavy damage. Parts of the ship were burning, and other visible wounds of mangled metal and structural damage were visible outside the ship. Inside, Natalie knew, the crew of the floating city was fighting a difficult battle. But still it steamed forward, its many cannons firing away at distant targets.

Suddenly, the great machine began taking heavy flanking fire, and Natalie turned to see multiple New Federation armada battleships approaching from the right. *Trinity* began to rotate, but it had already taken an immense amount of punishment from the armada battleships, as well as earlier engagements prior to Natalie's arrival. Fire streamed from multiple wounds, and it appeared as though some of the thrusters were beginning to shut down.

Behind the enemy armada battleships, Natalie could also see one of the New Federation's own leviathans, slowly rotating to also face *Trinity*. They were putting a stop to the ancient, powerful ship, a ship that had destroyed hundreds of Halerian ships. As round after round entered *Trinity*, it began to accelerate, not slow down. It continued to return fire and crippled or destroyed multiple Halerian ships before it was even close to them. Natalie, as well as many other Spectres, continued to fight alongside it, willing to die in defense of the century-old fortress.

As the range closed, *Trinity* still did not slow down. Having continuously accelerated from the point of contact with the frigates, the massive ship now carried an immense amount of speed, a speed well beyond the safety limits. The armada battleships, with their bows toward the leviathan, could not maneuver away quick enough.

The first armada battleship met the starboard wing hangar, which was the size of a battle cruiser. The hangar bay was cleaved off *Trinity* in a thunderous, violent display and tore into the armada battleship. The two became entangled, and Natalie watched the two, now one entity, begin to spiral out of control. Debris flew in every direction, some hitting and destroying strike craft in the process. The engines of the stricken ship flickered out, now just an uncontrollable, rotating mass in space.

The second armada battleship met an even worse fate. It crashed into the nose of *Trinity*, being impaled on the four massive cannons. Even though they were damaged, Natalie could see them fire, one final time, into the enemy ship. Each massive cannon let lose a crack of thunder, pumping a round each into the smaller ship. The armada battleship was instantly torn asunder, taking *Trinity's* main weapons with it, as well as a portion of the frontal hull armor.

Natalie could hardly bear what she was witnessing as she weaved through the debris moving fast and slow and at every vector. *Trinity's* crew had given up any chance of their own survival, and now only served to do as much damage to the Halerian fleets as they could before their demise. If there was a sign that the battle was over for the Altherians, this was it. They were fighting an enemy that outnumbered them nearly two to one, and Natalie had known from the moment she exited *Endurance* that the Halerians had gotten the best of them at the onset of the fight. It was a tragedy to witness, and she was helpless to stop it. Instead, Natalie was stuck in the thick of the defeat of the 3rd Mobile, fighting for survival.

Trinity steamed onwards, fires raging all over. Only after passing the armada battleships did Natalie understand its true target: the Halerian Lion-class leviathan, facing directly toward *Trinity*, with all its weapons brought to bear. The remaining weapons on *Trinity* continued to fire away, and the many cannons of the Halerian ship returned fire, devastating the stricken vessel. Natalie pursued an enemy Shrike, her engagement taking her momentarily away from *Trinity*. As she made her kill, she turned back toward *Trinity*, which had continued past her. She was now facing the rear and could see the main engines. They were no longer glowing orange, the typical Altherian-built engine color; instead, they were a bright blue, almost white, an indication of engines being overloaded.

This was *Trinity's* final attack, Natalie realized. At close range, the detonation of *Trinity's* engines would obliterate both *Trinity* and the Halerian leviathan. If Natalie stayed as close as she was, she would be caught in it as well. Immediately, Natalie turned and accelerated in the opposite direction of the two leviathans.

For *Trinity*, its final moment had come. Most of its crew had been evacuated, leaving only the personnel required to fire the guns, steer the ship, and run its engines. Each one of them had accepted their fate, knowing that their sacrifice may do something to salvage the situation for their brothers and sisters in the fleet. *Trinity* pushed ahead, ramming its hardened nose against the enemy leviathan with such force that the Halerian leviathan began rolling over. Around the two were many Halerian cruisers, frigates, and battleships, which had joined the fight to aid their leviathan against *Trinity*. Now, they had all been led into a trap from which there would be no escape.

The faithful engineers in *Trinity* performed the final safety overrides, destabilizing both the main engine cores, as well as the MAD drive. As the engines and the MAD drive destabilized, the rear of the ship began glowing a blue that penetrated the void, a blue that attracted the attention of all those on the battlefield. For the capital ships close to *Trinity*, there would be no time for escape. The many strike craft in the area darted away, casting aside their conflict to attempt an escape.

Within a few seconds after the peak of the piercing light, it vanished, and at once the whole of *Trinity* exploded in a violent, blue sphere, expanding in all directions and consuming everything in its path. The Halerian leviathan was the first to be consumed, followed by the many capital ships and strike craft within the immediate area. The sphere dissipated soon after, but the Halerians had lost a great many ships by *Trinity's* sacrifice.

Natalie Annikki escaped the blast, her Spectre's frame being pushed to the limit it could take in terms of speed. Natalie's mind had fallen blank, having just witnessed the sacrifice of her comrades. The battle around her had seemingly come to a halt. Farther off, the battle raged on, but in the relatively small space around *Trinity's* grave, there was an eerie silence. Every surviving strike craft—fighters, bombers, and marine transports alike—had no care for combat; not now. Now, they simply ran, ran to survive, to escape, simply out of fear for some, and for others, simply because their minds wouldn't allow them to do anything else.

Natalie's silence was broken by her Spectre suddenly jerking right under a heavy impact. She saw a bright flash rush past her cockpit and into the void as her flight stick was ripped from her hands. Her Spectre was left spinning off at high speed, Natalie becoming dizzy from the spinning mess of black void, stars, and ships in combat. Gripping the stick and trying to counter the spin, she found no response from her controls. The impact had caused her Spectre's engine to shut down, and she was in an uncontrolled spin.

Focusing solely on the instruments in her cockpit, she slowly recovered from her dizziness. All the internal lighting had been silenced. The only light came from the nearby star, but as Natalie's Spectre spun, her vision flashed from visible light to a blinding darkness. Moving by muscle memory and the brief half-seconds of light, she began to run through the startup sequence. The Spectre grumbled but did not fire. Another try, and it grumbled and whined before falling silent once more. Natalie cursed, running through the sequence again. There was no telling where she would end up if she couldn't get it started, not to mention being a sitting duck for any passing enemy. This time, as she hit the startup switch, she applied some throttle. The engine grumbled once again before settling in a low growl. The stick came back to life, applying a heavy pressure on Natalie's hand, but she was able to straighten out the Spectre. Slowly, she regained control, like an experienced rider bringing an unruly horse back under their reins.

Natalie undid her harness to move around in the cockpit, trying to examine her ship's damage. She could see the striking point, a deep impact into the right side of the fuselage and right wing. Bits of metal hung off the ship, and others were bent back. The Spectre had been opened like a can, but with the violence of an animal. She could feel it in the controls as well. The Spectre couldn't turn nearly as sharply, nor could it roll as well. Natalie slowly brought the Spectre around, facing toward the battle that continued to rage on. She was far out from the fight now, the many ships blurring together with explosions and fire. She began speeding up, trying to make her way back. She knew that she would have to find *Endurance* and land for repairs. As the speed increased, the control difficulty did as well. She would not be able to fight in this state.

Natalie's radio suddenly crackled and filled her helmet with a voice. "Hey, are there any OSC pilots in the area?" a male voice asked, worry filling his words. "My long-range radio is broken, and I need to return to my carrier for repairs. Can anyone help me?" Natalie noticed that the voice was familiar, and soon put the voice to a face.

Keying her radio, she replied quickly. "Swordfish, this is Wildcat, I've got you on short range comms." Glancing down at her L-RaD display, Natalie saw that the impact had permanently put it offline. "I've no radar, what's your position?"

"Thank god you're here, Wildcat. Your range is about a klick and a half. I'm going to come up on your left."

"Roger, Swordfish, please hold position off the left for visual reference." Despite the chaos Natalie had just been in, she found it easy to slip back into standard operating procedures, like a comfortable pair of shoes. Within a handful of minutes, Jinsu was flying off the nose of Natalie's Spectre, exactly where she had asked.

The radio crackled with Kislo's instantly recognizable voice. "All pilots, all pilots. Return to base immediately. I say again, RTB immediately. *Endurance's* beacon is up on your L-RaD; follow that vector home." The radio went silent.

"Swordfish, your long-range radio is down, correct?" Natalie asked soon afterward.

"Affirmative, Wildcat. I see *Endurance's* popped her beacon. Guessing we are to RTB?"

"The order just came down from Archon, but I'll need you to guide me home."

"Roger that, Wildcat, just follow me," Jinsu said calmly before adding, "Don't get too far away; we each only have half a ship." His voice carried a hint of laughter, and Natalie soon found herself more relaxed, having reunited with a friend.

Along their way, Jinsu and Natalie passed hundreds of powerless hulks of former ships and millions of small chunks of debris, floating in the void. As they weaved through, they could see many of the Altherian ships breaking contact and moving away from the battlefield, soon mass-accelerating away. The 3rd Mobile was retreating to friendly territory. Some stayed behind, however, attempting to slow the enemy. Natalie witnessed countless ships tragically fall attempting to hold off two Halerian fleets.

Not long after *Trinity* had fallen, the two pilots reached their home. They made visual contact with the OSC *Endurance* from some distance away, the nearly one-and-a-half-kilometer ship being quite easy to spot in the black void. However, as they neared, Natalie could see visible external wounds on her home. Thick smoke poured from the engine housing, and multiple hull wounds were visible along the top and sides of the ship. *Endurance*, although a rear-line ship, had not escaped the battle.

As the pair of White Tails came closer still, they could make out the shapes of many Dolphin-class transports entering the hangar bays, as well as the occasional Spectre-class fighter. Natalie guided her own damaged fighter into the hangars, which were crowded with far more strike craft than the regular capacity. Many were transports, carrying the squadron signs of other ships.

As Natalie exited the hangar and walked toward the White Tails' locker room, she passed many defeated-looking men and women carrying rifles and wearing camouflage clothing. She began to feel defeated herself as she neared the locker room. The 3rd Mobile had been defeated both on the ground and in space in just over an hour by the combined might and countless ships of the New Federation Space Fleet's strongest fleets, *Juggernaut* and *Storm Bringer*.

CHAPTER 18

The hangar of *Endurance* was, in a word, chaos. Natalie weaved her way through masses of soldiers, engineers, technicians, and other pilots on her way to the exit. Her Spectre was already being rolled back to the elevators to be taken below for repairs. All around her, Dolphins and Hunters, forced to land in the primary Spectre hangar, were being rolled to the elevators as well. Already, moments after the carrier had turned away from Dogor, the entirety of *Endurance's* crew was being mobilized for a possible attack. Natalie had already heard the news before she had touched down: the carrier's MAD Drive was offline, damaged beyond safe usage. The Tempest-class carrier was making for the border on engine power alone.

Natalie stepped around a Dolphin that had just powered down. Its markings told her that it wasn't from her carrier. Likely, it had returned from Dogor like many others only to find that its home ship had been obliterated in the melee over the moon. The soldiers stepping off it didn't even have any equipment, and Natalie could tell that the plane had been filled beyond the number of seats it had. When the ramp had come down, she had glanced inside. The looks on the faces of the soldiers were a variety of emotions, none of them good. At least two soldiers were still seated, their faces in their hands. One soldier being helped off the transport was sobbing.

Natalie made her way to the pilots' mess hall. Here too was overcrowded. Pilots from other carriers flooded the room, which made it difficult to find any place to sit down. The air in the room wasn't any better than she had seen in the hangar. The pilots, just like the soldiers they had carried, weighed the room down in fear and sadness, and more than one showed lasting confusion brought on by the chaos of their return to the fleet.

After a little while, a familiar figure appeared in the mess. She was looking around rather frantically, but Natalie saw her shoulders drop in relief when she finally spotted her friend.

"I've been looking everywhere for you," Varya said as she came to Natalie's table.

"Sorry," Natalie responded, smiling sheepishly. "I had to get out of the hangar. I guess this is where my feet took me."

Varya scooted onto the edge of the booth. Even though Natalie had found a table, she wasn't by herself. She was sharing the booth with seven other pilots, all of whom had come from other carriers that had been destroyed. Now the two White Tails were tightly squeezed together at the end of the seat and in a space only big enough for one person normally. When Varya started speaking, she was only a couple of inches from Natalie.

"I heard your plane was hit, but you're okay," she said, smiling. "I had to find you to make sure."

Natalie couldn't help but laugh. "Well, here I am!" she said. "I think I'm okay at least."

Varya looked at her from head to toe in their tight little space in the booth. Once she was done, she laughed. "I'm not a doctor, but I don't see any holes in you, so you must be fine."

"Thank you, Dr. Kishpin," Natalie joked. "I'm glad to see you're okay too, but I'm not really surprised."

Varya smiled, but her eyes betrayed a hint of worry, which was reinforced by her tone. "Natalie, if you can get hit, then any of us can. I got lucky."

"I got unlucky then," she responded. "It was a piece of debris from *Trinity* that hit me. It was really scary up there, and now…" The fear was beginning to suddenly overtake her. "Varya if we can't jump away—"

Varya gave a reassuring smile. "We're going to be okay." She placed a hand on Natalie's, which were together on her lap. "They say that we can continue accelerating on the main engine. They can't catch up to us. We already had a head start."

"You always know what to say, don't you?" Natalie laughed to her friend. "Thank you."

Varya blushed. "I think I've been getting my optimism from you," she said. "I wasn't like this before you arrived."

This time it was Natalie's turn to blush. "Please, from what you've told me, this was in you the whole time."

Varya shook her head. "You remember what I was like when we first met," she explained. "After Myath, I was such a cold, mean person for so long. You are the one that's been bringing me back to how I was before he died."

Natalie wasn't sure what to say. Something inside her stirred faintly, something familiar, like when she was with Darren. Her vision dropped to Varya's side, to where their flight suits were pushed together like one piece of fabric. When she looked up, Varya's golden eyes were looking back at her, her vision seemingly hovering just above Natalie's own.

"I," Varya paused. "I guess what I'm trying to say is…"

There was a deep, mechanical groan that made its way through every hall and room of *Endurance*. Then the lights went out. In the immediate darkness, Natalie heard Varya's voice cut into a gasp. Her hand gripped Natalie's, her fingers gripping between Natalie's hands. After three full, silent seconds, the lights came back on. People around them were already whispering to each other, asking one another what just happened. When Varya and Natalie looked at each other, they wanted to ask the same questions.

Varya stood up, letting go of Natalie's hand. "Stay here," she said. "I'll go find out what's going on."

At once, Varya was off, leaving Natalie alone in the crowded booth. Only a few minutes later, an announcement came over the ship-wide comms calling for all available Spectre pilots to return to the hangar. Natalie knew Varya wasn't coming back to her anytime soon, and she wasn't going anywhere for awhile. With her Spectre damaged, she had no business returning to the hangar with the others. Instead, she wondered if Jinsu would turn up. He was the only other White Tail with a damaged plane.

In the hangar, Varya sat on a metal stool close to her Spectre. The call to the hangar had told them everything they needed to know. *Endurance's* engine was gone. They weren't accelerating anymore, and they had to be ready to fly at a moment's notice, when the enemy arrived. Inevitably, they did, and now they were only fifteen minutes out. Varya wanted to go back to the hangar. She wanted to let Natalie know what was going on, but more importantly, she wanted to finish telling her what she had been so close to saying.

Instead, she sat in the hangar, quietly watching the argument taking place before her. The three men, engaged in their debate, seemed far removed from the chaotic scene around them. Engineers and pilots ran every which way, some pushing carts of ammunition and others spare parts. Some simply ran with tools in their hands, trying to help in any way they could. As flights were readied, the Spectres began to take off, careful not to hit the multitude of transports crowding the hangar deck. The White Tails should already be out there, but here she was, watching the argument that was holding them all up.

"The only thing wrong with my bird is the radio!"

"We all know that's a lie, Hyltide," Kislo spoke calmly, unfazed by his subordinate's tone. "If you go up there, you're going to die."

"If I stay here, I'll probably die as well," Jinsu spat back. "I'd rather die fighting to protect *Endurance*."

The engineer spoke up. "Sir, your Spectre has at best 60 percent of its former turn rate. You'd be wise to listen to your captain. Your plane is in no flying shape. My crew and I can have it ready to go in a few hours. *Then* you can go fight."

"A few hours is too long. We could have lost—" Jinsu was cut off by Trisha approaching from behind the others.

"Kislo," she said firmly, getting his attention. "The enemy is going to be here in less than fifteen minutes. We don't have time for this."

Kislo sighed. "Hyltide, I advise you to reconsider. With the state your plane is in, you're only bringing danger to yourself." The leader of the White Tails turned away, adjusted his flight helmet for comfort, and walked to his plane.

As Jinsu watched his leader walk away, Trisha tapped on his helmet. "It's your call, but you know he's not often wrong." She left him with that, walking to her own plane.

Jinsu stared at the hangar floor. Suddenly bolting his head upright, Jinsu turned not toward the exit, but toward his fighter. Varya shook her head and slowly stood up. Turning around, she climbed the ladder into her Spectre's cockpit. Settling herself into the cockpit, Varya did up her straps and began the startup sequence. From the corner of her eye, she could see the other White Tails lifting off and exiting the hangar.

Varya took a deep breath, exhaling slowly. She had been ready to believe that Natalie was right, that they had managed to make it through the battle without losing any members. Now, with two enemy fleets bearing down on the lone carrier, Varya was not so sure. It seemed they'd be lucky if any of them made it out alive. The Spectre roared to life as she pushed the startup button. Such thoughts did not matter to Varya now.

Outside, the entirety of *Endurance's* fighter contingent was forming up, ready to fight the enemy that was en route. Varya quickly located the rest of the White Tails and took her place in the formation. Glancing to her right as she slowed to a halt, she frowned at the empty space where Natalie's Spectre was supposed to be. Her attention was turned away by Kislo's voice over the radio.

"Alright, everyone, the fight parameters are pretty straightforward, but this will be the most important battle we've ever fought." His voice was calm and calculated as he gave his team their orders. "We're sticking close to home this time. Make full use of *Endurance's* turrets to help you out as much as possible. It's going to be crowded and hectic, but that shouldn't faze anyone here. We'll switch up the line in Wildcat's absence. Wyvern and Swordfish, you are paired for this fight. Everyone stay close to your pairs, keep each other safe. We have the home field advantage, but they have the numbers. Come home safe everyone. Good luck."

The White Tails quickly took up their new formation, spreading out the pairs from one another. Moving into her new position, Varya adjusted her L-RaD display to show an increased range. Picking a point ahead of her, her Spectre's onboard detector focused more energy on that point, reducing the detection range behind her. In doing this, she could see much farther ahead of her, but the farther she increased the range, the less of her three to nine o'clock she could see. She increased her range until she picked up the mass of red symbols quickly moving toward her. They were only seconds away from *Endurance* now. Varya tapped the reset button on the L-RaD and stared ahead. The wing commander in *Endurance's* bridge had positioned all his fighters on the far side of the carrier from the enemy. This guaranteed that the enemy would move into the range of *Endurance's* defensive turrets, while not sacrificing the Spectre's intercept speed.

As the enemy moved into the battle sphere set out by the tacticians aboard *Endurance*, Kislo, leading the White Tails as the vanguard, throttled up. Every pilot in the squadron, then the rest of the wing, seeing the brightening glow from his exhaust, followed suit. Nearly two hundred Spectres rapidly reached intercept speed, diving on the enemy fighters below, who were now meeting the high explosive rounds of *Endurance's* Aegis Point Defense turrets.

Varya smirked as she fired a missile off at her first target. The Halerian force was already in disarray, its formation breaking up under fire from *Endurance's* turrets. Many Shrikes were wide open for attack as the carrier's fighter wing dove on them. The Spectre swept past the fireball, Varya's eyes already fixed on her next target. Glancing at her L-RaD, she could see that Jinsu was hanging back but still following, watching Varya's back. The White Tails were so in tune with one another that they hardly ever had to say any words to each other in battle. Each pair worked together flawlessly against their foes.

As Varya gave chase to her new target, she could see in her peripheral vision that the area around *Endurance* had already fallen into chaos. Spectres and Shrikes flew at high speeds, dancing around the carrier and the other fighters. Explosions from the defense turrets were everywhere, looking to catch an unsuspecting Halerian pilot. Varya and the Shrike in front of her danced through the chaos, just like the many other pairs in the battle. Soon enough, however, Varya's dancing partner had a misstep. Varya countered, firing a small burst from her cannons into the Shrike. The rounds clipped the left side, sending it into a spiral from which the pilot could never recover. The Shrike smashed into the deck of *Endurance*, bursting into thousands of tiny pieces of fiery metal. Varya soared by, her Spectre unfazed by the tiny bits of metal bouncing off its skin.

***

The Shrikes attacking *Endurance* were beginning to seem endless. Varya and the rest of the Spectre pilots had been flying for forty minutes now, and still there were Shrikes everywhere. Varya had never been out of combat for more than five seconds before engaging in a new duel. As she recovered from her most recent engagement, however, she caught Jinsu's voice over the radio.

"Wyvern, I'm in a tight spot here." His voice was strained. "I'm chasing one, but I've got two latched on my tail."

"Roger that, Swordfish. I'm on my way," Varya replied, glancing at her L-RaD to find her flightmate's position.

Pushing her throttle to maximum, Varya turned her Spectre to intercept Jinsu's pursuers. The group was fighting near the upper structure of the Tempest-class carrier, to the right of the bridge. Varya, coming from the bow of the carrier, could see the duel as it flowed between the many linked building-sized structures that made up the area of the Tempest-class known as the upper structure. Getting closer still, Varya maneuvered herself above the fight before diving down at the perfect moment to catch the rearmost Shrike.

Varya fired a burst as she came into range before coming level behind him. The rounds had flown by and into the armor of *Endurance*, and now the Shrike jinked right, with Varya in pursuit. Taking a glance at the L-RaD, Varya confirmed that the Shrike had broken off from Jinsu. Varya relayed this to her flightmate whilst following the Shrike around the upper structure.

The Halerian pilot was skilled with his plane and knew exactly where to put it so Varya couldn't line up a good shot. Making full use of the maneuvering thrusters on the body of the Shrike, he dove between and around observation towers, heat sinks, and more almost faster than Varya could react. But still she followed, never giving an inch of ground. However, as the seconds turned into minutes, Varya was beginning to get frustrated by the Halerian's antics and denial of a kill. Gritting her teeth, she became even more determined to catch the Shrike, which was slowly moving toward the bridge of *Endurance*.

Varya came to anticipate his moves. After a few more of his dives into gaps in the structure, she was countering, finding half a second here and a quarter of a second there where she could let off a burst of machine gun rounds toward him. The Halerian was good, but Varya Kishpin was better. Still, she wasn't finding the contact she was looking for. No rounds had impacted key parts of the Shrike, which continued flying as if nothing had hit it at all.

A Shrike traced the deck of *Endurance* at top speed, weaving between turrets and observation towers alike. Following close behind was a Spectre, and farther behind, another Shrike. In the Spectre, Jinsu battled his own plane as much as the enemy. In every turn to follow the Shrike around a structure, the Spectre fought against the stick. It took all of Jinsu's energy to turn the plane and to continue the chase. He knew that breaking off meant certain doom. With a Shrike already behind him, the other would simply turn around and line up on him, who would be powerless to maneuver against both Shrikes. Jinsu leaned on the stick as he forced his Spectre through another turn. He could feel the sweat in his flight suit and on his face, dripping from his forehead onto his cheeks and lips. *Wyvern, get here soon.* The thought ran through his mind over and over as he relentlessly pursued his enemy.

The Shrike dove between the upper structure and the bridge, following the sides of *Endurance*, before coming level with its belly to the underside of the Tempest-class carrier. Varya followed, still chasing close behind. The Shrike was flying only a few meters off the hull of *Endurance*, still attempting to lose her by jumping between structures. But she continued to follow, using each opportunity she could get to let off a handful more rounds in the direction of her foe.

The Shrike weaved past a communications structure but was caught off guard by the presence of large cylindrical beams and antennae protruding from the hull of *Endurance*. Having to suddenly change direction, the Shrike lost ground to Varya. The Shrike pushed deeper into the turn, trying to keep her from getting her guns on him. If he flew straight, for even a second, she was now close enough to hit with every round from a burst of machine gun fire.

As the pair rounded another set of structures, an Aegis Point Defense turret caught sight of the Shrike. The firing computers made quick work of the firing solution, and the gunner squeezed his trigger from his station inside the gunnery deck, deep inside the carrier. The 80mm high explosive round flew straight at its target, perfectly placed for a guaranteed hit. The round detonated its warhead just ahead of the Shrike's nose.

The shock, the fire, the alarms, and the noise of her Spectre meeting large pieces of metal hit Varya all at once. The Shrike ahead of her had vanished into a ball of fire, and Varya, flying closely behind at high speed, could do nothing but fly through the exploding Shrike. Larger parts of the fighter hit her Spectre, damaging critical components and setting off a flurry of alarms inside the cockpit.

As Varya raced to switch off the alarms and analyze the damage, she was thankful that the battle was relatively quiet underneath *Endurance*. Some of the maneuvering thrusters had been damaged, but she could still land the plane inside *Endurance* with ease. She double checked her plane's more critical functions and then scanned the L-RaD for Jinsu. She spotted him near the bow of *Endurance,* still racing along the deck in pursuit of an enemy Shrike, with another in tow close behind. Varya turned her Spectre in that direction before picking up speed. She calculated that she would come out from underneath *Endurance* just before reaching his position.

Flying to the left edge of *Endurance*, Varya began an inverted loop, following the contour of the carrier's hull to reach the top side of the deck. The battle up here was far fiercer; however, she could tell that the number of Halerian fighters was dwindling. With a glance, she checked her L-RaD, making sure Jinsu was where she expected. Deciding to take the same approach as before, Varya continued to gain altitude over *Endurance* and Jinsu's pursuer before diving. She had a visual on the three fighters, their colors standing out against the gray deck of *Endurance.* They were weaving between parts of the upper structure but appeared to be turning back toward the more open main deck where they had come from. It would only take a few seconds for her to reach them and be on the back of the tailing Shrike. Varya placed her thumb on the missile fire button in anticipation.

Jinsu leaned on the stick, putting all the weight he could into it. He was following the enemy Shrike through its turn; a sharp 90 degree turn back toward the bow of the Tempest-class carrier. Nearing the exit of the turn, however, there was a metallic shudder, followed by a warning alarm. Scanning the Spectre's onboard telemetry display, Jinsu saw that the right wing was on the verge of failure. The continued use of the directional-assistance thrusters, already damaged from the earlier battle, had finally reached a limit.

He needed to make this kill and get to Varya now or face his own Spectre ripping itself apart. The leading Shrike escaped the upper structure of *Endurance,* soaring low over the open deck space toward the bow. Jinsu followed, attempting to line up a shot, mindful of the other Shrike still behind him. The lead Shrike flew by an observation tower on its right, making a hard turn to the left to weave around it. Jinsu followed, applying as much force as he could to try to cut the turn on the Shrike. As he reached the midway point in the turn, he caught the Shrike. A quick burst of the 25mm cannon rounds easily tore the Shrike apart, sending its debris to smash on the deck of *Endurance.* He smiled, bringing his Spectre out of the turn, ready to combat the Shrike behind him.

As the Spectre rotated back to level, Jinsu heard a loud bang, followed by several alarms. The telemetry display showed red all over the right side of the Spectre. The thrusters had given out and appeared to have damaged a number of components as well. The Spectre shuddered, rocking to the right. Jinsu gripped the stick, attempting to bring the Spectre back into control. There was only a hint of response in the controls. The Shrike behind him came out of its turn.

Varya's heart skipped a beat. Sparks burst from Jinsu's Spectre, and the plane suddenly jerked to the right and started flying straight. She could also see the enemy Shrike adjusting for the turn of events. Her missiles couldn't establish a lock at this range, lost in the flames and hot metal that littered the battlespace. Even with the throttle at maximum, she couldn't catch the Shrike in time. The burst of machine gun fire hit Jinsu's Spectre easily, more sparks bursting from the rear all the way to the front.

The pain hit him for only a split second, then subsided into numbness. Jinsu's right hand, still on the stick, slowly pushed down, sending the Spectre into a shallow dive toward the deck of *Endurance*, only a few meters away. He could feel the warmth of blood running down his upper body, stemming from somewhere in his chest. The Spectre scraped along *Endurance*, initially bouncing off before returning, grinding along its metal surface before coming to a halt.

Jinsu glanced upwards. The Shrike flew by at high speed, and less than a second after, a Spectre followed, its six machine guns and twin cannons all alight in fury. The Shrike didn't make it far before combusting into fiery debris. Jinsu smiled before resting his gaze on another Shrike, this one coming directly toward him. The Shrike's underside missile bay opened up, dumb dropping an armed missile as it flew by.

Varya watched the explosion replace Jinsu Hyltide's Spectre. The Shrike that had carried out the attack had dropped a missile as if it were a bomb, using *Endurance's* generated gravity against the stricken fighter. Now, it turned and scurried away from *Endurance*, in the direction from which it and the other Halerian fighters had attacked.

Suppressing her shock and anger, Varya glanced at her L-RaD. There were less than forty red markers on her display, and all of them were quickly moving away from the Tempest-class carrier, escaping back toward what Varya guessed was their fleet. Varya cursed the Shrike; she wanted to chase him but knew she would never catch him before meeting the rest of the Halerians. All she could do now was return to the hangar bay of *Endurance*, alone and without her wingman.

Trisha waited near the edge of the hangar bay, watching the Spectres come in to land after the battle's close. She had been one of the first to return after the call for all fighters to return to their hangars.

"Four, five," she whispered to herself, counting the Spectres with twin white tails entering the hangar. She continued to wait, even for two minutes after seeing the last Spectre enter the hangar. *Where's the last one?* She had counted herself, and now recounted the White Tails in the hangar. Six planes of seven, including Natalie's damaged Spectre. Trisha felt the realization and grief sweep over her. One of them hadn't made it. Trisha turned away from the hangar, racing toward the White Tails' locker room.

Trisha ran into the airlock, pushing aside a pair of engineers who were on their way out of the hangar. Before the airlock had even pressurized, Trisha's flight helmet was off, and the moment the green light came on, Trisha was out the door, sprinting down the hall. The locker room wasn't far, only a few turns down some corridors away. She had to know who she had lost, which of the people she loved hadn't come home.

Bursting into the small, partitioned locker room, Trisha caught the attention of everyone in the room. She was sweating profusely from the long battle and from her sprint through *Endurance*. Her black hair, usually tightly done up in a bun, had fallen loose and was clinging to her cheeks and neck. She panted as she took stock of the surprised faces.

"Where's Jinsu?" As she said this, she caught Varya glance away to the floor. "Wyvern, where is he?"

Trisha began walking toward Varya, who remained silent. Varya continued to look away.

Trisha was right next to her now. "Varya!" Trisha threw her helmet on the floor. It bounced and rattled loudly, rolling toward the male side of the locker room. Varya wouldn't look at her, but what was visible of her face bared every emotion she was attempting to hold in.

Trisha grew angry, her hands grabbing Varya by the shoulders of her T-shirt. "You dumb lizard, where is Jinsu Hyltide?!" Trisha heard the startled voices of both Kislo and Claire calling to her, but she paid them no mind. "You were supposed to be with him, what happened to him?!" Her voice started to choke, and her vision was blurred by tears. "Please just tell me what happened..." Trisha's voice trailed off as she collapsed to the floor, breaking down into sounds of crying.

Varya still stood, but as she looked down at her friend, she struggled to fight back her tears. "I'm sorry," she choked out. "I wasn't fast enough."

Natalie was in good spirits as she approached the locker room. When she had left the wing command deck, the Halerian numbers had been diminishing, and it looked like everyone had fought off the attack without her. She wasn't sure if she would make it to the locker room before her friends or not, but she wanted to congratulate them once they had all landed.

Natalie was caught off guard when she entered, however, by the sight of Trisha on the floor, with Claire and Kislo crouching next to her. Varya was against one of the lockers, her right arm suspending her head only an inch from the metal locker door, her left holding her helmet. Darren was the only one to meet Natalie's eyes when she entered the room. His own were clouded in grief and shock.

As Natalie stepped forward into the room, he quickly came forward. "Wha—" was all Natalie got out before being smothered in her best friend's arms.

"It's Jinsu," Darren whispered, his voice clearly fighting his own emotions. "He didn't make it back."

But the battle was... It was almost over. The realization hit Natalie like an ocean wave. She wrapped her own arms around Darren, holding him tight. She knew how hard the loss must have hit him. He had lost his friend, his closest confidant, and the only person he spent more time with than he did with Natalie.

After nearly a minute, Darren let go of her. As they separated, Natalie looked up at his face. She wanted to smile at his two days unshaven face and his messy brown hair, remind him of his disregard of standards, but that face was full of grief. She wanted to say something to comfort him, but she couldn't find any words.

She felt lost and hopeless, unable to comfort her best friend. Natalie put her hand on his heart for a moment, hoping that it would convey what words couldn't before she turned her attention to Trisha.

She was silent, crouched on the floor. As Natalie approached, she saw the light reflecting off the tears on the floor. Claire had her arms around Trisha, holding her steady from her left side. Natalie was about to crouch down next to the pair when she made eye contact with Kislo. Silently, he signaled her to the hallway. Natalie nodded, making her way outside the locker room. On her way out, she noticed that Darren had already left.

Kislo soon met Natalie in the hall, just outside the door to the White Tails' locker room. "So, you know what happened," he said, his usual confident tone showing signs of cracks. Natalie nodded. "How are you handling it? Are you okay?"

"I'll be alright," Natalie answered quietly. "I lost my father almost the same way four years ago. Show up to greet nothing. I'm sad; Jinsu was a friend of mine just as he was anyone else's, but I'll be okay."

Kislo nodded. "You're strong, which is good." He glanced back toward the locker room door. "I'm worried for Valentine, though."

"Who isn't?" Natalie asked. "She just lost the love of her life. We know how messed up Varya was after she lost Myath."

Kislo was silent for a moment, running his right hand through his thick, dirty-blond hair. "So, she did tell you." His voice dropped low. "And now it's happened again."

"I'm sorry, I know it was hard on you as well." Natalie shook her head. "It's not something anyone wants to go through."

"If Valentine can't fly," Kislo started suddenly, the confidence and commanding tone immediately returning to his voice. "If we have to go out there again… I want you in her Spectre."

Natalie's eyes widened in shock. "No, I can't, her setup is completely different from mine."

Kislo rested his right hand on Natalie's shoulder. "I can have the engineers bring her Spectre to your set up in under an hour. That's enough time from when we detect the enemy to when they arrive in combat range. I can't go out there with five planes."

"No one is in my seat before I'm dead." Neither had heard the locker room door open, but they heard Trisha's voice as she stepped into the hall. "And I'm pretty sure I'm not dead yet."

"Are you in any mental state to fly right now?" Kislo asked.

"I know two things that matter right now." She took a step toward Kislo. Claire had also entered the hallway and was standing behind Trisha. Her eyes almost reflected the same anger that Trisha's did. "I've got an undamaged plane armed to the teeth, and I know those savage fucks are coming back. I'm going out there when they arrive. You aren't going to stop me."

"And what if I say you can't?" Kislo's voice was stern now as he came closer to his second in command.

"You didn't stop Jinsu, why would you stop me now?" The pair were inches from one another now.

The ship-wide intercom suddenly sounded overhead. "All flight leaders report to command deck Julia. All flight leaders report to command deck Julia."

"They're back," Trisha said, smirking. "You'd better get a move on, *sir*."

Kislo gave away nothing about his mood as he stepped around Trisha and then down the hall. Claire quickly grabbed Trisha's arm, leading her away. As soon as they left, Natalie turned back to the locker room and stepped inside.

As she expected, Varya was still inside, sitting on one of the benches. Her black flight suit was undone to her waist, hanging limply off her hips, and her brown hair, usually in a ponytail, was loose and tangled, reaching to her shoulders and the white of her T-shirt. Varya was staring down at the floor, and an overwhelming silence filled the room.

Carefully, Natalie stepped toward her friend. She was still several steps away when Varya spoke. "I remember when I was the young scrapling in the White Tails nine years ago, so out of place when I got here." It was hard to tell whether she was talking to Natalie or herself. "Myath fit right in, since his brother was the second in command already. I didn't know anyone but him, just like you and Verra. The first of the White Tails I really met was Hyltide. He wasn't the recruiter then, but he was the first one that really talked to me. I remember all he ever wanted to do in his spare time was show me the ropes. He showed me all of *Endurance*, and he taught me combat maneuvers I had never even heard of. He was my first friend besides Myath…" Varya stood up, her helmet in her hand. Natalie could see the tears beginning to stream from Varya's eyes before she turned away and toward the locker. "I was supposed to have his back," she said to seemingly no one other than the locker in front of her. "But instead…" Varya collapsed, dropping her helmet in the process. It clanged and rattled on the floor, and Natalie rushed to her friend, catching her.

Varya turned to face her, for the first time acknowledging Natalie's presence. "Natalie…," she tried to start, clearing her throat. "Why us?" Her fearful eyes searched Natalie's for answers.

Natalie shook her head. "I don't know what you mean."

"Why do they have to target us? Why do the Halerians want to destroy *Endurance* so badly…?" Her voice trailed off again. Her eyes were welling up with tears.

Natalie paused, searching for answers. "I really don't know." After a long wait, she still had nothing. "I wish I did, believe me, but I just don't know."

"We're just one carrier." Varya was crying now, falling into Natalie's arms and against her chest. "Why send so much for one carrier?"

Natalie knew that no answer she could come up with would satisfy the question. Instead, Natalie grabbed Varya by the shoulders, forcing Varya to look up at her. "It doesn't matter." Her voice was firm but soft, finding an answer that would reassure the both of them. "What matters is that we fight harder than ever before. We'll make sure we leave this hell alive, okay?" Varya choked back her tears, nodding. "Good, now stand up with me."

Slowly, Natalie picked Varya off the ground until they were standing in the room together. "Now go get cleaned up. Kislo will be calling us back down here soon for new orders." Varya nodded again, and Natalie handed her her helmet, which was now scratched. Natalie smiled at her friend, a reassurance for herself as much as it was for Varya. Varya forced out a smile, taking the helmet, and quickly left the room.

Natalie sat down on a bench as she watched her friend leave. *If this continues*, she thought, *The White Tails will fall apart before the enemy can kill us.*

CHAPTER 19

Natalie leaned on a metal railing, and from the control deck watched the hundreds of flyable Spectres in *Endurance's* fighter wing take off. With the detection of a second mass of New Federation strike craft approaching, they began streaming out of the hangar. The first Spectres out were those on the immediate deck, with the exits before them. Following them were then the Spectres in the closed hangars. These hangars were the deeper storage that allowed the Tempest-class carrier to hold its six hundred strike craft. As she watched the rest of the White Tails exit the hangar, Natalie gripped the rail tighter. Her chief engineer had told her that she still couldn't fly, not for at least another hour. As the last Spectre flew out of the hangar, Natalie turned away in frustration.

Yet again, she would be the only White Tail not fighting. She only hoped that this time, they would all return home safe. Deciding to see something of her friends' battles, Natalie made the long trek to the opposite end of the 1400-meter-long carrier and up to the bridge of *Endurance*. The Tempest-Class carrier's bridge was divided into multiple decks for ship command, engineering, and strike craft operations. Natalie arrived on the *Endurance* Fighter Wing bridge deck about ten minutes later.

The incoming Halerian battle group had yet to make contact, and Natalie had time to reach the White Tails command post. The EFW bridge deck was covered in desks with large, semi-circular displays, showing information for the squadron the desk was assigned to. Each desk was manned by a lieutenant, who was tasked with logging all important squadron information as well as relaying any wing-wide orders.

In the center of the bridge and on a raised platform was the wing desk, manned by four officers. They were surrounded by a dozen screens, which gave them a 360-degree view of the space around *Endurance*, displaying all friendly and hostile fighters. The entire deck was alive with chatter, and enlisted crewmen passed information between the squadron posts and the wing desk.

Natalie wandered through the bridge, scanning the screens until she found the desk displaying the five currently active Spectres in the squadron. The displays had a list of the Spectres and their diagnostics and conditions as well as the condition of the pilots. On another display was a smaller three-dimensional display of *Endurance*, similar to the display on the center wing command post. This display, however, highlighted the White Tails in white lights, separate from the green of the rest of the wing and red for the enemy planes. The lieutenant at the desk took note of Natalie's presence, offering the stool next to him. Natalie took a seat; she had just under an hour before she would have to return to the hangars, hopefully to find a plane ready to join the fight.

Claire ran through her Spectre's systems one last time as Kislo gave his usual rundown prior to the battle's start. Once again, the lineup was shuffled around. Kislo, Verra, and Kishpin were to run together, while Claire and Trisha paired off. If Natalie became airborne, she would take Varya as her partner. Claire half listened to the orders as she continued to run her checks. She was more concerned about something failing on her Spectre than listening to the same set of battle orders as before. After all, the time they had between flights was not sufficient for the engineers to complete a thorough check on her plane's systems. Combat flying put a lot of stress on every component of the Spectre, and the risk of a failure would only rise after each subsequent flight without proper maintenance.

Satisfied that everything was working well, Claire returned her focus to what was around her. Glancing at her L-RaD, she could see the tip of the incoming enemy group. They were still a few minutes from the engagement zone set by wing command, but their numbers had grown. Claire frowned as she then looked at the orange and green markers representing the *Endurance* Fighter Wing. The mass of fighters had shrunk yet again with their last battle. Even more outnumbered this time, Claire was unsure just how long they could sustain a defense.

As the mass of Halerian planes neared the engagement range of *Endurance's* defense turrets, they suddenly fanned out, turning right and left and running parallel to the carrier, just outside of range. Quickly, hundreds of strike craft began encompassing the drifting carrier.

"Looks like they've cracked our plan," Kislo said over the radio. "If we can breakthrough into *Endurance's* defensive sector, they'll follow us in."

Claire keyed her radio. "We're outnumbered three to one. Why not wait for them to engage *Endurance* first?"

"They already know where we are, and what our plan is," Kislo answered. "If we don't engage now, they'll just increase their numbers until we can't engage."

"Then it's settled," Trisha spoke up, her voice firm. "We attack now at speed or not at all."

Kislo gave his affirmative and increased his speed, leading the remnants of *Endurance's* Fighter Wing into a shallow dive toward the carrier, now completely surrounded by Halerian strike craft. Coming from the starboard side, the wing spread out just enough to reduce the chance of friendly fire, and then opened up their cannons on the Halerian fighters between them and their carrier. The moment the Spectres broke through the shield, the Halerians, in their Shrike fighters and Cobra-class bombers, descended on the stricken carrier, and all hell broke loose yet again.

Keeping tabs on her L-RaD, Claire stayed close to Trisha, some tens of meters behind and off to her left. From here, she could watch for any enemy Shrikes attempting to attack Trisha, while also being in a position to make an attack on an enemy that proved too troublesome for her partner. All other pairings in the White Tails used a more distant strategy, with both planes flying separately and coming to each other's aid when called upon. Claire and Trisha, on the other hand, flew like a single entity; they were so well in tune, even communication between the two was minimal.

The chaos that they now flew in, however, tested the pairing. "The battle over Dogor wasn't even this messy," Claire said to her flying partner between maneuvers. "I'm struggling to visually track anything out here." Planes, Altherian and Halerian, fighter and bomber, flew at high speed in every direction, often coming within meters or less of Claire's Spectre. It took as much effort to track the enemy as it did to avoid every other plane in the battle.

"You're right," Trisha responded. "Dogor was messy for the caps, but it was so big us small fry could spread out. This is just stupid now."

Stupid doesn't even begin to describe it, Claire thought. Hundreds of planes concentrated on one capital ship. Throw *Endurance's* own Aegis Point Defense Systems into the mix, and the risk of friendly fire, ramming, or stray rounds became all too high. Claire wondered if the Halerians were questioning the risk they were taking. *They would be alone in that,* she thought. Not a single Altherian aboard *Endurance* would say no to flying in such a mess if it meant defending their home. Every pilot, even at the cost of their lives, wouldn't hesitate to fly against such terrible odds.

As Trisha picked up a new target, Claire refocused. This Shrike was proving to be a bit of a handful, dodging and weaving around every burst of machine gun fire and missile that Trisha threw its way. The dueling fighters raced along the left side of *Endurance,* toward the bridge of the carrier. Claire pushed her Spectre to a higher speed, tracing the top deck of the Tempest-class carrier, weaving between the small towers and Aegis turrets, which peppered the surface of the carrier. Claire knew she didn't have to say anything to her flying partner; she just had to be in position in time.

Knowing what Claire intended, Trisha shifted her angle of attack to the right of the Shrike, feigning a prediction that the Shrike would turn right when they reached the bridge of *Endurance.* Reacting to this, the Shrike instead turned left, climbing between the bridge and the main hull, arriving above the hull of the carrier and straight into the waiting jaws of Claire's Spectre. Trisha rolled right, looping over the bridge to meet up with her partner.

"Good kill, RedSky," Trisha radioed. "That guy cost me a lot of ammo."

"All thanks to your setup, Valkyrie," Claire responded as she took her formation position some distance behind her. "We'll have to start conserving ammo; it doesn't look like we are running out of enemies any time soon."

"You've got that right. Hell, it feels like there are more of them than when we started an hour ago."

Claire glanced at her L-RaD, frowning. "You might be onto something. It definitely looks that way on my display."

"If that's true, we're going to be in serious trouble soon. We don't have the liberty of landing for a resupply in this shitshow."

Natalie Annikki's attention was suddenly taken from the display by Kislo's voice over the squadron-command radio. "*Endurance,* this is Archon. Can you give us a confirmation on something here?" His voice carried only a hint of audible worry in it, undetectable to anyone who didn't know him well.

The lieutenant next to her was already responding when Natalie looked at him. "This is *Endurance*, go ahead Archon."

"*Endurance*, it feels like there's more Halerians here than when we started this engagement. Can you confirm if more are flying in?"

"Copy, Archon, I will check the displays, wait one." The lieutenant rapidly pressed a few buttons on his controls, switching the multiple displays on his screens to one large display, *Endurance's* full detection field. Natalie's heart sank. *Endurance* was covered in green and red markers, but coming from the left side of the display were hundreds more red markers. Halerian fighters and bombers were streaming in almost endlessly, just to destroy one carrier.

The lieutenant stared at the screen for a few moments. He didn't move a single muscle, not even a finger. He simply stared at the facts in front of him. "Archon, this is *Endurance*," the lieutenant said, his voice wavering slightly. "You are correct. More Halerians are flying in."

"How many more?" Kislo responded.

"Too many to count."

"Roger that, *Endurance*, I guess we'll have to switch to a more conservati—" The sounds of alarms suddenly cut Kislo off. After a few tense moments, he spoke again. "*Endurance*, it looks like I've caught a couple of stray rounds. Doesn't look like any control damage, but my diagnostics aren't giving me any readings on my cooling unit, can you confirm?"

Again, the lieutenant swiftly changed the screens around, bringing up Kislo's detailed Spectre diagnostics. "Archon, confirmed, it looks like the rounds struck your cooling unit. It's completely offline."

"Well, that's a bummer, isn't it?" Kislo responded flatly.

"Archon, you'll have to bring your Spectre in for repairs, I recommend immediately."

"We both know a cooling unit change takes upwards of six hours, in ideal circumstances. We don't have six hours to have a Spectre grounded."

"If you stay out there, you're going to burn up!"

"But if I stay out, there's a chance we'll fight them off." Kislo's voice remained calm and collected, as he always was. "How much time do I have?"

"If you keep running at a combat pace, an hour, maybe two if you're lucky."

"Wing command just broadcasted we are evacuating, confirm?" Kislo asked suddenly.

The lieutenant took a short glance up to someone on the central platform that Natalie couldn't see. He then turned back to the display. "Confirmed, Archon, the Dolphins are loading up all non-essential personnel now."

"Seems like I've still got a job to do then. Archon out." The radio fell silent. Natalie immediately stood up, causing the lieutenant to look up at her.

"Where are you going?" he asked.

"To the hangar," she responded, turning from the desk. "To go save my team."

Kislo sighed, switching his radio back to squadron level. "Alright, everyone, we've got new orders, straight from wing command." He glanced at his L-RaD, making sure that all his Spectres were still in the air. Satisfied, he continued. "They're evacuating *Endurance*. Dolphins full of our people will be flying out of the hangars and making a run for Altherian Empire space. Our job is to protect those planes now. We'll be the first line protecting the Dolphins, operating about a klick away from them. I want a pair per group they send out. Let's not lose a single one. I know we can do this!"

He reformed with Darren and Varya, and the three moved toward the largest hangar on *Endurance* in the center of the ship. Here were most of the transports, and it was also the closest to where any non-essential personnel would be. Without asking, Kislo knew they would begin sending them out from this hangar.

In the short time before the Dolphins began taking off, the squadrons of Spectres assigned to protect them began converging at the central hangar, working quickly to clear as many enemy fighters as they could before the Dolphins took off. The White Tails were no exception, the two flights working separately to down as many Shrikes as they could. As Kislo made another kill set up by his flying partners, he looked at his instruments. *The plane is flying as if nothing happened*, he thought, scanning over the temperature readings. *But the engine core is going to reach critical levels soon.* He sighed. He knew no Altherian ship would find *Endurance* in time. If he didn't land soon, he wouldn't get to evacuate. Kislo sighed again. *Natalie, get out here soon.*

"Ma'am, you're just going to have to wait," the chief engineer said, his voice stern. "Another hour at the most, then your Spectre wi—"

"That's too long!" Natalie shouted, cutting him off. Though he was at least half a foot taller than her, the ferocity in her voice caused him to take a step back. "You have to be able to get me out there sooner!"

"Ma'am, there's nothing more we can do. We're trying to get your plane prepared as quickly as we can."

"There have to be some parts of the plane that aren't mandatory repairs." Natalie's voice eased off but was still serious. "Some pieces that I can fly without or fly even if they aren't completely fixed."

"I'm not sure if there's anything like that available."

Natalie raised her voice again. "Then just make it flyable. I'll fly with a damaged plane, just let me get out there!"

"If you go out there without our repairs, you'll end up just like your friend." It was the chief engineer's turn to raise his voice. "I'm not losing another one because I didn't do my job."

Natalie fell silent, recoiling from the chief's harsh words. She had been acting just like Jinsu, she realized. If he had waited for his repairs, he may still be alive now.

"I'm sorry." Natalie's voice was quiet, and she struggled to maintain eye contact. "How long will it be?"

"Under an hour—just wait here." He patted her shoulder as he pulled his helmet on. He then turned and left, pushing through the door that led back to the hangar.

Natalie stepped slowly toward the glass, overlooking the hangar deck. Gripping the metal rail, she leaned forward, spotting her Spectre in the space below. There were few Spectres left now; only the damaged ones, like hers. Unlike the massive central hangar, however, this hangar was not active with Dolphin transports loading for takeoff. Instead, the Hunter-class bombers were being wheeled from the storage decks and into the main takeoff deck. *Even the bombers are being sent out,* Natalie thought. *How long can they last?*

Just as Claire made another kill, a burst of machine gun rounds flew past her canopy and into the darkness of the expanse. Instinctively, she jerked her flightstick hard left, rolling and turning sharply away from her attacker. Diving closer to *Endurance*, she sought the cover of the protruding structures that made up the area close to the carrier's bridge.

"Valkyrie, I've got one on my tail," Claire said through her radio. "I'll lead them to you."

Trisha responded almost immediately. "Copy that, RedSky, I'll set the trap."

While managing her maneuvers, Claire glanced at her L-RaD to find her flying partner. While Trisha had remained close to the Dolphins they were escorting, Claire had chased down an enemy Shrike that had come for their transports. Unfortunately, Claire was now near the rear of *Endurance*, flying through the narrow cut-outs in the engine housing. Trisha was still with the Dolphins, near the front of the Tempest-class carrier, and moving away from her.

Keeping her Spectre away from the enemy's guns, Claire maneuvered between the many structures that dotted the landscape of the near kilometer-and-a-half long carrier. The Shrike, being far less maneuverable, often had to climb above the structures, using its superior speed to gain lost ground before making a diving attack on her. Aware of this, Claire always made sure to make her maneuver just as the Shrike committed to the attack; her Spectre would swiftly turn away, and the Shrike's machine gun rounds would strike the armor of *Endurance* with no effect. This cat and mouse game continued, racing across the top of *Endurance*.

As the pair cleared the carrier's bridge structures, the number of hardened metal protrusions Claire could use for cover began to decrease. Weaving between Aegis Point Defense Systems and control towers, she soon reached the main hangar of *Endurance*, the massive rectangular opening where the Dolphin transports were lifting off from. With no structures to cover herself from the Shrike's diving attacks, Claire evaded in the only direction she could: down.

The central hangar of the Tempest-class was only fifteen meters deep, but it was enough for Claire to escape the guns of the Shrike behind her, if only for a moment. Slamming the flightstick forward, the Spectre plunged into the hangar bay. Almost in the same moment, Claire pulled back on the stick, fighting the momentum of the fighter from slamming into the hangar floor. Even then, the hangar floor wasn't the only obstacle. Many Dolphins dotted the hangar, and crews and evacuating troops boarding covered the space. It took everything she had to pull out high enough to not kill any of her comrades below. As she cleared the other side of the hangar, she let out an exhausted breath. Checking behind her, Claire saw that the Shrike was absent.

She had only enough time to breathe a sigh of relief before machine gun rounds flew past her canopy again, this time coming perpendicular to her. Making sudden evasive maneuvers and darting away, Claire checked her L-RaD. It was the same Shrike as before, coming at her yet again.

Who is this guy? she thought, bringing her Spectre back down to the deck and weaving between control towers. Making a tight turn through the structures between the two forward hangar bays, Claire caught a glimpse of the Shrike climbing to make another diving pass. The markings on its tail, an orange bird of prey on the gray vertical stabilizer, told her everything she needed to know. She was up against a pilot in the Orange Hawks, the best squadron in the New Federation Space Fleet, residing in the fleet *Juggernaut*, the largest and most powerful fleet in the New Federation.

Realizing that she was up against an equally skilled, if not more skilled, opponent, Claire keyed her radio. "Valkyrie, I hope you're coming in soon; I've got an Orange Hawk on my tail." She didn't even try to hide the urgency in her voice.

"Circling in now; I'll have it in no time," Trisha responded quickly. "Just hang on for a moment longer."

Giving an affirmative, Claire swept around another control tower. Trisha was closing in, and still the Shrike hadn't seemed to have noticed her. *Just a little longer, and she'll have it.*

Trisha came in at high speed, closing rapidly on the Shrike. The Shrike, maneuvering around to stay on Claire's tail, had shed much of its speed; now Trisha could swoop in, making a quick pass on the Shrike and save her best friend.

Three, two, one, now! Trisha counted down to gun range in her head, squeezing the trigger. In the same moment, her rounds began exiting the 12.7 and 20mm barrels on her Spectre; the Shrike suddenly jerked to the right, quickly changing angle and dodging her rounds. Trisha cursed as she flew past, having no choice but to circle around and re-engage.

A second pass, and the pilot easily brushed her attack off again. A third, fourth, still the Orange Hawk wouldn't be caught. Worse still, even as it was shaking these attacks, the Shrike kept its grasp on Claire. As Trisha brought her Spectre around to face her opponent yet again, she heard the beeping of an alarm; looking to the source, she saw her ammunition reserves flashing red. Trisha was out of ammo, with no way to save Claire below.

Claire pushed her throttle to maximum as she cleared the leading observation tower at the very bow of *Endurance*. The Shrike followed her through, and now there was no longer any cover for Claire to put between herself and the Orange Hawk. The only thing she had going for her now was the superior turning ability of the Spectre.

"Trisha, I need you to take this guy now!" she shouted over the radio. Claire checked where her enemy was now after the pair had cleared the carrier. The Shrike's pilot had been smart; they had used the final tower to mask them distancing himself from her. Now, all they had to do was pick the right opportunity to push forward for an attack. From this distance, the Orange Hawk could follow Claire through any maneuver she tried to pull, cutting her turns and meeting her at her exit, making an easy kill. If she kept flying straight, she would be an easy pick for one of the enemy's squadronmates. It only took a few moments for the other pilot to see the outcome. Claire rolled her Spectre and made for a sharp left turn, back toward *Endurance*.

The Shrike was coming in fast from Claire's left, easily cutting the turn. Claire had to time it exactly right to shake them off and buy herself some breathing room. If she missed this next turn, she would be dead. Just as the Shrike closed to gun range, she reversed her throttle, sharply cutting the Spectre right and up. The Shrike came wide, but soon began closing on Claire again. She had bought herself a few seconds, hoping that it would be enough for Trisha to have repositioned and come in to make the kill. But Trisha was nowhere near the position she needed to be in.

"Trisha, what are you doing!?" Claire shouted at her friend. "They're coming back behind me!" There was silence over the radio for a few seconds, long enough that Claire reached for the button again.

Just before she could press it, Trisha responded. "I've got you."

Confused by this short statement, Claire almost didn't see the other Spectre coming straight toward her. Quickly jerking the stick, her Spectre barely jumped out of the way in time. As she did, Claire caught the white of the other Spectre's massive vertical stabilizers. A White Tail, traveling at maximum speed. Claire looked around, trying to spot the plane, but it was gone. Looking down at her L-RaD, Claire no longer saw Trisha Valentine's marker. Looking closer, she couldn't see the Orange Hawk's marker either. Swiftly circling back around, Claire saw the dissipation of a fire, and the expanding field of tiny bits of aircraft. As the realization began to set in, Claire ripped out the clips on her flight helmet and threw up in her cockpit.

CHAPTER 20

Natalie's black and crimson striped helmet lay at her feet as she gazed out over the hangar bay. Next to it was a small green bag, barely the same size as the helmet. Her hazel eyes were fixed on the engineers who were busily loading her Spectre, the last Spectre in the hangar, with machine gun rounds and missiles. The engineers began mounting additional pylons for missiles as well as pods for extra ammunition. The door to her left opened, and the chief engineer stepped into the observation room.

"You've given me well over the standards for ordnance, Chief," Natalie said, turning to face him. "What's your plan?"

The chief was stone-faced, his voice just as emotionless. "We're closing shop after you leave, ma'am. Orders have come down that it's time for the engineers to evacuate. So, we've given your Spectre four extra Challenger missiles, putting you at ten, and with the extra two pods mounted on your fuselage, you'll have about 100 extra 20mm and 400 extra .50 cal rounds to send to the Halerians. We're giving you as much as we can since you're the last one we'll service on *Endurance*. You'll be ready to go in about fifteen minutes."

Natalie smiled then immediately frowned at the desperation in the situation. "Thank you, Chief. When we make it back to Jontunia, I owe you and your crew a drink." Glancing back down into the hangar, Natalie saw the other engineers beginning to finish up their work on the Spectre. "I guess it's time for me to leave too. Kiss the old girl goodbye for me, Chief." Natalie picked up her flight helmet and the little bag, smiled at her chief engineer one last time, and exited the observation deck.

From the cockpit of his Spectre, Darren watched the flight of four Dolphins as they escaped into the dark expanse, heading toward Altherian space.

"That's another four gone," Darren said over the radio. "Archon, have you picked up our next flight?"

It took only a moment before the squadron leader responded. "The next flight is still prepping for take-off. We have time to fly back to *Endurance* before they are out." The pair of White Tails were over fifty kilometers from the ailing carrier, far removed from the intense battle for survival taking place around the ship.

For a brief minute, there was silence between the two Spectre-class fighters as they flew at speed toward their carrier. Whatever thoughts that were in Darren's mind at that time were, however, quickly dispersed as Kislo's voice re-entered his helmet. "Phoenix, there's something we need to talk about before we get back to *Endurance*."

Darren was a little confused by his superior's tone of voice as he keyed his radio. "Is now the time?"

"It's as good a time as any." Darren noticed that Kislo's tone was suddenly much less formal.

"Alright, Archon, go ahead."

Kislo let out a sigh before he began. "A while ago, my plane was hit by a Shrike." A slight pause. "The only thing that was damaged was the cooling unit, which went completely offline. I've been flying despite it for the last two hours. Unfortunately, my time's almost up." Another pause. "Soon, the core of the engine is going to overload, and my Spectre will combust. There's nothing that can be done."

Darren's head dropped, and he looked down at the bottom of his cockpit, shaking his head. When he lifted it up, he looked straight up through the canopy at the distant stars and spoke. "You just have to make it back to *Endurance*, right? Then you can get on a Dolphin with the crew."

"We're too far out. Even if I made it as far as *Endurance*, lining up to land would take too long, not to mention the risk of the plane going up inside of the hangar bay." Kislo paused, and when his voice came back, so did his usual commanding voice. "This isn't about my survival, that's a fate already decided. This is about the survival of the White Tails."

Darren understood. If Kislo thought there was any chance for him to survive, they'd be working on that. "You have my attention, sir." It was difficult to accept that his superior, his mentor, would be gone soon, but Darren had to put aside those thoughts and emotions for now.

"I've thought about this for a while now," Kislo said. "In fact, I first started thinking about it a year ago. You're going to be the next commander of the White Tails."

Darren waited a long moment before responding. "Are you sure? Why not a better pilot, like Annikki or Kishpin?"

"It's not about flying skill. You're skilled enough if you made it into this squadron. I've seen it in you, the same ability to lead that my predecessor saw in me. You're able to keep a level head and see clearly through even the most troubled of situations. Like I said, for a year now, I've been thinking that you'd be a good commander. If not after me, then after Valentine, but we know what happened an hour ago. In a few minutes, we'll both be gone, so you're going to have to take up the reins."

It was another long moment before Darren spoke. "Okay," was all he said at first. "I understand and deeply appreciate your faith in me. I won't let you down, sir."

"Good, now let's get this done." Kislo's voice had returned to normal. "By the light of the Omasye, granted to me as an officer in the Omasye Space Council, I, Captain Tanner Kislo, hereby grant Lieutenant Darren Verra the rank of captain and assign him as the squadron commander of the White Tails, the 3rd Mobile's most decorated fighter squadron. By the Omasye's guidance, I know that he will lead the White Tails to many victories, and as captain, further the Omasye's influence, bringing more under his unifying light."

"I accept this responsibility and will do all that is in my power to further your, and the Omasye's vision of me and the White Tails."

"I know you will." The impromptu promotion ceremony was over. "I've seen a lot in you that reminds me of myself at your age. And I've seen things in you that I could only dream of possessing. I know the White Tails are low in number now, but you've got three great pilots to support you when you rebuild. Not to mention that Kishpin and Annikki are the two best pilots to ever serve in the White Tails."

"Thank you for the kind words, sir. Together we'll rebuild the White Tails to full strength."

"You have the command of the White Tails now, so I'll leave you to it." Darren knew the end was nearing as Kislo paused again. "My last order is for you to make your way to the Spectre hangars; Annikki is about to lift off, and she's going to need a wingman."

"I'm on it." Darren paused as he saw Kislo's fighter beginning to take a different course. "Good luck, sir, and thank you, for everything."

Kislo looked at his instruments. The flashing warning lights steadily increased their frequency, giving him a timer for his own death. Instead of focusing on this grim reminder, he flew along as he always did, scanning his L-RaD for a new target. He had finally made it back to *Endurance* and was approaching it from behind. He grimaced slightly as he looked at the main engine's exhaust port, which usually glowed a dim orange but was now simply dark, a tunnel of blackness ever since the engine had shut off. Scars of the Halerian bomber attacks littered *Endurance.* While they had been able to protect every transport thus far, the fighter pilots of the doomed carrier had been unable to keep the hundreds of attacking bombers at bay.

As Kislo neared the rear of the bridge structure, he saw one of these bombers moving to make an attack on the armored joint between the bridge and the rest of the carrier. Banking to the left, Kislo began to sweep in line behind the bomber. The red flashing glow of the warning lights provided the only lighting inside his cockpit as his fingers moved on muscle memory, arming the final two missiles inside the Spectre's internal bay. The onboard computer quickly scanned ahead, searching for a path through the millions of bits of metal that littered the space. As the locking tone became solid and the firing computer confirmed a good path, Kislo flicked the small red fire button on the top of his flightstick. He felt the missiles as they were discharged from underneath the fighter, then watched as they streaked off toward the bomber, which was still committing to its attack. Kislo knew that the Challenger missiles would reach the bomber before it could launch its own payload, and he began to pull up above *Endurance.*

As the bomber's signal on Kislo's L-RaD disappeared, confirming his kill, he suddenly became aware of the silence of space. The locking tone had faded, and as he throttled back on his engine, his cockpit filled with silence. Inside, the red warning light continued its slow, bright flashing. Outside, silent explosions surrounded *Endurance* as her fighter pilots continued their desperate fight. Kislo smiled, though, knowing that the remaining pilots of the White Tails would get all the transports to safety together, and they would rebuild his fighter squadron. He still smiled even as he felt the cooling unit begin to combust and consume the Spectre, which shared the name *Archon* with its pilot. Tanner Kislo leaned his head back into the seat and awaited the inevitable.

Though she had seen it from the observation deck, the hangar felt even more empty once Natalie began walking across it. Almost every fighter and bomber were gone already. Near the center of the hangar, however, was a particular white-tailed Spectre sitting on its haunches, heavily laden with missiles and waiting to enter the battle. As Natalie approached, it seemed to her that her Spectre wanted to get in the air just as much as she did. Readjusting her flight helmet for comfort, she checked its seal with her suit out of habit, though she knew everything was well sealed. Satisfied with its fit, Natalie walked up to the left side of the Spectre, twisting the handle to release the ladder. As it deployed, she made a satisfied smirk at the extra four missiles mounted on the wings, as well as the two ammunition pods just behind the internal missile bays. Natalie climbed into the cockpit and into the familiar seat.

Without thinking, Natalie moved her hands about the cockpit, flipping switches and pushing buttons to prepare the Spectre for takeoff. Once the plane was ready, she reached behind herself, grabbing a small air tube and connecting it to the back of her helmet. She heard the quiet hiss of the two sealing together, and at once the plane began feeding air into her suit. She flicked a switch inside, simultaneously retracting the ladder and sliding the canopy closed around her. Only a second later, she heard the low hiss of the cockpit filling with air. The moment the small green light came on, signaling that the cockpit had pressurized, Natalie flipped the final two switches to prime the engine of her Spectre. Then she moved her right hand to a round, red-outlined button, and pressed it.

The Spectre immediately rumbled to life, sending vibrations throughout the plane. As the engine settled into a low growl, Natalie gave the plane a moment to warm up before putting it through what she knew would be the fight of its life. She reached behind and fastened the bag she had with her to the back of the seat, to stop it from bouncing around the cockpit in battle. Satisfied that everything was ready to go, she switched the plane to vertical takeoff mode and began to throttle up. Within moments, Natalie could feel the weightless sensation of the Spectre's reinforced rubber wheels releasing from the hangar floor as the aircraft began to rise toward the hangar exit. Pushing farther on the throttle, the Spectre began to climb more rapidly, and Natalie exited the hangar at high speed to throw off any waiting enemies.

From within the Tempest-class carrier, Natalie had been unable to see with her own eyes the chaos unfolding around *Endurance*. The displays on the wing command deck only told so much of the dogfight happening all around between hundreds of fighters and bombers. The moment she exited the hangar bay, however, her senses were alive to the true nature of the battle over the OSC *Endurance*. As her Spectre rose out of the hangar, another one streaked by overhead with a hail of machine gun fire trailing behind it. In a moment that lasted only a few seconds, the machine gun fire caught the leading Spectre, sending it spiraling into *Endurance's* deck.

As the chasing Shrike flew over the hangar, Natalie instinctively ripped back on the stick and jerked her Spectre upwards. Her machine guns traced the bottom side of the Shrike, which caught fire and exploded just after passing the hangar opening. Natalie now disengaged the VTOL mode and slammed the throttle forward. Immediately, the Spectre climbed high above *Endurance*, and Natalie leveled out over the battlefield. Below her, a fight the likes of which she had never seen raged on. She couldn't believe that it had been this way for the past three hours straight.

The battle over Dogor had been a chaotic mess of capital ships fighting at point-blank range, caused by the dangerous entry of the New Federation fleets *Juggernaut* and *Storm Bringer*. They had mass-accelerated not to orbital-entry range like the 3rd Mobile had done when making its initial attack, but directly to orbital range and on top of the Altherian fleet. During that battle, the strike craft of both fleets were almost nulled by the close proximity of the battling capital ships. Here, however, there was only one capital ship, and with each passing moment, that ship was becoming less and less of a factor in the battle. Around that ship were, by a quick scan of her L-RaD, around eight hundred strike craft, and to Natalie's despair, less than a third were friendly. Those eight hundred strike craft created a whirlwind of furious and brutal fighting, as Altherian pilots fought twice their number just for a chance at survival, and Halerian pilots fought to overwhelm and brutally crush every Altherian they saw. In such an open space, no pilot was safe from any angle, and they were just as likely to be hit by stray rounds as they were by an attacking enemy.

Natalie watched for only a few seconds before picking an opportunity to dive toward an enemy bomber flying near the hangar bays. Rolling her Spectre, she dove toward the carrier deck and the unsuspecting bomber. The Cobra-class bomber was heading directly for the central hangar, where Dolphin transports were evacuating crew members. Natalie knew that if the bomber reached its target, many transports and, more importantly, many defenseless Altherians would be consumed by the payload of the bomber. As her fingers ran through the arming sequence for her Challenger missiles, she began to focus solely on the bomber. It was flying approximately 30 meters above the hull of *Endurance* and was flying mostly straight, with some weaving every now and then to avoid debris.

Natalie throttled back slightly and adjusted course to maintain a decent height advantage about 150 meters behind the bomber. As she listened for the tone of the missile lock, every fiber of Natalie's being focused on the bomber and that tone. The battle around her, in all its chaos, seemed to drain away until there was only her own Spectre, the Cobra in front, and *Endurance*, the home she had to protect from these malicious attackers.

It was a split second between the lock being established and Natalie firing the first missile of her defense of *Endurance*. The moment the missile streaked away from Natalie's *Wildcat,* her focus was ripped away by the flashes of machine gun rounds passing by her canopy. Cursing herself for making herself such an easy target, she quickly throttled up to maximum and dove toward *Endurance's* surface. She could see the marker of an enemy Shrike behind her as she flew past the wreckage of the Cobra on her way to just a few meters off the hard metal surface of the Tempest-class carrier.

The Shrike, following in behind, picked up speed to match, firing off another burst, which glanced off *Endurance* after narrowly missing Natalie's weaving Spectre. Natalie cut her Spectre hard to the right, hoping to use the superior turning of her plane and her unpredictable flying style to increase the distance between herself and the Shrike behind. As another burst flew past, she cut left, then quickly right, up, left, right, and back down in quick maneuvers designed to maximize the turning ability of the Spectre when against a Shrike. It was a set of turns linked together and perfected over three years of practice, now executed in a matter of life and death. While it increased the distance between her and the Shrike, it did not shake it. Natalie had another maneuver, designed specifically to use when close to *Endurance* or another Tempest. Regaining her speed, she banked hard right toward the bridge of the carrier and passed underneath with the bottom of her fuselage facing the bottom of the bridge. From aboard *Endurance*, it would have appeared that Natalie was flying upside down, but in space this was merely a reversal of perspective.

Now underneath the bridge, Natalie waited for the moment she passed into clear space again before pitching her nose down and sending the Spectre climbing up the side of *Endurance's* bridge. Again, as she reached the next corner of the bridge's exterior, she pitched down to continue tracing it. The Shrike was still following according to her L-RaD, which was part of the maneuver.

As she reached the edge of the bridge's topside, she pitched down again, but the moment she was out of sight, she cut hard right, angling herself to return to the top of *Endurance* again. If everything went according to plan, the Shrike would have dove to follow Natalie but then lost her when they reached the bottom side and realized she was no longer there. But the Shrike wasn't so easily fooled. Its pilot had taken much wider turns around the bridge of the carrier, meaning they were still higher above the top of the bridge when Natalie re-emerged. From her L-RaD, it had appeared that they had flown to the underside, but they were in fact still above.

Natalie became suddenly aware of this when she heard a loud, beeping missile lock tone indicating that an enemy lock was being established on her Spectre. Ripping her flightstick back, she activated the underside vertical thruster controls. By adjusting which of the four thrusters received the most power, she was able to flip her Spectre backward and quickly spiral away from her opponent. As she cleared *Endurance's* bridge, she straightened out to prepare to fly at high speed along the hull of the carrier. While her maneuver had broken the impending lock, it had caused her to shed almost all of her speed. Her opponent had been able to quickly follow and was now finding her slow-moving Spectre, an easy kill for his machine guns. Just before he could fire, however, his Shrike was suddenly ripped apart by cannon rounds. Natalie watched as his fireball dissipated, leaving only millions of tiny pieces of metal behind.

"That was a close one there, Wildcat." Relief washed over her as she heard the voice of her best friend over the radio.

"Thanks, Phoenix. I don't know why I couldn't shake him. Who the hell was that guy?"

"An Orange Hawk, same as the one that got Valkyrie." Natalie was silent in her shock. She hadn't even checked her display to see how many White Tails were flying. When she did, her heart sank; there were only four, including her. Sensing what Natalie was doing, Darren keyed his radio again. "Archon is gone as well; he's left me in command of the squadron."

Natalie felt anger, frustration, and sadness building up inside her all at once. She suddenly wanted to get her hands on as many Halerians as she could. She was thankful she was given the extra ammunition and missiles. Shaking her head, she brought her mind back into focus. She could catch and kill as many as she wanted, but she had to do it with a clear head. A blind rage would get her killed instead.

"What's the plan then, Captain?"

Verra shook off the goosebumps of being addressed as his new rank. "We're going to meet up with Wyvern and RedSky." His voice was reinforced by his new duty. "I've got wing command to put us on guard duty over the hangar entrance. We'll be keeping it clear for the Dolphins loading up and taking off. The rest of the wing is guiding them down the line and out to safety."

Natalie gave her affirmative as she pushed her throttle forward, accelerating to follow behind Darren's Spectre. The pair moved across *Endurance*, approaching the hangar bays from the carrier's bridge. It was only moments before the pair reached Varya and Claire, who were flying together over the central bay. With the arrival of their new commander and Natalie, they regrouped and formed up behind Darren's Spectre.

"Alright, everyone." Darren tried his best to apply confidence to his voice. "Here's how it's gonna work: We won't be breaking into two teams. Instead, the four of us are going to work as one unit. Each Dolphin that lifts off from that hangar deck needs to be secured until it can be passed on to the rest of the wing. So, keep one eye on your L-RaD and the other on your sights so we can stop any Halerian from coming within half a klick of our transports. Back each other up, and if you get yourself in trouble, call out and fly to your nearest friend. Let's all get through this together."

Darren didn't need a response to know the others would follow. Instead, he picked up his throttle and moved to engage the closest threat. The other three followed close behind before dispersing to cover the entirety of the hangar bay, as well as an extra two hundred meters on each side. If any enemy were to approach, the closest White Tail would swiftly move to engage and down the enemy before they could reach the Dolphin transports taking off.

Varya watched as the Shrike she had been chasing accelerated away from her, and away from *Endurance*. With it out of the immediate area around the hangar, she turned her sights on a new target.

Before she could engage, however, Varya heard Claire shout over the radio: "Wyvern, break right!" Instinctively reacting to Claire's command, Varya snapped her stick to the right. A hail of machine gun rounds, followed by a Shrike then a white-tailed Spectre, flashed past her. Punching the throttle, she followed behind the dueling pair, waiting for an opening.

Claire smoothly controlled her flightstick to keep pace behind her target. She had already noticed that Varya was behind them and watching for a good chance. As the Shrike flew along the top of *Endurance*, Claire fired a burst off the right side. While she knew it would not hit him, she placed her rounds to force him to go left around the upcoming Aegis turret, currently burning and disabled. The moment the Shrike darted to the left, he moved straight into Varya's path, and without the pair ever speaking, the two White Tails destroyed another enemy fighter.

No sooner had the Shrike been destroyed than Natalie flew past perpendicular to Claire, a Cobra-class bomber ahead and two Shrikes in tow. Claire immediately maneuvered to follow and, without taking so much as a glance at her L-RaD, knew that Varya was following as well.

Natalie weaved her Spectre, dodging machine gun bursts while attempting to establish a solid lock on the enemy bomber. Hearing the solid tone, she flicked the missile trigger. As the missile streaked off in search of its prey, Natalie ripped back on her flightstick, looping her Spectre backward and over the two enemy Shrikes.

That's two missiles, Natalie registered in her mind as she searched the top of the carrier below for the enemy planes. *I'll need to use my guns more to make them last.*

However, she found that she hadn't need for any weapons for the two that were chasing her. So quick to try to react to Natalie, neither pilot noticed the two Spectres coming behind them. From farther back, both Varya and Claire had time to follow the Shrikes up as they tried to loop like Natalie. As she spotted them, she saw the missiles slam into the center of each Shrike, and each in turn combusted in a bright explosion.

Rolling level, Natalie scanned her L-RaD for a new target. She saw Darren's icon in the midst of four enemy bombers. Though they posed little threat to him, Natalie knew Darren would have trouble downing all four before they reached the hangar. Natalie took a route at altitude, adjusting her vector to approach the bombers from the side and above.

Darren watched briefly as the Cobra descended in flames before impacting the deck of the carrier below. Its payload detonated, and Darren grimaced. Though it was clear of the hangar bay they were protecting, he knew that *Endurance* couldn't take much more structural damage. As he adjusted his sights to the next Cobra, Darren reminded himself to make sure this one exploded *before* hitting the carrier.

The bombers were getting close to the hangar now. Soon they would be angling to fire their torpedoes, but Darren knew they wouldn't make it. After all, Natalie was on her way. As he squeezed the trigger, sending his rounds toward the Cobra, they crossed with a hail of rounds from the left, which traced across the tops of the other two bombers. Simultaneously, all three bombers were wiped out, and Natalie's decorated Spectre flashed by Darren's vision. He watched for a moment as it banked left, rolling down to the carrier deck. Natalie was already on her way to another target, and Darren smiled. With pilots as good as her, there was no way they could lose a single transport.

After maintaining the shield around the central hangar for twenty minutes, Darren and the rest of the White Tails began to notice a change in the way the Halerians were attacking. The bombers stopped coming and no longer attempted to reach the hangar bays at all. Further, the enemy Shrikes, which had been attempting to engage the four White Tails to keep them busy for the bombers, were no longer seeking prolonged engagements. Now, the Shrikes simply approached the area covered by the White Tails at speed before firing off a long burst of machine gun rounds and turning away.

Darren watched from his Spectre as the fifth Shrike in a row turned away from him before he could engage. The machine gun rounds streaked harmlessly past his plane, some fifty meters to his right. They were not alone, however. Around him, bursts of machine gun rounds flew in all different directions. Simple bad luck and bad timing could result in two dozen rounds entering Darren's Spectre.

"Dammit, I almost had that one." Darren heard Varya's frustrated voice over the radio. "Phoenix, do you have any idea how we can counter this?"

Though no one could see, Darren shook his head. "No, I don't have a clue." He brought his Spectre to face the next Shrike approaching his area. "They seem to be hoping that luck scores them the hits on us."

"Well, right now they aren't getting very far," Claire responded. "All they're doing is burning ammo. At this rate, they'll run out before they get any of us."

"There's four of us and an unlimited number of them," Natalie grimly reminded Claire. "They aren't running out of ammo any time soon, at least not as a fleet."

"Wildcat's right," Varya agreed. "Phoenix, we need some sort of solution, even if it's just an attempt."

Darren shook his head. What were they supposed to do? If they tried to leave the area over the central hangar, the Dolphins still loading *Endurance's* crew would be defenseless. Beyond that, once the four left the area, they would be open to all of the enemy planes, with little cover from their carrier to protect them. As he watched another Shrike turn away, its rounds flying by and into distant space, he cursed to himself in frustration. Is this what command was truly like? Did it exist only for those moments when everything had gone wrong? Those moments when no matter what decision you made, it seemed to be the wrong one? Darren looked at his L-RaD. Each of those little symbols marking the three pilots under his command was waiting for a solution. Each one was waiting for him, a man from a poor mining town, a man that by all rights shouldn't have been made captain for another five years at least but was here now, thrust into the position of command during his squadron's—no, his *home's*—most dire hour. *Why, Tanner? Why did you pick me?*

Kislo's words came back to him: *"I've seen a lot in you that reminds me of myself at your age. And I've seen things in you that I could only dream of possessing."* Kislo had trusted him with the lives of the other pilots. No matter how much his mind ripped, screamed, and tore, he knew that he had to ensure their survival, even if his was damned.

"This is what's going to happen." Darren's voice showed no signs of the turmoil taking place in his mind as he keyed his radio. "If we can shake their pattern, we should be able to open the door to start engaging them at will. All we need is the space to make this happen. So, I'm going to fly out away from the hangar toward the rear of *Endurance*. This will give me some cover even when the enemy fighters start turning on me. The rest of you, the moment they start turning on me, which they will, split up and start engaging any enemy you can. If we can create enough chaos, it will take them a long time to return to this hit-and-run attack pattern."

Darren knew in his heart the voice he would hear next. "You're fucking crazy. Look at how many are out there! We have *nobody* at the rear of *Endurance*. You'll be on your own against any and every Shrike that wants to see another White Tail dead."

"I know what the chances look like," he responded calmly to Natalie's concerned anger. "But if you all pounce on them as soon as they turn, their lines will be broken up, and I'll be able to regroup with you."

"Sounds like it's our best option then," Claire said, her soft voice putting an end to the debate. "Let's get going."

Without waiting for anyone else to respond with any other concerns, Darren snapped his Spectre around to face the rear of *Endurance*. From where he was, he could see the bridge structure and the connecting upper structure burning. He noticed that since taking charge over the hangar, he hadn't heard from wing command. But as he pushed his throttle forward, he let those thoughts go. They would do no good now.

Claire carefully watched her L-RaD in her peripherals while flying a small pattern to remain in her respective area. Darren's marker had reached the edge of their small sphere where no Halerian planes entered. Claire watched as at first the enemy planes moved away from Darren before they realized that he was committed to flying away from the rest of the White Tails. One by one, enemy markers turned back toward Darren. She could tell he had switched to evade and attack mode, and soon even more enemy planes turned, even from the sides of *Endurance*, including the side Claire was maintaining. As soon as they began turning on her side, Claire thrust her throttle forward and engaged the closest enemy fighter. While the random bursts from their hit-and-runs were still everywhere, Claire pushed forward. She saw that both Varya and Natalie had begun their attacks as well. *Perhaps this plan of his will actually work.*

The Halerian plan to use hit and run attacks had up to this point failed for a full twenty minutes. However, time was something that the Halerians of the New Federation Space Fleet had plenty of, as well as machine gun ammunition. Only a dozen rounds fired from high above *Endurance* came streaking downward and were to be the first bullets to succeed in this strategy. Claire Riftfell's Spectre, closing on a lone Shrike, was suddenly riddled across its top with those 12.7mm armor-piercing bullets.

Claire finally let out a breath after a few moments of shock, confusion, and fear. She couldn't feel any pain. Everything was dark inside her cockpit, save for a few intermittent electrical shorts. Using the dim emergency lights on the sides of the seat, she could make out the metallic surface of the Spectre's Occupant Survival Dome. The OSD was designed as an automatic backup layer for the Spectre's pilot in the event that their canopy was breached. While armored and effective, it offered no external vision without the aid of a small camera fixed to the top.

Feeling around, Claire reaffirmed that no rounds had hit her despite breaching her cockpit. She found the camera's feed switch, which was then projected by a small holo-projector built into the OSD's front. With the display, Claire could essentially fly her plane through a television screen and perform as though her plane hadn't been hit. As she settled into her seat to resume flying, she noticed a small force on her side, indicating that her Spectre was spinning. As the camera powered on and began feeding to the display, she confirmed this. Her Spectre was spinning to the right and away from *Endurance*.

Concerned by the idea of being alone and vulnerable, Claire looked down at her L-RaD to look for any enemy planes. To her surprise, the L-RaD wasn't displaying anything; in fact, it was as if it wasn't even on. As she stared at it, one of the intermittent electrical shorts sparked up from the base of the L-RaD's projector. If she had no L-RaD, she had to return to *Endurance* to be safe, she decided. Grasping her flightstick, she was a little confused when it didn't seem to have any pressure on it from the spin. Still, she pushed into the spin, hoping to bring it to a stop. When she pushed it to the left, she felt no feedback, and even as she held it in place, the Spectre's rate of spin remained the same. She moved the flightstick everywhere, but nothing changed. Her stick was simply dead. Looking for any indications on her instruments, Claire found only more electrical shorts.

But there is still air in the cockpit, and there are still lights, and the camera, so there must still be power, Claire thought to herself. *Which means the radio might still work.* Keying the radio, Claire reached out to her friends. "Any White Tails in my vicinity, respond."

Claire was relieved to hear Natalie's voice. "I read you, RedSky. What is it?"

"My Spectre has been hit, and though I am uninjured, I have no instruments or controls. I am unaware of any enemy planes in my area, and I am spinning away from *Endurance*."

Natalie's heart sank. Perhaps, though, Claire would still make it out. Natalie scanned her L-RaD until she found Claire's Spectre. It was far away from *Endurance* and completely alone. No enemy planes were nearby, as they all seemed to be wrapped up in the chaos Darren had started. Locking onto Claire's Spectre, Natalie used the computer's controls to project a path, something usually used for targeting and interception purposes. The computer drew a white line from Claire's Spectre in the direction it was traveling. While spinning, it was traveling more or less straight.

Natalie took the vector given by her L-RaD and switched her display to a sector map. *Endurance* was in an area of gray space, uncontrolled by either the New Federation or the Altherian Empire, though the borders of both were close by. By plotting Claire's vector, Natalie could see where the Spectre would end up. When the computer displayed this white line, however, Natalie's felt despair wash over her. Claire's Spectre was drifting along the gray space and would never enter the territory of either the New Federation or the Altherian Empire. Eventually, she would reach the end of plotted and claimed space, and enter the vast, dark unknown.

Natalie keyed her radio, knowing that her friend was waiting for her. "RedSky, I've got some good and bad news." Despite the situation, and despite Natalie audibly forcing back the hopelessness in her voice, she wanted to keep her words at least somewhat lighthearted, for herself as much as it was for Claire. "Phoenix's plan worked; the Halerians aren't surrounding the hangar anymore. You're also clear of any enemy planes; no one is coming after you from what I can see."

Natalie paused long enough for Claire to respond. "So, what's the bad news?"

"You will never reach Altherian space." Like dropping an anvil to the floor, Natalie took a direct approach. "You're traveling along the gray space between the Altherian Empire and the New Federation. If your course can't change, you won't enter either one."

This time, there was a lengthy silence before Claire responded. "So, that's it then I guess." She was surprisingly calm. "I guess I'll just be drifting out here until my oxygen runs out."

"There's a chance someone will find you." Natalie couldn't just let her best friend die like this and refused to allow her to simply give up. "Be it Halerian or Altherian, some ship must go across the border. You'll be found and rescued!"

"Do you really think that?" Claire's voice almost sounded angry, as though she were scolding Natalie for being so hopeful. "The gray space is huge, and I'm in a single fighter plane. Even if the Halerians come across, they aren't going to slow down for a drifting fighter. It's over for me, Natalie."

Natalie still refused to give up hope. "You never know, maybe your luck will come around. How long will your air last?"

A small pause as Claire checked the gauges located behind her seat. While the instrument panel in front of her was shot out, the Spectre's air supply always had a backup gauge for engineers working on the plane. "Enough for six hours, twenty if I enter deep sleep." Deep sleep was the name given to the practice of decreasing the oxygen feed to the cockpit to just enough to keep the pilot alive. They would fall unconscious, but a rescue crew would be able to recover them alive.

Varya's voice entered the channel. "But if you enter DS, then you'll really just look like a drifting carcass to anyone else. You'll have to stay awake to make contact."

"So, six hours then." Claire paused. "I don't have much of a choice but wait it out right? Maybe you'll be right, Natalie, maybe I will get picked up."

Natalie's voice came over the radio, and Claire could tell she was pushing back tears. "Then I'll see you on the other side. All four of us, back on Jontunia soon enough."

Natalie was looking at her L-RaD; Claire was nearing the edge of her radio range. Soon she would go silent. But Claire's voice betrayed no fear of the unknown as she keyed her radio. "Even if I don't make it, I'll see the others soon enough. But you three, you better not show up for a long time."

"You got it, RedSky," Natalie responded.

"I'll see you later, Wildcat." Claire undid the latches on her flight helmet, disconnecting it from her suit. The Occupant Survival Dome had allowed the interior of the cockpit to repressurize, allowing Claire to breathe freely now as she took off her helmet. She ran her left hand through her red hair, damp with sweat from almost nine hours of battle, the last four of which had been continuous.

Placing her helmet between her seat and the right-side interior wall, Claire panned the camera outside. She was far enough now that she could hardly make out the shape of *Endurance*. It was a distant shining speck, reflecting the light of the nearest star. Soon, it would vanish from view, and Claire would be left alone to drift through the expanse. Though she appreciated Natalie's hopefulness, she knew the likelihood of being found was almost nil. There was only time now to await the end, when her Spectre, *RedSky*, would run out of air for its pilot. *I'll be home soon, Trisha*, Claire thought, relaxing into her seat. *Don't take off without me.*

CHAPTER 21

Darren flipped through settings on his L-RaD, watching as the remaining fighters of *Endurance's* fighter wing gathered over the hangar bay. He stopped when the L-RaD displayed the wing in different colors, each determined by squadron. To his dismay, most of the squadrons were down to two or three, and sometimes even just a single fighter. But with just over thirty planes left, it would have to do. As Darren flipped back to the regular settings, he heard his radio crackle to life.

"Phoenix, this is command, respond."

"Command, this is Phoenix. Go ahead." The thought briefly flashed in his mind that this was the first time they had spoken on the radio since he had regrouped with the others after Kislo's death.

"Phoenix." There was a slight, strange pause. "This is Commodore Vystra, captain of *Endurance*. The bridge has been evacuated. The bridge staff is on their way to the hangars, and you have about a dozen more transports to take care of. Get them to safety and get out of here."

Endurance had been under the captain's command for thirteen years. Darren knew that he would not evacuate with the others. "Understood, sir. It's been an honor."

"You have command of the wing until you are safe with the rest of the fleet. Good luck, Phoenix." The radio made a beep signaling the radio line from the command deck had been shut off. Vystra would spend the last moments of his life with his ship in silence.

Darren sighed as he looked around. He had never asked for the positions he had been thrust into. He couldn't measure how much he wished Kislo was still alive, and he was simply following *his* orders, not his own. At least the New Federation had provided a lull in the battle for him to organize what was now *his* wing. Some five minutes ago—thirty since they had lost Claire—the enemy fighters and bombers had pulled back and were now amassing nearby. Darren knew that they, too, were reorganizing, but instead of thirty-odd planes, they had hundreds. When they came back, *Endurance* would be finished.

"I'm down to three missiles," Varya said over the radio, glancing at the display reading "WPN" for her weapon status. "You'll have to take the lead for any longer-range fights."

"With my six, we should be alright," Natalie responded. "Both my ammo pods are still full as well."

Varya watched on her L-RaD as the remaining Altherian fighters gathered around the hangar bay. "With Verra in command here, we should be good to run the line ourselves."

Almost as if he had been listening, Darren came over the radio. "Wyvern, Wildcat, there's a transport heading out now." His voice sounded just like Kislo's now, Varya noticed. They were under his command, and command them he would. "Pick it up and escort it forty klicks off the bow. The Halerians are still regrouping, so you shouldn't have any contacts on the way."

Both responded one after the other with a quick "affirmative" before spinning their Spectres in the direction of the outgoing Dolphin. Right on time, the Dolphin rose from the hangar bay and engaged its twin-engines in forward thrust. The pair swiftly caught up to it as it accelerated, flying about fifty meters off the surface of *Endurance* below. Varya shifted her Spectre to the right of the Dolphin and then slowed to follow some hundred meters in behind. She saw Natalie take her own position on the Dolphin's left, a hundred meters ahead.

Darren throttled up his Spectre in unison with the rest of the wing. He had counted his fighters at thirty-three, not including the pair of White Tails away with a Dolphin. The enemy attack was starting now, and his wing would meet them head-on. As the two battle lines met, the space above *Endurance* exploded into chaos for the final time. Darren's wingman was an experienced pilot, but of a far less prestigious squadron. This didn't matter to Darren, so long as he had someone to watch his back.

As he and his wingman engaged their targets together, he reflected on their fate. More than likely, most of them would be killed, even though they were so close to finishing the evacuation. Darren felt a pang of regret as he thought about what his fate may be. After all, he could have just stayed in his hometown and become a miner like his father and brothers. He would have found a wife there and raised a family of to-be miners. It all would have been so simple. But his heart shivered at the thought, returning him to his senses.

If he had stayed, he would never have met all his friends and, most importantly, Natalie. He reminded himself that he'd left home with a dream, a vision that he had to fulfill. He would make a name for himself and bring his children up not as miners, but as anything they wanted to be. Darren Verra wanted to give his family the stars.

Varya watched the two planes before her as they glided over *Endurance's* hull. They were just clearing the forward hangars, now silent and absent of their fighters and bombers. They just needed to clear the bow of the Tempest-class carrier, and then it would be a straight shot to the border where the transport would be safe. Varya dropped her eyes to her L-RaD. The Halerians had begun their attack again, and with well over four hundred fighters, Varya knew the end of *Endurance's* Fighter Wing was close.

Varya's eyes scanned the area immediately around her; everything was still quiet. *This transport will be safe at least*, Varya thought. She couldn't say the same about the others though, or any of the fighter pilots left.

Natalie was still staring out at the blackness of space when out of the corner of her eye she saw an orange light appear. Her brain immediately registered it as a marker on her L-RaD, an enemy marker. Quickly glancing down, she saw the marker was coming fast behind her small flight, and only meters from engagement range.

"Wyvern, break now!" she shouted.

Varya heard Natalie's words and reflexively snapped her stick right. In the same moment, machine gun rounds raked her Spectre, sending alarm lights blazing and sounds blaring. Her plane's OSD activated a split second before the searing pain registered in her brain. Her hand, gripping the stick, suddenly went limp. Varya could feel pain across her back, stomach, and legs. As her Spectre began drifting off to the right, Varya cursed to herself. *I was too slow*, she scolded herself, like it was a training exercise and she had found a fault. *I'm sorry, Natalie.*

Natalie had spun her Spectre around almost in the same moment she saw the enemy Shrike appear on her L-RaD. As she came around, her heart sank, and her breath caught. The Shrike was circling away, and Varya's Spectre was drifting away from *Endurance*. From Natalie's position, she could see the holes across the fuselage and the sparks of damaged electricals.

How? Her mind raced. *How did he get the jump on her?* A single Shrike had snuck up on the two best pilots in the wing and had already downed one.

"Wyvern, this is Wildcat," Natalie called through her radio. "What's your status?" She waited, but as seconds passed, there was no response. "Wyvern, respond!" Still nothing. Natalie felt the strength in her body dwindle as she slumped back in her seat. *This can't be happening.* As Natalie coped with her shock, she almost didn't see the Shrike bank toward her.

Natalie snapped her stick and rolled the Spectre, diving toward *Endurance* only some seventy meters below. Everything had jumped back into her mind as she realized she was far from out of danger. Swiftly reaching the deck, she engaged her VTOL thrusters, pushing the Spectre from the hard surface and keeping it from smashing into the carrier. The Shrike was still tucked in close, but above Natalie, having not committed to the full dive.

Natalie weaved along the carrier's surface, maintaining an unpredictable nature to keep the Shrike from making an attack. While she had been able to buy herself several seconds, she was unable to turn the fight before the Shrike began to adapt. Making shallow dives, the Shrike fired bursts of its machine guns off the right or left side of Natalie, commanding her next turn. Natalie cursed; every slight advantage she made to try to turn the fight on her opponent was taken away. She knew her opponent was leading her to the edge of *Endurance* where she would be easy to chase for a kill. Becoming increasingly desperate, Natalie settled on a plan, pulling the flightstick back into her stomach.

Natalie's Spectre turned vertical, climbing before the enemy Shrike. As she passed him, she saw the markings of an Orange Hawk. The Orange Hawk raced by, and Natalie slammed the stick forward, bringing her Spectre behind her opponent. Only, he wasn't there. Frantically, Natalie searched outside her canopy and then her L-RaD. The Shrike was nowhere to be found. Seeing that they were at the edge of *Endurance*, Natalie concluded that the Shrike probably broke contact under the carrier.

But if he went under to re-engage, Natalie suddenly realized, *he'll come up behind me.* Natalie began furiously turning just as the Shrike reappeared on her L-RaD. He was behind her and coming in fast. Natalie knew she couldn't turn in time. *Is this it?* Had the Orange Hawks finally gotten the better of her? Is this where she, like the other White Tails, fell?

Varya coughed. Blood, still affected by *Endurance's* gravity, spilled over her mouth, chin, and neck. Some of it splashed onto her visor. Quickly unhooking everything, Varya cast the helmet to the side. She coughed again. More blood, this time onto her flight suit. Not that it made a difference. Blood had already soaked through two exit wounds on her midriff, and she could feel the blood on her back. Her legs showed similar damage. Carefully, she touched the exit wounds, wincing in pain. There was a small med kit inside her Spectre, but Varya suspected her wounds were greater than its capability.

Slowly unzipping the top half of her flight suit, she carefully passed over her wounds. With time and willpower, she revealed her wounds. The machine gun bullets had ripped through her skin and tore through the black tank top she wore under her flight suit. The black now had a twinge of red as the blood from her body soaked into it. The med kit wouldn't do, she confirmed. She would bleed out soon if she couldn't get proper treatment, treatment that was no longer available on *Endurance.* The best thing she could do was fight, she concluded. At least no rounds had hit her arms or hands.

Varya slowly reached for the flightstick with her right hand, using her left to peel her blood and sweat soaked brown hair from her skin, letting it drop behind her. As she scanned her instruments for damage, she wiped the blood from her lips, but unconsciously smeared it across her cheeks as she wiped away tears of pain that had now stopped.

Finding her plane to be mostly functional, Varya checked her scanners: Natalie was under attack from the Orange Hawk that had hit her. The transport had continued flying and was close to escaping. Varya throttled up, determined to help her friend.

As she righted her Spectre and began flying, she saw the Shrike escape from Natalie, disappearing below *Endurance.* She was still farther from the carrier than she needed to be. Varya pushed the throttle to maximum, disabling the safety limiters and engaging the emergency intercept mode. Rapidly, she grew closer, but then saw the Shrike reappear behind Natalie. If she didn't make it in time, Natalie was too far out of position to survive. Arming her last missiles and disabling the weapons safeties, Varya would be ready to engage at the earliest opportunity. She coughed again, blood falling across her chest. Some sprayed onto her instruments. The pain was constant but was now beginning to fade. She knew she would bleed out soon. *One last thing*, she told herself. *There's just one more thing I need to do.*

Natalie couldn't hide her shock as the Shrike suddenly caught fire from cannon rounds, half a second before a pair of missiles slammed into its rear. Natalie saw her savior's movements on her L-RaD. She couldn't believe it.

"Wyvern!" Natalie exclaimed with relief. "I thought I lost you!" No amount of thanks could ever amount to how grateful Natalie was that Varya arrived in time.

"Not so fast, kiddo." Varya laughed through blood. Spitting onto her legs, she continued. "I won't disgust you with my injuries, but—" Another cough of blood, this one audible over the radio. "It looks like this is where my fight ends."

Natalie felt something in her break, shattering into tiny pieces. "What? What are you saying?" She knew exactly what Varya was telling her and what the sounds of her choking cough meant. Still, she refused to believe it.

"I'm sorry, Wildcat." Varya felt the strength in her arms slipping, dipping the flightstick ever so slightly as her hands slid from their grip. "I asked you not to die for me, but I so selfishly never considered keeping myself alive for you." Everything was beginning to slip away now. Varya could no longer feel the pain from her wounds. Instead, she felt relief as the pain faded. "You'll have to live for both of us now, kiddo; we both knew it would end this way." The world around her was darkening. Varya thought she saw Natalie's Spectre come near, but the only thing she could make out for certain was the hard metal surface of the OSC *Endurance*, which she was slowly descending toward. "You know, I took up flying because I wanted to save people."

Natalie didn't want to listen anymore. Small tears were on her cheeks already, the same sort of small tears that mixed with blood as they ran down Varya's face. "I think I lost that somewhere along the way; it became less about saving people and more about killing my enemy. You joined for the same reasons I did." Each word was beginning to become difficult. They stuck to Varya's throat and mouth, fighting against escape.

"I think I found what it's like to save people again. Natalie..." Varya dropped her usual perfect radio procedure. "Save the people you can, for me, and for yourself." Varya's eyes tried to shut, and her mouth closed. She forced them into action again with whatever spirit was left in her. "Don't become the killer I became. There's so much more to life than that. Goodbye, Natalie." Varya let herself slump in her seat, her spirit finally succumbing to her body's wounds.

Varya fell into the forever-unconsciousness that leads to death just seconds before her Spectre met its end. From Natalie's cockpit, she couldn't bring herself to look away as her friend's Spectre slammed belly-first into *Endurance*, its fuselage shattering before combusting into several small explosions as fuel and ammunition ignited and detonated from the impact. In an instant, *Wyvern* and Lieutenant Varya Kishpin were gone, a field of debris spread across *Endurance's* hull.

***

Darren suppressed his emotions as he saw Natalie's marker returning to the wing alone. Another of his pilots, another of his *friends*, was gone.

Darren's radio crackled with life. "Phoenix, this is Wildcat. The transport is clear, ready to reform with the wing." Her voice betrayed a hollow, emotionless state, the one one reaches when they've expended all the feeling they can give.

"Copy, Wildcat," Darren responded. Realizing that he hadn't updated the status of the wing in a while, he shortly added, "Wait one for formation order." Continuing to fly defensively to ward off any potential attackers, Darren closely examined his L-RaD. To his dismay, of the thirty-three fighters he had, only a dozen remained now. Darren's own wingman had been killed moments ago when a Shrike blindly collided with his Spectre in the chaos of the battle. Looking up from his L-RaD, Darren keyed his radio. "Ground, this is Phoenix."

"Go ahead, Phoenix," a voice responded. It was unfamiliar to Darren, but it must have been one of the last crew members still in the hangar bay control room.

"We're running low on manpower up here. How many transports are left?"

"The last transports are prepping for takeoff now, Phoenix; we're getting out of here."

"Phoenix copies, out." Switching his radio back to his squadron's channel, Darren spoke again. "Wildcat, form up on me; the two of us will stick together from now on."

"Wildcat copies, moving now," Natalie responded quickly, and Darren watched her marker begin to move in his direction.

It wasn't long before Natalie and Darren were flying in a defensive formation together, each one warding off any attacks on the other. If an enemy plane were to approach one of the pair, the two would move rhythmically, with almost no words spoken, and place the enemy between the two of them. An enemy would have to break off from the attack or face certain death. The pair of White Tails kept this up for nearly ten minutes, swapping back and forth over a dozen times. Of that dozen, only four of them had realized their mistake before becoming debris drifting through space.

Natalie, with the ease of an experienced and highly skilled pilot, slid her Spectre to the left, cutting in just behind the Shrike ahead. Her movements were so fluid and calm that only a pilot with many years of experience would have realized soon enough that she was coming for them. Ahead of the Shrike, which was itself only fifty meters from Natalie, was Darren, and the Shrike trailed just over a hundred meters behind. It took only moments for the missile's targeting computer to find a path, and an even shorter moment for Natalie to pull the trigger. The missile was violently ejected from its holder on the Spectre, dropping a few meters below before the fuel inside ignited, sending it streaking toward its target. As the Shrike exploded and the Spectre sped overhead, Natalie reported to her squadron commander. "That one puts me down to three," she said, her eyes glancing down to the instruments to double check.

"That's fine. The transports are taking off now. We'll be out of here in a few minutes."

As though the Dolphin light transports had been waiting for those words, they began to appear from *Endurance's* large central hangar bay as Darren finished his sentence. As they rose, staggered but together, Natalie counted six of them, each one rising with their powerful twin engines being rerouted through their thrust pods. Natalie smiled then frowned. This was it, the final group of transports. Natalie, Darren, and the other fighter pilots would follow them away from the stricken and doomed carrier and never look back. If only they had been ready sooner. How many of her friends, and how many of *Endurance's* pilots, could have been saved?

Natalie found herself saddened at the prospect of abandoning *Endurance* as well. This had been home for the past three years, and now it was doomed to be ripped asunder by the New Federation's bombs and torpedoes. It was truly an unjust fate for a single, lonely carrier and its crew.

Just as the six transports began to move forward, Natalie caught a glimpse of a Shrike diving on them at high speed. Already, a few of the remaining Spectres were moving to intercept it. Natalie instinctively hit her throttle, tracking the enemy with her eyes while her hands guided the plane toward the Shrike. Mere moments before friendly planes could reach the Shrike, it fired off a burst of rounds and banked hard to its left, attempting to flee. Natalie, not in a position to chase and seeing friendly fighters already engaging, instead turned her attention to the transports.

Five of the six Dolphins were continuing to accelerate away, but the final Dolphin was moving slower, a trail of dirty black smoke trailing behind it. While it was still flying, the rounds from the Shrike had clearly hit something major in the Dolphin's engines, keeping it from accelerating with the rest of its flight.

"Wildcat, this is Phoenix," Darren said over the radio, continuing without a response from Natalie. "One of the transports has no engines. The others will carry on with the wing. We will stay to defend this one."

Giving her affirmative, Natalie maneuvered above the Dolphin to better guard it. She watched as the rest of the wing, some ten planes now, carried on forward with the other five Dolphins. Many of the attacking Shrikes soon moved to follow the larger group. Darren formed up just behind Natalie, and the pair waited, watching the Dolphin attempt to get its engines running again. While it could continue forward like this, it had not had enough time to accelerate to a reasonable speed. At this rate, it was barely moving faster than *Endurance*.

Natalie, who had been studying the smoke and small signs of life in the Dolphin's exhaust ports, was suddenly brought back to her immediate surroundings by Darren's voice.

"Looks like we've got an enemy squadron forming up on our left," he said calmly, quietly, as though speaking louder would alert the enemy. "Eight planes. Probably the Orange Hawks; they'll have known the White Tails would stay behind."

"Sounds like they're inviting us to destroy their squadron," Natalie responded. "We'll see how they like losing everyone they know."

Darren held his tongue, knowing that something, some primal motivator based on revenge had triggered in Natalie. He only hoped that she could still fly smartly in her anger. The Orange Hawks moved toward the three Altherian planes over *Endurance*. All eight Shrikes maintained altitude against the two Spectres. As they neared, Darren and Natalie began their counter; turning away from each other, they pushed their throttles to maximum simultaneously and corkscrewed above the Shrikes. While well timed to dodge the initial attack, the Orange Hawks were quick to dissolve their formation and begin the dogfight in earnest.

Natalie was quickly upon one of the Shrikes as it turned over and dove toward *Endurance*. The Shrike was faster, being lighter and having turned and dove first. But Natalie wasn't the one making the kill; acting on silent chemistry and instinct, Natalie knew she had set up the enemy Shrike for Darren, who came sweeping across the top of *Endurance*, catching the Shrike at the bottom of its dive.

Natalie at once ripped her flightstick backward, bringing her Spectre level in under a second. In what appeared to be one fluid motion that was really a succession of smaller movements, Natalie switched her VTOL on, stopping her Spectre in its dive while keeping it from moving forward horizontally. A chasing Shrike flashed by, unable to react in time. In the same pair of seconds that had begun the maneuver, Natalie rolled her Spectre belly-up, pulled the stick back, and slammed the throttle forward. The chasing Shrike was now the Shrike being chased. This Shrike, however, did not dive for the cover the carrier provided. Instead, it stayed high, using its speed to keep distance between the two planes.

As Natalie gave chase, she heard Darren's voice. "The transport has one engine working again," he said quickly, as he was concentrating on his current engagement. "Prepare to break off and follow."

Natalie reached for the radio key with her left thumb but was cut off when a burst of machine gun rounds flew across her canopy perpendicularly. While maintaining chase on her target, she gained all the information she needed from the L-

RaD's display in half a second. "Wildcat copies, but be advised, the rest of the enemy wing is returning." Deciding it best to break off and work closer with Darren, Natalie made a hard left, her attacker flying by in the opposite direction.

"The rest of our wing is coming back to us now," Darren said. "There are four planes left, but all transports made it out safe."

"Tell them to get back quick," Natalie responded. The area around her was beginning to fill with planes. She found Darren near the transport and chasing off enemy planes. Natalie quickly moved to engage, diving toward a Shrike making its approach. Firing off a missile, Natalie logged *two* in her mind before turning to a new target. The Dolphin was nearly clear of *Endurance* now; then, it would be a straight shot to Altherian Empire space. *Almost there*, she thought.

Spotting another Shrike moving toward the transport, Natalie came in at speed to intercept. The Shrike was directly perpendicular to Natalie and preparing for the turn. In response, Natalie rotated her Spectre so its long wings stood vertical over *Endurance*.

"Transport's clear!" she heard Darren shout over the radio. "Resistance should start going down now. We've got this!" There was a noticeable air of relief in his voice.

Natalie Annikki never got to share that relief with her friend. Moments from making her turn, a second Shrike swept by, raking her Spectre with machine gun rounds. Many hit the fuselage of Natalie's plane, but three found their way through the blue tinted canopy of the Spectre *Wildcat*. The first round embedded itself in Natalie's left leg, burrowing with the violence of a badger. The second round shattered her right hand, ripping it from the flightstick and sending it limply to the side. The final round tore through the plastic and metal of Natalie's black and crimson-striped helmet, glancing off her left cheek, but not before carving a deep pink and red trench in it from the base of her ear to the edge of her mouth. The OSD closed just as her consciousness returned to reality.

Natalie's first response was to cry out in pain, though this brought only more pain. Her second response was to right her Spectre, which had been sent spinning by her right hand. This was a struggle, as Natalie was forced to manage the throttle and stick with only her left hand. Bringing her Spectre around eventually, however, Natalie began to reorient herself. The transport was a fair distance from *Endurance* now and would soon escape. The rest of *Endurance's* fighter wing was coming across the carrier, and Darren was flying toward Natalie.

"Wildcat, respond!" he shouted desperately over the radio. Natalie realized he must have made several attempts for contact by now.

"I'm... Wildcat's here," Natalie responded, the pain making words difficult. "I've been hit, unsure of my wounds. The plane feels fine though."

"Fuck, we're almost out of this, Natalie. Can you still fight?"

"I'm not sure... My right hand doesn't feel like it's all there."

Darren breathed in deeply, searching for a solution. "Fly toward the transport, Wildcat," he ordered. "There shouldn't be any more enemy planes."

Natalie appreciated that idea and throttled up toward the Dolphin. Then she noticed Darren flying the other way. "Phoenix, where are you going?" she asked.

"The wing is going to need my help, and I can get some of the ones still here off your back. Just keep flying."

Natalie felt an uneasiness building in her, but she kept going. Darren soon passed her, heading toward the dying carrier. Halfway to the transport, Natalie keyed her radio again. "You're coming back... right?" Something was triggering every fear in her.

Darren didn't respond right away. When he did, his voice was low. "I'm not sure, to be honest." He laughed curtly. "I didn't really come up with an escape plan."

"What plan did you come up with?"

"I've a gut feeling that *Endurance's* core is about to go." Natalie's heart sank with each word. "I thought that if I pulled them off you, they wouldn't come back after the carrier was destroyed."

"But you'll get caught in the explosion," Natalie blurted out as her mind put two and two together. "You can't reasonably do this!"

"If I do, but you live, then so be it." Darren was calm and determined and was now coming over *Endurance's* bow. Natalie became sure that Darren wasn't planning on returning.

"You can't leave now, not when we're so close." Natalie felt tears beginning to well up in her hazel eyes.

"Wildcat, I'm no good at these ceremonies, but I'm naming you commander of the White Tails. Kislo told me to rebuild, so that order falls on you now."

"No! I won't do it!" Natalie cried. "You're supposed to live; we can rebuild it together!"

"You don't need me to do that," Darren continued. "The White Tails is now your future. Rebuild, and keep fighting to protect what's important to you."

"What about your plans?" Natalie demanded. "What about changing your future?"

"I've already done that, Nat." Darren dropped his voice low again. "I became a better man than I ever could have hoped to become. I grew up, Natalie, and I met the most important person in my life."

Natalie could hardly bring herself to respond. "So, that's just it then?" she asked. "You're going to let yourself die here for no reason?" From the OSD's camera, which Natalie pointed toward *Endurance*, she could see the growing blue light of a core collapsing.

"I'm not dying for no reason," Darren responded. "I'm dying so you can live, and that matters more to me than my own life."

"Please don't. Just come back."

Darren responded as though he never heard the plea. "Ah, it looks like *Endurance's* day is over," he said flatly, a cool edge against his fate. "Everyone is turning away, but they won't make it. Looks like it's the wing, and about twenty Halerians in it to the end. This isn't so bad. At least I'm not alone."

Natalie couldn't speak. Only the sounds of tears and sniffling came over the radio and into Darren's cockpit.

He relaxed in his seat, keying the radio again. "I love you, Natalie; I never stopped loving you. Promise me you'll live a long life, long enough to be buried on Jontunia. Space is no burial ground for you."

Natalie choked back her tears for the last time. "I… I promise," she forced out, each word having to fight to escape. "I love you, Darren. I'm sorry I couldn't save you. I'm sorry… I'm sorry."

"No apologies, Nat," Darren responded. His voice sounded choked now. "Don't *ever* regret living, Natalie. This is goodbye now."

The OSC *Endurance's* core, emanating a piercing neon blue light, collapsed in on itself. In its expanding sphere of destruction, *Phoenix*, the four other Spectres of *Endurance's* Fighter Wing, and some twenty-five Halerian planes were captured, along with *Endurance* herself. Within seconds, the Tempest-class carrier was gone, replaced by a field of debris. Somewhere in that field of debris were Darren Verra's remains.

Natalie only saw the marker appear because she was staring down at the floor, with her L-RaD in front of her. A single Shrike, caught on the wrong side of the explosion, had decided to give chase. *You've killed them all*, Natalie thought. *But that wasn't enough? You have to come for each and every last one of us?* Now, Natalie reached for her flightstick, sitting up straight in her seat. It hurt, gripping the stick with her right hand. With her undamaged left hand, Natalie slammed the throttle on her Spectre forward.

"You'll wish you died in the explosion; at least that would've been quicker!" Natalie rolled her Spectre with a quick snap to the right and spiraled her Spectre down toward her target. She didn't feel anything other than blinding hatred. She would kill this Shrike.

The Shrike was caught off guard by the sudden movement of the enemy Spectre. For its entire approach, the Spectre had been quietly gliding along some four hundred meters behind the real target, the Dolphin light transport ahead. But discipline told the pilot of the Shrike to engage the escort first. Now, as he dove away from the charging Spectre, he wished he hadn't provoked such a foe. With speed, the Shrike pulled up, climbing out of his dive. He hoped now to catch the Dolphin before the Spectre caught him.

Natalie cut the Shrike's dive, pulling back slightly on her stick but using the Spectre's belly-fixed exhaust ports to push the Spectre back up. The Shrike realized his mistake quickly and suddenly cut to the left in a hard turn. Natalie smiled viciously, one that comes only from a just kill. The Shrike had made his second, and final, mistake. Natalie cut her stick to the left, relying now on the full strength of her hands. Her left augmented her crippled right, but her right still had to do most of the pushing. Now the pain returned, but Natalie bit through it. She could see the Shrike on her display slowly lining up with the targeting computer for her remaining two missiles. She only had to push a little more.

Natalie cried out in pain and anger, pushing her Spectre harder in a bid to turn faster. Her right hand was ready to quit, ready, she felt, to break away from her wrist and fall to the floor of her cockpit. *Push,* she told herself, then swore she heard it again in six other voices. She reminded herself that that's who this was for: her friends, killed in the violent rage of the Halerians. For the six of them. This Shrike would have to do for now. Natalie had to prove to them that she would continue for them. The pain in her hand seemed to subside, and the Shrike slid into the targeting window.

Out here, away from *Endurance's* grave, there was no debris, no wreckage to impede a missile's path. As the locking tone became solid, Natalie hit the missile release. She hit it a second time for good measure. *Zero,* she counted in her mind. The two missiles, identical Challenger air-to-air missiles, dropped from the internal bay of Natalie's Spectre. As they rolled some two feet clear, their guidance systems activated, and suddenly they leveled out and their engines fired, all in under a second. The missiles streaked off, the first slamming into the front of the Shrike only three seconds after firing; the second impacted the cockpit a split second behind. The Shrike was consumed in fire and disintegrated as Natalie swept by without a second glance.

As Natalie flew toward the Dolphin transport, she took a long look at her L-RaD, using the controls to increase its directional range ahead, behind, below, above, and to each side in turn. Ahead, only the Dolphin existed. Behind, where *Endurance* had fallen, the Halerians were reorganizing and flying away, back toward their originating fleet. Natalie sighed in relief; no more enemy planes were coming for them. The nightmare was finally over. The fall of *Endurance* was over, and Natalie Annikki was the only pilot still standing from the Tempest-class carrier's prestigious fighter wing.

She glanced at the small clock on her instrument panel. It was just after half-past five in the evening. Almost twelve hours ago, she had sat down with Jinsu for breakfast. *Feels like a year ago…* With the realization that she was alone, and that the battle was over, she felt all her energy leave her body. The pain came back in earnest, and Natalie slumped in her seat, tears of anger, pain, and loss floating in the cockpit.

CHAPTER 22

Natalie listened to the low hum of her Spectre-class fighter's engine as it flew along at a low speed, matching the Dolphin-class transport two hundred meters diagonally to her left. It had been twenty minutes since *Endurance* had met its sudden, violent end, and the battle had concluded following the withdrawal of the New Federation strike craft.

She continued to watch her L-RaD for the appearance of anything other than the Dolphin's and her own Spectre's markers. With no sign of any enemy for now over twenty minutes, Natalie allowed her mind to drift toward her personal situation. Small inky spheres of blood drifted across her cockpit, occasionally impacting something, bursting, and sticking to it. She allowed herself to notice the pain she felt for the first time since the end of the battle. She was slumped to her side in her seat, with no strength to do anything anymore. Knowing how shameful it would be to just give up and die, especially after what Darren had done for her, Natalie had to do something. At the very least, she would find out how bad her wounds really were.

Slowly sitting up in her seat, she looked down at her left leg. Blood had soaked into the fabric of her flight suit, darkening it to a crimson hue. She then looked to her right, down at her hand that lay limp at her side. The sight of blood and bone forced her to look away.

Using only her left hand, Natalie reached up to her neck, unclipping the six clips that sealed her helmet to her flight suit. Then she reached for the small tube connecting her Spectre's oxygen supply to her helmet, unfastening it, and letting it retract into the fuselage. Now she could take off the broken crimson-striped helmet, which she did by carefully lifting it from her head. The left side of her face hurt, and she could feel blood. She ignored it as it was by far the least severe of her injuries. As the helmet came off completely, her sweat-soaked hair falling from inside to her uniform, Natalie took a deep breath. The cockpit had fully re-pressurized with the activation of the Occupant Survival Dome, signaled by a green "air" light displayed on the instrument panel.

Hooking her helmet on the right side of her seat, Natalie reached over to the left in search of her med kit. Locating it, she brought it onto her lap. Still working with one hand, she opened the small white metal box. She scanned the contents and found a few bandages, some sterilizing cleaning liquid, some stitching thread, and a knife. The knife was a standard survival knife for pilots to use in the event they crashed somewhere without help. Natalie knew that it could also cut clothes in an emergency, and so she took it out of the box before closing the lid and placing it back in its holder.

Now Natalie looked down at her left leg. Based on the blood, the bullet impacted her at about mid-thigh, and so she placed the knife just above. Gripping the fabric of her flight suit to make it taut, Natalie began cutting, careful not to slice her leg open with the sharp knife. Slowly, she worked her way around her leg, until she'd cut the left leg of her flight suit loose just above the mid-thigh. She folded the knife and tucked it under her right leg.

Taking a deep breath, she grabbed the edge of the disconnected pant leg and slowly peeled it from her leg. On the first tug, she stopped instantly, a cry of pain forcing its way out of her mouth. The fabric, soaked in blood, stuck to her wound and tugged on it as she tried to peel it away. Natalie tried again, but it still stung as the fabric released its grip on her leg. At least it hurt a lot less than before. She carefully moved it downward along her leg, exposing more of her wound until she could see it all.

She wanted to vomit. The bullet had embedded itself in her leg, and there was a crater of blood, muscle tissue, and shards of metal and bone. While she tried to remember the basic medical training she had received all those years ago on Jontunia, the sight of the wound sent her mind in a spiral. Instead, Natalie grabbed the med kit, fishing out the largest bandage roll and the cleaning liquid. Had she even known how to stitch a wound together, she imagined that the wound was too big for some basic stitching.

Inspecting the bottle of sterilizing cleaning agent, Natalie wondered how she should best apply it. She took one of the soft fabric squares, which had been next to the bottle. Opening the bottle, she quickly placed the fabric over the top, allowing some of the liquid to float into it. Feeling that it should be enough, she immediately replaced the cap to prevent any of the liquid from floating out of the bottle and into the cockpit. She then tried to clean the edges of her wound where the blood had spread over her leg as it soaked into her clothes. Progressively, she came closer to the wound until she was at its very edge. Using a newly soaked cloth, she touched the edge of her wound.

The stinging pain was intolerable as Natalie groaned through gritted teeth. Recoiling, she let go of the cloth, letting it float a way to somewhere in the cockpit. Cleaning the wound would be left to the professionals, she quickly decided, putting the bottle and the cloth squares back in the med kit. All she could do now was bandage the wound to slow the bleeding. This was not a pain-free process either but was far more manageable than the hell the sterilizing agent had brought on. After ten minutes of cursing in pain, Natalie managed to tighten the bandage around her leg to a satisfying degree. The thick wad of fabric pressed on her wound would last long enough, she believed.

Sitting back in her seat, she noticed the pain in her leg had subsided, at least a little bit. Instead, Natalie now noticed just how cold it was in her Spectre. While the planes that flew in space were heated, they were heated only just above freezing. The toll of flying a fighter in space caused the pilot to sweat anyways, especially under the layers of the flight suit and whatever clothes they wore underneath. But now, Natalie's left leg was completely exposed to the cockpit air from her mid-thigh to her knee. Now, she began to feel the cold air begin to work its way down the cut-off pant leg to her lower leg, as well as up the rest of her flight suit. She needed something to cover it up.

Unzipping her flight suit's top half, Natalie pulled her left arm from the thick, warm uniform. Underneath, she always wore two layers; a thin long-sleeve sweater and a black tank top. The sweater would have to be sacrificed for the sake of her leg. Then she could zip up the flight suit, and it and the tank top would be enough until she and the Dolphin nearby were rescued. The only issue was her right hand. It still throbbed with pain, and she couldn't move anything from the wrist down. She would look at it after she freed her right half from the flight suit.

Slowly, she began backing out her right arm. As her right hand touched the end of the sleeve, the pain got worse then subsided as it gently glided inside the sleeve. Occasionally, the pain worsened as the hand was touched by parts of the fabric. She cursed, and tears of pain formed and floated away. The pain was definitely worse than her leg had been. Too often, she was forced to stop to recuperate, the pain simply too great.

After several grueling minutes, the full arm, including the right hand, was free from the flight suit. Now, Natalie was forced to look at it. While the hand was still shrouded by the black flying gloves she wore, something was clearly amiss. She could not move any of her fingers, which were not sitting in a uniform pattern like a limp hand would. Some were dislocated in appearance, pointing off in unnatural directions. In the center of her hand, she could only see a mess of blood, fabric, and metal. The damage was similar on both sides of her hand.

Natalie knew that it was best to bandage the hand in a way that none of the fingers would move independently of the hand, and the hand would not move independently of the wrist. Over the next twenty painful minutes, she wrapped and bandaged her hand to the point where she couldn't see the wound any longer. From her fingertips to her lower wrist was a mess of white bandages. The pain was dulled into a constant throb, but still better than the sharp, intense pain of before.

Satisfied with her work, she took off her black sweater. Everything except for the right arm came easy. It took several minutes longer to roll the sleeve across the bandaged hand. Even through the bandages, Natalie felt like she was in some sort of torture chamber, or hell.

Now sitting in her Spectre with only a tank top covering her upper body, she remarked that the cold she felt on her leg hadn't been all that bad. No, it was much colder now. She laid the center of her sweater over the top of her left leg, and then used the rest of the main body to cover the underside. Though she could use only one hand and her mouth, she worked quickly, motivated by the thought of returning to the warmth of her flight suit. Using the arms to secure the sweater, she finished the job. Several more minutes passed as she forced her right arm back into the flight suit. Natalie did up the rest of her flight suit at a record-setting pace, especially for someone using only one hand.

Even with the flight suit it was still cold, but at least it was better than without it. The pain of her hand and leg began subsiding to reasonable levels, and Natalie relaxed in her seat. Her face may still have been cold, but that was far more bearable; after all, it was no different than the cold days in Rikata.

She looked down at her L-RaD. Still nothing but the marker of a Dolphin just ahead. The pair were still in the gray space between the New Federation and Altherian Empire, and Natalie wasn't sure exactly how far they were from friendly space now.

Calmly, she keyed her radio. When Natalie had taken her helmet off, the plane's systems immediately switched radio input and output to the cockpit's microphone and speakers built into the instrument panel. "Dolphin, this is Wildcat. Just checking in, over."

The Dolphin didn't take long to respond. "Wildcat, this is Cockroach," a male voice said, the sound filling Natalie's cockpit. "Still running on one engine, but it is stable. We have twenty-three passengers on board, all in good health. What's your status?"

"Cockroach, Spectre is undamaged as far as I can tell. I have zero missiles, but a decent amount of cannon and machine gun rounds left. There hasn't been anything on the scope for the last forty-five minutes, though."

"Wildcat, we're getting the same readings on our scanners. We see that your OSD is up. Was your Spectre hit?"

"Yes, but as I said, it seems undamaged. I was hit twice by the rounds though." Natalie ignored the stinging on her left cheek. That was probably more from the helmet breaking than a bullet, she believed.

"How are your wounds? Are they critical?"

"I've patched them up to the best of my ability," Natalie said. "I should be okay for now."

"Hang on, we've got medical staff in the back." The pilot wasn't taking chances with the health of his only protector, it seemed. "I'll patch you through to the hold's comms."

You're kidding me, Natalie thought to herself as she waited for the channel to switch. *Of course they'd have had medical the whole time.*

The radio crackled to life once more. "Hello?" The voice of an older man came through. "Is this the fighter pilot?"

Natalie sighed. "Yes."

"I'm a doctor," the man said. "Our pilot told me that you were wounded. Can you describe the injuries?"

Natalie was certain the doctor couldn't do much from another plane, but she decided to humor him. "Two .50 caliber rounds, one into my left thigh, the other into my right palm." She assumed what the next question would be, so she skipped ahead. "I've applied basic bandaging to each, but there is nothing more I can do with the med kit I have."

"I'm familiar with the standard issue med kit you have." The doctor was calm and professional, which made Natalie feel a little more at ease. "What you've done should be sufficient for a few hours. Do you have any extra bandage to change the old with?"

"I don't think so," Natalie responded flatly. "The wound on the hand was pretty bad and took up most of it. I don't have enough for a proper change for either wound." Now that she was talking more regularly, Natalie noticed the pain in her left cheek beginning to worsen. She dismissed it as nothing more than some extra stress from the act of speaking.

The doctor sighed. "Well, hopefully someone finds us soon then. In the meantime, you can use what you have left to add onto what is there once that becomes thoroughly soaked."

Natalie was about to respond when the sound of an alarm cut her off. "Affirmative, Dolphin, wait one," she hastily responded before looking at her instruments. The alarm was a loud but slow beeping, and there was a small, circular yellow light blinking on the right side of the panel. Upon closer inspection, Natalie realized it was the oxygen warning light.

"Shit," she muttered. Her eyes quickly panned to the oxygen gauge nearby. Metered in hours, the Spectre had a maximum of twenty-six hours of oxygen on board. Natalie's gauge showed only two. "You're fucking kidding me," she muttered again.

Now she looked down at the L-RaD, which was also the Spectre's computer display. Hitting a few buttons with her left hand, she brought up the plane's onboard systems display. While it couldn't give perfect diagnostics, it could at least show the rate of oxygen usage on board. When Natalie zeroed in on the oxygen display, she saw that the rate of depletion was far greater than normal.

"Cockroach, this is Wildcat."

The pilot of the Dolphin answered the hail. "This is Cockroach. Go ahead, Wildcat."

"I've just discovered a leak in my oxygen tank." She tried to hide the disappointment and frustration in her voice. "My computer says I have less than two hours of air."

There was a long silence before the pilot responded. "Copy that, Wildcat." He sounded more let down than Natalie felt. "What are your options?"

The only two options she had had already gone through her mind. "Well, the first is to keep flying like this, and in less than two hours suffocate," she said bluntly to Cockroach. "Option two is to power down and switch to emergency feed."

"If you do that you'll pass out," Cockroach responded quickly. "What if a Shrike shows up?"

"If nothing's shown up for this long, I think we'll be safe." Natalie paused, turning her right hand over left and right and back again. "Besides, I'd rather maximize the time I have and risk a fighter arriving than suffocate for no reason."

Natalie heard a sigh through the radio. "Alright, I guess I can agree," Cockroach said quietly. "I sure hope you're right."

"You and me both, Wildcat out." Natalie reached forward and switched off her radio. Relaxing back in her seat, she used her left hand to bring up her Spectre's systems again on the display. Flipping through the different systems onboard, she soon arrived at the settings for the feed of air into her cockpit. At the bottom of the display was an option: "Emergency Feed" in red lettering with an on/off display. Flicking a small button, "on" became the highlighted option. Natalie tapped another button, bringing the display to its default state, showing the markers of both *Cockroach* and *Wildcat* as they sailed along together. Natalie leaned back in her seat, adjusting herself to be more comfortable. Her injuries pulsated with pain, but they were far better than they had been.

As the minutes ticked by and Natalie used the extra air still in her cockpit, she felt herself becoming weaker. Whether this was from the slow decline of air available or the blood loss from her injuries beginning to set in, she did not know. *We'll be found soon, right?* Natalie found herself wondering. *We must be; that's all that's left.* Natalie shut her eyes, letting darkness envelope her mind. Soon it was replaced with Rikata and herself, staring out the window of her home at the sun as it set over the town. As unconsciousness began to set in, Natalie remarked at how foreign it all now looked.

CHAPTER 23

"Mommy, where are you going?" Natalie asked curiously as her mother set down a second bag before the door. Her mother didn't respond, instead turning to face the sound of Natalie's father coming down the stairs behind them.

"So that's it then?" he shouted from halfway down the stairs. "You're just going to leave us here?"

Natalie's mother ignored her husband, grabbing a jacket from the wall and pushing her shoes into the open with her feet. Natalie watched, her hazel eyes darting from her mother to her father and back.

"Jennifer, answer me!" Natalie's father shouted. "Where are you even going?"

"If I told you, you'd trap me here," Jennifer Annikki replied. Her voice carried the same angry tone as Natalie's father, but none of the panic. "There's a better life for me."

"But not for your six-year-old daughter? Think about her at least."

Natalie's mother looked down at her. Natalie had no idea what was happening in that moment, but she wanted it to end.

"She can't come with me." Her mother looked back at her father. "I can trust you to take care of her." She put on her shoes, sitting on the bench by the door. Natalie in turn sat on the bottom step of the stairs behind her.

"I just want to know why you're leaving, Jen." Natalie's father suddenly sounded defeated. "That's all I want to know."

"You wouldn't understand, Mika." Jennifer stood up and looked him in the eye. "Your work has and always will prevent you from seeing that."

"So, it's the New Federation." Natalie heard her father's voice darken, and she pushed herself back along the step, farther from both her parents. "You are going to abandon your family for those violent, vengeful people? They would see this planet, and all that humanity has built, razed if it meant they could see Altheria's oceans one time!"

Natalie's mother shook her head. "I knew you wouldn't understand. If you had seen what I've seen, Mika, you wouldn't be so quick to judge them."

"I've seen plenty, you and I both know that."

"Everything you've seen has been through a lens, a lens set by the Councils. I've seen the truth, the *real* truth."

Mika put his arms out in front of him in plea. "Then show me!" he begged. "Show me this truth that you've seen. Take us with you if this *real* truth is so much better."

"If I did that, we'd be hunted forever." Jennifer opened the door and picked up her bags.

"Then at least take Natalie!" Natalie's father pleaded one more time. "Why won't you take her? Take her to this better life!" Natalie stood up as if called upon.

Jennifer paused, holding the door with her left hand. Then she shook her head. "I can't." Natalie's mother closed the door on Mika. Natalie sat back down. Her father stayed a long time at the door, staring at it from only inches away.

"Daddy, is Mommy coming back?" Natalie spoke in the silence.

Her father shook his head. "No, sweetie." His voice was choked. "I don't think she's ever coming back."

***

The bright ceiling light caused Natalie to squint as she opened her eyes. It felt as though it would blind her, and it made her head hurt. Turning her head to her left, she saw a medical machine humming quietly away, its display showing things she had only seen in movies.

With her left hand, she carefully lifted the bed sheet. She had been left in the black tank top and shorts that she always wore underneath her uniform. She could see the white coloration of a bandage on her leg.

After a handful of minutes, Natalie slowly pushed herself up with her left hand, sitting up on the white medical bed. Looking around, she frowned. Nothing in the room could help her discern where she was. Judging by the absence of windows, she assumed she was on a ship, somewhere in space. *Whose* ship it was, Natalie was anxious to know. She looked left at the medical machine again. Nothing it displayed told her about the ship she was on.

Her questions were soon answered when the white door to the room slid open with a mechanical glide. Behind it was a doctor in a white coat and a young nurse in a military uniform. Natalie recognized the camouflage pattern as Altherian. She breathed a sigh of relief.

"Oh good, you're awake!" the doctor said, stepping inside, the nurse following. The door quietly slid closed behind them. As the doctor walked from the door to the machine, he caught Natalie's questioning stare. "You have questions, but I need to give you a quick examination first." He laid a clipboard on the small table next to the machine. Studying the machine, his focus flipped from the machine's display to the clipboard and back several times. Each time, he wrote something on the clipboard's paper.

"Where am I?" Natalie directed her questions to the young nurse, who was standing next to her bed.

"Ma'am, you are on the Altherian Oracle-class cruiser *Light the Way*," the nurse responded as she checked the level of fluid bags hung up near the end of the bed.

Natalie thought for a moment but couldn't place the ship in the 3rd Mobile. "Which fleet do you belong to? Where is this ship?"

"*Light the Way* belongs to Jontunia's 3rd Defensive, and we are currently on the border of the Altherian Empire and the New Federation." The nurse took the clipboard as the doctor handed it to her.

"That's a long way from home." Natalie watched as the doctor knelt next to her bandaged leg.

"The whole defensive fleet was called up to cover the retreat of your fleet," the doctor said. "We're here to find survivors and make sure the Halerians don't pursue too far."

The nurse quietly spoke the words of the 3rd Defensive: "We stand ready."

Natalie looked from the nurse to the doctor, who was carefully beginning to unwrap Natalie's bandages. "Can I know your names?" she asked.

"Dr. Adrian Tulo," the doctor said. Natalie looked up to the nurse to her right.

"Corporal Dustra Sinclair, ma'am." She spoke firmly, like a member of the army rather than that of the OSC, Natalie thought.

Suddenly, there was a sharp pain, causing Natalie to wince. "Ah sorry," Dr. Tulo said. "This last layer of bandage touches the wound, so it might sting." Slower, he began to peel off the bandage. Natalie was too disgusted to watch, instead turning away, gritting her teeth to hide the pain. "It's healing nicely," Tulo said after a few moments when the pain had stopped. "You'll need a hydro-brace to take the weight off, but you should be able to start walking again tomorrow, though, with a bit of a limp. By the time we return to Jontunia, we'll be able to take the brace off."

Tulo began to apply some new bandages. Natalie watched, carefully studying the pattern he spun the fabric around her thigh. "How long was I out for?"

"Well today's the eighth, so… four days," Tulo responded without slowing his hands. "You were found extremely late on the third. You didn't get into my operating room until the wee hours of the fourth, actually. They took a long time extricating you."

Natalie didn't pry. She wasn't sure if she wanted to know what he meant. Instead, she watched as he finished wrapping up her leg and then moved around to her right, Sinclair stepping back to make room. Tulo began the same procedure on Natalie's right hand, slowly unwinding the bandages.

"You're lucky you still have this hand at all," Tulo said, setting down the last of the old bandages. "It took hours to reconstruct the tendons and knuckles, even with a machine guiding."

"Does it still work?" Natalie asked, looking at her intact left hand.

"Well," Tulo paused. "Try squeezing your hand. Slowly."

Natalie did as he said. It didn't take long for searing pain to shoot from her hand up her arm. At once, she released her grasp on the air.

"This one will take a lot longer to heal than your leg, I'm afraid."

"Will I fly again?"

Tulo sighed. "It's too early to say. With the right rehab, maybe. But you're not on the winning side of the odds."

Natalie stared at the floor as Tulo began to rewrap her hand. The room was silent, save for the machine, which was idly humming away.

When Tulo finished bandaging her hand, he stood up. "Do you have any other questions for us?"

Natalie looked at her hand and then up at him. "When do we get back to Jontunia?"

He shrugged. "Hard to say," he said. "If the Halerians don't counterattack into Altherian territory, we might be heading home in a few days."

"And if they do…" Her voice trailed away, knowing the answer.

"Try not to worry about those possibilities, ma'am," Sinclair said. "You went through a lot. You should focus on resting for now."

Natalie nodded. "Am I to stay here then?"

"Just until tomorrow," Tulo explained. "Then we'll fit you for your hydro-brace, get you walking around, and then send you on your way to your temporary quarters. Until then, you'll just need to stay here."

"I'll be bringing you all of your meals," Sinclair said with a smile. "Is there anything else I can bring for you?"

Natalie shook her head. "No, I should be fine for a day."

Soon after, both Tulo and Sinclair left Natalie on her own in the room. She laid back down and looked up at the plain ceiling. There was nothing complex about it, nothing intriguing, nothing worth a single thought other than to note its color and distinct lack of interesting features. Despite this, Natalie stared at the ceiling for a long time. To her, it may have been hours, but in reality, it was probably barely thirty minutes before there was a knock at the door.

Carefully pushing herself upright, Natalie called to the door, "Come in."

The door slid open with the same mechanical sound as before. This time, however, it was a man in an OSC uniform that walked into the room. His patches were that of a commodore, and his ashy black and gray beard told Natalie that he had at least two decades of experience under him. She saw his nametag read "Krusswell."

Natalie tried to push herself up a little straighter, but he waved her down. "You don't need to push yourself just for me, Lieutenant," he said. "Commodore Krusswell, captain of *Light the Way*. I'm just here to check in on you." His voice reminded Natalie of the stereotypical father-figure, though not *her* father. More like the ones in old TV shows, she thought.

"Well, sir, I'm alive," Natalie said.

Commodore Krusswell smiled and pulled a small stool to the edge of the bed and took a seat. "Yes, and I'm happy to see that. You were out for a long time." There was a slight pause as he looked around at the medical machines in the room. "But I never lost faith in either my ship's doctors or in your strength."

Natalie wondered what this man could possibly know about her strength. But she couldn't ask. "I'm sure it was the skill of the doctors more than anything that saved my life," Natalie said with a forced smile. *Whatever he thinks of my strength, he's probably greatly overestimating it,* she thought.

"In any case," Krusswell went on, "you are alive, which is excellent news. How much did the doctor tell you?"

"About?" Natalie cocked her head slightly to the right.

"About your arrival on this ship," Krusswell said. "You know it has been four days since you got here, right?"

Natalie's eyes shifted away from Krusswell's face and toward the floor behind his left side. "Yes, sir, he mentioned that, but that was about all."

"It was quite the chaotic moment," Krusswell said, smiling as though reminiscing the scene. "I was there myself when they pulled your Spectre into the hangar."

"There was a Dolphin with me when my Spectre was discovered, right, sir?" Natalie asked, suddenly remembering the people she had been escorting when she had fallen unconscious.

"Yes, a damaged one. Don't worry, they all made it on board just fine." Krusswell smiled. "I wanted to ask you about the battle though."

Any relief in Natalie vanished in an instant. "The battle over Dogor, sir?"

"No, I want to know what happened to the OSC *Endurance*." His voice grew serious. "You're the only one to make it back that witnessed the whole battle."

Natalie was quiet for a few moments. "There's not a lot to tell, sir," she began. "They overwhelmed us, simple as that. We evacuated the carrier, but not before losing all of our fighters, except for mine, and well, you saw the state my Spectre was in when it came aboard, and you see me now." She motioned with her right arm; the hand covered in bandages.

"And Commodore Vystra? None of the ships in the fleet have mentioned retrieving him yet."

"He stayed aboard, sir." Natalie was quiet. "He, like every fighter and bomber pilot that died, did so to buy time for the transports to escape."

Krusswell sighed, looking away from her. "Alright, thank you, Lieutenant." He looked at the machine monitoring Natalie's vitals. "You should get yourself some rest. I can't imagine what you went through back there. All I know is, based on what the passengers of Dolphins we've picked up have said, it's amazing you made it out at all."

Natalie didn't respond. She looked away from Krusswell then to the cold floor of the room. The tears came so fast and suddenly, she didn't have time to excuse herself. Krusswell patted Natalie's shoulder as he stood up. "Give yourself the time you need," he said quietly as he turned to leave. "You've done your duty for now."

The moment the door slid closed, Natalie collapsed onto her back. The ceiling's dull features were blurred and obscured by the tears pooling in her vision. They began to overflow, streaming down the sides of her face toward her ears and onto the white pillow under her. With her left arm, she tried to wipe the tears away, but more replaced the ones now smeared on her wrist. And so, she lay still, sniffling and with her arm blocking her vision and any tears from breaking free.

Why had she lived? *How* had she lived? Why did she live instead of any of the others? Natalie realized all at once that she was now utterly alone. There was no one to comfort her, no one to tell her that things would be okay. No one to bring her friends back.

Never again would she be able to play sports or go on leave with her friends. She would never join her friends in the mess hall for drinks ever again. Kislo would never be there to give her advice. Jinsu and Trisha's smiles and laughs as they sat together were gone. Claire would never be able to listen to Natalie's problems and give her the comfort she needed ever again. There would never be anymore flying talk with Varya. Darren, her best friend, had been torn out of her heart and would never return.

It could have been any of them here instead of me, Natalie thought. *So why am I here?* As if activating to answer her sickening questions, her memory began playing fragments of the battle. Natalie was left as a passenger in reliving the worst moments of her life.

Darren sacrificed himself to save me in the end, she thought. *He hadn't been hit. He should have stayed instead of me.*

In reverse order, her mind moved from *Endurance's* final moments to the previous moment Natalie could have, or *should have*, been killed.

She saw Varya save her from the Orange Hawk instead of landing to get medical attention. She used her final breaths of life to save Natalie's life.

She saw Darren save her when she had made the mistake at *Endurance's* bridge. A moment later, and the enemy would have killed her for her own stupidity.

She saw the engineer stopping her from taking off with a damaged plane. *Why couldn't he do that for Jinsu?* Natalie questioned.

Finally, she saw the moment she had been hit by *Trinity's* debris. The ancient leviathan, and her own plane's fragility, had prevented her from flying in the initial moments of *Endurance's* desperate bid for survival.

If I never had that damage, I would have flown when the first attack happened, Natalie thought. *Maybe I would have died then, in the first wave, with Jinsu.* Her mind began piecing together an alternate reality, a dreamworld where she was long dead.

Darren wouldn't have had to save her when she took off. *Would the extra ammunition have saved him? Or someone else? Who else could have been saved instead?*

Varya wouldn't have used the last moments of her life to save her. *Maybe if she had a different wingman, she wouldn't have been hit at all.*

Finally, Darren wouldn't have had to fly back to *Endurance* to distract the Halerians from Natalie and the Dolphin. *He would have saved them by himself and would have made it here instead. Maybe others would be with him. If it weren't for me, how many would still be alive now?*

Natalie shook her head. She tried to block the images from her mind, to derail the thoughts that were overwhelming her. When she finally did, she only felt the dull, throbbing pain of her leg and hand. She removed her left arm from her face and looked back up at the ceiling. The ceiling tiles had small perforations in them. Natalie started counting. If she could focus on counting each tiny hole, she wouldn't think of her friends.

There were 625 holes on each tile, assuming she hadn't counted wrong. Then, she started counting the tiles in the room. When she exceeded her vision, she moved her head slightly to count the rest. In the far-left corner, the room angled, and the tiles were cut into triangles. Some were exactly half a tile, but others were bigger or smaller. Natalie decided to leave these for last. Only when she had counted all the whole tiles in the room did she try to math out the total, minus the imperfect triangles.

"Six hundred, twenty-five times 192..." she whispered. "Is..." She wished she were quicker at math. Or at least had a piece of paper. "Six hundred, twenty-five times two... That's 1,250... Plus ninety times 625?" She sighed. Maybe she could ask Sinclair for a calculator when she came by next.

Giving up on her math expedition, Natalie resorted to watching her own vitals on the monitor beside her bed. She wasn't sure how long she watched the rhythmic way the green lines rose and fell, but at some point along the way, she fell fast asleep.

***

Natalie woke up to the sound of the door sliding open. When she opened her eyes, she saw Corporal Sinclair standing in the door with a tray of food.

"Sorry to wake you, ma'am," she said apologetically. "But your dinner is ready, if you want to eat."

Natalie gave a sleepy nod and sat up. "What's for dinner?"

Sinclair smiled and brought the tray over to her. "Nothing special today, unfortunately." Holding the tray with one hand, she reached under the bed and produced a small white stand, which she unfolded with a flick of the wrist and set on Natalie's lap. "Just some smoked meat, potatoes, and some green beans. I brought you some water as well." She set the tray atop the stand. The food was plated in an appetizing arrangement, and the plate's contents steamed.

"This looks delicious, thank you," Natalie said, looking from the food to Sinclair.

"Is there anything else I can get you, ma'am?"

Natalie thought for a moment and even glanced up at the ceiling tiles before shaking her head. "This is just fine, thank you."

Sinclair bowed her head slightly. "Of course, ma'am," she said. "You enjoy your meal. Doctor Tulo and I will be back later this evening just for a checkup."

Only once the door closed behind Sinclair did Natalie turn to her food. Just glancing at the meat made her mouth water. For a moment, she thought about the last time she had physically eaten, rather than whatever nutrients the doctors had been pumping into her. When the image of eating breakfast with Jinsu that morning flashed through her mind, she suddenly felt all the loneliness of earlier rush back. Trying to hold back the onrushing emotions, she flung her arms out to reach for her cutlery. The faster she started eating, she believed, the faster she could disconnect from the unwanted thoughts.

Those thoughts were dispelled rapidly the moment her right hand tried to wrap around the knife resting on the tray. The speed and force at which Natalie tried to close her hand sent a searing pain through the center of her hand, as though someone had shot it a second time. She recoiled, flinging the fork from her left hand across the room and falling backward until her head landed on her pillow.

Once again, Natalie found herself looking at the ceiling and its 192 tiles with 625 tiny holes in each. Resting on her chest, she clutched her right hand with her left. The pain, still fierce, was now beginning to subside into a dull throb.

Not on the winning side of the odds, Natalie thought. *That's what he said.* She raised her right hand until it was between her eyes and the ceiling. It was still wrapped in a layer of bandages, but she knew that there was nothing good underneath. *If I can never fly again, what will I do? Will they send me home? Will my career be over?* She dropped her arm to her side.

Natalie started thinking about home, Elle, and the reason she had joined in the first place. *I wanted to protect people. I wanted to keep people from being killed like my father.*

Suddenly, she shot up in her bed. *The notes,* her mind began racing. *I still don't know what those notes are about, or what they are saying about my father.*

"Varya said that we'd look for the truth together," Natalie whispered. "But she's gone now..." She felt the tears starting to come back. *I should keep looking. I have to. For Dad and for Varya. She wanted me to find the truth.*

With her left hand, Natalie brushed the tears off her cheek. She didn't want to think of Varya anymore. Just like the others, she found herself wishing that she could forget her, forget all of them, forget *Endurance.* After a few moments, she refocused her vision on the tray in front of her.

Eating took a while. The fork was lying on the floor near the door, far out of reach for someone incapable of walking. Natalie fed herself by stabbing the meat with her knife, and the potatoes and beans she ate carefully by using her knife as an inefficient spoon. When she finally finished, she laid back on the bed and shut her eyes. She didn't want to stare at the ceiling anymore.

CHAPTER 24

The next morning, after breakfast and a routine checkup, both Tulo and Sinclair returned to Natalie's room. They hadn't said anything the evening before about the fork on the floor or the way that her eyes had betrayed the number of tears she had shed while they had been away. And this morning, when those same eyes continued to betray her, they said nothing. They simply smiled, and Sinclair carried a flat gray-colored hydro-brace into the room.

"Let's get this on, shall we?" Tulo said when they entered the room. "No sense in waiting around. All indications point to your leg healing well, and your vitals show that you have recovered quite rapidly. Once this is on, you'll be on your way to your new quarters."

Natalie didn't speak. She simply nodded at him with a dull expression and reddened eyes. Still, both he and Sinclair smiled at the prospect of getting Natalie fitted for her brace.

"All I need you to do is lie back on the bed," he said.

She did as he said, lying flat on her back. She tilted her head to watch what he was doing. Sinclair passed him a black brace with a joint in its center and small tubes on its exterior. She then carefully lifted Natalie's left leg, just high enough for Tulo to slide the brace underneath and onto the bed. As Sinclair lowered Natalie's leg, he did up the straps over the front of the leg, and within moments the brace was unified with the leg as he did up the last strap.

"There you are," Tulo said, stepping back from the bed. "The brace is pressure sensitive, so it'll move with you with little effort. And it will take the load off your wound too. You'll be hobbling around for a bit, but it's better than a wheelchair."

"Why don't you give it a test run, ma'am?" Sinclair asked chipperly.

Natalie slowly pushed herself off the bed and onto the tile floor, putting most of her weight on her right leg. Slowly, she allowed her left to take more of the weight. Silently, the brace acted and reacted, taking the new pressure off her injured leg.

Sinclair remained close by. "Try taking a couple of steps, ma'am," she said. "Go slowly, I'm right here to catch you."

Natalie did as she was asked and stepped forward with her left leg. She stumbled, but Sinclair grabbed her arm and steadied her.

"Just a few more, ma'am," she reassured Natalie. "You'll get the hang of it in no time."

It took Natalie another fifteen minutes to walk on her own without stumbling every few steps. By the end, she could limp from one end of the small medical room to the other and back without Corporal Sinclair's assistance.

"That's great," Tulo said, watching from the edge of the room. "At this rate, you'll be able to walk from one end of the cruiser to the other!"

Sinclair laughed. "Let's not let her get ahead of herself."

"Well, she's going to be on her way to her quarters soon," Tulo said, drawing a piece of paper and a keycard from his clipboard. "It's yours until we get to Jontunia. Here's the location." He handed the items to Natalie.

"Let me get you my jacket," Sinclair spoke up. "It's just hanging in the office. I won't need it until we get home." Natalie nodded, and Sinclair was immediately out the door, with it sliding patiently closed behind her.

Sinclair was back in less than a minute, a camouflage jacket in hand. She handed it to Natalie and helped keep her steady as she put it on. The jacket was a little big for Natalie, covering her to just past her shorts. As she zipped up the jacket, Sinclair tore off the rank patches and the nametag, which read "Sinclair." In their place she gently pressed on lieutenant ranks, and a nametag reading "Annikki." The nametag was in the color and style of a flight suit rather than an army uniform.

"We pulled the tag off your flight suit when we took you out of it," Sinclair explained, noticing Natalie's attention to it. "We did have to wash a bit of blood off of it, but nothing too bad."

"Thank you," Natalie said quietly, placing the paper and the keycard into the jacket pockets.

Tulo opened the door. "You'd best be on your way then. We'll be in touch soon." He pointed at Natalie's right hand. She nodded and limped out the door, glancing down at the room number on the paper before determining the direction of her new quarters and starting off toward her new room.

Luckily for Natalie, the residential sector was directly adjacent to the medical ward, and with the Oracle-class cruiser being almost half the length of a Tempest, Natalie was able to hobble her way to the room indicated on the paper she was given, two decks down and close to an elevator, adjacent to the stairwell. On her way, she passed the occasional crew member going about their day. Natalie noticed them giving her some odd looks, every now and then staring until Natalie made eye contact with them.

Have they never seen an injured person before? Natalie wondered. She tried to dismiss it as some sort of nonsense. After all, she wasn't a crew member on *Light the Way*. She was essentially a foreigner, or someone from another town. An interloper in a tight community, one that stood out like a sore thumb on account of her brace and bandaged hand.

By the time that she reached her room, however, the stares had been enough. Natalie didn't waste any time unlocking the door before swiftly stepping in and shutting it behind her. Moving on muscle memory, she reached for the light switch, which happened to be in a familiar location on the wall. At once, all of the lights in the kitchen and living area turned on and bathed the room in the same soft light as that of the medical room.

The quarters were eerily similar to Natalie's own on *Endurance*. In fact, as Natalie walked unsteadily through the space, she noticed that they were exactly mirrored, making them identical in every way to Darren's instead. All that was missing was the disorganized way he piled his dishes in the little kitchen and Darren's personal effects that he had brought from Jontunia or bought over three years of flying—and Darren himself.

When the same feelings that had tormented her yesterday, the ones which had kept her awake long into the night, and the ones that had woken her well before she should, began to well up again inside her, Natalie cast her vision at once to the floor and hobbled with all the speed she could to the bathroom door. Before she allowed any thoughts into her mind, she occupied herself with what she saw as the next priority: a shower and a clean change of clothes.

Natalie took the towel from the wall as she stepped out of the shower. She closed her eyes and dried her face and hair as she took the few short steps from the shower to the bathroom counter. As she began patting her hair with the towel, she opened her eyes and looked into the mirror. All movement, even her breath, ceased when she saw her face.

Reaching from just before the base of her left ear to just to the left of her mouth was a long, deep, hideous scar. Though thin at either end, it widened toward the middle to the width of Natalie's smallest finger. Whatever the wound had been, the medical staff had attempted to patch it up, but it still looked and felt horrendous as Natalie ran her finger along its length. It was rough and coarse, her finger feeling every bump and groove. Natalie couldn't bear to see it any longer, turning from the mirror to face the wall behind her.

Oh gods, her mind raced. *Is this what those people were staring at? This is what happened to me?* Natalie stared at the tiled floor then the towel that had been dropped to her feet. After a few moments, she spun around and looked at her mirrored face. *Is it permanent?* She turned away again. Images of her friends flashed briefly in her mind. She could never show her face to any of them. Her mind focused on Darren, and she felt tears beginning to well up in her eyes.

Then thoughts seemed to come all at once: the others would never see her face or the scar. Darren wouldn't be able to respond to it. They were all dead. This scar was the mark of their deaths. Natalie rushed forward, collapsing to the floor as her left leg gave out. She pulled herself the last foot to the toilet and puked.

The bedroom was cleanly set, with a made bed and some items on the shelves, such as clean towels and soap. On the bed itself were Natalie's things recovered from her Spectre. Her flight suit was folded and set next to a brand-new standard uniform. On the new uniform, Natalie's nametag was visible, facing the ceiling. Farther toward the head of the bed were Natalie's flight helmet and the bag Natalie had taken with her when she departed *Endurance* for the last time. She grabbed the new uniform and got dressed, willing her mind to remain blank.

Natalie limped across the room and sat on the edge of the bed next to her bag. She drew everything out from within it and examined them for any damage. Much of the contents were simple things that Natalie had bought or taken from home. Decorations and mementos, she took each one out and placed them on the bed.

Natalie found a small sleeve of photographs and flipped through each one. They were pictures of her and the White Tails from the last three years. Natalie didn't spend much time looking at them, just enough to make sure they weren't torn or damaged in any way, before replacing them into their protective sleeve.

Next was the notebook with all the messages she had received from the anonymous source. She thought about opening it but decided instead to place it back in the bag.

That will have to wait for now, Natalie thought.

The last item in the bag was the stuffed cat her father had given her. It had been the first thing she put in the bag when deciding what to keep. Its synthetic fur was still soft to the touch, and though it now smelled of military bag, Natalie didn't mind. She put everything back in the bag and closed it up, setting it aside on the nightstand next to the bed.

Natalie picked up her flight helmet and looked it over. For the most part, it was undamaged, and had been cleaned since her recovery onto *Light the Way*. On the left side, however, was a patchwork job to repair the hole created by the Halerian bullet. Natalie spent little time looking it over as she placed it on the shelf below her bag. Keeping her flight suit folded, she placed it under the helmet and stood up. As much as she wanted to sit in her room waiting for the fleet's return to Jontunia, she knew she had something still to do.

Natalie limped through the halls of *Light the Way* as she made her way toward the cruiser's bridge. She tried to ignore the glances, stares, and quiet remarks as people walked by, her scar ever present. Natalie dropped off the jacket loaned to her, leaving it hung outside the medical room she had woken up in. When she arrived at *Light the Way's* bridge, it had been fifteen minutes since she had left her quarters.

The bridge was quiet, with only the sounds of footsteps occasionally moving from desk to desk and the low whispers of information being passed. There were under two dozen staff working the bridge, a sign that the threat of a Halerian counterattack had long passed. Commodore Krusswell was watching the slow pace of events from his chair in the center of the upper floor of the two-floor bridge. He was silently sipping on a mug of coffee and reading reports as they scrolled by on his personal terminal. Natalie approached from behind before snapping herself to attention and bringing her right hand up in her attempt at a salute.

"Sir, Lieutenant Natalie Annikki, reporting for… uh…" Natalie trailed off. Just what *was* she reporting to him for? It certainly wasn't for any duty; her body was still a wreck.

Commodore Krusswell smiled as he turned around. "At ease, Lieutenant." He placed his mug of coffee on the small surface next to his chair and stood up. "I'm glad to see you're walking."

Natalie glanced down at the brace on her leg. "The miracle of technology, sir," she responded. "I was surprised to be able to walk myself."

"What brings you to my bridge so soon?"

"Sir, I was hoping you could find something out for me." Natalie shifted her weight away from her left leg. "One of my colleagues was still alive, last I heard from her, but was adrift. I was hoping you could check with the rest of the fleet as to whether or not anyone has recovered her Spectre."

Krusswell motioned to one of his staff officers to come over. "Of course we can, Lieutenant," he explained as the other officer approached with a transparent tablet. "The fleet has been compiling a list of recovered strike craft in the area, even debris that has drifted through. If they've found your friend's plane, it will be in here." Krusswell took the tablet from the young officer and dismissed him. "I'll just need the ID of the Spectre in question."

Natalie felt a rush of hope through her chest. "Yes, sir, it's EFW-164."

Krusswell nodded, scrolling through the tablet's thin screen. Natalie glanced away from just how many lines he scrolled through. After a few moments, he shook his head. "Nothing," he said, turning toward Natalie. She didn't meet his gaze, instead looking at the metal floor. "There are a few still missing. It's possible your friend will turn up before we leave. Do you want me to check any of the others?"

Natalie shook her head. "No, I know what happened to the rest." She looked up at Krusswell. "Thank you for checking."

Krusswell smiled. "Is there anything else I can do for you?"

"Not right now, sir." Natalie was quiet and struggled to look her superior in the eye. "When are we setting off for home?"

"In four days," Krusswell responded. "With the three strongest fleets heading back for repair and rebuilding, the OSC is calling up the seven of the remaining nine Mobile fleets to continue the war without them. I don't know what's in their plans, but once they arrive, the Defensive fleets that were called up to the border will return home." Krusswell looked longingly to the wall, where a Jontunian flag had been hung.

"Is this the farthest you've ever traveled from Jontunia?" Natalie asked, glancing between Krusswell and the flag.

"This is the farthest almost any of us have been from Fury's Gate, Lieutenant." Krusswell motioned to the whole of the bridge, and the ship itself as he said Jontunia's other, more sacred name.

Natalie looked around at the others on the bridge. Natalie doubted that any of the crew had even been to planets other than their own. "Home was supposed to be just a few hours away, right?"

Krusswell sat into his chair with a sigh. "When I wanted, I could go to the observation deck and look out at the walls of the Salerum Cloud, and I could see Jontunia, not as a speck of light in the distance, but as a world. And I could see Tralis as it quietly watched over our home, like we ourselves were trained to do." He shook his head. "This isn't the place for us."

"I suppose not, but it's your duty, sir, isn't it?"

"Duty's the only reason any of us are here, Lieutenant. Without the Nine Claws, the fleet just feels… weak."

He was right, Natalie knew. The nine Hard Mobile Retention stations surrounding Jontunia made up the bulk of the defensive fleet's combat power. Without the HMR stations, the fleet would prove little more than a speed bump for any attacking Halerian fleets. *But the OSC should know that,* she thought.

Natalie stepped back. "It's only four more days, sir. Hopefully nothing happens." She didn't feel like being a part of another slowing operation. Once was enough. "If you'll excuse me, sir." Commodore Krusswell nodded to Natalie's attempted salute, and she turned and exited the bridge.

Light the Way's cafeteria wasn't particularly busy when Natalie Annikki limped through the entranceway and toward the meal line. She tried to ignore the second glance the server gave her when she was handed her meal. She limped from the meal line toward the tables. Natalie saw some soldiers among the few dozen people already seated, ones that must have been on *Endurance* and escaped on the Dolphins. They were laughing and joking, seemingly unaffected by what they had just experienced.

Natalie turned away from them and toward an empty table when she was stopped by a voice. "Excuse me, ma'am. Are you the pilot that saved us?"

Natalie turned to face a woman no older than herself, her eyes looking sheepishly through glasses as she tugged nervously at her brunette hair. Her simple dress clothes told Natalie nothing about who she was.

"You're the pilot from *Endurance*, right? It's just that you look like… you might be." Natalie saw the woman's eyes flick over the scar disfiguring her face. "Sorry, I don't mean to offend."

Natalie didn't want to talk to this girl, but she was only asking a question. "Yeah." Natalie spoke quietly.

The young woman's eyes lit up, and she smiled brightly. Natalie glanced around, meeting the looks of others in the cafeteria. "Would you please come sit with us? There's a few of us that really wanted to talk to you."

Us? Natalie could feel the apprehension rising, but it was too late to back out now. The woman was already leading her to a table with four others.

The woman motioned for Natalie to sit down across from her, and she did. Setting her tray down, Natalie reached for her ponytail, subtly stroking it. The others were all watching, surely wondering who she was.

"Dr. Browning, I've found her!" the woman called to a middle-aged man seated on the far end of the table. "This is the pilot that escorted us here!"

Dr. Browning smiled at Natalie. "I'm so glad my assistant found you," he said. "I wanted to know if you had survived your wounds and pay my thanks for protecting us like you did."

It clicked immediately for Natalie, who couldn't hide her surprise. "You're the doctor I spoke to from the damaged Dolphin?"

Browning nodded. "These are all people from that Dolphin," he said, motioning to the other four seated with him. "My assistant who found you is Ava. This is a colleague of mine, Dr. Lys." A woman close to Browning's age gave a courteous wave to Natalie. "And these two young men are the pilots of the Dolphin."

"On behalf of all twenty-five lives you saved, we thank you," the young man sitting next to Natalie said. "Without you, I don't think any of us would be here."

"You're… Cockroach then?" Natalie asked.

"That's right." The man smiled. "Lieutenant Ian Thein, but you can just call me Ian. And you must go by something besides Wildcat, I presume."

"Uh, yeah, Lieutenant Natalie Annikki. Just call me Natalie." She felt unsteady. She simply wanted to eat in silence, alone. She stabbed at her food, eating what she could. As questions came to her, she answered in short, clipped sentences. Mostly, she stared off at the white walls, counting the tiles and ignoring the people around her. She just wanted to be left alone. Eventually, the question Natalie dreaded, but knew was coming, was asked.

"I heard the fight was pretty desperate. Did you lose many planes?" Dr. Lys asked.

How many planes? There were people in every single one of them. Don't speak like they were just objects to be thrown away. You, how many of you *lived?* Natalie repeated the question over in her mind. *You may as well have asked: how many pilots died so we could have this meal?* "Just me," Natalie said in a low voice. "I'm the only one that 'got away.'"

Most at the table, other than Ian, were shocked. *What? Did you hear about any other fighters flying with us? Look at me, dammit; if there were others, do you really think I would have been the one to stay behind with you?* Natalie tried to weather the irrational anger swelling up inside her. But with every moment of stunned silence that passed, she gave more ground.

Ava was the first to speak again. "I'm so sorry to hear that. I'm glad you made it back in one piece, though." She smiled.

Why, so you could feel safe, knowing that at least one pilot was still ready to save you? Natalie had to grind her teeth together to keep from snapping back. *Do you have any idea how many people died? Apologies mean nothing now. The lives sacrificed so you, so I, could sit here and eat this meal and say sorry that they had to die for it? What the fuck gives you the right over them to live? Who decided that the lives of you people were worth more than the lives of the pilots?* Natalie realized that everyone was looking at her in silence. She looked down at her half-finished food and abruptly stood up.

"Natalie?" Ian called to her as she began to turn away.

Natalie didn't answer him. She didn't even pick up her tray and instead hastily limped out of the cafeteria and all the way to her quarters.

In the silence of the dark, empty room, Natalie screamed. Not a single light was on, and instead the room was lit only by the dim bluish glow of the screen facing the couch. Natalie was pacing from the living room to the small kitchen and back, tears and screams of anger and agony penetrating the stillness of the room.

"Why was it me?" she asked the room. "Why am I still here?"

The room didn't answer Natalie's sorrowful questions.

"Why me?!" She grabbed the first thing within reach, a small white mug. "Why are they still here and not us?!" She whipped the mug across the room, shattering it against the solid wall. For a moment, Natalie felt relief, as though the mug contained the souls of each of the people she had saved from *Endurance*. When the moment passed, Natalie slouched over the counter and sobbed.

"My friends were no less than any of them, so why did they have to die? Why were we so expendable?" No answers came to Natalie. She was greeted only by the silence of the room, a silence that was far too much to bear. She cried out again, grabbing another object and shattering it against the same wall.

"None of them will ever know how I feel," she spoke viciously toward the door, thinking of Ava and the others. "'I'm so sorry.' Fuck off. How about I kill all your friends at that table in front of you? Then you'll know how I feel. Then you'll know how worthless petty bullshit like that is. You couldn't understand."

She grabbed a plate off the counter and aimed for the door. She wound up with all of her strength and threw the plate. Her throw set her off-balance, and she stumbled to the floor. She rolled onto her back and looked down at her braced leg.

"I hate you," Natalie spat at her leg. "Why can't you, and *you*," she looked at her right hand, "just get better, so I can fly away from this hell hole. Get better so I can go find Claire dammit." Natalie dragged herself across the kitchen to its center.

Propping herself up against the side of the counter, she saw Claire's face flash in her mind and cried.

"I'm sorry," she whispered. "I failed you. I failed you all. You all put so much faith in me... Why? I failed you from the very beginning. If I hadn't chased *Trinity*... maybe you would all be here instead of me." Natalie looked from the floor to the ceiling. "I hate you, Varya, Darren; why did you have to save me, just so I could be alone like this? I hate you both." Natalie paused, tears overwhelming her briefly.

When she spoke again, her tone had shifted from anger to sheer torment and sorrow. "Are you all together right now? I don't want to stay here alone." She pushed herself off the floor and turned toward the sink. "Is this a reward or punishment?" She plugged the sink, turned the water on. "What kind of reward is living if there's no one else?" Natalie watched water slowly fill the sink. "Why should I be rewarded for failing everyone?"

She forced her head into the water. She held it there even as the rest of her body quaked in fear when the air was gone. Her reflexes, desperate for air, inhaled the water instead. The moment Natalie began choking, something in her threw herself from the sink, and she fell back onto the floor, coughing up water and gasping for air. "No," she growled when she could speak again. "No more..."

Natalie half-crawled, half-dragged herself across the room to the shattered plate next to the door. Rolling up her right sleeve, Natalie grabbed the biggest, sharpest piece of shattered porcelain she saw. She placed it against the soft skin of her right wrist and slowly began pressing into it, sliding it ever so slightly across her skin. She winced at the pain but kept pressing until she saw the first bit of blood rise around the penetrating edge of the porcelain. Natalie went to press harder but stopped. Her left hand dropped the piece of shattered plate, and Natalie fell to her side in tears.

"Please, Darren, take me to you, somehow..."

Natalie lay motionless on the floor for hours. After the first two, the tears stopped, and Natalie simply stared at the ceiling without thought. She couldn't bring herself to move, to get up, to even roll over. She just stayed on the floor, thinking of nothing. She didn't even know if she ever blinked. Perhaps this was as close as she could get to being dead.

Eventually, Natalie found enough strength to drag herself to the edge of the wall between the kitchen and the living room. She stared blankly at the screen, which still idly lit the space in a light blue hue. The clock said it was close to the middle of the 10th. She had been lying on the floor for nearly an entire day. It was nearing lunch time again aboard *Light the Way*, but Natalie didn't move. She didn't feel hungry, or thirsty, or tired even. Instead, she felt nothing, nothing but the rise and fall of her own chest as she unconsciously kept herself alive.

It took another full day for Natalie to reach the entrance of her bedroom. She wasn't sure why she was moving this way, but every time she had any strength, she pulled herself another foot forward. Perhaps there was some comfort in the bedroom, or maybe the farther Natalie got from the door to her quarters, the farther she felt from the sad reality she lived in. Whichever the case, Natalie pulled herself into the bedroom. Here, there was no glow of the screen; instead, it was dark and somehow more silent than before.

Natalie's eyes scanned the darkness from just inside the doorway. As they adjusted, she began to make out familiar silhouettes scattered about the room. Even in the dark, she could make out her helmet resting on the shelf inside, and as her eyes moved upwards, they spotted the bag she had brought with her sitting on top of the little table. Natalie suddenly remembered the bag's contents. Possessed by some newfound energy, she attempted to stand before falling on her injured leg and crawling across the floor. She reached for the nightstand and pulled the bag down to the floor with her.

She opened the bag one-handedly and turned it over, scattering its contents on the floor. Feeling around in the dark, Natalie's hand passed over familiar objects, including the photos of her deceased friends, but she couldn't see their faces. Eventually, she felt what she was looking for: an object soft to the touch, whose fur now smelled more like combat than home. Natalie clutched it in her good hand and brought it to her chest.

"Dad," she whispered in the dark. "What am I supposed to do? I want to keep flying, and now I want to know what happened to you. If you could just tell me what *really* happened, then… Please, Dad, I don't know how to go on anymore." She felt the first tears in days beginning to form. "I don't know how to go on like this, Dad; I've lost everyone, and I don't even understand what for." The tears began to gently slide down her face, those on the left pooling on the edges of her scar. "If only you could speak to me, maybe you would know what all this fighting is for." Natalie paused as realization set in. "Were you connected to this war? Who betrayed you, and for what? If I knew, would that tell me why we had to have this war? Please, Dad, I need to know why..." Natalie hugged the stuffed cat before falling to her side, sobbing. Only two feet from her bed and after two days, she finally succumbed to sleep.

***

Natalie tucked her hands under her armpits as the cold wind blew around her. She was standing in a street, in a town that seemed as foreign as it did familiar. The roads, lawns, and rooftops of houses were blanketed in snow. Natalie turned around and saw a house behind her, one which she quickly recognized as her own. She was in Rikata, she realized; she was home. Natalie turned away from the cold and walked up the few steps to her front door and stepped inside.

In the entranceway, Jinsu was waiting. He was dressed in casual clothes, and he smiled at Natalie. "Hello, Natalie," he spoke softly as he approached her. "You look like you've been through hell."

"Who says I'm through it?" Natalie replied. "I'm starting to think it never ends, honestly."

Jinsu placed a hand on her shoulder and said, "This is the end—or at least, an end. But don't worry, you are strong enough to keep going."

"I'm sorry for what happened to you." She couldn't think of anything else to say.

"Don't be," he assured her. "There was nothing you could do to change the outcome. Now please, get going." Jinsu motioned for Natalie to continue through the house. He didn't follow.

Natalie found Trisha sitting in the kitchen. She jumped up from her seat the moment she saw her. "The kitten is finally home!" she exclaimed, bounding over to Natalie and giving her a tight hug.

"Hi, Trisha," Natalie said as the two separated. "You look well."

Trisha scanned Natalie's face. "I certainly look better than you," she said. "You look like you've been lost in the woods for weeks."

"I feel like I've been through worse." Natalie stared through the kitchen window at the not-so-familiar town.

"I know, kitten, but that's behind you now." Trisha stepped in front of the window to get her attention. "You should be proud you made it out. You're the best damn pilot I've ever seen, and now you have the opportunity to prove it again and again to the Halerians."

"How could it be behind me if every day I have to face being alone?" Natalie was on the verge of tears. "How am I supposed to be proud of losing all of you?"

Trisha placed her hands on Natalie's shoulders. "That's not what I'm saying. You need to put the *battle* behind you. Put what happened to you behind you, but don't forget what happened to us. And don't forget the Orange Hawks, ever."

Natalie nodded. "I won't. And, Trisha, I'm sorry."

"What for?"

Natalie glanced away. "I should have protected Claire better," she said quietly. "It's my fault she's gone."

Trisha was quiet for a moment and then smiled. "I think you're wrong, Natalie." She turned her friend toward the kitchen door. "But you'll have to ask Claire yourself." She gave a gentle push to Natalie's back, forcing her forward. When Natalie turned around at the door, Trisha was gone.

Natalie walked to her father's study. She stopped at the doorway when she saw Kislo in the room, admiring her father's book collection. She watched for a minute or two as he scanned the back of each book, stopping occasionally on ones that he must have found interesting or recognized. A few times, he reached up to touch the book with his fingertips.

"Hello, sir." Natalie broke the silence and stepped into the room.

Kislo turned around and smiled. "There's no need for that, Annikki." His voice was soft and carried none of the usual seriousness to it that it usually did. "I'm not your superior anymore."

"That's not true."

"Of course it is. You are the leader of the White Tails now."

"But you put Verra in charge," Natalie countered.

"And he served admirably in the short time he had to lead," Kislo said. "But he is not alive to lead anymore, and he placed *you* in command."

"But why have a leader at all?" Natalie questioned. "I'm the only one left."

"That's why it's important for you to lead," Kislo responded. "Our memory, and the history of the White Tails. All of that is your responsibility now. It's up to you what happens to our name. Rebuild our squadron or renew it as something else. I'm leaving it in your hands."

Natalie was quiet for a moment. "I understand." She looked up at her former commander. "I won't let you down."

Kislo nodded. "You never have. I know you'll bring more glory to our name. I'll be forever proud of you."

"Thank you, si—Tanner." Natalie turned to leave.

"Good luck, Natalie," Tanner said as she left the room.

Natalie walked down the short hallway to the house's living room, where Claire stood admiring the art on the wall. Her red hair was as vibrant as Natalie remembered. Claire turned around to see her friend and smiled.

"Claire..." Natalie spoke softly. The two embraced for a long time.

"I've missed you," Claire said as she rested her head against Natalie's shoulder.

"I'm sorry, Claire." Natalie wanted stay in this room forever. "I wanted to go find you, save you, but I—"

"It's okay." Claire suddenly pulled away, her blue eyes staring straight into Natalie's. Tears were pooling at their base. "You never would have found me."

"What?"

Claire shook her head and paced around the room. "You could have flown for days and never found me. I don't blame you for anything. You were lucky enough to escape at all."

"But I still should have looked for you," Natalie argued.

Claire stopped and looked Natalie dead in the eye. "You would have died," she began, her voice serious. "Don't think for a second that something so stupid would have worked."

"But—"

"Let it be, Natalie. Stop holding yourself responsible."

Natalie was silent, and Claire took the few steps to cross the room. When she stopped before Natalie, Natalie nodded. Claire wrapped her arms around her friend one last time.

"Good," she said. "Now go on, there are others still waiting for you."

After leaving the living room and Claire behind, Natalie took the short walk upstairs. Standing in the hallway near the top of the stairs was a woman with long brunette hair done up in a loose ponytail. Her golden eyes were set alight when she saw Natalie, and she smiled.

"You've finally made it," Varya said.

"I wish I could have been here sooner," Natalie replied as she took the last step of the staircase.

"Don't," Varya said flatly. "And it better be a long time after this visit before I see you again." Though she was serious, her voice betrayed pain as she finished her sentence.

Natalie stood quietly in thought, watching Varya toil with her own emotions. "Why'd you do it, Varya?" she asked at last. "Why die for me when you could have made it to the hangar? You could have made it home."

This time it was Varya who stood silent in thought. Eventually, she sighed. "Because I was tired, Natalie," she began. "I was tired of the never-ending war, tired of fighting, tired of killing and seeing people I cared about get killed. And… I couldn't just let you die."

"Why? What makes me so important?"

Varya glanced to the side. "Aside from being a great pilot? Once I got to know you… something changed… I wanted to make sure you lived. It became my goal."

"I wish you hadn't…" Natalie's voice trailed off.

"Don't say that!" Varya shouted, more so in fear than anger. "The truth is… is…" Varya's words failed to flow. She shook her head and tried again but couldn't speak. It was as though something in her were rejecting the words she so desired to say. Instead, Varya approached Natalie, coming closer and closer to her until she brought her face in close to Natalie's and suddenly kissed her on the cheek. "Do you remember my wish? Don't die… Please, just don't die," Varya whispered before stepping around Natalie and descending the stairs. When Natalie turned around, she had vanished.

Natalie slowly pushed open the wooden door to her bedroom. Darren sat on her bed in worn jeans and a dirt-stained T-shirt. He was holding a picture of himself, in those same clothes, with his family. He looked up at Natalie as she came into the room.

"It's good to see you again, Nat." His words pierced the stillness of the dimly lit room.

Natalie immediately felt the tears welling up in her eyes. "You bastard," she said. "Why did you have to leave me?"

Darren placed the picture on the bed and stood up. "So you could live," he responded, walking toward Natalie. "Only one of us was going to get to."

"But why choose me? I didn't even get a say in it."

"Because I love you." Darren wrapped his arms around her. "How could I choose my own life over yours?"

"But you left me to live… *alone*," Natalie cried into Darren's arms. "Do you have any idea how hard it's been?"

Darren kissed the top of Natalie's head. "I do, and I'm sorry for that," he said softly to her. "I wish I could be there with you. I wish that one of us could be there with you, and if there had been a way, it would have happened. But there wasn't, and so I won't apologize for saving you. That's something I will never regret."

"But life is impossible now, Darren. Living without you all is a waking nightmare. I don't know what I'm supposed to do or where to go without you and the others at my side."

Darren pushed Natalie away just enough so she could look up at him. "I can't tell you what to do. No one can. But I can say that you should keep flying. Never give up on the thing you love so much."

Natalie looked down at her hands. Though the right hand was healed in this dream, she knew it wouldn't be when she woke up. "I can't fly," she said. "My hand will never heal."

"Yes, it will, trust me." Darren held Natalie's face in his hands. "You'll fly again. And you know what? You'll be taking each and every one of us up there when you do."

Natalie nodded, tears streaming down her face. "I want to fly again."

"You will, Natalie, sooner than you expect." Darren moved forward and pulled Natalie in, kissing her. When she felt him release his grasp, she opened her eyes. Natalie was standing in the room alone. When Natalie blinked again, all was dark. She blinked a few more times. Silhouettes of objects started to become clearer. Her body was sore. She was thirsty and hungry. Natalie realized she was back on *Light the Way*, alone in her bedroom, on the floor, surrounded by her belongings.

***

Laying on her couch, Natalie watched the ship-wide news scroll by on the wall display. On the coffee table was a full plate of bread, slices of meat, and cheese. Next to it was a tall glass filled with water, and in Natalie's left hand was a half-eaten sandwich.

Across the top of the display a notice scrolled by: " TIME UNTIL DECELERATION: 4:03.34." The seconds ticked downwards as the message slowly disappeared off the left side of the screen. Soon after Natalie had woken up, *Light the Way* and the rest of the 3rd Defensive was recalled from the frontline. In a few days, they would arrive over Jontunia, and Natalie would finally be home—whatever that really meant now.

Rehabilitation, she thought, glancing down at her right hand. *Rehabilitation for who knows how long. And then maybe, maybe I'll get to fly again.*

"Well, looks like you'll be calling me a liar," Tulo said as he took off the last of Natalie's bandages.

"Excuse me?" Natalie cocked her head to the right, glancing from her hand to Tulo's face and back. She sat at the edge of the medical bed, the same room that she had woken up in a week ago. To her right, Sinclair stood, silent but brimming with happiness.

"I'd imagine that in just a few cycles time, you'll be able to fly again just fine," Tulo explained as he examined her right hand.

Despite the positive news, Natalie sighed. "But I'll be limited to Phantoms forever, right?"

"On the contrary." Tulo pointed his right index finger to the ceiling as he spoke. "While it may be a good place to ease back into flying, I think that your hand will be fit enough to fly Dolphins only a cycle later."

The Dolphin is certainly better than the alternative, Natalie thought. *But the Dolphin can't fight.* "What about the Spectre?" she asked Tulo.

"Well, we aren't completely sure about that one yet." Natalie's heart sank. "Your rehabilitation will have to go exceedingly well."

"But there is hope!" Sinclair interjected. "Don't give up, ma'am."

Natalie nodded. "Thank you, Corporal."

"I think we're all good here." Tulo stood up, letting go of Natalie's hand. "I'll see you the same time tomorrow for your next session."

"What happens when we get back to Jontunia?" Natalie asked after she stood up.

"A week from now, you'll be transferred to a medical institution planetside to continue your rehab. You'll stay there until you're fit for duty again."

"Thank you, Doctor." Natalie nodded to both Tulo and Sinclair. "I'll see you both tomorrow."

Natalie left the medical room and walked back to her quarters. Her leg was bothering her less and less each day. *Soon, the brace will be gone,* she thought. *And soon after, I'll fly again.*

CHAPTER 25

The retro-thrusters of the Oracle-class cruiser *Light the Way* slowly faded out until they had shut off completely. The cruiser now floated seemingly motionless in the blue-green expanse of the Salerum Cloud. No sooner than it had stopped did its small hangar bays, both located on the underside of the ship's hull, rotate downward to reveal themselves to the void. They locked into position, and a moment later nearly two dozen Dolphin light transports streamed out and made for Tralis.

Each one had a similar destination: one of the many pads and hangars that covered the surface of the moon, each one making up a crucial part of the interlinked complexes that wrapped and wound their way across the moon. Inside the vast complexes, men and women of the OSC and OGC moved with purpose to bring supplies, wounded personnel, and parts to their destinations. At one of the complexes, an unending number of shuttles landed and took off, each returning from or heading to the surface of Jontunia.

Many more Dolphins and Phantoms joined those of *Light the Way*. The 3rd Defensive, having returned from its emergency duty at the Altherian-Halerian border, now began the unloading of extra ammunition, planes, and recovered personnel from the shattered 3rd Mobile. On the other side of the moon from the 3rd Defensive, the remnants of the once great fleet sat in eerie stillness. The only movement among the hundreds of ships was the scurrying of many more hundreds of little engineering ships, each assigned to heal a wound from the opening act of the new war.

In the center of the fleet sat the sole surviving leviathan in the fleet, the flagship *Heart of Jontunia*. Around it, a fraction of its former fleet remained. Of the nearly three thousand ships that had set out for Gystamere, only six hundred had returned home. All had some sort of damage, but some were worse off than others. For some of the ships, these homes of hundreds or thousands of people, the damage was too great to be repaired. These ships were towed off to another area, an area where large engineering ships sat in orbit and were dismantled. Their parts would be used to rebuild the 3rd Mobile, so that in a few years it could return to its former strength and stand again as one of the strongest fleets in the sector.

Natalie sipped on a coffee. She was sitting in an office in Garun. The central desk was flanked on either side by tall bookshelves filled with books. On one side, the book subjects were entirely philosophy. On the other side, they were all medical. At the corners closest the door, there were two small potted trees.

The wooden door opened with a click, and in stepped a captain from the OSC. He carried a small red folder in his right hand. "Sorry about the wait, Lieutenant," he said, hurriedly rounding the desk to sit down in his office chair.

He slapped the folder down on the desk and opened it. His fingers ran through pages in a flutter until he reached the one he was aiming for. With a satisfied expression, he drew it from the folder, closed the folder, and laid the paper on top of the red folder.

"Here we are," he said. "As I'm sure your ship doctor mentioned, you will have to continue undergoing therapy and rehabilitation until your hand heals, or until it is clear that it won't get any better. This document is what you'll need to bring with you to the center the OSC is sending you to. Give it a read over and sign at the bottom please." He spun the paper around to face Natalie, who placed her coffee on the desk before taking the paper in her left hand.

The form read with an amount of medical nonsense that she found herself skipping entire sections of it. What she took note of were the dates and the location of the specialist center. The OSC had allotted a full year for Natalie to regain the use of her hand, and the specialist center was in the south end of Garun.

Before she signed the paper, she looked up at the captain. "Am I to stay in the capital for a whole year, sir?" she asked.

The captain nodded. "We'll get to that right after this, but yes," he said. "The OSC has rented an apartment for you to stay in here in the capital."

"And the rehab starts immediately," Natalie continued. "Does this mean I won't have the chance to go home?"

"Unfortunately, the OSC demands your presence close by, so they can both monitor your progress and call you up in case of any duty requirements," the captain explained. "You could take up a staff posting here to allow for another officer to join the fleet, for example. Therefore, you'll need to be available in the capital for the duration of your rehabilitation."

Natalie frowned. "Sir, I want to be able to go home. I haven't seen my home in years. After everything that's happened, I think that going home would be best for me."

The captain's cheery demeanor suddenly faded. "Lieutenant, I understand what you are saying. However, you must understand that what you think is best for you is not what the OSC thinks. At the end of the day, the OSC is an arm of the Omasye himself. If the OSC says that being here is best for you, then *that* is what is best for you. Please sign the page."

Natalie stared at him for a few moments. She knew that there was no sense in arguing. She was practically being ordered to accept the treatment and remain in the capital. If she defied him, they would simply confine her to some sort of base housing and escort her to her treatment every day. They didn't really need her signature for anything. Taking the pen in her left hand, Natalie scribbled an attempt at a signature on the page.

The captain smiled again when he took the paper. He replaced it into the folder and stood up. "Now, Lieutenant, if you would follow me," he said. "We'll get your key, and I'll have a car take you to your new apartment."

Natalie didn't have much to unpack. After only an hour or two, she had the entire apartment set up the way that she wanted. She even had the captain send someone with groceries so that she could at least feed herself until she was ready to go shopping on her own. With her kitchen stocked, she wouldn't have to worry about anything other than her appointments for at least a week.

The apartment was near the top of the tall complex and offered a rather picturesque view of the city skyline and the distant horizon. Inside, it was relatively simple for a two-floor apartment. From the doorway, the laundry room was positioned on the left of the front hall with an open kitchen and dining area on the right. Next to the laundry room was a sizable closet. At the end of the hall was the living room, which itself contained two couches facing a large wall display and a sizable bookshelf on the opposite wall. A narrow staircase between the laundry room and the living room led to the bedroom and bathroom, which were both on the floor above.

With her unpacking completed, all that was left to do was give the place a good cleaning and make herself dinner. Natalie was happy to finally have something to keep her occupied for a while.

It was into the evening when she finally settled onto the couch in the living room, satisfied that her new house was how she wanted it. Still, she found little to do. Reaching for the remote on the coffee table, she turned on the wall display.

The display was already tuned to a twenty-four-hour news program. Today's top story was the 3rd Defensive's return to the system. Video feeds of capital ships sending and receiving transports were shown alongside an infographic displaying the losses sustained by the 3rd Mobile from the Battle of Dogor. The moment she recognized the statistics for what they were, Natalie closed her eyes and shut off the display.

Numbers so neatly organized for the public, she thought. *That's all we'll ever be to them.*

With her eyes still closed, she relaxed farther into the couch. She actively forced her mind to stop thinking about *Endurance*, but when she did, she only thought about her father and the messages she had received. She knew that the messages were written down in her notebook upstairs, but she tried to visualize each of them now.

The first two, the ones that came during training, she thought, beginning to see the letters. *They were…* She found it harder to remember the messages than she expected. *Maybe I rely on the notes too much.* She tried harder to remember. Then she imagined the closest thing she had associated with those first messages: Darren. Behind his picture, her mind flooded with the other messages and Varya. Through her own doing, Natalie was suddenly trapped with unwanted memories of both Darren and Varya, how they had helped her, and how each had ultimately saved her at the cost of their own lives.

Natalie suddenly wanted to lie down and go to sleep. She could stop thinking if she were asleep. She wouldn't have to think about *Endurance* or her friends. She wouldn't have to think about why her father had been killed and just who had killed him. The messages, the deaths, and all the pain and stress on her conscience would be gone if only she were asleep.

She felt as though if she could fall asleep, she would wake up the next morning home on the carrier she had loved, with her friends that she had loved, doing a job she loved. Yet, when Natalie closed her eyes, she only pictured death. She only saw the flashes of explosions and gunfire in the long battle, only saw the moment Varya was killed saving her, the moment Darren flew past her for the last time, and the moment *Endurance*, and all she had known for three years, was destroyed. It was a long, terrible wait until sleep finally came to Natalie.

***

Natalie wandered through the familiar hangar bay. It seemed surreal; the vast hangar bay so empty. The hangar felt overwhelmingly large without its population of strike craft. In its center sat a lone Spectre, distantly gazing to the sky. Natalie approached it, but when she came near, its canopy suddenly peeled back with a hiss of escaping air. The ladder, which had released in sync with the cockpit opening, soon resonated the thunk of boots on metal as the pilot climbed down. The pilot was a woman in an Altherian flight suit. She turned toward Natalie and began to approach while unfastening her helmet. She stopped short of Natalie just as she undid the last strap and lifted the flight helmet from her head.

Deep red hair fell to her shoulders as Claire dropped her helmet onto the hangar floor. It banged and echoed throughout the empty space.

"Claire?" Natalie could do nothing to conceal her shock, which quickly turned to joy as Natalie stepped forward. "You're alive! You made it out!"

"Why?" was all Claire asked. She didn't smile like Natalie had. Natalie stopped dead, her smile vanishing.

"Why what?" The sound of groaning metal swept through the hangar, causing Natalie to look around. Claire didn't share her concern.

"Why did you leave me?" Another, more violent groan. The floor shuddered. "You left me to die, Natalie." Tears began to fall from Claire's soft blue eyes.

"What? No… I wanted to save you; I swear!" Natalie desperately reached toward her friend.

"You left us all to die!" Claire's voice flared in anger as she took a step back. Fire burst through the ceiling at the far end of the hangar. "Why are you the only one? Why did you live? Why did you abandon me?" Claire's tears suddenly turned blood red as they ran down her cheeks. More fire burst from the ceiling, floor, and walls all around them.

Natalie fell to her knees in tears. "No, please, Claire," she cried. "I didn't want this. I didn't want to leave you."

Endurance groaned again, and the screech of collapsing metal echoed around them. Claire squatted down in front of Natalie. Her bloodied face smiled something sinister as she stared at Natalie. "You'll never have us back," she said quietly, her whispers somehow carrying above the sound of metal crushing and crunching together. "You abandoned me. You abandoned *all of us*." Claire stood up and turned away from Natalie as she cried, collapsing onto the hangar floor. As Claire walked away, the wall before her collapsed in white, explosive light expanding rapidly toward them both. Before Natalie knew it, everything was gone.

***

Natalie awoke with a start, sitting straight up on the couch. She was drenched in sweat, and her eyes darted around the room, trying to regain some sort of bearing. Only when she realized where she was did her breathing slow and her mind relax. She looked down at where her hands rested on her legs. Her left hand was shaking. Her right remained deadly still. Natalie took a number of deep, long breaths. In her mind, she kept telling and retelling herself that it was only a dream. Still, it was minutes before she was fully calm again.

From the couch, Natalie moved in slow movements, done with as little brain power as possible. She moved from the living room to the kitchen, flicked on her coffee maker, and then moved from there to her bedroom, where she took out a fresh set of clothes and went to the shower. When she was done, she returned to the kitchen, changed into a light-colored T-shirt and a pair of dark jeans.

She sat down with her coffee and glanced at the holographically displayed clock on the wall. She still had nearly an hour until the car arrived to take her to her first appointment. She wondered what it would be like. She imagined high-class spas and medical centers from movies, where every demand is taken care of by staff in pristine white coats. She knew that it was simply wishful thinking, but it still seemed nice.

For once, she thought, *I wouldn't have to worry about anything. Everything I needed and wanted, available at a moment's notice, and I wouldn't have to do any work.*

Right until the doorbell rang, Natalie seemed to simply daydream at the table.

Natalie was feeling much sorer than she had anticipated when she left the clinic. For nearly six hours, they had run her through a gauntlet of exercises designed to rebuild and reactivate the muscles in her leg and in her hand, and by the end she was exhausted. She wanted nothing more than to go back to her apartment and lie down. The car sent for her was already outside when she walked into the afternoon sun. She climbed in, and at once the black car set off for her apartment.

Halfway along the journey, Natalie saw something. The car was driving along the city's outer highway, a massive ring road that kept cars out of the busy city-center. In the distance, Natalie could see a monument that she had only heard of. It was a ship, about 400 meters long, and tall, like a large apartment complex.

The ship was the first ship to ever land on Jontunia with human life. It had been preserved as a monument in the early days of the Federation, and even during the Omasye Rebellion, it had been spared thanks to its cultural significance. As Natalie stared on, her mind drifted to her father, a colonial engineer. There would have been men and women just like him aboard that ship, the one which cemented civilization on the world that Natalie called home.

"Can you take me somewhere?" Natalie asked her driver from the back seat.

The driver didn't look up from the wheel. "Where to?" she said.

"The OSC archive," Natalie said. "Just for a little while."

"Sure thing."

It was nearly an hour later when the car stopped in front of a large, beige building. Windows wrapped around the entire building between layers of beige stone. There was little activity outside. It was already late afternoon, but Natalie suspected that even during the highest points of the day, not many people were visiting the archives.

"I shouldn't be more than twenty minutes," she told her driver. "Feel free to go get yourself a coffee or something."

The driver didn't respond, and Natalie hopped out of the car. She made her way up the steps from the sidewalk to the front door of the OSC archives. When she went inside, all she had to do was flash her OSC identification card to the receptionist. After that, she had free rein to head off into the archives themselves.

Part of the archives reflected an older style of log keeping. Here, double-sided bookshelves from the floor to the ceiling lined the building from one end to the other. On these shelves, one could read into the history of not just the Omasye Space Council, but militaries from Altheria before unification. Another section of shelves contained memoirs, both originals and copies, of the men and women who served in the OSC throughout time, though, the majority of the original memoirs were those of former members of the 3rd Mobile.

Natalie kept walking until she reached the end of the bookshelves. At the end of the hallway was a staircase, which took her up to the next level. On the second floor, the room was much more open; what filled it was desks and computers to access the real heart of the archives. Natalie made her way to a computer near the back of the room. Though there was no one else on the floor, she didn't need anyone to come up the stairs behind her and see her screen.

The computer booted up in only a couple of seconds. Being that the archives were open to all OSC personnel, there was no reason for any login credentials. The computer simply booted into a guest account and displayed a menu to begin navigating the vast archives. At once, Natalie went to work searching for what she needed.

It didn't take her long to navigate to the log of incidents on the Altherian borders. The log was updated frequently and displayed a long list of incidents ranging from pirate activity to trading ships crossing the Insubel Dominion border with the wrong passage codes. By typing in a few more keywords, Natalie brought the list down to an isolated selection of incidents on the Altherian-Halerian border that resulted in lethal action.

This list was much shorter, but still rather lengthy. *Even in peacetime we can't help but shoot each other,* Natalie thought. *I wonder who shoots first more.* She was quite sure she knew the answer as her eyes glazed over a pair of incidents in which Halerian patrols had destroyed Altherian ships.

She typed in the year her father died to bring the list down even further. Then she scrolled through until she reached the cycle he died. She wasn't sure of the exact day, but there wouldn't be many incidents in a single cycle, so it should have been easy to find.

Except it wasn't. Natalie studied the list, clicking on each incident and reading every part of them. Not even one matched her father's death. His name wasn't on any of the reports, and the name of his ship was never present. According to the database, the incident didn't even exist, or at least that was how it appeared.

Why isn't it here? Natalie wondered. She read through the list again. She checked the cycles before and after and still found nothing. *It should be here, shouldn't it? Why wouldn't it have been reported? The OSC would have known.* Hell, by some of the indications she had, Natalie wondered if the OSC had been involved. *If they were involved...*

Natalie glanced around the room. No one else was around. She backed out of the database until she reached the home page for the archives. Then she shut the computer down, stood up, and took the most direct route she could to the exit.

Varya told me not to trust anyone, she reminded herself. *And if the OSC* was *involved, then I definitely can't be talking to anyone in the OSC about it. And I probably shouldn't be snooping around an OSC database then either...* She glanced back at the building. No one else was around, but Natalie felt as though the building itself was looming over her, watching her every move and counting her steps until she, just like her father, crossed the line of what the Omasye deemed acceptable.

***

"Your clinic appointment was pushed back today," Natalie's driver said to her when Natalie reached the car. "I'll be taking you to a meeting at HQ first."

Natalie looked down at her clothes. She was wearing a light, olive colored button-up jacket over a white T-shirt and a pair of loose pants over her hydro-brace. "Do you think I should change?"

Her driver shook her head. "We'll be going to the clinic right after," she said. "I'm sure they'll understand."

Natalie smiled in response and climbed into the back of the car. The driver walked around to the front, climbed in, and the pair set off for the headquarters of the OSC on Jontunia.

When the car arrived at the massive office tower, Natalie hopped out and went straight for the office she was to report to. It was the same office she had reported to when she had first arrived. She didn't know what the captain might want with her, but she didn't think she should waste his time either. Running on simple memory, she retraced her steps back to his office and knocked on the door.

At once, the door opened for her. The captain was standing in a finely pressed uniform. He smiled.

"Lieutenant! Please, come in," he said.

Natalie followed him inside and sat down across from him once he had taken his own place at this desk.

"Would you like some coffee?" he asked, holding an empty mug up for her.

Natalie raised her left hand and smiled politely. "No thank you, sir," she said. "I had my fill of coffee over breakfast."

The captain nodded and set the mug down. "So, how have the last two weeks been? It's hard to imagine that time has gone by so fast."

"Things are well, sir," Natalie told him. "The rehabilitation exercises are hard, but they say that I'm progressing well. I might have the brace on my leg removed by the end of this cycle."

"And your hand?" he asked.

Natalie paused before responding. "They haven't said. Right now, the best estimate is the end of winter, but that's over half a year from now."

"Well, it's only the start of the 8th cycle now," the captain said in a calming tone. "A lot could change between now and the 3rd of next year. You could recover faster than they expect."

"Perhaps, sir. That would be nice." Natalie decided to leave out the negatives of the doctors' projections—the limitations, the expected slowdown in progress, the possibility of never being able to fly again.

"And how has living in your apartment been?" The captain changed the specifics of the subject. "I hope there hasn't been any issue getting everything you need."

Natalie shook her head and smiled. "I've adjusted to it well, thank you," she said. "The driver you assigned to me is very helpful."

The captain leaned far back into his chair and nodded. "That's all good news, but I'm afraid I have to tell you that you won't be in need of your driver any longer."

"What do you mean?" Natalie asked, her head cocked slightly to one side.

"Another officer from *Endurance* has offered to stay with you in order to attend to any needs or difficulties you may have," the captain explained. "She'll be moving in with you today."

"I don't have any difficulties or needs," Natalie responded flatly. "I don't think I need a roommate, sir."

"Well, Lieutenant," the captain responded with a firm tone. "Your driver is being reassigned, and this officer is the only person available to assist you from here on out."

Natalie didn't like that she had been backed into yet another corner. She hated the idea of having someone else live with her. She didn't need *anyone* in her life right now, let alone that close to her. Yet here she was, facing the invariable fact that she would be joined by a total stranger for the foreseeable future.

"Is that all, sir?" Natalie asked. She didn't try to hide her disappointment, or her rising anger.

"That is all, Lieutenant," the captain responded. "The officer will meet you outside the front door."

Natalie plodded back to the entrance of the building. Not once did she lift her head to look more than a few feet in front of her. Only when she was outside did she look out at the road, which looped back on itself some twenty meters from the front door. A car was parked next to the sidewalk with a familiar figure beside it.

"Lieutenant Annikki!" Captain Victoria Damos called to her, waving a hand to motion her to come to the car.

Reluctantly, Natalie made her way over to the car. "Good morning, ma'am," she said.

"It is wonderful to see you again, Lieutenant," Damos said with a bright smile. "When I heard that you had made it through the battle, I knew I had to find you again."

"What for?"

"Well, first I wanted to see how you were doing," Damos said. "And second of all, I wanted to thank you. Without pilots like you, us Dolphin pilots would never have made it out with everyone else."

Natalie let out a *hmph*. "Well, ma'am, all the pilots 'like me' are dead now. And out of all of us, I'm not the one you should thank."

Damos didn't respond right away. She looked down at Natalie and seemed to study her face for a few moments. "Let's get to your appointment, shall we?"

***

Damos had unpacked all her things while Natalie was at her appointment. She explained how she had arranged her things as they drove home, and Natalie sat in the passenger seat without saying a word. When they reached the apartment, Natalie grabbed a cup of coffee and plopped herself down at the dining table. From there, she watched Damos organize the last of her belongings.

There was no second bedroom in the compact two-floor apartment. However, one of the two couches in the living room had a pullout bed, which Damos had done up with sheets and a fine red blanket. She arranged the majority of her belongings, which came in only two large suitcases, inside of the central closet. As Natalie watched on, she saw that the closet was now divided in two by hers and Damos's things. The rest of what Damos owned she kept in one of the suitcases, which was lying on the floor next to her bed. Satisfied that everything was where she wanted it, she sat down across from Natalie.

Damos crossed her arms on the table. Natalie could feel her staring at her, but neither said anything. She simply kept sipping her coffee under the watchful gaze of her new roommate.

I don't need anyone here, she kept repeating in her mind. *I don't want anyone here. Why can't they see that I just want to be left alone?*

"I heard about your injuries," Damos broke the silence. "It was a tough battle. How are you handling everything that happened?"

"Why are you here?" Natalie asked not in response, but as though she hadn't even heard Damos's words.

There was a pause, and then Damos smiled, letting out a short, almost nervous, laugh. "What do you mean?" she asked. "I told you this morning; I'm here to help you with anything you need."

"I already had that." Natalie stood up from the table and grabbed her empty coffee mug. "The driver I had did everything that I would ever need from you.

The difference was that she didn't force herself into my life." She turned from the table and went to the kitchen.

"You need someone to talk to," Damos said over the sound of running tap water. "I know you are in a difficult time in your life, and I'm here to—"

"Don't tell me what I need," Natalie spat. "I lost *everything*. The only thing I need right now is to focus on getting back what I can. For me, that's flying. That's it. That's all I ever need to focus on right now. I don't need to talk to anyone about the things I won't get back."

Forcefully, she set the mug down on the counter. Then she turned from the kitchen and limped her way upstairs. When she got to her bed, she threw herself onto it. She felt like a child throwing a tantrum, but she didn't care.

Get out of my life. She imagined she was still in front of Damos. *Get out of my life and just let me fly again. I only need two things right now. Talking to a stranger about my friends isn't one of them. Why can't people see that? I need to know what happened to my dad, and I need to fly again. That's it. Nothing else matters, so stop bringing it up.*

Natalie didn't leave her room for dinner. She heard Damos set a plate down outside of her door, and after ten minutes, she reluctantly opened her door, took the food, and closed it again. She wished that the next time she left her room, Damos would be gone. Then Natalie could have her apartment back to herself; a place to get away from prying questions about the battle, a place to spend in solitude conjuring up plans to find out the reason her father had died.

***

The blanket was flung from her with such force that Natalie smacked her own hand off the wall. She sat up, panting heavily. Beads of sweat ran from her forehead to her jaw. Her clothes were clinging to her body, and for the briefest of moments she thought that she had awoken in a bathtub, or a pool, or on a sinking ship. Images of the nightmare she had just lived through flashed through her mind, and she frantically looked around the room, ensuring that nothing had followed her into the real world. When she did, she made out the silhouette of Damos crouching close to the bed.

The room was dark. Her apartment was opposite the morning sun, but her clock told her it was already morning. Damos was in just a T-shirt and sweatpants, and her pale green eyes caught what little light there was in the room. She looked worried.

"It's alright," she said softly. "See? You're here now."

Natalie took a few more moments before speaking. "Why are you here?" was all she could utter.

Damos kept her look of concern but moved slightly closer. "I heard you call out something in your sleep," she explained. "I ran up here and saw you squirming in your sheets and muttering things. When I touched your arm, you threw your fist at the wall and woke up. It was a nightmare."

"Oh." She didn't have anything else to say. What *could* she say?

"Are you alright now?" Damos asked.

Slowly Natalie nodded. "I think so."

"This isn't the first one you've had since..."

Perhaps it was the way Damos spoke to her, or perhaps it was simply the de-barring of barriers that happens when someone finds another in such a vulnerable position, but Natalie couldn't bring herself to not speak. "Almost every night," she admitted. "Always about *Endurance*, or my friends. Sometimes in this place, or sometimes on *Endurance*."

"I'm sorry," Damos said. "I can't imagine what that's like. I've been flying for a long time, but I've never experienced loss like you have. Even on *Endurance*, thanks to you and your friends, my whole squadron made it out safely." She stared down at the edge of the bed as she spoke.

There was a pause. "Why are you here?" Natalie asked.

Damos looked up at her. Natalie felt as though their positions of vulnerability had suddenly flipped as she looked into the other woman's eyes. "I wanted to repay you, I suppose." Natalie had to strain her ears to hear her even though they were only a foot away from one another. "I, my squadron, everyone who survived is indebted to *Endurance's* fighter pilots. I felt that if I could help you, maybe that would be enough to repay the sacrifice of all of them."

"You know that's impossible," Natalie said. "Just because I'm the last one left doesn't mean that I can channel your debt to them."

“I have to try.” Damos sounded like she was going to cry. When Natalie thought of the nightmare she had woken up from, and now this woman practically begging to help heal her, she thought she might cry too.

All she could do was nod. That seemed to be enough, and Damos’s expression reversed from her own sorrow back to her concern for Natalie.

“You don’t have to talk to me about anything right now,” she said. “Or ever, if you don’t want to. But if you ever do, I’ll be right here.”

“I’d rather try and not think about it,” Natalie responded. “I want to remember my friends for why I loved them, not for how they died.”

“Then let me help you do that,” Damos said.

“How?” Natalie asked. “I don’t even know how to do it myself.”

Damos smiled. “That’s okay. Wouldn’t you rather have someone else to figure it out with you?”

CHAPTER 26

The car was already outside when Natalie walked from the clinic. It was raining heavily, so she tried to quicken her pace despite her hydro-brace. Leaning against the driver's door was Captain Damos in a plain beige coat and holding an umbrella. When she saw Natalie, she waved but waited until she was closer before she hopped into the car.

Natalie climbed into the passenger seat shortly after her. She reached across herself to grab the door with her left hand, then did up her seatbelt. "How long were you waiting in the rain?" she asked.

"Oh, not long," Damos responded. She put the car in gear and pulled away from the clinic. "Maybe fifteen minutes."

"Victoria," Natalie said in a half-hearted serious tone. "I told you that you don't have to wait outside the car. Especially if it's raining as bad as this." She motioned ahead of her to the windshield, where the wipers were rapidly sweeping across, pushing away hundreds of droplets of rain, only for the glass to be covered by hundreds more.

"It's courtesy where I'm from." Victoria was focused on the road while she spoke. On the highway, the spray from other vehicles was nearly blinding. "You can't change my ways overnight."

"It's been an entire cycle," Natalie said flatly. "You aren't my servant."

"That changes nothing," Victoria responded. "Take it as a sign of respect. If I didn't like you, I would wait in my car without you."

Natalie knew she had no choice but to give in. If she had learned anything about her friend, it was that she was even more stubborn than she was. If Victoria wanted to stand in the rain, or rather, if it were justified by her own beliefs, then nothing Natalie said would change it. All she could do was change the subject.

"The news says that they've already laid down two leviathan hulls in orbit," she said. "More hulls will be laid down soon in order to bring the fleet to fifty percent combat power by next summer."

Victoria laughed. "Yeah, and I'll be the next Admiral of the Fleet. The leviathans *alone* will take five years. The other ships are dependent on how fast the entire supply chain on Jontunia moves, and let me tell you, it moves pretty damn slowly."

Natalie looked from the road to her friend. "When do you think we'll be at fifty percent then?"

"Three years," she said. "Two if we're lucky and every person in the entire chain puts on the right socks every single day."

"I won't hold my breath then," Natalie said with a laugh.

"Now you're learning," Victoria said. "Unfortunately, the fleet will have to rotate in eventually, which means we're going to be a sub-unit in another fleet."

Natalie frowned. "That sounds like a disgrace. When would that happen?"

"With the current rotations and the tempo of the war, I imagine you'll be all patched up just in time for us to ship out."

"That's better than missing out," Natalie said. "All I want is to get back in the fight."

For the first time along their drive, Victoria glanced over at her. "You're going to have plenty of chances to fight, Nat. You shouldn't rush into it."

"I have a year of downtime while my hand is fixed." Natalie's tone became serious. "That's long enough if you ask me. Too long, even."

Victoria sighed. "So be it then," she said. "In any case, the 3rd is most likely going to become part of one of the smaller fleets, so in a year you and I might be living on Thornisha or Shalurno for all we know."

"Do you think we'll end up on the same ship again?" Natalie asked.

"Who knows," Victoria responded with a shrug. "A lot of ships need pilots, not just carriers. And we fly different craft, so in reality it's a total crapshoot."

"I hope we're on the same ship again," Natalie said quietly.

"I hope so too, Nat."

The rain continued to beat against the windows of the apartment even as the pair sat down to eat dinner. Even though she wasn't religious, Natalie waited patiently with her hands in her lap as Victoria said her evening prayer before dinner.

"The Omasye, hand in hand with the Gods, guides our future," Victoria said, her eyes closed. "The Altherian Empire is shaped by His hand, which is in turn given direction by the Gods. Only He can understand their vision for our great Empire, and only we can trust in his unifying light. Without the Omasye, there would be no us, and without the Gods, there would be no Him. For that, we thank the Gods each day, so that they may continue to guide the Omasye in shaping the great future of the Empire." She opened her eyes, smiled at Natalie, and picked up her cutlery. That was Natalie's cue to take her own, and the two women began eating.

For the most part, they enjoyed their meals in silence, but along the way Natalie paused and looked across the table at Victoria. "Do you miss flying?" she asked.

Victoria stopped mid-chew. With her hands gripping her cutlery and placed flat on the table, she finished chewing as she processed her response. "I mean," she began, "wouldn't any pilot?"

"Would you rather be flying right now?" Natalie probed further.

This time Victoria shook her head. "Not at all," she said. "Remember what I told you when I moved here? This is what I want to do. In the same way that all your energy is dedicated to returning to flying, all of mine is dedicated to helping you get there. I'd do this over flying for as long as it takes."

"I'm not testing you," Natalie said. "You can be honest here. I won't be offended if you said you would rather fly. I'd probably agree with you, actually."

There was a longer pause this time. Victoria seemed to glance at her food, then the table, and finally back at Natalie. "I don't like flying anymore," she said with a quiet, ashamed tone. Her eyes fluttered as though she expected Natalie to reach across and slap her, or at the very least yell. But when that didn't happen, she continued. "I flew down to that horrible moon to gather up some of the soldiers. And no sooner did we think we were safe, *Endurance* came under attack, and we had to evacuate. The scenes on that moon, the things I saw when we left our carrier for the last time… I never want to see those things again, Nat. They say that OSC occupations are for life, or at least until you retire, but dammit, I can't bring myself to fly again."

The silence in the room when she finished speaking weighed heavily on everything. One could almost feel it causing the entire apartment complex to sway. The table their food sat on seemed to sink in the middle, and the chairs suddenly felt weak, as though they would crash down in wood splinters at any moment.

Then there was quiet, nervous laughter. Victoria forced a smile. "Which one of us is supposed to be broken again?" she asked.

Natalie was straight faced. Her mouth would have hung open in shock if what Victoria had said hadn't felt so real, so personal, so close to how she herself felt. "Are you going to be okay, Victoria?"

Green eyes shifted until they stared distantly at the wall behind Natalie. "Maybe we are both supporting each other in our own ways," Victoria finally said. "Even if one doesn't know it." She made a thin, strangely sad smile and then turned to her food.

Natalie watched her for a couple of minutes before she continued eating her own meal. Inside, she was scolding herself for ever thinking that fighter pilots could be the only ones scarred by what happened—that *she* was the only one scarred. *The fear in her eyes was real,* Natalie thought. *She lived through the scariest day of her life, just like me. She came off better, but it'll affect her for just as long as it will me.*

She wondered about the other pilots that survived. No pilot other than herself survived actual combat, but the others that did had to fly through it. Almost all of them were in unarmed transports, hoping and praying that people like Natalie would keep them safe. Fighter pilots, bomber pilots, they all at least fought back against the overwhelming enemy. But the transport pilots had nothing. All they could do was fly as fast as they could. Many, like Victoria, probably thought they were flying to their deaths. Few of them had probably ever flown in major combat before that morning. Natalie wondered how many would ever want to do it again, or how many were like Victoria, their wings clipped by their own fear of death.

***

Natalie's breathing slowed back to normal. She was on her hands and knees, staring straight into her pillow. Her hair clung damply together and was hanging down within her vision. She could feel the dampness of her white T-shirt on her back and the uncomfortable way her shorts had twisted and wrinkled.

Just another bad dream, she thought. *It's over now. It's morning. It's a new day.*

Slowly, she sat back until she was resting on her ankles. The now-cold sweat on the front of her shirt made her shiver as the fabric fell back onto her skin. She jumped out of bed, tearing the shirt over her head and tossing it behind her, at once reaching for a sweater within a dresser drawer. She pulled it over herself until it fell loosely over her, reaching just past the bottom of her shorts. She left her hair a mess and pressed her feet into a pair of black sandals, stepping out of her room almost in the same movement.

Natalie came down the stairs as quietly as she could. When she reached the bottom step, she peered around the corner and into the living room. As she expected, Victoria was fast asleep on the pull-out bed, a long bare leg sticking out from under the sheets as she slept widely on her stomach. Tiptoeing from the stairs, Natalie made her way to the front door where the day's mail had been dropped off.

The mail was sitting behind a metal panel in the wall. In the hallway was a similar panel, and both were locked by separate keys. The mail, be it an envelope or large parcel, would be placed into the compartment and locked inside, where the apartment's tenant would retrieve it from within their home.

Inside the compartment this morning was an assortment of junk mail, advertisements, and flyers. There was only one letter in the entire stack. When Natalie shuffled through the papers to find the envelope, she took it with a shaky hand.

The envelope, just like those before it, only had one address—hers.

How the hell do they even know where I live? Natalie glanced back at where Victoria slept, then back at the mail. On quiet, quick steps, she practically ran upstairs with the envelope.

In the seconds before she reached her room, she decided that now was not the time to read it. Her roommate would be awake soon and would surely be confused if the rest of the mail had been left strewn on the floor. Tucking it away deep within one of her dresser drawers under several layers of clothing, Natalie returned to the main floor without the envelope.

She let out a silent sigh of relief when she saw that Victoria was still sleeping. Natalie gathered up the junk mail and set it on the kitchen counter and then turned to the other side of the kitchen. The pre-programmed coffee machine had already brewed a fresh pot, which Natalie happily filled two mugs from. She took a sip and then began preparing breakfast. Keeping things simple, she reached for a loaf of bread, glancing across the counter to ensure that her toaster was on and ready for use.

She had just placed the bread in the toaster when she heard the ruffling of sheets behind her. Spinning around, Natalie caught the eyes of Victoria as she sat up in her bed.

"Good morning," Natalie said playfully. She smiled warmly at her friend's sleepy state.

Victoria simply made a low groan and reached across her bed to the other couch where a long, black blouse was lying.

"Pour me a cup, will you?" she said, climbing out of bed and pulling the blouse over herself at the same time. "And what's for breakfast?"

Natalie was already halfway across the room when she answered. "I already made you one, here." She handed the mug of steaming coffee to Victoria just as the latter pulled the collar of her shirt over her head. "Breakfast today is some hot toast and whatever you'd like on it."

Victoria stood up and stretched. "You really don't cook much, do you?"

"I cook plenty," Natalie said, already returning to the kitchen. "I just keep my breakfast simple."

"*Too* simple." Victoria followed her to the kitchen. "Anything in the mail?"

There was a slight, undetectable hesitation in Natalie's body before she spoke. "Nothing," she said before turning around. "Just some junk mail. It's on the counter."

Natalie watched Victoria sift through the mail before making a *hmph* sound. Satisfied that she hadn't given herself away, Natalie turned back to the toaster. Mostly, she turned her face away from her friend.

Like clockwork, the pair ate the breakfast over some idle chitchat about life and the news before returning to their respective places of rest to get ready for the day. Natalie showered first, followed by Victoria, and both reconvened at the front door in appropriate attire to go out into the world. Like a well-rehearsed act, they were both ready at the precise time that they needed to leave the house.

Victoria dropped Natalie off at the clinic before heading off on whatever errand she had told Natalie about over breakfast. Sometimes it was just shopping for the two of them—groceries, essential goods, sometimes specific things that Natalie asked for. Other times, Victoria told Natalie that she had to head to headquarters. To Natalie, it saved herself from having to go in to report on what little progress she had made in regaining the use of her hand.

When they returned home, the sun was hanging low in the afternoon sky. In an hour or two, one of them would be making dinner. Until then, Natalie went straight to her room and shut the door behind her. She dug through her dresser drawer until she produced the letter from that morning.

Sitting down at the edge of her bed, she tore it open and peered inside. She expected to find little letters like every time before. However, all she saw was the crisp edge of a folded piece of paper. Natalie pulled the paper out with her left hand and unfolded it on her lap. The message, like those before it, was curt, but longer than the others.

There is no time anymore.

Meet on the roof of East Towers - Business Block. 1100 2596.9 7

Natalie glanced at the wall displayed clock. Today was the 4th. She looked back at the letter. She examined it closely, turned it around, then on its side, anything that she could think of. There was no other information.

They want me to meet them in three days and won't even tell me who they are? Natalie read and re-read the short letter. *Who are these people? What do they want from me? Am I going to be killed?* She thought about when she had gone to the archives. *Are they worried that I've learned too much? Is this even from the same people as before? What is going on?*

She shoved the letter back into her dresser to prevent her brain from spiraling into oblivion.

What should I do? She thought. *If I go… they might kill me. Or maybe they know what happened to my father? No, they would tell me, right? If they knew…*

She shook her head violently. She wanted to scream to release the thoughts from her mind.

Do I take it to Victoria? No, I better not. I shouldn't let her know unless I really need her help.

Breathing out, then in, in long, deliberate strokes slowed her mind just enough to regain her composure. Her thoughts may be running rampant, but she wouldn't show it. She couldn't show it.

Natalie found that she did remarkably well keeping herself in a seemingly natural state. She had pleasant, normal conversations with Victoria over dinner, and they watched the evening news and a television show without her cracking under the pressure of all of the questions and thoughts that continued to stir in her head.

Sleep, however, wasn't so easy. Natalie tossed and turned for what seemed like the entire night. The only reason she knew she had slept was because she woke up in the morning scared and drenched in sweat from another new nightmare. Luckily, by breakfast the nightmare had faded into fragments. Bits and pieces of Natalie standing in some unknown office building. Men with guns coming from every door and corner. *Endurance*, her father, and all her friends on the same page—and Natalie's own blood staining the page.

"Was it a bad one last night?" Victoria asked over breakfast.

Natalie's eyes snapped up in her direction. She had been staring off at the wood table, almost like someone concentrating too hard on a test. Except it was just her thoughts taking up all her attention. "Huh?" she muttered. "Did you say something?"

Victoria made a polite smile and rested her head on her right hand. "You've been spaced out all morning," she said. "Do you want to talk about it?"

Natalie knew she meant the nightmare, but she found herself longing for Victoria to ask about the greater issue, an issue that she was completely unaware of. For the briefest of moments, she considered spilling everything to her. But she stopped herself.

It's best that she doesn't know, Natalie thought. *It's best that nobody else gets involved.*

"It was nothing," she said.

Victoria frowned but turned to her food. "Alright. If you change your mind, just say so."

Natalie nodded but told herself that she never would. She meant it too. The only other people that had ever been wrapped up in Natalie's mysterious messages were dead now. Natalie herself may be next. If someone else was brought into the mix, their life could be in danger just as much as her own. She wasn't going to be responsible for the blood of someone she cared about. At least that's what she told herself.

It was only the next day when she finally broke down. With the meeting the next day, her mind just couldn't take it anymore. Both Victoria and Natalie were home since it was the weekend. Victoria had just sat down with her lunch when the envelope was thrown down in front of her.

"What's this?" Victoria said, her eyes wide. She looked from the envelope to Natalie, who was practically steaming from her ears.

"I can't take it anymore," she said in anger. "I didn't want to get you involved, but I don't know what to do anymore."

Victoria picked up the envelope and drew the letter from inside. She never once took her eyes off of Natalie, who, after a moment of breathing out the last of her overboiling anger, sat down at the table. After reading over the letter once, Victoria set it down.

"I don't understand," she said. "I don't know what any of this is about."

"It's about my father," Natalie explained. "His death wasn't an accident. At least, I don't think it was. Someone wanted him dead."

"And this letter?" Victoria asked, holding the letter by the corner with her thumb and index finger.

"Whoever sent me this is either going to tell me what happened, or they are going to kill me for trying to find the truth."

"Why would they kill you?"

Natalie slouched forward, resting her head on her left hand. "Because I think it was the Councils that ordered his death," she said flatly. "If they and the Omasye were involved, they'll surely kill anyone who tries to uncover the truth."

"That isn't the way that the Intelligence Council does things," Victoria said. She stood up, leaving the envelope and the letter on the table. She took her plate in one hand.

"How would you know?" Natalie asked, her head and eyes tracking her friend as she walked toward the kitchen.

Victoria stopped next to Natalie and placed a hand on her shoulder. "I have what, nine, ten years on you?" She carried on to the kitchen sink.

"What should I do then?"

For a moment, the only sound between the pair was that of water rushing from the tap. "Throw it away," Victoria said over the noise. "Pretend you didn't even get it."

Natalie stood up from her seat and carefully picked up the letter. She walked until she was standing just outside of the kitchen space. "I shouldn't report this to someone?"

Victoria turned only her head to face Natalie. "If you don't go, they'll get the idea. Besides, are you really the kind of person that would report someone to the Councils?"

Natalie thought for a moment and then frowned.

"Didn't think so," Victoria said. "Throw the letter away, and you won't have to think about it ever again." With her foot, she pried the cupboard door open under the sink. A small garbage bin was underneath.

After taking one last look at the letter, Natalie did as she was told. She took three limping steps across the kitchen and then dropped the piece of paper into the garbage. Victoria lightly kicked the door closed. She smiled.

"Trust me," she said. "You're going to feel a lot better with it behind you."

"But what about my father?" Natalie asked. "What if I never know what really happened?"

Victoria thought for a moment. "How do you know anything really happened?" she asked. "What if the report they gave you was accurate, and these people sending you letters were just trying to set you up?"

"That can't be," Natalie said. She started pacing between the kitchen and the dining table on the other side of the half wall. "I went to the archives and checked the border incidents. There was nothing there about my dad. If it was an accident like they said, the incident should have been there. But it wasn't, Victoria—nothing was there." Her speech was getting quicker with each breath, and her eyes were alight. She couldn't look away from her friend, but she felt like she wanted to run.

Victoria approached and grabbed her by both shoulders. She made a long *shh* sound, and only spoke once Natalie stopped fidgeting. "Slow down, relax, breathe," she whispered. "If something really happened to your father, something that has been covered up, we can try to find it together. But you need to approach it with a clear head, okay?"

Natalie subtly nodded. She looked away.

"Good," Victoria continued. "You'll see. Everything is going to be okay. I'm here for you." She let go of her friend.

Natalie took a step back. "Thank you," she said in a low voice. Then she turned away and went upstairs, limping with her braced leg all the way to her room.

The door was closed almost silently behind her. The only sound was the click of the door's latch against the wall. Natalie made her way to the desk in her room and sat down. She opened one of the drawers next to her and took out a familiar notebook. She then began flipping through pages until she saw what she was looking for.

She read the messages over a few times before dropping the notebook onto the table. She set her head down on her left arm and looked out at the wall.

We can find it together, she thought, imagining Victoria's voice. *We'll find the answers for you.* Varya's voice suddenly echoed in Natalie's mind. *That's right*, she thought. *Someone else already promised the same thing…*

Natalie imagined long brown hair on the head of a woman who smiled softly at her, though hid more behind her golden eyes. She saw Varya in front of her, her hands overlapping at the front of her waist. Her smile, the way her eyes fell on Natalie; it made her feel comforted. She could have told herself that everything would be okay, and she would have believed it because it would have come from Varya's lips and not her own mind.

She lifted her head. On the corner of her desk was a small clear package of photos. She had been meaning to get them framed for her room on *Endurance*, but now they were the only photos she had left of her life. Natalie carefully took the package in her hand. Tilting it downward, the stack of photos slid out and onto the wooden desk. She placed the clear, plastic package nearby and then began sifting through the photos.

All the photos were recent, and not a single one contained anyone that wasn't a White Tail. Photos of the squadron in the bar or on Claire's beloved soccer pitch. Photos of their most recent leave—photos of Darren, Varya, and Natalie together in Garun.

In one of the photos, Natalie and Varya were standing together on the balcony of Varya's apartment. The photo had been taken by Darren candidly from behind them. Both women were leaning on the railing of the balcony, overlooking the city. They were in the middle of a conversation. From the angle the photo had been taken, most of Varya's face could be seen. Her head was turned toward Natalie, and she was smiling brightly at whatever it was that they were talking about.

Natalie stared at the photo for a long time. She studied every detail of Varya's face, trying to understand and recall every complex emotion she displayed. At some point, Natalie felt a tear slide down her cheek. In a rushing flutter of movement, the photos, including the one she was holding, were pushed to the back of the desk. In their place, Natalie dropped her head onto the cold wood and sobbed.

"Varya..." The name came out through choked breaths. "We were going to find out together, you told me so. But you're gone, and now I've told another... What have I done, Varya? Have I thrown away our only chance?"

You said not to tell anyone, she thought, imagining she could speak to Varya here and now. *But that was when you were alive. I can't do it alone, but please, Varya, how do I know that I'm doing the right thing?*

CHAPTER 27

Natalie walked through the woods, weaving her way around thick trees this way and that. Unimpeded by a brace or the fear of hurting her right hand, she stepped confidently, leaning her hands against trees if she ever found herself off-balance. The forest canopy, a dense ceiling of large, green leaves, shaded the forest floor from the sun. What light came through the leaves dimly lit the area. At night, Natalie was sure that one wouldn't be able to see their hands in front of their face.

She continued through the forest in some aimless direction for what felt like hours until she reached a small clearing, still shielded from the light by the canopy above. The grass here was greener than the leaf-covered moss and grass elsewhere, and the ground gently rolled over some sort of mound, raising the level of the forest beyond by a few inches. Though the grass was unimpeded by the fall of leaves, it was still short and not overgrown, and when Natalie sat down on it, she found that it was soft and cool to the touch.

She sat there only for a few minutes before she heard something in the woods. Moments later, Varya emerged from her right. Natalie jumped to her feet.

"Varya?" She called her name hesitantly. She glanced around her, left and right, past Varya deeper into the woods and even over her shoulder. They were the only two around.

Varya never really spoke. She only looked at Natalie, her golden eyes moving between Natalie's own, searching for something. After a minute, she stepped closer but still never said anything.

"Varya, I'm sorry," Natalie said. She already felt like she was going to cry. "I let you down, I betrayed you. Please… say something."

Yet still, despite Natalie's pleading, the woman she cared for so much wouldn't utter a single word to her. Even her facial expressions were emotionless. She seemed instead to convey everything through her eyes, which were searching for something in Natalie just as much as they seemed to be trying to say something—say something that her mouth simply couldn't.

Natalie had to force herself to pull back her emotions; she had to force back her tears, force back all the terrible thoughts welling up in her mind, until she was left with only a lump in her throat.

"I... I didn't know what to do. I..." The words stuck in her mouth. Every emotion was increasingly present with every second that ticked by. She wanted to reach out to Varya. She could feel her hands shaking. "I'm weak." The words seemed to fall out of her mouth. "I couldn't... I just couldn't handle it on my own, Varya. Since you and the others... Since you've been gone, my mind is a mess. I can't sleep properly, and most of the time the only thing I can think about is you and everyone else."

Varya's eyes dropped low, like she was looking at Natalie's stomach or her feet. The rest of her face remained as expressionless as before.

"When I got that letter," Natalie tried to continue. "I... I..." She shook her head. "I'm so weak, Varya. That letter was just too much. I needed someone to help me, and... well, you aren't here anymore. You aren't even real now."

Varya's eyes darted back to Natalie's face. This time, her expression was obvious. Everything about her suddenly betrayed a pain and sadness that made Natalie regret ever opening her mouth. Varya stared at her with that unbearable look of sadness for a few moments and then took a step back.

"Wait...," Natalie whispered. But Varya had already turned around. "Please, Varya, I'm sorry!" she pleaded as Varya started walking back into the forest. "Don't go... I'm sorry..." Tears were pouring out now unimpeded. Natalie fell to her knees. "I need you, Varya. I..." Her voice trailed off. She opened her eyes and wiped away her tears. Varya was gone. Natalie fell forward, cupping her face in her hands. "Come back," she said. "I love you."

***

Natalie was slow to open her eyes. Already, she could feel the dampness of her pillow and the lines of now dry tears on her cheeks. She wondered if she cried as much in her sleep as she had in the dream.

I probably would have drowned, she thought. She pictured Varya walking away from her and felt like she might cry again. *I let her down. She'd never forgive me if she were...* Her mind hesitated, but she forced it to think the words. *If she were still alive.*

Natalie rolled over until she was face-down into her damp pillow. She remembered the last things she said in her dream, when Varya had already left her in the woods. *I wasn't dreaming then,* she thought. *That was what I really wanted to tell her.*

Her thoughts were interrupted by a knock at the door. Natalie lifted her head just high enough to speak clearly.

"Who is it?" she asked.

"Who do you think." Victoria's voice came back through the door almost immediately. "We're going to be late for your appointment if you don't get out of bed."

Natalie took her seat at the table without a word. In front of her was a plate of fried eggs and a small pile of potatoes. Next to it was a glass of pale red juice.

"Was it a bad one?" Victoria asked. Her voice was delicate, and when Natalie looked at her, her green eyes betrayed her concern.

"Sort of," Natalie said. "It was about one of my friends."

"I'm sorry," Victoria said. "We don't have to talk about it."

"Thank you."

The rest of breakfast, and even the drive to the clinic, was done entirely in silence. While it was certainly well beyond the norm, Natalie appreciated it. She didn't want to talk about anything today. She didn't even want to think. If a skip button had been presented to her the moment she had woken up, she would have pressed it without hesitation.

Instead, she had to live through the day. She lived through her daily clinic visit: exercises and therapy to get her using her leg again and to get her right hand back to some semblance of functional. Every week, there was progress, but every day felt the same. Still, by the end of her session at the clinic, she had had enough time to process her dream with Varya, enough that she could at least think of things other than the brown-haired woman with golden eyes.

"How was today?" Victoria asked. They had been on the road for five minutes.

Natalie was staring out her window at the distant skyline. "It was fine," she said, her response like a pre-set reflex.

"Did they say anything about your progress?" Victoria was undeterred by her friend's lack of enthusiasm.

"I'll be out of the brace in three weeks," Natalie responded in the same flat manner. "Assuming that everything continues as is."

There was a small pause. "What about your hand?" Victoria asked when she was sure that Natalie wasn't going to continue.

Another, longer pause. "Little progress," Natalie said. "It's always the same."

Victoria let out a quiet sigh. "I'm sure you'll start making progress soon," she said. "But I'm glad to hear about your leg! That's very timely, too."

"Why's that?" For the first time since getting in the car, Natalie looked over at her.

This caused Victoria to smile. "I only found out about this today," she explained. "But next cycle there's going to be a ceremony to commemorate the Battle of Dogor."

Natalie didn't respond. She turned back to her window and continued staring at the passing buildings. Minutes passed.

"What does it matter to me?" Natalie finally asked. Victoria glanced over. She could see the reflection of her friend's face. She looked unwell, like she could have thrown up or burst into tears right then and there.

"They want you to present the flags of *Endurance* and the wing," Victoria said delicately.

Natalie didn't move. She didn't speak, make any sound, or even change her expression. The words may as well have gone right over her head or may as well have not even been spoken. Victoria returned her eyes to the road after taking one last look at her friend. She wouldn't pry. Not today.

Natalie followed Victoria into their apartment. Victoria went straight toward her bed, pulling the jacket of her uniform off and tossing it on the couch as she walked. Natalie shut the door and crouched down to the mailbox. With a swift hand, she unlocked the metal door and swung it open. Leaving the key in the door, she reached in and retrieved the stack of mail. Then she shut the door and locked it.

Still crouched on the floor, she quickly sorted through the mail. She almost passed over the blank envelope without a thought. It was halfway to the small pile of other envelopes when Natalie suddenly realized what it was. With one motion, she jerked her left hand back toward her right, causing the envelope to fall out next to her, out of view from Victoria.

Her heart was already racing. She glanced across the room to the living room, where Victoria was sitting on the edge of her bed, looking at something on her phone. With even greater urgency, Natalie sorted the rest of the mail then replaced it all in one neat, sorted stack. She placed the blank envelope into the waist of her pants and pulled her shirt over it. Then she dropped the mail at the kitchen counter and, with a combination of panic and attempted subtlety, made for her room.

The bedroom door was closed and locked. The envelope was torn open as it was carried to the desk. Natalie peaked inside; there was just one sheet of paper.

Why another one? she thought as she slid the letter out. *Why can't this just be over?*

The letter, just like the one before it, had been folded neatly in three. Natalie spread it flat on her desk and read.

Police arrived at the last meeting site.

We are not your enemy.

Meet behind the furniture shop south of Larring Station. 1300 2596.9 25

This is the last chance. If you want to know the truth, come alone.

Trust us.

Natalie shut her eyes and looked toward the ceiling. She knew it was already the 24th.

Why? she asked no one and nothing. *Why, why, why, why, why? Why can't they just leave me alone? Why do I have to deal with this? Why? After everything that I've lost, why does this have to stay?*

She opened her eyes and looked at the letter again.

I should just throw it away. Just like the other one. Throw it away and be done with it. Then I'll never have to think about it again.

Natalie shook her head and stared at the letter. What if I talk to Victoria? She'll tell me the same thing—get rid of the letter. Don't think about it. But is that the right decision anymore?

She remembered the dream she had. She saw Varya turn away from her, leaving her behind in the woods. What would she have told me to do? she thought. What would she say now?

Natalie stood up and walked from one end of her room to the other and back again. She had to move, do something, expel some of the rush of energy she was now feeling.

"Varya told me not to tell anyone," she whispered. "She was supposed to be the only other one that could help me. But she's gone now…" Natalie stopped in the middle of the room. "If there's nobody else to trust, then I have to make the decision, right? Varya, is that what you want me to do?"

Spinning on her better leg, Natalie faced the letter lying on the desk. Then she started toward it.

No one else can know, she thought, reaching for the letter with her left hand.

And that means that this is my decision. She picked up the letter and read it over. Once she was sure she had each word committed to memory, she dropped it on the desk again.

From one of the drawers, Natalie produced a small lighter, which she swiftly applied to the edge of the paper. As it began to burn, she took the envelope and placed it on top so it would burn too. Within moments, any sign of the letter had become smoke in the room. Natalie breathed out in a relieving sigh.

It's gone, she thought. I'm the only one that knows now.

When dinner came around, Natalie took her usual seat across from Victoria. Her friend had already made and set dinner out, and she was waiting patiently when Natalie arrived.

She smiled at Natalie. "Feeling any better?" she asked.

Natalie did her best to show some sort of positive emotion, but if anything, it came across more neutral than anything. "I'm alright," she said. "Just needed some time to think."

"If you need anything else, don't hesitate to come to me," Victoria said before shutting her eyes for her daily prayer. Across from her, Natalie waited until she was finished to eat.

There was little to talk about over dinner. Where normally the two would have discussed the news, or anything that Victoria had heard at work, there was now silence, interspersed by small talk and short, often one-word answers. Natalie hated it. She knew that Victoria was trying her best to dance around a delicate and difficult day for Natalie, but she wished that the two could just eat without talking on days like today.

Tomorrow we'll be able to talk normally again, Natalie assured herself. Tomorrow everything will be better. Maybe then she could even tell Victoria about her dream and about Varya.

***

Natalie moved along with the crowds getting off the maglev train at Larring Station. Most were faster than her own limping speed, and they weaved and dodged around her as they made their way to the station exit. Natalie made her way there too, slowly climbing the steps to the world of the planet's capital above.

This area of Garun was one of the many residential sectors of the megacity. Tall apartment buildings surrounded the city's streets, blocking the view to the sky except for that directly above an individual on the ground. Like much of the city, cars were a rare sight. Busses and trams took up most of the traffic, with the occasional delivery truck. Every so often, a car would be hidden amongst the flow of traffic. Natalie paid little mind to any of it as she limped down the street. She was heading south, on the lookout for a store she had never seen before, in an area of the city that she had never been to.

Luckily, the store was fairly obvious. Three blocks from the station, Natalie was waiting to cross the street, staring at a beige building with a blue roof. Its branding, and from everything she could see in the windows told her that this was a furniture store—the first one since leaving the station. Between it and the next building over was a small entranceway for delivery trucks.

Once across the road, Natalie followed the entranceway to the back of the furniture store. In behind, the entranceway opened into a wide space of asphalt ground and tall concrete walls. There were no vehicles and no people around. Natalie wandered through the space until she reached the far wall, then turned around. She was alone.

This is the right place, she thought. Isn't it?

She flicked her phone out of her pocket. With another flick of her wrist, the two small metal ends, which were snapped together, separated. The top metal piece extended out, guided by thin rails on either side. With a subtle click, the phone locked in position, and the holoscreen was displayed between the two ends. At the top, the time was displayed.

1302. I wouldn't have missed them, so where are they?

She flicked the phone closed and dropped it into her pocket. Slowly, she paced around the space, waiting for something to happen, or for someone to show up. The early autumn sun was beating down on the little lot from cracks between tall buildings. In these beams of light on the pavement, Natalie could feel a still-strong heat.

It's not nearly winter yet, she thought, stepping out of the sunlight. She flicked her phone out again. *1318. How long should I wait?*

Just as she was contemplating how much more time to give, she heard the sound of tires turning up gravel on the entranceway and the low hum of an electric motor. Moments later, a silver-colored car came around the corner and stopped in the middle of the lot. Natalie was standing some ten feet in front of it, and for the first time realized that she was now trapped in the back of the lot.

One of the rear passenger doors opened. A man in a simple colored shirt and a pair of black pants stepped out. He was older, with graying hair and some visible wrinkles on his face. His gut, though probably once slim, was beginning to pressure the belt of his pants. Without much pause, he approached Natalie, only stopping once the two were only a handful of feet apart. There was a long silence. The man seemed to look at Natalie from head to toe. Only once he had finished did he frown.

"I am sorry to see you in such a state, Ms. Annikki," he said. "It is a tragedy that this has happened to you."

"You're right." Natalie's first instinct was defensive, reactionary, and volatile. "I could be dead just like everyone I know. Then you wouldn't have to look at my scars."

"Don't speak that way," the man said. His old, tired voice was quiet, but unstrained. "Your father would hate to hear you speak that way."

"What do you know about my father?" Natalie asked aggressively. Her eyebrows furrowed, and she scowled at the old man. "What do you want with me?"

The old man sighed. He turned away and looked out at the surrounding skyscrapers. "Your father was one of my best friends," he said. "He was one of the best men I ever knew."

His words silenced Natalie. They subdued the flame in her eye, if only temporarily. She could do nothing but stare at the man, waiting for him to continue.

"Do you know who I am?" the man asked.

Natalie shook her head.

He laughed. "I'm sure you are just like your father," he said. "You stay away from politics as though it were a plague. My name is Julius Tyvell. I'm the Chancellor of Jontunia."

Natalie stood in stunned silence. He didn't *look* like Jontunia's leader. There was no flashy suit, no motorcade, no security around him. Just an old man in plain clothes.

Tyvell knew what she wanted to ask. "Your father and I went to school together," he continued. "Though he went into engineering and I politics, we were always close. Even after we both rose to the top of our fields, it only kept us closer. We had excuses to meet. When we weren't talking about business, we talked a lot about family. I still remember the day he came to me after your mother left. And I remember how much he talked about you; about how proud he was of the young woman you were becoming. He told me about how excited you were to join the OSC, and how much you wanted to fly. And then he left for his next trip, and he never came back…"

Natalie looked away. She stared at the pavement under her.

"I'm sure that losing your best friend is easier than losing your father, but still." Tyvell paused. "I still feel that void every day. I know that the incident surrounding his death was covered up. I know what really happened, and I know that what they told you wasn't the whole truth. That's why I sent you those letters."

"None of them made any sense," Natalie said, still looking away. "Nothing makes sense."

"I had to keep them vague," Tyvell responded. "Even someone like me isn't immune to the Omasye's way of keeping secrets."

"So why tell me at all?" Natalie lifted her head to look at the man. "Why take such a risk?"

"Because you deserve to know..." Tyvell trailed off. "You deserve to know the truth. After everything you've gone through, especially now... I cannot even begin to imagine what pain you've suffered."

Natalie simply let out a *hmph*. "What is the truth then?" she asked.

"Three days before your father left the Halerian colony he was overseeing, there was another incident at the border," Tyvell explained. "A Halerian passenger liner strayed out of its transit lane and into an OSC patrol's lane. I don't know the details of what transpired, but the patrol destroyed the ship. The OSC was firm in its belief that the Halerians were in the wrong, and the Space Council convinced the rest of the Councils, as well as the Omasye himself, that there was no blame on the side of the Altherians."

Tyvell paused. He sighed and looked down at the ground. Then he lifted his head and spoke again.

"As you can imagine, the Halerians were very angry," he said plainly. "Your father left the colony three days later with his usual escort, a pair of Shrikes from the squadron called the Orange Hawks. And, in the middle of gray space, the escort destroyed *Future's Dream*, with him on it."

"An act of revenge is an act of war, Chancellor," Natalie said, her voice fluctuating in anger. She dismissed the mention of the Orange Hawks for now. "Why would the Omasye cover this up?"

"Because, like it or not, we didn't want war then," Tyvell responded. "We agreed with the Halerians that we had learned a valuable lesson, and the incident wasn't recorded by either side. If it had gotten out, there would have been millions like you saying that it was an act of war. Then we would have had no choice but to go to war."

Natalie was furious. "What difference does it make?" she asked, straining herself to not yell. "You decided to go to war anyway. If you had gone to war right then, maybe I wouldn't be fucked up." She raised her bandaged right hand. "Maybe I wouldn't be sitting here every day, mourning the loss of every single one of my friends, of people that I loved. You 'not wanting' to go to war three years ago has taken everything away from me. If you didn't want to go to war then, you should have never gone to war now."

There was silence between them for a time. Chancellor Tyvell stared at Natalie, his expression drooping.

"I wish I had the power to decide when we go to war, Ms. Annikki," he said, the pain in his voice lowering his voice to that of a whisper. "If it were up to me, this war would never have happened. Unfortunate as it may be, however, your father's death was the first drop in a series of drops into a glass, which, once overflowing, meant that we had to go to war."

Natalie turned away from him. "But my father alone wasn't worth it."

"Not every injustice in the sector can be met with vengeance, I'm afraid," Tyvell said. "It is the hardest part of my position, but it is the reality of this world. Individual injustices are but small drops in a wider scheme of politics."

"I don't need your bullshit speech, Chancellor." Natalie was ready to walk away. She had what she needed. Nothing else he said would matter anymore.

"Ms. Annikki, what do you intend to do?" Tyvell asked.

Natalie was mid-step but stopped. "Fly again," she said. "I have nothing else left." She started walking again.

"I hope, for your father's sake, and your own," Tyvell said before she got out of earshot, "that you find some sort of peace before it's too late."

Natalie didn't stop. She simply kept walking past the car and around the corner, away from Tyvell and the furniture shop.

CHAPTER 28

Natalie looked up at the backside of the large stage wall and then back down at the neat, freshly trimmed grass. Soon, it would be time for her to come out from behind the temporary stage, climb the stairs, and be part of a "celebration." It had already begun. She didn't care to listen, but the voice of a man, probably the fleet commander of the 3rd Mobile, was addressing the crowd that had come to commemorate Jontunia's dead.

Few, if any, will know any of us. Natalie thought about the White Tails. *And I'm to be the symbol of our defeat?* Suddenly, Natalie felt sick. She grabbed a member of the stage's steel skeleton and vomited underneath. As she stood back up and wiped away any evidence from her face, she heard the man on stage begin to introduce her.

Natalie came up the steps on the stage's left side, which were now much easier without her hydro-brace. The applause of the large crowd filled the area. The man on the stage was indeed the fleet commander, an admiral dressed in his OSC ceremonial dress, unlike Natalie. They had requested her to be in her flight suit for reasons Natalie didn't fully understand.

Something about connecting me to the battle for the people, she reminded herself as the question resurfaced.

When she reached a suitable distance from the fleet commander, Natalie halted and gave him a sharp salute with her now unbandaged but heavily scarred hand. When he returned it, Natalie took a pace forward while he was being handed the items to be presented. Natalie was handed two folded flags, the smaller of which sat atop the larger. This was all a rehearsed motion, the entire event being planned and recited to Natalie a dozen times in the lead-up to today. With the flags in hand, Natalie began walking to the right side of the stage as the fleet commander began his speech for her part of the ceremony.

"Lieutenant Natalie Annikki is a young, skilled pilot in the 3rd Mobile," he began. "Four cycles ago, she took part in the Battle of Dogor flying with the White Tails, but her recognition today is for her actions in the aftermath, when the New

Federation so viciously pursued the carrier that she served on, the OSC *Endurance*." Natalie reached a flagpole on the side of a monument listing the names of those lost from *Endurance*. Somewhere on there, the names of her friends had been carved. She attached the larger flag to the pole first and slowly began raising it. The flag was that of *Endurance*, a dark green and white flag with a top-down view of a silver falcon flying over the Tempest-class carrier's silhouette.

As Natalie raised it, the fleet commander continued. "During the Fall of *Endurance*, the New Federation launched over a thousand fighters and bombers to destroy the lone carrier. Against such terrible odds, the *Endurance's* brave pilots took to the sky while the captain of the ship ordered an evacuation." Natalie now began raising the second flag, a simple dark green flag with white lettering reading EFW / EBW to commemorate both the fighter wing and the bomber wing of the lost carrier. "Due to the sacrifice of these brave pilots, every single Dolphin transport launched made it safely to friendly territory with members of the crew on board. Lieutenant Annikki personally escorted the final transport even after suffering life-threatening wounds and crippling damage to her fighter. Lieutenant, if you would please return to the stage."

Natalie walked along the same route back to the stage. She halted next to the fleet commander but did not salute this time.

"Lieutenant Annikki flew with the elite fighter squadron, the White Tails," the fleet commander said. Natalie took a side glance at him but said nothing. The script she had been given ended here. She was to be dismissed to the back of the stage with the other officers of the ceremony. Yet the fleet commander continued. "She is unfortunately the last surviving member of the 3rd Mobile's best squadron. For her actions in battle, and to take command of such a revered squadron, Lieutenant Natalie Annikki will be hereby promoted to captain, and each of her squadron mates will posthumously be awarded a one rank promotion." The fleet commander turned toward Natalie. "Captain Annikki, I will also award you with the Star of Garun, the highest honor the 3rd Mobile can bestow upon any member. You saved hundreds of lives even in the face of almost certain death." He held out a small medal in his hand, beautifully crafted and well shined. He stepped forward and pinned it to the left shoulder of Natalie's flight suit, where the ribbons of other commendations were sewn in. Finally, he shook Natalie's hand. The crowd applauded.

So, it's the survivors that get celebrated, Natalie thought as her eyes emotionlessly scanned the crowd. *I did nothing more than any of the others did. Now I just have another reminder of how I lost them all.* Natalie caught the expressions of some of the crowd, especially those in the front. She was noticing both the eyes that avoided looking at her face and the ones that lingered, visually tracing her scars. Natalie shifted her left hand over her right to hide the scars, but there was nothing she could do about the one on her face.

Is that all they see? Just scars and undeserved medals? She looked to the right of the crowd, where the monuments for everyone lost in the Battle of Dogor stood. In the center of the circle of monuments bearing the names were the monuments for the "heroic" ships, including *Endurance.* The leviathan *Trinity* was the largest monument at the very center of the circle. *So much sacrificed for nothing.* Natalie suddenly wanted to cry. *They all died for nothing. My friends, traded for absolutely nothing.* Natalie turned away as the applause died down, saluted her fleet commander, and went to the back of the stage to sit with the others.

***

"How has the capital been treating you, Captain?" the admiral of the 3rd Mobile asked her. He was flanked on either side by the other two fleet commanders, both vice admirals. The three were sitting on one side of a long desk facing Natalie, in a sort of office inside the 3rd Mobile's headquarters.

"I've yet to see much of it, sir," Natalie responded. "But from what I have seen, it is very beautiful."

"Well, you must see more of it before you leave. This is the perfect time of year." The admiral shifted in his chair. "We wanted to bring you here to discuss your career."

"What about it?" Natalie asked.

"What do you wish to do in the OSC? You were severely injured in battle."

"I want to fly again." Natalie's voice was firm. "I want to get back in a Spectre, sir."

"That may not be possible," one of the vice admirals said. "Your hand was nearly destroyed."

"Then put me in a Dolphin until I can prove that I can fly a Spectre again."

The admiral sighed and then smiled. "You have a lot of spirit, Captain," he said. "I'm sure we can arrange that. But if you can't fly Spectres ever again, be prepared to take a ship's staff position."

"I can accept that," Natalie responded. "I just want the opportunity to try."

"Good. Now..." The admiral shifted some papers. "Is there anything you want?"

"I don't understand the question, sir."

"Is there anything we could do to support you during this time?" the admiral asked. "Any luxuries we could provide, or places you want to go? See family or provide for them while you are away. Or we could give you a private yacht. You could fly to Fortuna from here in a matter of days with such a thing."

"What about information?" Natalie asked. "There is something that could ease my mind."

"If we are allowed to share it, then yes, we can even provide information."

"I want information on the Orange Hawks," she said bluntly. "Their numbers, markings, fleet, anything you have."

"For what purpose?" the admiral asked.

"For when I am back in a Spectre," Natalie said. "Why else?"

The admirals exchanged glances. Then the head admiral faced her again. "We can have that arranged," he said. "We will get a folder collected of all the relevant data and leave it with Captain Damos to bring to you. Is there anything else we can do for you?"

"No," Natalie answered. "That was all I wanted to know." She stood up, saluted the three fleet commanders, and left the room.

***

By the time Natalie made it back to her apartment, Victoria was already there. A beige folder was lying on the table. Victoria was in the living room, her black suitcase open. She was packing.

Natalie walked by the folder and stopped at the edge of the room. "What are you doing?" she asked.

Victoria dropped a shirt into her suitcase and looked up. "They've called me back," she said. She stood up straight and brushed her hands on her pantlegs. "You're able to take care of yourself now. You don't need me anymore, so I'm rejoining the fleet tomorrow."

"Who decided I didn't need you anymore?" Natalie asked, raising her voice slightly. "Just because my leg works, doesn't mean that I'm alr—"

"The information you requested is on the table," Victoria interrupted. She walked by Natalie and began pulling things from the hall closet. "The car will be left here for you so you can get to your appointments each day. Nothing else will change. Go into HQ once a cycle to give them an update, and other than that, just try to take care of yourself."

Natalie was staring at Victoria, who was turning from the closet to the living room, a jacket and some shoes in hand. "I don't want you to leave," Natalie said. *Another thing taken from me,* she thought. *Like everything else.* "Why can't you just stay?"

Victoria sighed. "If it were up to me, Nat," she said, frowning, "I wouldn't be going anywhere until you told me to. But it isn't up to me. This is reality. This is how it works. You don't need a guardian anymore, Nat."

"I think I do," Natalie whispered.

Victoria walked by Natalie again, this time on her way into the living room. "I know." She started placing more things in her suitcase. "But the OSC doesn't see what I see every morning, and what *you* see every time you sleep. Your nightmares and how you feel don't exist outside your own mind, and to the military, it therefore doesn't exist at all."

There was silence in the room for minutes. Eventually, Victoria went back to packing as Natalie stood nearby watching.

"Hey," Natalie eventually said. Victoria, who was facing away from her folding clothes, stopped moving but didn't turn around. "How about we go out tonight? Once you're done packing, that is."

"You want to go out? After everything you've had to do today?" Victoria turned around and faced Natalie with an astonished and concerned expression.

Natalie forced a smile. "I'd rather that we both have fun on our last night rather than sit around here being sad and upset."

Victoria smiled. "Alright," she said. "I'll make sure I'm done packing by dinner. I know a restaurant we can go to, and after that, I know a few good bars around here."

Natalie gave her a thumbs up as she turned to head upstairs.

"Be ready for six!" She heard Victoria calling up after her.

***

Natalie stumbled into the apartment behind Victoria, who was guiding herself along with her left hand on the wall of the hallway. The two were laughing incoherently even before the door was closed.

"Did you see that guy's face when you turned him down?" Natalie laughed out in a loud voice. "I think you broke his heart!"

"I know!" Victoria yelled from only ten feet ahead. She drew out the *w* for several seconds. "He was so nice too! Any other night I probably would've given him a chance."

"You shouldn't let me get in the way of your fun, you know!" Natalie said, turning to go upstairs.

"I'll have my fun another time," Victoria responded. She began to follow Natalie upstairs.

Natalie stopped halfway up the stairs and looked backward. "What are you doing? Your bed is down there." She pointed down to the first floor.

Victoria shook her head. "Your nightmares," she said. "I'll sleep on the floor."

Natalie didn't argue. In her drunken state, she couldn't even formulate a proper response. Instead, she continued up the stairs with Victoria behind.

The lights never came on. In just a few minutes of shuffling around in the dark, Natalie had given Victoria a pillow to use, and she was on the floor fast asleep using her jacket as a blanket, and her shirt was wrapped around her bare feet. Natalie simply dropped both her shirt and pants at the foot of her bed and crawled under her blanket, where she passed out almost immediately.

When she woke up, the room was still dark. The first thing she felt was her splitting headache and then her parched throat. Natalie rolled over and looked out at the floor of her room. The pillow was still there, but Victoria was gone.

Did she already leave? she wondered as she climbed out of bed. *Maybe she had an early shuttle…*

Natalie made her way across the room, grabbing her towel on the way out. When she returned from the shower, she felt better, but still had the terrible headache. With whatever speed she could muster, she got dressed and headed downstairs to confirm if her friend had left.

When she turned the corner of the stairs halfway down, she made immediate eye contact with Victoria, who was sitting at the dining table.

She smiled. "Did you think I already left?"

Natalie came down the rest of the stairs. "It was within possibility," she said. "When do you leave?"

"Pretty soon." Victoria motioned at her packed luggage. The suitcases were next to the couch that had once been her bed. It was now folded up and returned to its original state. "But I wouldn't have left before you woke up."

"Thanks," Natalie said. "Do you have a headache too?"

Victoria lifted her coffee. "It's on the way out."

Natalie laughed and went to the kitchen to get her own.

"How did you sleep?" Victoria asked.

Natalie knew what she was really asking about but paused. She didn't dream about *anything* last night. She didn't really remember falling asleep, but, as far as she was aware, she had come home and woken up in the morning. There was nothing in between.

"I slept fine I think," she said. "I didn't dream about anything."

Victoria at once jumped to her feet. "Really?!" she exclaimed. "You didn't dream about anything at all?"

Natalie shook her head. "I guess I just blacked out," she said with a laugh.

"I don't want to say that's why," Victoria said quietly. "If it is, be careful. The nightmares are better than having a drinking problem."

Natalie smiled. "Don't worry," she told her friend. "I'm sure that that wasn't the reason. Maybe I just felt safe with you on the floor next to me."

This caused Victoria to blush slightly. "Well, whatever the reason, I'm glad you didn't have a nightmare for once. Hopefully it's a sign that they'll end for good soon."

Natalie nodded.

"Oh!" Victoria said, raising a finger. "This is the folder you requested." She grabbed the beige folder from the table and handed it to Natalie. "I haven't gone through it, but they told me what it was. It's all of the information on the squadron that killed your father, right?"

"And my friends," Natalie said, taking the folder. "As far as I see it, they're responsible for taking everything from me."

"Not everything," Victoria said softly. "You're still alive. Do what you will with that information, Nat. Just make sure that you are sure that what you are doing is the right thing."

"I will," Natalie responded. She glanced from the folder to Victoria and back. She caught Victoria's green eyes searching for any kind of indication on her face. "I'll have plenty of time to think things through before I'm back at the fleet."

Victoria smiled. "Speaking of." She glanced back at her luggage. "I'd best get going. I'll have someone drop the car back off here later today."

At once, she started moving her luggage to the door. Just as when she moved in, she only had her two large suitcases. She pulled on her shoes and turned around to face Natalie, who was still standing at the edge of the kitchen.

"Well," Victoria said. Natalie could tell that her voice was choked. "I guess this is goodbye. At least for now, I hope."

Natalie nodded. She didn't want to speak. Her throat was tightening just as much as her friend's. Luckily, she didn't have to. Victoria took two bounds to reach her and wrapped her arms around Natalie. She held on tightly and rested her head on Natalie's left shoulder. Natalie placed her left hand on Victoria's back. Neither said a word but held each other for almost a minute. When they separated, Victoria merely smiled, stepped back, grabbed her luggage, and left. Even after the door shut, Natalie stood still, staring at the door for awhile longer.

***

Natalie sat on her bed, her back against the wall that her bed was next to. The sun was beginning to set over Garun, the tall skyscrapers obstructing much of its beauty. Below, thousands of buses, trucks, and cars moved about the streets, and the city's maglev system wound its way through the buildings in some parts before diving underground.

She imagined that by now Victoria was long gone, off world and probably already on Tralis. Her next few days would no doubt be busy: she had to get her next ship posting, then transit to that ship and move into her new quarters. *Eventually,* Natalie thought, *I'll do the same.*

Her focus returned to the city outside. The ceaseless activity never seemed to show any signs of routine, though she knew that's what it was. The city was always in a state of organized chaos as millions of individuals went about their own routines within the great expanse of buildings and roads. Natalie enjoyed watching the capital's activity. It was far greater than anything her hometown had ever seen.

Natalie pulled her ponytail up to her left cheek as she thought about her old town. *I guess there's nothing left for me there, is there?* She ran the tips of her hair along her scar. *Such a quiet, peaceful town. It wouldn't want someone like me anyways.*

Natalie's attention was brought up to the sky as a civilian shuttle took people toward Tralis. Her mind wandered to the day when her and Darren, fresh-faced graduates from the flying school, rode a similar shuttle. It was then they properly became White Tails—the day they were introduced to the people who would become their closest friends.

She thought of Darren and Varya. She could almost feel the love and affection they showed to her in the last days before the war began. *If only I could have told them how I felt, without fear, without hesitation.*

Natalie remembered how Varya had spoken to her just before the battle began and what she said just before she died. *If we made it through, would Varya have confessed? What would I have said then?* Briefly, she remembered the dream in the forest. She knew the answer now, but things were so different now. Would things have been the same between them if they had lived?

Natalie could feel tears beginning to pool at the edge of her eyelids. She saw images of the White Tails in *Endurance's* bar. She saw each of their faces. *I'll be the last one forever, won't I?* She started to feel sick. The shuttle was climbing toward the high, thick clouds.

Why me? The question had returned. At once, Natalie shook her head. She suspected the question would never be satisfied. It would linger forever.

Suddenly, the tears stopped. *Even if these thoughts never leave me, I can at least do something about it. If I can ever fly a Spectre again, I can promise you one thing, Orange Hawks: I promise the White Tails will outlive you, even if I'm the only one.* Her right hand quivered. She held it still with her left and continued to gaze out the window at the setting sun, and the shuttle heading for space.

EPILOGUE

A light snow fell over the market. The tiny snowflakes melted when they touched the cobblestone path, and a cool wind gently blew. It was only days before winter on Altheria, and the capital was receiving an early sign of things to come.

Natalie wandered down the street, passing by many little shops of different kinds. Hundreds of people were moving through the small shopping district. Natalie walked along in the flow, slower than most, taking in all the sights and sounds. All around the shops were towering buildings, apartment complexes larger than she had ever seen, business headquarters, and government towers. Ardenia was just like her father had described: a massive, sprawling city, far bigger than any city on Jontunia.

As she continued, Natalie heard a man's voice calling out to the passing shoppers. "Altherian jewelry!" he yelled. "All sourced from here on the home world!" Natalie often heard people like this shouting, advertising their products. Natalie carried on down the street, and the voice, like others before, faded behind her.

Eventually, Natalie's eyes caught a store of interest, one which Natalie had been searching for. The store was called "Miyano's Indigenous Pets," with a neat, small storefront nestled between two larger stores. Natalie went inside, and the front door chimed as it swung open. The store was small, the center of it full of shelves holding various objects. Natalie supposed they were for pets.

"Hello!" A chipper, small woman appeared from Natalie's left. "I'm Miyano! Is this your first time here?"

"Uh, yes," Natalie responded. "This is actually my first time on Altheria at all."

"Ah, you are from Jontunia?" Natalie nodded. Miyano smiled. "I can hear it in your accent. What brings you to the capital?"

"I'm just visiting. I leave tomorrow," Natalie told Miyano. "I wanted to see a place like this before I left."

"You've come at a good time. Today is the first, so we just restocked for the thirteenth cycle. Take your time. The pets are at the back." Miyano turned to walk back to the front counter. "If you have any questions, just call me over."

Natalie said her thanks and began walking through the store. On the right-hand wall of the pet store, there were multiple small glass enclosures and cages. Natalie slowly inspected each one as she passed. The glass enclosures had soft dirt and wood chip floors, with rocks and logs on top. Natalie saw in some of them small creatures with scales and leathery skin. Some had legs and long tails, which Natalie figured were the "lizards" her father had told her about once, and the long ones with no legs must be "snakes." Most of the snakes and lizards moved slowly or not at all, some hiding in the darkness of their hollow logs.

The cages had similar floors but had little soft-looking beds, tubes, and wheels. In most of them were small furry animals, which Natalie realized were the domesticated rodents of Altheria. She recognized the mice, which had come to populate Jontunia long before Natalie was born. Natalie looked around and saw birds and fish in cages and tanks around the store, often remarkably similar to those common to Jontunia. Turning around, Natalie looked at the other small animals. She read the names of their species, written on the glass with markers. "Ferrets" rolled around and played in the largest cage, and "gerbils" lay lazily in their soft bedding.

Natalie moved along until she reached the very back of the store. Here were the largest glass enclosures. In the bottom ones were what Natalie immediately recognized as young dogs as she squatted down to look at them. Natalie had seen dogs before, as they were a popular pet of high officials on Jontunia. She had seen them early in her life when watching broadcasts of politicians, and her father had told her what they were. Some of the young ones were sleeping, others played with each other, bouncing around and tackling each other. Natalie watched them play for a bit before she stood back up and looked into the top enclosures.

Instead of young dogs, there were many kittens spread across the three enclosures. In the first one were three small white kittens, all nestled together sleeping. Natalie watched their fur rise and fall with their breaths, the three of them completely at peace together. In the next enclosure was a litter of four kittens of all different colors who were making full use of the connected platforms they had. They jumped from one to the other, often pushing and shoving each other, playfully fighting to see who could control the highest platform. In the final enclosure were another three kittens. Two of them were a beautiful orange, and they sat in the corner together licking each other's ears and faces. The third, however, was a fluffy brown-haired kitten, which was sitting on the other side on an elevated platform watching them. Its fur was long, mainly a dark brown with tiny freckles of light brown and black all over.

When it saw Natalie, it hopped up and bounded over to the glass before sitting down again. It stared up at Natalie, small green eyes full of wonder, staring into hers. Suddenly, it mewed through the glass at Natalie. It mewed again, and Natalie could hear it ever so faintly as it came through the glass. It mewed a third time at her before raising a paw and pawing at her but hitting the glass. When it mewed again at her, Natalie smiled.

THE END

ACKNOWLEDGEMENTS

This novel began as something else entirely fourteen years ago, and, when it finally began to take shape as the story it is now, I was helped along by a small group of individuals who will remain precious to me for the rest of my life. Without any of these people and their contributions, be it large or small, this novel might not have existed without them.

The first is my father, who made sacrifices no father should be asked to make so that his children could have the widest opportunities in life. Through his military career and the time he spent away from his family that he can never have back, he gave to us the opportunity to try and do anything we wanted, and ensured that we would always have a home to return to if things didn't pan out. When he was home, he passed onto me his love for military history, rural living, and the values that made him the greatest man I've ever known. Though for better or worse I followed in his footsteps, his experiences in the military and now mine have lent themselves greatly to both this novel's military and political themes.

Of course, Histria Books for giving me the opportunity of a lifetime in publishing this novel. Wildcat was a dream, a treasured fictional reality of mine, and something that for many years felt as though it would remain as my own idea rather than something shared. By giving me this opportunity, Histria has opened the door for me to tell the story of characters so dear to me and of a tragedy that reflects so much more of my own thoughts and values than I could ever clearly tell.

My friend Lucy, and two of my professors, Dr. Huw Osborne and Dr. Dale Tracy, the three of whom this book is dedicated to. Without their time, honesty, and support, this book would never have made it to where it is today. Each gave their most professional and unbiased advice and criticism to my work when it was in its most critical stages of editing, and each in turn helped shaped my writing style into what it is now. Words will never do enough justice to thank them for the time they took to read my work and provide the edits and suggestions that I would never have found on my own.

Lastly, I want to thank the many other people who were involved in making this dream a reality. My mother, brother, and sister, who collectively formed the rest of my support structure through the good times and bad, and reminded me that if everything fell apart, I'd still have family to turn to. Jadnn, my best friend who proves that no matter the physical distance, true friends will never actually be apart. Mary, my childhood friend and avid reader who helped to give me the "reader's perspective" in all my writing over the years. Jordan, my only friend with as much love of sci-fi and technology as I have, and Liam, who inspired and motivated me to tread onto the rocky path of publishing.